romances be
reckless!

Anne
Dec 2019

ANNE MARSHALL

BALBOA.
PRESS
A DIVISION OF HAY HOUSE

Balboa Press books may be ordered through booksellers or by contacting:

Balboa Press
A Division of Hay House
1663 Liberty Drive
Bloomington, IN 47403
www.balboapress.com
1 (877) 407-4847

Because of the dynamic nature of the Internet, any web addresses or links contained in this book may have changed since publication and may no longer be valid. The views expressed in this work are solely those of the author and do not necessarily reflect the views of the publisher, and the publisher hereby disclaims any responsibility for them.

The author of this book does not dispense medical advice or prescribe the use of any technique as a form of treatment for physical, emotional, or medical problems without the advice of a physician, either directly or indirectly. The intent of the author is only to offer information of a general nature to help you in your quest for emotional and spiritual well-being. In the event you use any of the information in this book for yourself, which is your constitutional right, the author and the publisher assume no responsibility for your actions.

Any people depicted in stock imagery provided by Getty Images are models, and such images are being used for illustrative purposes only.
Certain stock imagery © Getty Images.

Print information available on the last page.

ISBN: 978-1-9822-3326-6 (sc)
ISBN: 978-1-9822-3325-9 (hc)
ISBN: 978-1-9822-3327-3 (e)

Library of Congress Control Number: 2019912059

Balboa Press rev. date: 08/27/2019

August—London

Music blaring, lights flashing, the gallery was a happening place. Maddy walked through the well-dressed crowd, wondering how they could stand in their high heels and tight garb. They were probably wondering how someone with a simple frock and flats obtained an invite to the event. The very thought made her laugh. This was mad. The art on the wall was clearly avant-garde and priced very high. *Not much here for a working girl to consider, she thought.*

As she turned the corner, she caught a glimpse of a tall, brooding man in a well-appointed suit staring intently at the wall. The elaborately framed art piece was so hideous that Maddy wondered if he was related to the artist. Who else could look at the mess on the wall for more than a second? His silver hair was a little too long, resting on his starched shirt collar. Handsome? Perhaps, but in a dangerous way. He appeared to be age sixty or so but well preserved. His arms were crossed, and as he moved his hand to his chin in contemplation Maddy realized she was staring at him. She shook her head but was drawn by the way he was standing, one ankle crossed over the other. *Why am I even looking?* she wondered. As she moved closer, something about this man looked complicated.

She approached the figure and in a loud stage whisper asked, "Would you really consider buying that for your wall?" He turned slowly, and her heart fluttered. Maddy was sure she was burning up with a fever, and her legs felt weak. Surely *he* was a piece of art.

He cocked his head and stared quizzically. "You don't like it?" As he moved his head, the light defined his features—a fine face with character, and yet his eyes looked distant and sad. Posture—ramrod straight. Boarding school, she guessed.

They stared at each other for what seemed like minutes before a shrill voice broke the spell. "Ah, Sebastian, there you are. Where have you been all night?" The voice was getting closer. Maddy heard a groan escape his lips and saw the grimace on his face. His eyes darted towards the voice. At least now he had a name—Sebastian.

"Just kiss me," Maddy said as she leaned forward and grabbed the lapels on his jacket and pulled him to her. The kiss was long and stirring. He had not hesitated or faltered.

The voice behind them was indignant. "Well, I might have known you would disappear and find a place to hi ... oh, my." The smartly dressed raven-haired woman stopped short, hands on hips, shaking her head in disbelief. She turned quickly and spat out the words, "Easily distracted I see. Perhaps you might call when you get your senses back."

She walked away, leaving a trace of strong perfume, tossing her long hair. "Don't bother seeing me home; I'm leaving for the lounge with the tennis crowd. Not your thing, I know." she said in a cruel voice. "By the way, that piece is perfect for you ... dark and confusing."

"Well, that might have been awkward," Maddy said as she shook her head and straightened her long scarf.

Sebastian stood in silence, watching her, unsure what he could possibly say, his eyes dancing, his mind racing, a smile forming on his lips.

"Indeed." He paused. "Reckless as well."

"Maybe, but it was fun." Maddy laughed easily, rolling her eyes and arching her eyebrows.

"Let me show you one of the artist's early works. I think that style might be better suited to your tastes." Maddy held out her hand and turned to walk through the crowd. After a moment of hesitation, Sebastian took her hand and followed, wondering what this woman thought his taste might be. His hand was cool and smooth, she noticed. *Her hand is warm*, he thought.

They wound around the art groupings and crowds until they came to a small alcove where a less-modern, more-studied series of art was displayed. He had to agree the area was more appealing to his sense of colour and form. "Well done. Who are you?" he asked after studying the canvas options.

Maddy held out her hand, curtsying slightly. "Maddy Davis, Canadian.

Just an ordinary person. I wanted a midlife crisis, so I ran away from home—just like Shirley Valentine—to find myself and really experience London. Emerson said, 'When a man is tired of London, he is tired of life.' Is that true?"

"How did you get in?" he asked warily. He had not taken her offered hand.

"Purely by chance. Two gentlemen were having words on the street as I walked by. They handed me their invitations as they hailed a cab. They did say I would need several glasses of champagne to appreciate the work. How serendipitous for me!"

"Indeed."

Sebastian watched her with awe. This woman was so confident. She seemed perfectly natural and at ease in the sea of designer dolls and stiff conversation, as if she were in her own world. She was fit—*Rubenesque,* he thought—perhaps forty to forty-five years old. Her hair framed her face, blonde with natural-white highlights, no grey. He noticed her big blue eyes; she wore no make-up. Her simple linen dress, leggings, and bright scarf seemed perfect. Her smile lit up the area around her, and she looked as though she could not stand still. She was so … so … he searched for the right word in his mind. She was so … alive. Yes, "alive"—that was the word. He felt comfortable around her, and that was disconcerting. Her "kiss me" scheme had worked at keeping the wolves at bay, for the moment. Without thinking, he suggested she might enjoy the ballet next Friday evening. Her enthusiastic response made him feel grand and generous. He found himself looking forward to the performance. She hadn't asked who was performing; she just accepted.

"Oh dear, I should get going," she said suddenly.

He was reminded of Cinderella leaving the ball before midnight. "My driver can see you home," he offered.

"I'm in the West End; I can take the Tube; I have an Oyster Pass. Thank you. Much appreciated. See you Friday, Sebastian." She breezed out of the room, leaving him feeling lost and incomplete.

"Indeed," he mumbled to himself as he headed for the door.

Sebastian stepped out of the gallery and into the car, humming a light tune. His driver, a handsome young Indian man, Daveesh Singh, looked back in surprise. "You're in a mood, sir. Did you find something of interest?"

"No art, Daveesh, but I did have quite a chance encounter. Left me rather breathless …"

"Very well, sir. Home?"

"Hmm, yes, home." He stared out the window, distracted by the memory of her kiss—their kiss—and how light-hearted he felt. He saw a figure dancing on the street, oblivious to the walking traffic but clearly enjoying the music from her earphones. "Stop, Daveesh. Stop here."

Sebastian lowered the window, cleared his throat, and shouted. "Please get in before you get arrested or attacked." She stopped moving forward but kept dancing. She removed the earphones and brightened up the night with a wide smile. Sebastian felt like a child who had been given a great reward.

"Care to walk with me? It's a beautiful evening." She pointed to the sky.

"I'd rather get you home safe and sound." He shook his head, smiling.

Daveesh ran around the car and opened the door for her. Maddy shook his hand and introduced herself, asking where he was from and what he was reading, as she had seen him reading in the car when she left the gallery. She asked if he was married before she sat in the back seat next to Sebastian.

"This is very kind of you. Not necessary, but very kind." She kicked off her shoes as soon as she sat down, tucking her feet under her on the seat.

"It's the least we can do after you saved me from Deirdre Fontaine. That was quite the move, by the way."

"My pleasure. Lucky for you I was there to assist."

"Indeed."

The saloon seemed very quiet after they dropped Maddy at her rental flat.

"Daveesh, did we just agree to have you meet a nice girl at a coffee shop? Did we just invite a woman we met less than an hour ago to join us for a property tour—a crazy woman we saw dancing on the road? Did we agree to have pizza after the ballet? Did I dream this?"

"Yes sir. Ah, no sir, no dream. You … ah, we … did agree to all the new adventures," Daveesh replied, chuckling. Perhaps his boss was finally returning to the land of the living. It was a good sign.

4

The next morning, Daveesh arrived at the corner coffee house and was introduced to Grace, a petite Caribbean woman with a wonderful lilting voice. He was immediately smitten with her baking, her chai, her voice, and her big brown eyes. She was taken by his quiet, polite manner and his dark brown eyes. Maddy was delighted to see how well they got on, becoming instantly comfortable with each other.

Grace ran the coffee house on a busy corner, offering the best chai, frothy coffees, and fresh baking every morning. She was too focused on her business; Maddy worried she was letting life slip by. Maddy had found the coffee house on her first day in London. Jet lag had her up early, scouting the neighbourhood. She watched Grace handle the baking and the customers, and after a few days Maddy suggested minor efficiencies for ordering and seating, which Grace was pleased to try, throwing an apron at Maddy and pointing to the tables needing clearing. The shop was moments from Maddy's temporary flat, making it convenient for her to arrive early. Although the morning clientele was steady, Grace wanted to expand her luncheon trade. Maddy had offered to help, designing new menu flyers and updating decor. She and Grace had become quite close in the past month, working together. Daveesh would soon become a regular at the coffee shop, sharing recipe ideas and joining Grace in the kitchen. Maddy was delighted.

After indulging in the aromatic chai, en route to collect Sebastian at his office, Daveesh talked animatedly about his college courses, his family, his aspirations and his admiration of Grace. Maddy was a good listener, and he couldn't believe how much he wanted to tell her. They exchanged favourite authors and chatted amicably. He told her how he had come to be the driver for Sebastian and how his father had been in service for the family, caring for the young Sebastian and beautiful Aunt Belle before him, until the grandparents passed. Daveesh had looked up to Sebastian, and when his father passed away, he had been offered a position within the company as a driver, eventually becoming the personal driver to Sebastian so he could study and obtain his degree. He spoke reverently of Sebastian, and it made Maddy like him even more.

"Davi ... I think I will call you Davi; it's less formal ... do you mind?" she asked the driver.

"Davi, Davi … it sounds very American … I like it." He smiled in his rear-view mirror at her.

Today they were visiting properties Sebastian was considering divesting, as the market was active. He had asked Maddy to accompany him and provide a woman's point of view. Lambert, his assistant, would be joining them as well. Maddy and the flamboyant Lambert were easy together; he loved her enthusiasm and direct approach, and she loved his creative side. Lambert laughed when Maddy complimented his suit and tie and called him a perfect metrosexual.

The holdings, as they were addressed, were magnificent. The first condo was a penthouse near Canary Wharf. Maddy thought it would be ideal for a foreigner who came to London for only a few days a month. The outdoor patio was lovely but not family friendly. *Wow, lots of windows to clean.* She asked if there was secure parking for a scooter or small vehicle. Lambert made notes. She also timed the lift, commenting on how quickly the tenants would be at their door.

Next they visited an older Victorian terrace house with large windows and panelled walls, fireplaces in all rooms, a small kitchen in need of updating, a safe neighbourhood, but no parking. The Regent Street address was impressive. Maddy suggested the first floor could be an office. Lambert made more notes. Sebastian didn't add any thoughts, wandering through the buildings, listening to Maddy and Lambert commenting on space and decor. Once or twice he asked Maddy directly what she would do with wall coverings in a certain room or how she would fill the space in another.

Georgian and overgrown with ivy, the next house was on a quiet boulevard in Maida Vale. There was a long tree-lined drive, a three-car garage with lodging overhead, and an abandoned garden apartment. Maddy headed straight for the garden and planned a quick layout for the one-room space, before looking elsewhere. Lambert was fervently taking notes. She was so effusive in her plans for the garden apartment that the group never did tour the main house, merely opening the grand front door and appraising the winding staircase. When Maddy saw the sweeping staircase, she envisioned a young debutante in another age making an entrance at a grand coming out-party. There was laughter and the raising of eyebrows before they returned to the car.

The final holding was a small cottage on the outskirts of the city.

Aeroplanes flew over, leaving patterns in the sky. Maddy thought the stone walls and rustic decor would be ideal for air crew who wanted to be close to the airport and the city. It was chilly inside, but the large fireplace would heat the space quickly. The backyard shed needed repair, but otherwise this was ready to live in. *Who wouldn't love those thick-walled window seats?* Maddy thought.

Lambert noted the repairs, and the group headed back to the city.

"Have you done this before Maddy?" Lambert asked as he flopped into the car. "You were so fast and so definite."

"No, but it was fun. You two are the experts; I'm sure I was just here to break any ties." Maddy responded.

"Heavens no, we usually walk around the properties with an estate agent and can hardly wait to get out; it's very tedious." Lambert shook his hands in the air and rolled his eyes.

Sebastian was quiet, contemplating the notes and reviewing the day. "Put them on the market, high-rise condo first. Try foreign ownership; let's see how that works. We can also list the cottage. Let's not spend any money on renovations, just move it. Any thoughts on dinner?"

"How about Greek? There's a new restaurant near Grace's place that smells amazing when I walk by. Mr Spanakis comes into the coffee house every morning; he's such a lovely man. Are you game?" Maddy was quick to respond.

Davi added his vote, and Lambert said he was happy to take a recommendation from Maddy. Sebastian shrugged; he was preoccupied with his notes. They agreed to go Greek.

The Athena was busy and noisy when they walked in, but Mr Spanakis was delighted to see Maddy and ushered them to a booth immediately. Maddy introduced the group and suggested the chef prepare his favourites for the table. She looked over at Davi and requested a vegetarian choice; he was pleased she had remembered. The owner brought a bottle of ouzo and glasses to the table, and Maddy ordered saganaki for the group, assuring them they would love it. Sebastian watched the group settle in. Maddy, with her legs tucked up under her, never stopped moving. Her shoes were under the table; she never seemed to keep them on for long. Davi called Grace and asked her to join the group at Maddy's request. Soon the table was covered with steaming platters of food and a variety of drinks.

Sebastian wondered if the practice of sharing food was a North American custom. Maddy held up forkfuls of moussaka for tasting, and the group followed suit, reaching over and tasting each dish. Lambert and Daveesh—or Davi, as he had been renamed—seemed comfortable enough with the process, and by dessert he, too, was digging his fork into the flaky pastry in the middle of the table. At some point Maddy leaned over and asked Sebastian how he was doing. Before he could respond, she continued. "This must be a different night out for you. I hope it's better than eating alone." She looked up at him with a broad smile, and he felt, at that moment, he would go anywhere with her.

"It's very enjoyable." He hoped he sounded sincere. She touched his hand and thanked him for including her in the day. He wanted to tell her he had enjoyed her company, appreciated her comments, and hoped for more days together, but she had turned away and was insisting she could walk home from the restaurant.

The group walked out arm in arm, laughing, shouting "Opa!" to the owner.

Maddy and Grace, still arm in arm, sauntered off, deep in conversation. Davi was concerned, so Lambert ran up to them and escorted them around the corner to the coffee house, continuing to Maddy's flat while Davi waited on the main road. On the ride home Davi and Lambert reminded Sebastian he had agreed to accompany Maddy to the market in the morning. Davi smiled when his boss asked what time they were to meet. He couldn't remember Sebastian ever being to an outdoor market.

The next morning, Maddy waved at the vendors, tasted food from the stalls, and wandered without aim through the market, dragging Sebastian behind her. She stopped abruptly and turned to Sebastian, breathless. "What's your favourite flavour?" He was surprised by the question and shrugged, wondering if he had a favourite flavour. "How about lemon?" she asked as she pointed to some icing-sugar-covered blocks. "Here, try this." She held a jellied square up to his lips, waiting for him to bite into the rich treat. He moved back, not familiar with the tasting experience. "It's Turkish delight; it's wonderful." She bit into the square and licked the icing sugar on her lips. Sebastian immediately pulled his handkerchief out of his pocket and wiped her face. She laughed, throwing her head back, and touched his hand. They shared a look and carried on.

"I love the market. It's so full of hope and fresh smells." Maddy turned quickly.

"Hope? I'm not sure what you mean." Sebastian was following her through the narrow alley, his arms out to protect her from the crowd.

"Hope. It's not something you discuss with someone you just met." She smiled, looking up at the sky, her eyes bright. Sebastian pushed his hands into his pockets, which he never did, to stop the sudden urge to hold her face in his hands.

As they walked through the stalls, she turned to Sebastian, her face serious. "Does it hurt?"

He looked perplexed. "I'm sorry?"

"Does it hurt to be so uptight all the time—to be so proper?" She stopped and watched his face, her head tilted, eyebrows arched in question.

"There are rules of conduct, good manners, and structure ..." He couldn't find the words to describe his upbringing.

Maddy laughed. "I know. I get it; you're English. I think your feelings are all locked up somewhere." She placed her hands on his chest. "I hope you find them someday. You're like, hmm, like the Tin Man." She nodded, pleased with herself for finding the right metaphor.

Sebastian continued walking, not sure if he was amused or angry with her. She touched his hand, and he felt a light shock go through his arm. His fingers closed over hers, as if they had a mind of their own. He managed to look over at the owner of the hand in his and he gasped when she looked up, smiling brightly, her lips apart and her eyes daring him to respond. He took a deep breath and wondered why he felt light-headed.

Davi was amazed at how quickly Maddy became a part of each day. Sebastian invited her to lunch one day, to job sites in and out of the city following lunch, to dinner at places he had never tried before, for drinks after work, for walks in the park—it was a new Sebastian. He stopped staying late at the office after Maddy noted everyone stayed late because they were afraid to leave before the boss. He accepted invitations for exhibits and cocktail receptions. He seemed a healthier version of himself. Maddy challenged him constantly with questions and alternatives. They seemed very compatible and happy together. Davi told Grace he thought Maddy made Sebastian a nicer person, to which Grace replied, "That's what we women do." Davi thought it best to simply nod as if he understood.

Maddy was trying to sit quietly in the car as they headed south to the sea. Sebastian was due for a visit with his aunt Belle, his only living relative, and he had invited Maddy to see the cliffs, although he couldn't quite remember why he had extended the invitation. Sebastian was scanning a report, his glasses perched on his nose, and his pen circling phrases. Maddy removed her earbuds and studied his face. They had spent every day together since the art gallery meeting, but he wasn't a talker. He was difficult to read, and she was unsure if he remembered she was there.

"Sebastian, would I be disturbing you if I asked a few questions?" she asked tentatively, smiling sweetly.

He removed his glasses, lowered the report, and looked over at her, eyebrows raised. *How could a face have so many dimples?* he mused.

"I just wondered if I could ask you simple things that your friends would know, like, do you drink coffee or tea in the morning? Are you a morning person or a nighthawk? Do you buy your own clothes? Do you cook your own breakfast? What do you have for breakfast? Do you always go to your club for lunch? Do you always drink lager? Any special brand if I were to order you a pint? Do you cook at all? What's your favourite food? Favourite music? Do you like reading? What makes you laugh?" she stopped for a breath. She had so many questions, such as why he carried large reports rather than work on his laptop, but Sebastian cleared his throat and responded.

"Coffee in the morning, tea with milk during the day; as you have pointed out, I am English, after all. I wake up to take international calls, so I would say I am a morning person. I see my tailor twice a year. Lager or Guinness. Don't order for me. I don't cook. My housekeeper prepares a full English breakfast twice a week; otherwise, it's just coffee. Lunch at the club, of course … unless I go out with a client or you. I enjoy Asian food, jazz and classical music. I do read war stories and mysteries, as well as the masters. As you can see, I have a fair amount of report reading. My old eyes prefer print to computer screens. I don't laugh. Anything else?" His voice was flat, almost bored. "I suppose you want to know my Zodiac sign."

"Not especially. I wouldn't think you'd fit the profile. You're such a private person. I hope you don't mind my asking, but as I spend time with you, I just want to know you better. You really should eat breakfast. Maybe

I could interest you in a tasty smoothie recipe …" Her voice tapered off as she saw him glance at his report.

There was no response, so she continued. "It's not easy meeting people at our age. We know what we like and don't like, and we get set in our ways. It takes time to know how you think, how you handle things, where the boundaries are, and what's comfortable. I was just interested." She waited.

"Do you want to know anything about me?" she asked, as there was no response. Removing his glasses, Sebastian looked out the window in deep thought and began speaking.

"You drink tea with milk or green tea lattes, no coffee. You have a high energy level, so I would guess you are just as chipper in the morning as you are late in the evening. I don't quite know what to make of your wardrobe. You can't seem to keep your shoes on or sit still. You're a healthy eater, so I imagine you enjoy full English breakfasts as much as those egg muffin things. You like to try new things, and you always choose an ethnic restaurant when asked. You eat off other people's plates, and you take samples from street vendors. You treat crisps as if they are a defined food group. You listen to and dance to all kinds of music, and you read everything, including road signs, as though they were classics. You are kind and generous, and you talk to anyone, anywhere. You smile often and seem very happy with your life. You seem reckless; you don't follow rules. What more do I need to know?" He quickly turned away, suddenly interested in the countryside. He knew that if he looked over at Maddy he would want to kiss her.

Maddy looked down, feeling admonished. She understood the chat was over.

She shook her head and replaced her earbuds, looking out at the passing scenery. She considered his evaluation of her and smiled. Then, suddenly, she felt tears on her cheek.

Sebastian returned to his report but could not concentrate. It was clear, even to him, he had hurt her feelings. He leaned back and looked over at Maddy. She was curled up in the seat beside him, her back to him. Her shoes were off, her feet under her. He felt a strong desire to hold her and shook his head, surprised at his thoughts. He reached out and touched her shoulder. Maddy turned, removed her earbuds, and looked so darn receptive he had to take a deep breath to keep his hands from holding her face. He felt as if he were drowning in her bright blue eyes. Were there tears on her cheeks?

"I'm sorry; I didn't mean to sound so pompous. In fairness, when you speak to people, they do respond. I also enjoy having dinner with someone who actually consumes the food instead of moving it around his or her plate. I'm sure you have more research questions. Go ahead." He hoped he was sounding sincere and encouraging.

She didn't skip a beat. "Which football team do you support? She held her breath.

"Manchester United at home or Munich Bayern." He was trying to play along.

"Favourite thing to do on Sunday morning?" It was killing her to stop in between questions.

"Read the *Times*, *Economist*, Bloomberg, and Al Jazeera to compare the reporting."

"Do you hunt or fly fish?" *Don't all English gentlemen hunt and fly fish off the banks of the river?*

"I have gone to the lodge to shoot pheasant, and I belong to a Speyside club croft, but it's been years since I've gone up to throw a line." He wondered why he didn't fish more. "I've never been on a fox hunt, if that's the next question."

"Why do you work so much at this point in your life?"

"I don't. I sit on several boards and committees, and I'm needed only for final quotes and special projects any more. I seem to do more entertaining these days." He seemed wistful.

"Were you ever married?"

He hesitated, looking out the window. "Yes. Once," he whispered.

Maddy touched his arm. "I'm sorry; I didn't mean to pry. Tell me about your aunt."

Sebastian brightened, happy to change the subject. He had just begun to describe his aunt Belle when they arrived at her Victorian cottage.

Sebastian introduced Maddy as his friend, and the two women walked away, arms locked, bonding instantly. Sebastian looked over at Davi, who was smiling broadly, and followed the women into the house. Davi had certainly taken to this woman and his new name. Sebastian was confused; he needed a drink.

This was new ground for Sebastian. His friends, or acquaintances, didn't ask questions about his life or his habits, and he was unsure whether this was because they didn't care or because they accepted him just the way he was. Maddy was so curious about everything. Perhaps he was taking her interrogation too seriously. Hadn't she accused him of being too serious? She had a way of telling him he was a dinosaur by making him sound charming. Something told him she was trouble. He had loosened his tie in response to her observation that perhaps a cardigan would be more appropriate than a business suit when visiting his aunt. Nothing was sacred ground in her mind. Had he imagined it, or had Maddy inquired about accompanying him to the tailor to update his wardrobe? "Just to jazz it up a bit," she had said. He had smirked at the thought. Angelo, his tailor, would never want to collaborate with a woman ... or would he?

He watched the women, heads together, amiably chatting, and realized it had been a long time since he had brought anyone to meet his aunt. Belle was clearly enjoying the conversation, and he was glad he had introduced her to Maddy. In many ways, they were alike. They both saw images in the clouds and would stop mid-sentence to point out a bee attacking a flower in the garden or comment on the sound a bird had just made.

Aunt Belle was overjoyed to meet a female friend of her beloved boy. She was fussing over Sebastian, linking arms, straightening his hair, holding his hand, touching his knee—there was a shared fondness between them. High tea was served on the garden terrace, and polite conversation ensued. Belle was delicate, like a bird, with a mass of white hair and catlike hazel eyes outlined in kohl. She wore flowing costumes with sparkling jewels and ballet slippers, which gave her the appearance of an ageing film star. She was very engaging, and before long the little tea party had taken on the light mood of friends enjoying a sunny afternoon together.

When the doorbell rang, Belle jumped up and planted a large kiss on the cheek of George, a tall, stooped older man with white hair and hooded eyes. His face was ruddy from the sea and wind, and he had a crooked smile reminiscent of a leprechaun's. George had business matters to discuss with Sebastian, leaving Belle and Maddy to ponder dinner arrangements, the weather, and how to stop Sebastian from working so hard.

Dinner was a pleasant affair with laughter, storytelling, and shared memories. Maddy asked why Belle and George weren't married, and they blushed. "I asked for her hand in marriage sixty years ago. What if I ask and she says no? I would be devastated," George responded with a twinkle in his eye.

Maddy laughed. "Maybe she's had enough time to think about it. You won't know if you don't ask."

Belle reached over and touched his hand. "We'd make a good pair, wouldn't we?"

It was a tender moment, and Maddy noticed that Sebastian looked uncomfortable, while Davi smiled and nodded. Maddy was delighted Davi was considered part of the family; his adoring looks at Belle made her smile.

As they were leaving, Sebastian noticed Belle and Maddy huddled together.

"You must come back and walk the beach with us; you seem to have lit a spark in my beautiful boy. Please say you'll come and visit," Belle pleaded as she held Maddy's hand in hers. They agreed to stay in touch now that Maddy had set up a Facebook account for Belle.

"That was a lovely way to spend the day, except for missing out on the beach walk, which I'm sure we'll do next time. Thank you so much for bringing me here," Maddy gushed as they drove off, waving frantically to the older couple.

Sebastian nodded, also pleased with the outcome.

"It was lovely to see how much they care for you; they're so proud of you," she pointed out.

"Indeed."

Maddy sat back and wondered why both Sebastian and George used the word "indeed" as if it were a complete thought, but she shrugged and giggled.

"What's so funny?" Sebastian asked, watching her and trying hard to control his smile.

"You. You're so formal, even with your aunt and George … don't you ever just let go? Do something spontaneous?" she teased.

He leaned over and kissed her lips slowly and softly. Her lips parted, and her heart fluttered. Her eyes were closed, and she was floating. Then, as suddenly as it had begun, he pulled away, clearing his throat. In a gruff voice, he asked, "Is that spontaneous enough?"

"Hmm. Very good, shows promise," she responded with a mischievous grin, cocking her head to one side. Sebastian turned to the window and seemed fixated on the darkness.

Outside the flat, Davi opened the car door, walked Maddy to the apartment gate, apologizing for the change in Sebastian on the return trip. He had retreated into his silent world, checking messages and reading his reports, making it clear he was done talking.

"No worries, my friend" Maddy assured him. "He seems like a loner, and I can be a bit much. See you tomorrow. Oh, by the way, Grace found a superbly rich breakfast recipe to try in the morning; you should come by. Good night." She waved as she walked through the gate.

Friday evening Sebastian watched her run up the steps of the ballet, wondering if he should send his regrets and go home. She was wearing a long, flowing scarf over a plain cotton dress; she looked like a fresh flower. She smiled at everyone, and people turned back to smile at her obvious enthusiasm. She would be wondering where he was, waiting for him at the will-call window for the tickets. He saw Davi watching him curiously in the rear-view mirror.

"Sir?"

"Yes, well, I guess I should go ... I'll look for you here later."

The ballet was a mix of classical and contemporary dance—interesting enough. It was made all the more fascinating for him seeing it through her eyes; her comments on colour, costumes, and interpretation, and her asides on the crowd, turned what was usually a long night in the loge into a new experience. How did she do that? How did she make everything around her new and exciting? It was exhilarating, yet risky. She was playful, irreverent, and funny; when she whispered in his ear, he got a tingling sensation. She offered Sebastian a lemon bonbon, placing it in his mouth, explaining that the icing sugar would leave dust on his suit. He smiled, recalling the memory of lemon bonbons as a child. At one point she grabbed his leg, as she was so caught up in the story. He looked over and saw her brush a tear from her cheek. He handed her his handkerchief, which she accepted with a giggle. She once leaned into his shoulder and clapped her hands, delighting in the outcome of a scene. She clasped her hands together at the finale, holding them under her chin as if the production had been hers to direct. He couldn't believe how enjoyable the evening had been, feeling embarrassed at his initial hesitation. Her enthusiasm made him feel warm inside. But as they walked out of the theatre, he was debating whether he was ready for more. His world was very predictable, and she was certainly not.

Sebastian could not recall when he last ate pizza, but here he was, sitting on the banks of the Thames. It did cross his mind that he was safe here; no one he knew would be walking by or wondering what he was doing eating pizza from a box on the banks of the river. He felt a sudden urge to hold her and dance with her as he watched her taking in the sights of the city. She made him see things in a new light—the street globes, the reflections, the boats slowly passing by. She was fascinated by everything new. It was easy to get caught up in her world; this woman could hurt him if he wasn't careful.

In the car, she rested her head against him, and he felt he needed to protect her, to be sure she was cared for. This was new ground, and he cautioned himself to go slow. As they approached the flat, he kissed her forehead and told her he was going away on business for a few weeks. His expression and voice made the statement a dismissal. It was difficult to watch her sad, forlorn reaction to the news, and he almost changed his mind. He needed time to think about what was happening.

"No, Davi, it's okay. I'm fine. Don't." She opened the door. She didn't want Davi to come around and open the car door and see her reaction to the apparent dismissal.

"Thank you for a lovely evening, Sebastian." She stepped out on the curb, wondering what she had done to make him act so mean. She had never thought about the future, but as she watched the car drive away, she felt an aching sadness flow through her.

His heart flipped when he dared to look back and thought he saw her brush a tear from her cheek.

September

"Sir, will you require the car after I drop you at the office?" Davi asked.

"No, I don't think so. Why?"

"I have to meet a train this morning. I mean, I would like to meet a train this morning, if it's all right with you."

"Family arriving?" Sebastian looked up from his paper.

"Well, no sir … a friend,   actually—Maddy. Maddy returns today, and I know everyone at the coffee shop is anxious to hear of her trip." He nervously looked away.

Sebastian had purposely not asked after Maddy since the ballet weeks ago, and Davi had not offered any intel (as directed by Grace). Davi explained that Maddy had gone to Spain to walk the Camino alone, as a pilgrim. Grace had worried about her state of mind and was anxious to have her return.

"I see." A long pause ensued, and then Sebastian said, "Is it possible I could make the pick-up with you? I think I have some explaining to do."

"As you wish, sir." Davi smiled, hoping he was doing the right thing.

Three weeks of agony had passed since Sebastian had left Maddy outside her rental apartment. It had been three weeks of questioning himself, not sleeping, snapping at anyone in his path, and generally feeling as if he had lost a vital organ. It was just not reasonable or even sane, he told himself, to miss someone so much when you hardly knew her, but he had to see her. It was sure to be emotional. He didn't handle emotion well.

Victoria Station is a grand old building reminiscent of a time when train travel was in vogue. Now commuters and strangers with backpacks arrived and left as quickly as possible. Sebastian walked towards the train—"Track 6!" Davi had shouted—and saw her immediately. She was saying goodbye to a group as they disembarked, all carrying backpacks and looking very fit in their walking shorts and hiking boots. Several young men were laughing with her and helping her with her pack. He felt a pang of jealousy as he watched how easily the group interacted and jested with each other. Of course they would love being around her too!

He continued walking towards the group, an imposing figure in his tailored suit—overcoat flowing behind him as he took long strides, his expression purposeful. As the travellers dispersed, Maddy started walking backwards while waving. She then turned and fell into his arms.

"Oh, pardon me," she gasped. As she looked up, her smile was replaced by a look of confusion.

He held her and controlled the urge to wrap her in his arms. *Difficult to do with the backpack*, he reasoned.

Maddy was frozen in his arms, taking in the smell of him. He was so handsome, causing her thoughts to confuse her more. Hadn't she just spent three weeks trying to get over him? Why was he here? *Breathe. Breathe. Run away. Breathe. Breathe. You won't have a chance if he starts talking …*

Sebastian was looking at her tenderly. "Maddy, please don't run away; hear me out." Their eyes locked. Her body wasn't responding to her urge to flee.

"I was such an idiot. I know I hurt you. If I could turn back time, I would; believe me, I would." He had to turn away, as her eyes were swallowing him. She looked so hurt; a tear was tracking down her cheek, and that was unbearable for him to watch. "I was afraid of you and the power you had over me, but I want you in my life, and I can change. Will you ever be able to forgive me?" he pleaded.

The group of hikers walked by and eyed Sebastian suspiciously. "You all right, Maddy, love?" one of them asked. She nodded, trying to smile and assure them she was fine. She waved.

"Please, Maddy, forgive me and give me a chance to make this up to you. Please." He was holding her shoulders tightly.

Tears now streaming down her cheeks, she looked up at him, blinking to stop the flow. Her head and heart were in turmoil.

"I know it will take time, but I want you to know I'm going to fight for your forgiveness." he whispered into her hair.

Her head was spinning, her heart was bursting, and a voice within her was screaming, *He hurt you; he'll do it again! Get away!*

"Maddy, come back into our lives. Lambert hasn't been able to look at me since you left, Daveesh is missing his friend, and I miss having you around. We need you. Please?"

Maddy was confused, but the pleading in his eyes won her over.

"Just kiss me," she said softly. "A kiss never lies."

He loosened his grip on her arms and gently held her face, kissing her tears, kissing her eyes, and kissing more tears. His lips touched hers, and it was as if a spell joined them in a long, slow, hungry kiss—a kiss that made them both gasp and move apart.

They looked into each other's eyes for what seemed like an eternity when the air brakes signalled the movement of the train, breaking the spell. They both laughed.

"Let's go home." He took her hand, and they walked towards the waiting car.

"Hmm, I'm not sure where home is just now. Davi's auntie and uncle have taken my rental flat until they find a bigger place. It's so convenient while they're helping Grace at the coffee house."

"I think I have the perfect solution," Sebastian responded, squeezing her hand. He felt like a teenager on a first date.

Outside the station, seeing Davi, Maddy ran forward, flinging her arms in the air to greet him as he walked towards her, excited and pleased to see her, yet cautious and hopeful his boss hadn't upset her. It was clear he was meeting a good friend.

"Grace is anxious to see you; let's go … so good to have you back." He winked at her, hoping she would understand his delight at seeing her and hoping all was well with Sebastian. Grace might not be so quick to forgive his boss; he was not looking forward to the lecture he was sure she would feel necessary to deliver.

"Auntie and Uncle are working full-time now; the new menu is keeping them all busy. Your suggestions were most helpful," he assured her, pride in his voice.

He took the backpack and walked jauntily to the driver's seat; this was just what the boss needed. He already looked less stressed.

It was good to have Maddy back … she made things come together.

It was a joyful reunion, although the regulars at the coffee house were suspicious of Sebastian and his motives. Hadn't their girl run away because of him? In the course of the excited sharing of news and experiences, it was clear that Davi's auntie and uncle were settled in the small flat near the coffee house, as they were now working full-time with Grace. Maddy had offered her little apartment while she was away, and it seemed mean-spirited, somehow, to displace them now that they had established a routine.

Sebastian was quick to offer a solution for all—Uncle and Auntie should remain in the flat and Maddy move into a separate apartment at his estate, no strings attached. Everyone felt this was a reasonable solution, although Maddy expressed concerns, which were quickly debated: "Save your rent money for travel", "Nice offer", Davi would be available for driving, Oyster Pass still valid, lovely to have Uncle and Auntie so close …

The talk subsided when Sebastian stood up and suggested they visit the new living quarters right now. He was adamant that they should take the Tube; he had purchased an Oyster Pass—a big step towards his transformation to win Maddy's friendship, he explained. A stop at the outdoor market for fresh vegetables was negotiated, and away they went, with everyone in the coffee house sighing in relief. Who doesn't love a happy ending? They all agreed.

As the cabbie turned into Bellmere House, Maddy felt she had been here before, and then it dawned on her—this was the house with the garden apartment they had looked at selling. The stately home, covered in ivy, looked like an old college dorm with set-in windows and a large entrance door. Surely there were ghosts. They walked past the garage, Sebastian pointing out the upper lodging where Davi lived, following the path to the garden. The sliding glass doors of the apartment were new, as were the patio stones and the deck. Maddy stopped, shocked to see before her a beautifully furnished apartment, exactly as she had laid it out for Lambert. Plants had been added to the patio, adding colour. The garden needed attention, she noted.

The apartment was perfect in every way; there was a kitchenette with counter seating, a desk and bookcase, a bed with a fluffy duvet, a sofa and flat-screen television, and a washroom with a rain shower as well as a washer and drying rack, the sliding glass doors across the front providing natural light and the small fireplace in the corner inviting.

"I feel like Alice in Wonderland." Maddy clapped her hands and twirled around the room. "Are you sure?" she asked. He nodded.

"Thank you, Sebastian; it's perfect." It was exactly as she had imagined it.

"Enjoy it. It's yours. No strings attached. Here's a phone for use in the UK, a credit card for expenses, and a reference book for anything else you might need, compliments of the ever-efficient Lambert." He looked pleased at her reaction. Maddy was still walking about the room, touching everything.

"Lambert stocked the kitchen as a welcome gift," he said as he opened the small refrigerator door. Maddy was clearly impressed.

"Yes, well, I'll leave you to get settled, I believe Davi delivered your bag - is that all you have?" He hesitated before walking out.

"I can only wear one thing at a time … it seems to be enough." She laughed at his confusion.

"Would you like to join me for dinner this evening? We have market fresh bounty," she asked shyly, holding up the shopping bags, hoping he would accept. "7 pm, in the garden, no jacket required."

"Indeed" he turned and bowed. He must remember to tell Lambert how pleased he was with the renovation and how positive Maddy had reacted.

The next morning, Maddy visited the neighbours on the street, introducing herself and inviting them to the garden for cocktails, and she became fast friends with beautiful, lonely Audrey across the boulevard. The two women connected immediately. Audrey was bored with her life at home, finding herself spiralling into depression. Maddy was so upbeat and demanding of her; she wanted to know everything about her past and her dreams. Audrey had never experienced anyone like Maddy, and after their initial visit she knew they would be friends.

Maddy brightened up the lives of the next-door neighbours Esme and Gordon, a retired couple who had convinced themselves they were too old to enjoy much of anything. Several of the homes were occupied by foreigners who kept a house in London. Maddy became friendly with their housekeepers, sharing recipes for ethnic food and getting to know where they shopped and more about their lives than anyone had ever bothered to ask. They all looked forward to visits from Maddy, and they were eager to share their fresh-baked wares.

Mrs Boronowski had been the housekeeper for Sebastian and his family for over forty years. She was very protective of Sebastian. When Maddy assured Mrs B she had no intention of moving into the big house, Mrs B relaxed and hoped the two of them would make it work, although Maddy insisted she and Sebastian were just becoming good friends. Mrs B. thought Sebastian needed a woman in his life—someone to care about— and thankfully Maddy wasn't a teenager or too fancy; she didn't seem like a gold-digger. Maddy was effusive over making pierogies, as she helped pit the cherries for the filling, earning high praise in the eyes of Mrs B.

Lambert called each day to assist with routings and to figure out which bus to take, which stop was best, and which restaurants she should try. He also provided advice on new exhibits or showings, and on purchases, and soon they developed a close friendship. He was looking out for her like a big brother. They enjoyed the same sense of humour and kidded each other mercilessly.

"Why do I have a credit card?" Maddy asked Lambert.

"You'll need to get things I may have forgotten, although Lord knows what those might be," he joked. "Sebastian wanted you to have an expense account because you saved us substantial fees with your assessments on the sale of the property assets. Consider the card your commission. Enjoy it, my dear."

He laughed when Maddy said it felt weird. "Just be sure to have a good single-malt whiskey on hand. Never mind; I'll send one over." Maddy smiled at how solicitous Lambert was towards his boss.

Sebastian returned home early a few nights later, disappointed to see the garden apartment in darkness. He was looking forward to updating Maddy on the action taken as a result of her questions, and he had a package from Lambert with tickets for various events she might enjoy. He had promised himself he would go slowly this time around.

He walked into his study, poured a single-malt scotch and settled in, feet up on the desk, to read the latest report on the possible sale of the South American operation.

He was well into the overly verbose written argument against selling when he heard soft music. He took his glasses off and walked over to the window. He saw lights and heard a pleasant melody coming from the garden. As he walked down the path and turned the corner, he was surprised at how light his step was and how anxious he was to see her.

At first glance he could not find her, and then he saw her feet sticking out from under a hedge.

"May I offer any assistance?" he asked after clearing his throat. She moved forward on the grass, sitting up, leaves and twigs in her hair. She smiled and clapped her hands together, looking pleased. "You're just in time. Did the music bother you?"

Sebastian reached down to help her off the ground.

"Not at all; I wondered how you were doing, and the music led me here."

"I am so happy to see you; I'm just about to turn the lights on, and here you are. You came at the best possible time." She grabbed his hand and dragged him towards the building. "I got all these lights from the neighbours and from your garage; hope you don't mind. I thought it would add even more ambiance to this beautiful little oasis."

Did she never take a breath in between sentences or thoughts? he wondered, a crooked smile on his face.

"Here we go. Hold on!" she called as she flipped the switch and jumped off the deck. "Okay, now." She ran towards him. The little garden came alive with white twinkling lights; it looked as if the stars had fallen into the trees.

"Dance with me?" she asked in a soft voice. "Please? You just close your eyes, feel the music, and hold me tight so I know what you want me to do. I'll try not to lead." She looked up at him with the wide eyes of a child at Christmas, her arms out in position, and before he could tell her he didn't dance, they were dancing to a Willie Nelson song. He was once again surprised at how natural it seemed, dancing in the garden under the stars, in this fairyland she had created.

Several songs later, he realized they were still dancing, and he was enjoying the moment. He made a note to remember the feeling—how to describe it—when Maddy next asked him if he had ever just enjoyed the moment. He was aware he must have missed many wonderful experiences by not being *in the moment*.

She looked up at him, searched his face, about to say something, and then smiled. No words, just a smile.

Sebastian blinked and shook his head. He was afraid that if he stayed one more minute, he would not be able to control himself. All he could think of was holding her all night.

He thanked her for sharing the "lighting of the garden" with him and for being such a patient dance partner. She laughed and offered an open invitation to dance whenever he heard the music.

He bowed formally and bade her a good night.

As he walked back into the house, he realized he was still humming the last tune and moving with a spring in his step. He also felt guilty for not having told her he had agreed months ago to escort Deirdre to the opening of a new show. He knew Maddy would love it, as it was a Bollywood interpretation of a Shakespeare play. Just one night, no strings attached—no issue. He wasn't looking forward to seeing Deirdre, but it was too late to cancel. A small voice asked him how he would handle knowing Maddy was going out with someone from her past. He shook off the feeling. How could you be jealous of someone you had just met?

Bollywood

The next morning, while baking at the coffee house, Davi mentioned his cousin had offered tickets to a production he was directing. It was a Shakespeare play with a Bollywood slant. The actors were East Indian, and his cousin was keen to fill the opening night with friendly faces. Maddy was thrilled; she loved all things Bollywood. They arranged to meet at the theatre early, as Auntie and Uncle were catering for the actors.

Ravinder Singh was a handsome figure in his long, beaded Nehru jacket, cotton pants, and silk shoes. He had directed the production in New York and Toronto with great success. The West End theatre was known for hosting privately funded works by foreign companies. Maddy and Ravi found many things to talk about, including the reviews on the Toronto production, visits to India, and how the translation board encouraged new patrons to the theatre in Hindi. Ravi knew of the village in India Maddy was supporting, and they were soon standing alone, having cut everyone else out of the conversation.

"Maddy, we do a director's q and a with the theatre manager at the beginning of the play—very informal. Would you please introduce us? You seem to have a connection with the play, and I love your enthusiasm. This evening is for patrons of the arts, so everyone here has participated in the funding of the production. I think it would add to the evening." Ravi was sincere in his request, as he was so enjoying her company.

The small theatre was filling, and the chairs were in place on the open stage. Ravi and Thompson Gell, the theatre manager, waited with Maddy as the lighting checks were done and the last of the guests arrived.

Maddy walked out on the open stage, her bright blue scarf wrapped casually around her neck, and the crowd quieted. She heard a gasp and looked down to be sure her kurta was straight. She introduced Ravi with such grace that he blushed, humbled by her accolades. It was clear he was delighted. She then introduced the theatre manager and welcomed questions from the theatre-goers, explaining why the Hindi translation on the reader board was important, and adding in an aside regarding how the translation changed to English when the actors spoke Hindi, although the audience would know what was going on by the wonderful facial expressions and actions. Her enthusiasm was infectious, and the crowd was anxious to ask questions. She concluded by bowing to the men and clasping her hands in front of her. "Gentlemen, the floor is yours." Applause erupted.

Deirdre was fussed to see Maddy, the woman from the gallery, on the stage, while Sebastian was mesmerized by her ease at the introduction and her playful rapport with the director. He enjoyed the play—its clever melding of two cultures, Shakespeare's words with the singsong accents, and the colourful costumes and simple staging. He realized he was enjoying watching Maddy for most of the first act as she delighted in every moment of the play. How he wished he were sitting beside her, feeling her excitement. He wondered if she had lemon bonbons with her. Deirdre noticed he was preoccupied. "How could you bring me here when your *garden mistress* is here?" she hissed. Deirdre had heard of the apartment setup and had named her nemesis "the garden mistress".

Sebastian turned to her and calmly replied, "Deirdre, you are a respected patron of the arts, not a fishwife. I had no idea Maddy—her name is Maddy, by the way—would be here. Please behave."

The intermission seemed interminable, as Sebastian was not keen on having Maddy and Deirdre meet. Ravi had gone straight to Maddy for her comments on the first act, and they were comparing notes in the back row, heads down, when Sebastian and Deirdre returned to their seats.

After taking their bows, the cast appeared in the reception hall to meet their friends and family. Sebastian saw Maddy standing beside Ravi. He had his hand on the small of her back as he was taking leave of a group of entertainment reporters. He was moving towards the door with Maddy, Davi, Grace, Auntie, and Uncle. No doubt they would be celebrating the success of the opening. Sebastian realized he was uncomfortable with the way Ravi was holding Maddy.

He watched her give her full attention to an older couple who had stopped her. Her head cocked to one side, her eyes intent on the conversation. She looked up, smiling, and saw him in the crowd. Her eyes widened and held his gaze for a second; she then looked over at Deirdre, blinking, the smile fading. She looked down and seemed to collect herself, concentrating on the conversation. Did he imagine she looked hurt?

"She's moved on, Sebastian; so should you. Let's go; I've had enough of India for one night." Deirdre took his arm and led him outdoors.

"Did you enjoy the play?" Maddy appeared from nowhere. She looked amused.

Somewhere in his head, Sebastian heard the word "busted".

"Would you like to meet Raveesh? He and Davi are cousins." Maddy reported, motioning to Ravi. "We're all heading out to the new restaurant A Taste of India; won't you join us?" Maddy was waiting for a response, having introduced Sebastian and Deirdre to the director.

"No thank you," Deirdre replied haughtily as she turned to go, taking Sebastian by the arm.

"Thank you, another time," Sebastian said directly to Maddy as he was dragged away.

Davi watched the exchange and turned to Grace, who had covered her mouth with her hand, her eyes wide. "That went well, don't you think?"

Maddy and Ravi were climbing into the limo with Auntie and Uncle.

"Let's go." Davi took Grace by the hand.

Maddy looked at Grace across the leather seats and shrugged. Grace leaned over and patted her knee. "I'm sure there's a reasonable explanation."

Maddy laughed out loud. "'No strings', he said. I am defined by my friends, and tonight, my friends, we celebrate the brilliant production of Ravi."

"Hear, hear!" the crowd in the limo agreed.

And celebrate they did, dancing until dawn.

Sebastian paced back and forth, watching for the lights of the limo to pull in. Eventually he fell asleep on the sofa, dreaming of Bollywood dancers led by Maddy and Ravi. He had taken Deirdre straight home; she had not enjoyed the fast patter of the play, unable to make out the words. Sebastian felt sad for her; she found the downside but didn't mention the bright colours, the facial expressions, the flirty dialogue, or the humour. She hadn't cried or clasped her hands together, offered lemon bonbons, or whispered in his ear …

Maddy and Davi returned home as the sun was coming up, the limo stopping at the driveway. They were still dancing and giggling, shushing each other so as not to disturb the neighbours. It had been a wonderful night of high-energy dancing with Davi and his family. Grace, Auntie, and Uncle had gone home hours ago, aware of the early morning opening of the coffee house. Maddy and Davi bowed to each other at the garage, sharing a namaste with hands clasped. Maddy padded barefoot into the apartment, dropped her shoes, and fell back onto the bed, tired but happy.

Only once during the evening had she wished Sebastian had joined them. She was not able to define the feeling of seeing him with Deirdre but realized he was an eligible bachelor and he had friends in the city. She had shrugged off Grace's concern for her, laughing at herself for feeling cheated on by someone who had clearly said "no strings". She had been determined to enjoy the evening. Her feet were aching, so she must have succeeded, she reckoned. Ravi had asked to see her again before the show closed. Maddy asked about his family, guessing he was married, and agreed to see him at the coffee house sometime during the next two weeks.

The loud piano riff alarm woke her at noon. She took stock: feet still sore, same clothes on, phone date confirmed. She stood up and checked the weather outside. *Ah, yes, I'm still in England, and it's raining.* It took a moment for her to remember why the alarm had gone off. She had agreed to fill in for someone, sitting with chemo patients at the hospital. *Too late to cancel.*

Starbucks cup in hand, she opened the door to the ward and was greeted by the staff; the two young men and the middle-aged woman she was visiting with today looked up, relieved to see her. The wan smiles on their faces made her feel ashamed for even considering staying in bed. She could hardly wait to tell them about the Bollywood experience.

Maddy dropped in to see Grace at the coffee house and stayed for dinner, realizing how much she missed seeing her friend. "First things first, Grace, I need to soak in your bathtub. I miss my bathtub. I do my best thinking in the tub. Showers get you clean; they don't relax you."

"Maddy, has this guy made any romantic moves or tried anything out of line?" Grace asked, concern in her voice, as she delivered a casserole to the table. Grace had seen the disappointment on Maddy's face at the theatre when Sebastian appeared with the skinny, uptight woman.

"Not at all. He's been a good friend. We have an easy time together, but he doesn't seem interested in more." Maddy took a mouthful of the chicken divan and smiled.

"Do you think he's gay?" Grace was careful to ask this.

Maddy laughed, arms on the table, head cupped in her hands. "No, but that could only happen to me." They enjoyed the evening, chatting and laughing and working on the menus.

Grace insisted Maddy sleep over, as there was a very real chance she would fall asleep on the Tube, never making it home. No argument. Maddy was too tired to move, citing old age as the culprit and thanking Grace for the use of the bathtub. Grace merely laughed, shaking her head. Davi had told her of their marathon Bollywood evening.

"I heard you were a Bollywood rock star. The family wants to adopt you."

"See, the offers keep rolling in. Good night." Maddy was asleep on the sofa before Grace could respond.

"Sir, are you all right this morning?" Davi asked his boss, who was looking under the weather.

"Sorry; I'm trying to deal with a dilemma, and I'm at a loss. It's easier closing an international merger than it is to understand personal relationships." Sebastian shook his head in frustration. He had not slept well and had not seen Maddy for several days.

"Sir, it's none of my business, but if you need help with relationships, I would suggest you speak with Maddy for advice. She is so great at listening, and I must say, she is a fixer. She wants to fix everything. Talk to her." Davi nodded, as if to agree with himself. "She's the one, sir."

Sebastian leaned his head back on the car seat, trying not to smile. *If only I knew where she was.*

"Indeed. Thank you."

Walking in the Rain

"Sebastian, would you like to go for a walk?" she asked, watching him read through a thick report. "Just to clear your head." This was becoming a Sunday ritual; after breakfast at a local deli, they would either walk in the park or attend a flea market, returning to the garden apartment to read on the sofa.

"It's raining," he said over his reading glasses, nodding at the garden.

"It's England; it's always raining."

He placed the report on the side table, stood up, and pulled her up from the sofa where she was sitting with her arms wrapped around her legs, her chin on her knees.

"A walk is not what I need, but a walk it shall be. Come on, then; let's get an umbrella."

She kissed his cheek and declared he was a great sport.

"Indeed."

After shaking their wet jackets off, they sat on the rug by the fire, warming up with colourful afghan shawls around their shoulders. Hot chocolate and sandwiches had never tasted so good.

They were staring into the fire when Maddy stood, dropping her blanket. The music was soft and sexy. "Dance with me?" She held out her hand. He stood beside her and took her in his arms. The music took them someplace far away. Maddy instructed him to hold her, close his eyes, and dance as if no one was looking.

Sebastian wondered if they would ever talk about the night at the play. He was aching to know why he hadn't seen her for two nights, but he couldn't ask; he had no right to ask. He looked down at her face. Her eyes were closed; she looked so content. She opened her eyes and smiled at him, melting away any doubt that she was enjoying his company. He kissed her forehead. She snuggled into his chest. He felt warm and safe. Maddy sighed, enjoying the feeling. This was new to Sebastian; he had never spent time with anyone who demanded nothing in return, and it was comforting.

A phone was ringing. They stepped apart, looking around the room to find the wicked object that had broken the spell. It was Maddy's phone. She answered. "Maddy here." She sat down, listening intently to the caller. "Of course, sweetie, I'll be there. What time?" She looked concerned. "No, of course not, no trouble at all; I'll be there by 9.00 a.m. and take care of everything. You go back to bed and get better." She ran her fingers through her hair and nodded into the phone. "No, no, I'm happy to do it. Bye." The caller did not want to hang up. "Yes, I do too. Ta-ta."

Maddy turned and smiled at Sebastian, shrugging her shoulders and raising her eyebrows in defeat. He cleared his throat and gathered his papers. "I should finish this report and make my notes so I can participate in the discussion tomorrow." He was busy collecting his papers and packing his briefcase. "Thank you for a lovely Sunday." He kissed her cheek and ran through the rain to the house.

Maddy cleared their dinner, tidied the apartment, and fell back on the bed, arms out, sighing.

Mah-Jong

Lambert smiled to himself as Sebastian announced he was heading home to complete reading the prospectus. Lambert nodded, noting that Sebastian had often been heading home early lately. Could it be his garden tenant he was anxious to see?

Sebastian arrived home to find a group of women around a table, playing a game.

Maddy rose to greet him as he stepped out of the car.

"Hey, Sebastian. We're learning to play mah-jong. Do you know the game?" He shook his head and nodded to the ladies. Mrs B was at the table, waving him away; he was disturbing the game.

"Would you like a drink?" Maddy asked, hopeful for a distraction. "I should have asked you if it was all right to have friends over. I'm sorry; it was presumptuous of me." She looked concerned and contrite, her cheeks flushed and her eyes begging for forgiveness. He had to turn away.

"By all means, it's your home. Do as you please." He turned and headed for the house.

"Everyone leaves in an hour. Would you like to have dinner with me? We made shepherd's pie and pastries today. It's not fancy, but it is hearty." Maddy sounded hopeful.

Sebastian turned to her and was about to decline when he heard himself say he couldn't remember the last time he had been offered shepherd's pie. He would see how far he got with his reading before committing.

Maddy shrugged and returned to the game table, sorry she had not introduced the women to him. He seemed shy; perhaps he would have stayed to have a drink if he knew them. She would apologize later.

"Maddy, it's your move," Esme remarked, not looking up.

Maddy quickly turned her attention to the game, surprised at how disappointed she felt.

Sebastian walked into his study, removed his tie, poured himself a drink, and sat at the desk, feeling disappointed, although he couldn't reason why.

Throwing in the Towel

Sebastian was whistling as he walked through the garden to the apartment. He heard the music, knocked on the glass door, and called, "Maddy, it's Sebastian. Hello."

"Hang on; be right out," she called.

Sebastian stepped in and noted how orderly the room was—everything in its place, tidy, and very welcoming. He sat on the sofa, loosened his tie, and closed his eyes, head back, thinking how comfortable the garden apartment had become.

He felt her presence before she spoke. "Sebastian? How nice. Drink? Audrey says every British home must have gin and tonic on hand. Would you prefer a beer?"

The room smelled fresh, like spring, as she appeared before him wrapped in a plush towel, drying her hair with a smaller towel. His mind was racing, hoping the towel would fall, resisting the urge to stand and wrap his arms around her. He cleared his throat and agreed that a gin and tonic would be lovely.

"Lemon or lime? I never quite know which is right." She smiled back at him from the small refrigerator.

"Ah, either is fine, but I prefer lime if you have it." He felt like a schoolboy, watching her, willing the towel to drop.

"Please help yourself when you come over; there's always something to drink or munch on." She handed him the drink, and he felt dizzy; she was too close.

"Cheers." He raised his glass and took a sip, enjoying the cool liquid going down his throat.

Maddy sat on the opposite side of the sofa, watching him and wondering why he had stopped by. She smiled and thought how comfortable it was to have him sitting here, on the sofa, sipping on a gin and tonic in the afternoon.

"Maddy, I should have called first, but I have tickets for a comedy at the Playhouse, and I thought—rather, I hoped—you would be available for an early dinner and the play. I'm sorry for not giving you more notice, and I understand if you have plans …" He sounded awkward to himself and wondered what he must sound like to her. He wasn't sure where to look.

"Great. I'd love to go. I probably should get dressed." She laughed a throaty laugh, and he smiled back, enjoying the sound. "I'll just be a minute."

He watched her move across the room, towel still intact, running her fingers through her hair, her scent wafting through the small apartment. He rubbed his forehead and smiled to himself at how naturally the scene had played out. Maddy had not been self-conscious greeting him in her home with just a towel wrapped around her and offering him a drink. He couldn't recall any other woman he had ever known who would wander out wrapped in a towel; even his wife, Claire, had dressed before appearing each morning. He was mulling thoughts of culture or personality differences when Maddy appeared in front of him in a simple blue linen dress, a long colourful scarf in her hand, her hair tied back with a ribbon. She wore ballet slippers and looked as though she had spent hours putting together a simple yet elegant look. He stared up at her, enjoying the sight of her.

"I'm ready." She smiled down at him, holding out her hand to help him up off the sofa. He stood quickly, again resisting the urge to hold her in his arms. He finished his drink, glad for a diversion. He nodded at her in approval and gently put his hand on her back and led her out into the garden.

Davi dropped them at a small restaurant near the theatre, where they managed a table on the outdoor patio. Soon they were watching the setting sun bounce off the wake from the boats on the Thames.

They chatted about the weather, the architecture of the buildings across the river, Belle and George, and current events. Sebastian was charmed by her facial expression when she didn't understand something; she would stop a conversation, not in an aggressive manner, by asking what he meant or encouraging him to explain something, and she always wanted to know why he felt the way he did about almost everything. She was quick and funny and very easy to be with, alone or in a crowd. At one point during dinner, she touched his hand while trying to convince him to see an alternative. He conceded, not because he heard her argument but because he enjoyed the intimacy of the gesture.

The play was entertaining, racy, and very funny. Sebastian wasn't sure if he enjoyed the comedy as much as hearing Maddy laugh out loud. During the intermission, they shared a flavoured sparkling water—a concept new to him. Maddy shared everything: food, drinks. Despite himself, Sebastian found he was enjoying it.

When they returned to their seats, Maddy immediately began conversing with those around her, sharing favourite lines and asking for recommendations on future shows and restaurants. As they were leaving the theatre, several people came over to suggest plays or trendy eating places. They were conspiratorial in their passing of information, and he had no doubt he would soon be visiting each location. He watched Maddy in the crowd and marvelled at her ease with talking to complete strangers. His world was insular, with club members and known business acquaintances; he wasn't as comfortable with strangers.

Maddy reasoned, when they spoke of it, that strangers were just friends one hadn't yet met.

Too soon, the evening was over, and they arrived back at the garden. Something about the way he walked her to the door told her not to invite him in for a drink.

"Thank you for a lovely evening, Sebastian. I'm so glad you thought of me." She reached up and kissed his cheek.

He smiled at her, thinking how much he wanted to kiss her.

"It was my pleasure, and I hope we can do this again. I will try to give you more notice next time." He was very polite.

"No worries; it was perfect timing. Good night." She waited until he walked through the garden to close the patio door. The butterflies in her stomach were flying into each other, and her knees were shaking.

Audrey

Maddy frequently visited Belle and George, or B and G, as she called them, usually by train or driving with her neighbour Audrey. Audrey was tall and slim, with flowing tresses and chiselled features. She feared she was becoming agoraphobic, staying indoors and waiting for her husband Jeffery to return home after his frequent business trips abroad. She no longer worked in television, hosting designer makeover shows, and was bored with her life of apparent luxury. She had first met Jeffery at an opening reception for an office remake; they had talked all evening, and the next day he asked her to marry him. He swept her off her feet, literally, she liked to say.

They had a busy life, and for many years they were happy to meet on the fly, whenever their schedules allowed. When Audrey had her second miscarriage, they decided it would be best for her to stay at home and give up her career to concentrate on being a mum. After several more attempts, they gave up. Jeffery took more international clients at his firm and travelled even more, staying away from home for weeks at a time. Audrey felt trapped in the house, alone, fighting depression. She couldn't make herself go out job hunting, despite her many contacts.

Then Maddy came along, and although she was older, she had enough energy for them both, it seemed. Maddy somehow saw the potential in Audrey and started giving her small design projects, asking for her help in choosing furniture, accessories, and colour schemes. Soon the two were involved in redesigns, using many of Audrey's old friends and contacts. They scoured markets, looking for treasures and the perfect accent note for a wall. They tried new restaurants and attended theatre and gallery openings, enjoying each other's company.

Maddy offered Audrey a much-needed distraction, forcing her out of her comfortable home and into the world of Maddy. They fell into a fast friendship, trusting each other and sharing their stories. Audrey warned Sebastian not to screw up; she didn't have many female friends, and Maddy was important to her.

One of their fellow train passengers commented on how the women reminded him of the *Absolutely Fabulous* duo, with their patter and dry humour. The comparison to the television sitcom brought gales of laughter from the women, who then acted in character for much of the ride home—without the Bolly, of course.

"Maddy, we have to dry clean those sweaters you and George wear on the beach; they smell fishy," Audrey said one night on the return train trip. "The locals talk about it. What does Sebastian say when you get home smelling from the walks on the beach?"

"I always shower and use whatever tropical fruit shampoo is on sale at Boots. I'm on a coconut roll just now. He seems to like it. No complaints, as a matter of fact." Maddy shot back.

"Maybe he's just hungry. Let me take you to my stylist," Audrey offered.

"One visit to your stylist would eat up my annual clothing budget," Maddy laughed.

"Oh please, let's not talk budgets. I always seem to go overbudget, and Jeffery gives me the lecture about cutting back and how money doesn't grow on trees." Audrey waved her hands in the air. "It's just too much for me."

"Oh, Audrey, I could live comfortably for a few weeks if I sold one of your beautiful gowns. Maddy said, laughing a laugh so contagious the other passengers were smiling.

"Oh no, Maddy, after the budget lecture I look contrite, and then a few days later, at breakfast, I say I'm perfectly happy to wear the same gown I wore last year to the event. Jeffery nods, kisses me goodbye, and I wait. It usually takes between eighteen and twenty-six minutes before he calls me back and says it would be wrong to wear the same dress as last year since he makes his clients so much money; they would be shocked to see his beautiful wife—that would be me—in the same dress twice. He then begs me to get a new dress—something sexy."

"Sexy is good."

"It's all good. Last week he intimated that I was not to go shopping with you. He's afraid you'll take me to one of your markets and we'll find the original gown the queen of Sheba wore at a famous ball and he'll be forced to defend the historical significance." Audrey was bent over in laughter.

Maddy laughed just as hard. They had found some rare, eclectic treasures, to be sure. Although she wore them, and they suited her, they were not de rigueur for the establishment. And Jeffery was the establishment. He didn't even own a T-shirt.

"I'm shocked but thrilled he thought I might have some influence on your wardrobe. I must research the queen of Sheba so I can tease him with a hint of what you might be wearing. He'll be beside himself." Maddy could hardly get the words out she was laughing so hard; tears were streaming down her face.

"Let's stop at Boots on the way home and I'll get you some new nail polish; yours is all chipped."

"Please, Maddy, my manicurist will have a fit if I walk in with a different varnish." Audrey looked at her nails. "Oh, they are in bad shape. I must call."

"Maybe she has queen of Sheba in a bottle." Maddy waved her hands around her head, attempting to mock exotic dancing. They fell back laughing.

"Do we have time to pop into Harrods for bouquet garni?" Audrey asked, leafing through a magazine.

"I only go to Harrods when all the other art galleries are closed for the day. I don't shop there, but I could go with you," Maddy responded. "Why don't I get you some herbs tomorrow at the market? You can strain them through your panty hose—more practical."

The sound of their unrelenting laughter carried throughout the train, and although not everyone was in on the joke, they were wishing they were; the disembarking passengers were smiling, and some whistling, as they hurried out of the station.

Laughter filled the air as they walked past his window, forcing Sebastian to look up from his report. Davi greeted them as he was leaving for dinner with Grace. "Would you like to join us?" he asked.

"No thanks, we've had quite the day on the beach. Davi, someone on the train told us we were like the girls in *Absolutely Fabulous* ... can you imagine?" Maddy laughed.

"Were you drinking on the train?" Davi asked in a serious voice, his head cocked to one side.

"Heavens no, but we were a wee bit loud," Audrey responded.

"I'm sure they just meant you were fun," Davi said in his quiet singsong voice as he turned to go.

"Thank you, my friend. Give my love to Grace." Maddy waved. "Oh, Davi ... wait a moment." Maddy ran over to him. "How did your exam go? I'm sorry I forgot to ask."

"Oh, quite excellent. I think I did well enough in the course, but I still have a problem with the afternoon class. Perhaps you would like to join me for a session so you can see how it flows. Your study guide was most helpful." He nodded, acknowledging her help.

"Excellent." She clapped her hands. "I'd love to attend the class. Just say when. Have fun tonight."

"I'm heading home too; sorry to leave you all alone, sweetie. I'm knackered. You tire me out." Audrey gathered her packages and headed for the path. "I'll confirm the pricing on the beams and let you know what I find out about the tiles. Good night. Are you sure you don't want to visit my stylist?"

Maddy hugged her friend, waved, and turned to plug in the lights and the music.

She was moving easily to the music, eyes closed, her arms in the air. Sebastian cleared his throat behind her. She turned and slowly opened her eyes, greeting him with that smile—the smile that started in her eyes and spread across her cheeks, lighting up the area. "Hi. Did we disturb you?"

"Not at all," he said softly. He had walked down to the garden, not able to concentrate on his report once he heard her laughing.

"Davi tells me you are a fixer—a person with solutions," he said, sitting beside her.

"Oh, really?" She chuckled.

"I have to agree, since you suggested I leave work early so everyone else could be more productive." He recalled how he had not appreciated her comments at the time, although the office morale had improved. "I have a dilemma, and I hope you can help me." He sat beside her at the table.

"What's wrong? Of course I'll try." She looked concerned.

"Nothing's wrong. I'm trying to include everyone on the team in a responsive, more receptive way, and I can't seem to integrate the shy or less secure team members into the group. Any suggestions?" He paused and continued. "I want to provide coaching so they can approach others and share their experience or ask for assistance. Do I start with the stronger members of the team or newcomers?" He fidgeted with the coaster on the table. He was not a fidgety person by nature.

"Hmm, not knowing the players, I can suggest some icebreaker exercises to introduce everyone, concentrating on their talents and past success. I can help you with that, if you like." She smiled at him, wondering if this was really what he wanted to talk about.

Sebastian looked away and nodded. "Maddy, how do you do it? How do you walk into a room and just start a conversation with a stranger?" He looked uncomfortable, but Maddy realized he was getting closer to the real question. She watched him patiently, nodding and encouraging him to continue.

"It's not difficult. You see someone in the room, and you watch them for a minute or two; see if they're as nervous as you are; watch how they view the crowd, how they hold their drink, how they acknowledge people passing by—you know; you notice their body language and expressions. Something about the person will attract you. Walk over and introduce yourself or start with a question. Just focus completely on them." She stood up.

Maddy pulled Sebastian to his feet and walked away from him, turning as she continued.

"Let's pretend we're at a reception. When you are ready, walk over and introduce yourself. You can say something bold—something unexpected— just to make me want to get to know you better. Okay?" She waited. "Don't forget to make eye contact and smile at me; a smile says so much. If they smile back, you walk over, very confident, not tentative." She gestured deliberately.

"You approach them; smile. It makes your face less tense. Practise—just smile." She was watching him smile. Realizing he was not moving, she walked towards him.

"You say something nice, like, 'I'm sure we haven't been introduced' or 'I couldn't help but notice you are standing here alone, brightening up the room.' Whatever you feel most comfortable saying—you know what I mean?" She gave him a concerned look.

Sebastian nodded.

"Okay, now you've made contact. You could keep on talking, but that could waste a lot of time if they aren't responding. This is where you make your move. You either invest or divest—stay or move on." She put her hands on his chest. "You either start a conversation, begin dancing, or direct them away from the crowd—get them alone." She waited. "Oh, don't forget the call to action. You must have an action plan. What do you want to happen next? You invite them for a drink somewhere else, dinner or something special—you know, to get to the next step, if that's where you were going with the question." She stepped back. "Does that help?" She could see his confusion.

"When you saw me in the gallery and kissed me, was that your bold move?" He asked.

Maddy smiled. "I can't lie; you were so handsome, and the light was creating a halo around you. You looked good." She was nodding, recalling the moment. "When I heard the irritating voice and saw your grimace, all I could think was that I had to do something to help this poor man; he already has bad taste in art, now women too. I had to think fast. We didn't have time or an escape route, so I kissed you. It wasn't planned or premeditated. It could have been disastrous."

"How so?" He asked, thinking back to the event.

"You could have pushed me away," Maddy responded.

"As I recall, I kissed you back. Ah, after the initial shock." He smiled. "Didn't I?"

"You can't kiss and tell." Maddy smiled, enjoying his discomfort.

Sebastian looked at Maddy standing beside him, the light just right, her eyes dancing, and her hands still on his chest. He was fighting with himself. He wanted to kiss her and test her theory on the bold move.

"Maddy, I'm sorry about the night of the play. Deirdre had asked me months ago to escort her. I don't know how to deal with these things.

When I saw you at the theatre, I wanted to sit with you and share your delight with the lines and the whole experience. I really didn't know you would be there." He hoped she would respond with a kiss.

Maddy stiffened and moved back. She looked down at her hands, rubbing them together, upset that Sebastian was worried only that she had seen him.

She looked up, and he could see her eyes were moist.

"Sebastian, it was confusing, but it's really none of my business. You have old friends and acquaintances, and I'm new to the hood." She was trying to make light of it. "I was disappointed you didn't join us after the show. It was unbelievably fun. However, you did say 'no strings', so I have to respect that."

"The director seemed very solicitous; will you see him again?" He hated himself for asking.

Maddy hesitated before answering. "Raveesh is very married, and he's a part of the family. I hope I see him again. He has a brilliant mind."

She was smiling again; that was a good sign. But she had moved away from him, and it was time to go.

October

"Davi, are you on your way home?" Maddy was walking through the garden, setting up the foot basins and chairs. "Yes, we are ten minutes away," he responded.

"Excellent. I need you both to help me with a mission of mercy, please?" Maddy whispered into her phone.

After a moment, Davi replied, "We will help you if we can. See you presently."

Maddy smiled at the young girls and gave the thumbs up sign. The ladies were already in their chairs, pedicures and manicures underway.

"Ah, here you are. Welcome to the Garden Spa." She ran towards Davi and Sebastian, both of whom were looking very hesitant and perhaps a little wary. "Birgit and Amelia operate the spa on the high street, and they want to add home parties to the menu down the road, and they need practise, so here we are. Your foot bath awaits." She pointed to a chair with a basin in front. "Thank you both; I appreciate your good sportsmanship." She smiled. "I'm helping them out so they can feel confident going out. Drinks and snacks are on the way. Enjoy."

Sebastian looked uncomfortable, and Davi was petrified as the girls removed his shoes and then his socks and directed his feet into the water.

The ladies at the other treatment stations were quick to welcome the men and include them in conversation. Maddy appeared with chai for Davi, single-malt scotch, for Sebastian and a tray of hors d'oeuvres for both.

The garden was festive, and the conversation was enjoyable. Mrs B, Grace, Esme, and Audrey were soon done, moving their chairs closer to the men, continuing the conversation, and encouraging the spa girls. It was a pleasant evening, and Maddy was an attentive hostess. As the Spa girls cleared their equipment and tables, the guests continued to visit and dine on the meal Maddy provided. Sebastian was surprised at how at ease she made them all feel—how she introduced inclusive conversation and kept them entertained.

After dinner, the group dispersed, most complimentary of the spa experience and food. Davi offered to drive Mrs B and Grace across the city; Audrey and Esme waved and walked home.

Sebastian was delighted to be alone with Maddy at last.

"Thank you for being such a good sport. I really wanted the girls to feel comfortable with men as well as women." She smiled at him and patted his shoulder.

"I must say, it was a first. I'm thankful you didn't require Davi and me to get painted up." He smiled back.

"Oh look, a shooting star." Maddy was pointing to the sky, her face flushed and her eyes bright. Sebastian didn't look up at the sky; he was too focused on her face.

Friday Night in a Foreign Land

Wondering where Maddy might be seemed to take up a great deal of his time lately. Sebastian sat back in his home office, feet up on the desk, his gin and tonic untouched. He had hurried home after his last client meeting, hoping to whisk Maddy off to a pleasant evening. He smiled as he thought of the conversations and comfortable silences they shared. She was the consolation prize for having worked hard all week.

He heard Maddy arrive, walking by his window, speaking on her mobile.

"Don't be silly; of course I miss you all. Look, you have lots of wonderful friends around, you and you're crazy in love with Jonah. Why don't you come and visit me here? I'd love for you to meet my new friends." There was a pause. Sebastian couldn't help but hear the conversation.

"Well, if it makes you feel better, here I am, a single woman, arriving to a lovely garden, where I will sit by myself on a Friday night, in a foreign country. You, on the other hand, are surrounded by loving friends and family at a fantastic lakeside cottage. Say hello for me, and assure everyone I'm fine. I'm truly fine, honestly. Mary, you should go back to bed. Everyone will be expecting your wonderful turkey dinner tomorrow, and you'll need to be up early. I'm sorry to miss it." Another pause. "Me too. Big hugs. Happy Thanksgiving." Another pause. "I promise. Bye for now."

Sebastian walked into the garden slowly, unsure of what he would say or do.

"Maddy?" he called. It was unusual to find her in darkness since the lights had been installed.

He saw her sitting on the deck, staring out at the garden. He wanted to run over and hold her; she looked so vulnerable.

She peered up with a sad smile. "Hey Sebastian, are you just getting home? Are you hungry? Can I get you a drink?"

"Hello. No. I wondered if you would join me for dinner. I thought I'd take the MG out for a drive and find a small pub. You're so right; I enjoy the car, and I should drive it." He was standing beside her, his hands behind his back.

She looked up and smiled. "That would be wonderful. Do I need to change?"

"No, you're perfect. Oh, you might want a scarf if we leave the top down." He reached out for her hand. He felt giddy holding her hand and walking towards the garage.

They drove in silence, Sebastian wishful that she would talk to him about her friends over dinner, and Maddy feeling homesick for her friends but enjoying the car, the man, and the irony of not being alone on a Friday night.

The Firkin and Toad Pub was inviting and noisy as they stepped in and found a seat by the electric fire. Sebastian ordered from the bar and sat across from Maddy, holding her hands in his. "Thanks for coming with me; it's certainly more enjoyable taking the car out and exploring with someone else."

Maddy looked around the room and then back at Sebastian, her eyes moist. "I'm glad you asked me. I had a call from a friend tonight, and I'm afraid I would have spent the evening wallowing in self-pity. Thank you."

He wanted to hold her face and assure her she would never be alone when the drinks arrived and the moment passed.

It was damp, and the air was chilled when they left the warmth of the pub. Sebastian put his arms around her as they walked to the car. The evening had been lively as the locals involved them in the weekly trivia contest. Several of the older men suggested they stay in the lodging upstairs. Maddy endured endless queries about Canadian relatives she might know and where they lived in relation to her home. They were exhausted as they said good night to the crowd.

The drive home was filled with laughter as they revisited incorrect answers and wild guesses, characters, and accents. Sebastian walked Maddy to the patio door and kissed her good night, and with all the British reserve he could muster, he turned and walked to the main house. Maddy fell into bed, smiling and wistful. It was a great feeling to be a single woman in a foreign land on a Friday night.

It's Who You Know

"Sir, I have good news to brighten your day." Davi was worried about Sebastian; he had seemed tired and distracted these last few days. At one time Davi would have remained quiet, realizing work was stressful for his boss; now he knew Sebastian was this way because Maddy had been away and he didn't know where she was.

"I could use some good news. Fire away." Sebastian leaned his head back in the seat, half listening to Davi.

"Sir, Maddy is back. She was working on a project with Mr George, but she came home this morning. It was her turn to host the neighbours for morning coffee. She has promised us tea and cinnamon buns. It's a lovely gesture." Davi was almost singing.

"Indeed." Sebastian sat up. "A lovely gesture, indeed." He was looking forward to seeing Maddy; he missed her welcome-home smiles and dancing with her and having her ask about his day.

As the car pulled into the garage, Sebastian stepped out and walked towards the patio, which was set for tea. Maddy came out with oven gloves, holding a warm tray, her face flushed from the heat of the kitchen. She blew a rogue wisp of hair away from her eyes and moved her shoulders up to graze her cheek, and in that instant Sebastian wanted to run his hands through her hair and kiss her on her flushed cheeks.

Maddy invited the men to the table. "Hey, so good to see you. Come and try my first attempt at cinnamon buns."

"They smell delicious." Davi was keen.

"Indeed," Sebastian managed, preoccupied with his thoughts of kissing her. "Davi tells me you get together with the neighbours once a week." he said as he poured the tea at Maddy's request.

"Yes. I introduced myself the day after I moved in and invited the ladies to come over for coffee. Several of the homes on the block are staffed, but their owners live abroad for various reasons. It was fun to meet everyone, and now it's a regular thing. It can be very interesting." Maddy smiled as she served the warm cinnamon rolls.

"I think I may have sold your penthouse in the city."

Sebastian had taken a first bite and was enjoying the soft, sweet roll. He stopped chewing and stared at her. "You what?"

"The folks two doors down, next to Audrey, have never lived in the house. They bought it so their teenagers would have a place for university, but the teens don't want to live so far from the heart of the city and have resisted moving in. I gave Jasmina, their housekeeper, a copy of the prospectus you had on the penthouse and she passed it on to her owners. They love it and want to purchase it immediately. Who should I put them in touch with? Is Lambert able to help them? Are there any other interested parties? They don't care about negotiating; they just want to buy it and sell this house. Is that all right? I should have asked you first, but it happened so fast, and I haven't seen you for a few days." Maddy finally took a breath.

Sebastian slowly sipped his tea, looked up at Maddy and started to laugh. "You sold a very exclusive penthouse in the heart of London through the housekeeper, and you want to know if it's all right? Maddy, that's amazing. Lambert can act as the agent; he has his papers. The two of you can share the commission. I can't believe it. Well done, Maddy."

"Well, I'm glad you're pleased, and how nice for Lambert to have the commission; he'll be doing all the work. What about the house across the street? It sounds like they want to dump it as quickly as possible. I got the details from the web site—it was worth *mucho dinero* when they purchased it three years ago. It needs some updating. It's very brown." Maddy handed the listing over to Sebastian, who was still in shock.

"You amaze me, Maddy. You simply amaze me." He shook his head, doing the maths in his mind. Buying houses, renovating, and selling were what he enjoyed most these days. He could easily make an offer and turn it around quickly. He decided he and Lambert would discuss it in the morning.

The party of three chatted about the weather, world news, the recent terrorist attacks, and how delicious the cinnamon rolls had turned out. When the tea was done, Davi excused himself, giving Maddy a thumbs up.

"Let's not be so quick to show interest in the house across the way; we have to be transparent, and we don't want to take advantage of the situation. Lambert will be thrilled. Will you call him with the contact information?" Sebastian asked.

Maddy nodded, pleased with his reaction.

"Location, location, location, they always say, but I think it's who you know."

Sebastian leaned over and kissed Maddy on the forehead. "I need time to process how someone so skilled at cinnamon buns can also move major real estate and make a great cup of tea. Good night, Maddy; it's good to have you home." Sebastian slowly walked towards the main house, not trusting himself to look back at her, knowing that if she smiled or gave him the least bit of encouragement, he would wrap his arms around her … *And what?* he asked himself. *And then what?*

The Assistant

"Maddy, that was a phenomenal referral. Let me take you to lunch." Lambert was beside himself; he had completed the sale—documents signed, keys exchanged. It was his first solo transaction, and he felt a debt of gratitude to Maddy, who refused to take her share of the commission.

"Cheers, Maddy. You know, you and Sebastian have been so good to me." Lambert raised his glass and toasted Maddy.

"How so? You earned that commission."

Lambert looked around the restaurant and leaned towards Maddy. "When I was first an intern at the firm, not a person would give me the time of day. Sebastian always worked late and always spoke to me. He would ask me about school, my life at home, what my aspirations were, what I knew about the office equipment … He gave me challenges. He would ask me if I could handle getting copies and setting up the boardroom, if I could find a suitable show for clients coming in from America, if I could find him a superb restaurant where he could take a fussy client with food allergies, if I could program a spreadsheet. He always made it seem like a test, and I wanted to please him so badly."

"Is that how you worked your way up into this position?" Maddy asked.

"I guess I worked hard, trying to second-guess what he would need, what he might be looking for. He sent me on courses to learn financials, etiquette, and business management. I was my mother's son; I always looked for a better deal, for a better alternative." He laughed, shaking his head, thinking back to his early days. "Sebastian has changed over the years, but he has always relied on me to keep him up to date and in the know."

"You two have a great relationship. It's nice to see you working together." Maddy smiled.

"I think I owe my career to his wife, Claire. She was a tyrant. She would burst into the boardroom and ask Sebastian if he was sleeping with his secretary, Jean. If he laughed or tried to calm her, she would get louder and insist he fire the bitch. He was always very calm, watching her with a detached look, as though he were in another world. One day she said she was going to Paris with her friend Manon to buy maternity clothes. If he wanted to see their child, she said, he should fire the witch and come to France begging her to return. It was awful, Maddy—the boss man being yelled at by this woman who never showed an ounce of caring towards him. He watched her walk out of the office, turned back to the group at the boardroom table, and carried on with the proposal." Lambert shook his head. "It was just painful to watch … even more painful to know that's how he found out they were having a child."

"Oh my gosh. How does someone deal with a performance like that? That would leave scars, surely." Maddy tried to imagine someone being that callous.

"I remember Sebastian asking Jean if she was married. She smiled and said she was getting married in June to a boy she had known all her life. Sebastian nodded and asked her if he was a good chap and if he was to be invited to the wedding. He didn't fire her; he just made sure I was included in all the subsequent meetings. After the wedding, Jean left, as her husband was taking a better position in Manchester. Claire wouldn't go to the wedding … that's another story." Lambert rolled his eyes and took another sip of his drink.

Maddy didn't say a word; she just waited for him to continue.

"My mother came into the office; it was the most embarrassing day of my life. She asked to see Sebastian, demanding to know why he was being so good to me. She accused him of being my *fancy man.* He laughed and explained that I had potential and I was invaluable to him in the office. He told my mother his wife was touchy about his having a female secretary, so he was looking for a male assistant to keep the peace at home. He hoped I was helping my mother with the household expenses and looking after her. Of course, she melted and left, ensuring Sebastian I would be the best assistant he could imagine. Can you believe that?" He laughed but looked uncomfortable with the memory.

"Sebastian insisted I have a uniform—a new suit with five shirts and new shoes. I was to come to work with a fresh shirt and polished shoes. 'A man is evaluated by his shoes, not his intellect', he would say. I had two older brothers; I had only ever had hand-me-downs; having five new shirts was decadent. You see, I owe him a lot." Lambert looked up and smiled at Maddy. "He's been different since you came—softer, somehow. I knew when I first met you that my life would never be the same. Cheers!" They toasted again.

"Have you been to *The Rocky Horror Picture Show*?" Maddy asked, trying to lighten the mood. "I saw a flyer on the entrance board."

"No, what is it?" Lambert asked, relieved to change the subject.

"Are you kidding me? You don't know? Really, you haven't seen this iconic juggernaut of film culture?" Maddy was feigning shock. "Come on; it's on at 3.00 p.m. and we're going. You need a celebratory break. Come on; let's get out of here. It's expensive, and they're snooty. You need to have some fun. Come, come." Maddy stood and waited.

Lambert quickly asked for the cheque and followed Maddy out to the street. Who could say no to her enthusiasm?

"Sir, at what time do we leave in the morning?"

Sebastian looked up from his report, removed his glasses, and realized Davi was speaking to him. He had read the same page several times and was relieved to break the pattern.

"Sorry?" He seemed distracted.

"What time would you like to leave in the morning? I believe you have a meeting near Gloucester late morning. Traffic will be heavy leaving the city." Davi replied patiently. His boss seemed distracted lately, lost in deep thought. Grace suggested he was in love.

"Yes, of course. Let's be on our way by 8.00 a.m. That should give us time to spare." Sebastian realized they were home, in the driveway, and he was pleased to see the garden lights on.

"Sir, Maddy has friends near Gloucester …" Davi looked up in the rear-view mirror and noticed Sebastian searching the garden for her.

"Let's see if she'd like to join us, shall we?" Sebastian responded as he climbed out of the car. He was moving towards the garden, his reports still on the seat in the car.

Davi smiled. He would have to tell Grace she was right again.

Sebastian heard laughter as he approached the garden, and for a moment he hesitated.

"Ah … Sebastian, great timing. We're just about to sit down for dinner." Lambert was waving him over. "We've had the most marvellous afternoon. Can I get you a drink?"

Lambert seemed quite at home.

Maddy appeared with a platter of food, delighted to see Sebastian.

"Hi. You're just in time. We have so much food. Please, sit down. Where's Davi?" She leaned over and touched his hand. He felt warm from her touch, her dancing eyes, her welcoming smile, and her genuine pleasure at seeing him.

"Would you like to drive out to Gloucester with us tomorrow morning? I have a client meeting, and you could visit your friends," Sebastian said.

"Great. I'd love to come. I can take the train to Painswick. What time?" Maddy was bouncing in her chair. Sebastian laughed at her enthusiasm and found he was looking forward to the drive.

Lambert cleared his throat and lifted his glass. "A toast to the woman who makes our world a more exciting place … Here's to Maddy." He winked as they raised their glasses.

Maddy shook her head and shrugged, pleased with the sentiment and humbled by the words.

"Hear, Hear." Sebastian clinked her glass, making eye contact and holding her gaze for a moment longer.

"You will not believe what we did today." Lambert was anxious to share his adventure.

Sebastian reluctantly looked away from Maddy and gave Lambert his attention.

It was good to be in the garden, having dinner with friends, sitting next to Maddy.

Lonely Hearts Club

"Sebastian, why don't you drive down and join us for dinner. We're throwing a small dinner party for Maddy. She's been working so hard on the council issues; we just feel she needs to have some fun." Belle had called Sebastian to chastise him for not visiting more often.

"Maddy has lots of friends in the city, Belle; she always seems to be having fun." Sebastian responded absently, recalling how seldom he was able to sit alone with her.

"I think she's lonely in the city. You're so busy you don't have time for her. I really think she could have a grand life here. As a matter of fact, Rod—you remember little Roddy; he prefers to be known as 'Rod' these days—well, he asks about her all the time. They worked together on the council deal, and he is quite smitten with her. He and Josh Leonard are both single again, and I just know, I feel it in my bones, that given half a chance they would convince her to make the move here. We would all be so happy to have her closer; she brings us such joy." Belle sighed and continued. "Maddy and George walk the beach for hours, conspiring and planning things. She wears that dingy fishing jumper of his, and I swear the two of them are always up to no good. She stays at the old cottage on the beach—can you imagine? I think they plan to clean it up. She really is a part of the village now."

"Belle, are you setting her up at this dinner?" Sebastian gave the phone his full attention.

"Well, it could happen. Why don't you join us? We miss seeing you, and it would be such fun to have you and your old chums together, especially with Maddy in the mix." Belle was enjoying the thought. "I think Helen is coming as well."

Sebastian finally agreed to make the trip, under the guise of bringing George some renderings he had requested. As the call ended, Sebastian found he was angry—angry that Belle would want to introduce Maddy to someone else in the hopes she would find a mate—someone to spend quiet evenings with, someone to lure her out of the garden. *Roddy ... Heavens, why Roddy?* He gathered the drawings and headed for home.

Roderick Frampton, respected council member and solicitor, was already sitting with Belle and George when Sebastian arrived at the house. Rod, as he was now known, stood and embraced Sebastian as an old friend. They had spent many summers on the cliffs and on the beach before Sebastian left for his state school education. As they were reminiscing over single-malt scotch, Josh Leonard arrived with Helen Maloney. Both had been fellow pirates in the cliff gang in their youth. George was entertaining the group of old friends with his recollections of their shenanigans when they heard Belle from the front porch.

"Oh, my dear, just look at you; you're soaked to the bone. Why didn't you ring? We could have collected you, especially since the wind came up. As if the rain wasn't enough. Let me take your coat. You get to the fire. George, you must throw this old coat out. Hurry, my dear; get those wet things off. You'll catch a dreadful cold." Maddy had arrived. George leapt up quite ably for a man of his age and, with a twinkle in his eye, excused himself. The group of friends looked at each other, no longer predisposed to catch up with each other now that George had left the room.

They could hear a friendly banter from the porch—Belle fussing, George laughing, Maddy emphatic that the walk was great. Sebastian smiled as he heard her confess that she couldn't resist jumping in every puddle on the way.

Her clothes hung to dry, she walked into the room barefoot. As Maddy floated into the room dressed only in a black leotard with Belle's afghan swung casually around her shoulders, her hair loosely held high on her head with a tortoise clip, a cup of hot cocoa cradled in her hands, the men fought for position to welcome her. She graciously greeted each of them, asking a personal question and giving them her full attention.

She was surprised to see Sebastian and greeted him with a double-cheek air kiss. As he held her arm, he realized she was indeed soaked to the bone. George made a seat available by the gas fire, and Maddy immediately sat cross-legged, looking up at the group, thankful for the warmth. She began asking questions of the group, leading them to continue reminiscing, filling in the gaps since they had last seen each other.

As they took turns catching up, Maddy turned sideways and hugged her knees, allowing the fire to dry her left side. Sebastian watched as she slowly moved her hand up to her hair and released the hair clip. It was a simple gesture; suddenly it was a sensuous move as she slowly shook her head. Her silhouette against the fire was striking, and as her hair fell on her shoulders, Sebastian, Rod, and Josh were mesmerized. Helen continued to speak but suddenly realized she had lost her audience. Maddy turned, wondering why Helen had stopped speaking, and smiled in encouragement. Helen patted her short, dark hair and wished she could, for once in her life, let her hair down and hypnotize her old pals like this stranger had just done. She sighed and took a sip of her sherry, noticing that Maddy had lovely hair, with not a hint of grey; she probably didn't have to colour every four weeks.

George raised an eyebrow in amusement as he watched the scene before him. Rod stood and walked over to Maddy, sitting beside her on the bench. *Bold move.*

"Today was a first for me. I watched a master negotiator at work. Well done, Maddy." He smiled and raised his glass in a toast. His look of admiration was unmistakable. Maddy smiled at him, her face cupped in her hands. "Thank you for your help with the legal matters. You were so succinct and yet so warm. Now we just have to get the rest of the council to approve the lightbox."

Helen felt left out of the conversation and suddenly spoke up, with renewed confidence. "Oh Roddy, isn't it fortunate you got over the stuttering."

Maddy gasped and swung around on the bench. Sebastian closed his eyes, wondering what the fallout of the cruel remark would be. Josh groaned and moved closer to the hearth. Maddy looked up at George with a pained look. She turned and placed her arm across Rod's shoulders. She laid her head against him and whispered, "Hey, every superhero has to overcome adversity." Rod responded by touching her hand on his shoulder.

Helen seemed unaware of the faux pas and continued to speak. Josh stopped her with a raised hand and a stern look. Maddy shot him a grateful look, and he sat beside her, asking about her plans for the weekend. The mood in the room had changed, and Sebastian felt he was losing her, watching his friends sandwich her before his very eyes. He cleared his throat and made his announcement. "Maddy, I managed to secure theatre tickets for the opening of your long-awaited Broadway hit Saturday evening. We should leave after lunch." Maddy responded with applause and such delight, as it was clear she was leaving with Sebastian the next day.

"Shall we move into the dining room? I think I'm ready for you. George, please direct everyone into dinner." Belle was flushed and seemed totally unaware of the mood in the room. Maddy smiled at Sebastian, and suddenly he knew exactly what his future held.

As the group moved into the dining room, Maddy stopped Helen with a touch of her arm. "Helen, you are so fortunate to have your childhood friends here. My family moved every two years when I was a kid, and it wasn't always easy to parachute into a tight-knit group. I had to make friends fast in each new town; I don't have the history or memories you have. What a fantastic bond."

Helen nodded, her words lost in the collage of the four friends through the years. She had something Maddy coveted—childhood friends. She sighed and smiled as she sat in the chair Josh held out for her.

Dinner was lively; the wine and conversation robust. Between the main course and pudding, Rod realized that Sebastian had won the girl and he would have to settle for friendship. Josh and Helen reconnected on some level and made plans to take a long hike the next day. Belle winked at George across the table—mission accomplished.

"Tell us about the meeting this morning, my dear. How were the Russians?" Belle asked, anxious to hear what had transpired.

Rod was pleased to report on how capably Maddy had handled the negotiations. Despite her protests and proclamations of his fine legal work, he insisted on relating the story.

"Maddy and I arrived and sat across from the three Russians. Maddy produced a bottle of vodka (I think—I couldn't read the label) and shot glasses. She poured a drink for everyone and gave a toast in Russian—I presume—as they threw back the shots.

Maddy offered Milos, Mr Karazan, the opportunity to show the community his commitment to safety by providing the solar barrier lights at the crossing—proving his desire to be a part of the community and so on. She asked for a timeline, and he suggested, after consulting his team, the work would be complete in a month. Maddy countered by saying it would be better in place in a week. They countered with two weeks. Maddy still thought one week would be best. After much discussion amongst themselves, they offered ten days. Maddy considered this and suggested one week would be better. Again there was much discussion, and they agreed to have everything in place by the middle of the week. Maddy applauded this with amazement regarding their professional and caring approach to the safety of the children in the area. It was incredible." He paused for effect.

"Next we had to sign off on the contract. Mr Karazan asked Madushka—that's his name for Maddy—if it was a good contract, and she nodded, pointing out a few items like liability and maintenance clauses. He looked at his team and signed it—without reading it. He just signed it. Big bear hugs and away we went. A very interesting experience for me, I must say."

"Maddy, I didn't realize you spoke Russian?" Belle said, her admiration clear.

"Not well enough, any more. I'm afraid I used most of my vocabulary in the toast." Maddy confessed. "When Milos spoke to me, I looked over at Rod and asked him to speak English as a courtesy to my English friend. I got lucky." Maddy blushed.

"Well, no matter. We will have a safe crossing from the beach, and that's worth all the vodka in town. Cheers, Maddy and Rod." George raised his glass.

Helen cleared her throat and asked why a Russian businessman would allow Maddy—or Madushka, as he called her—to approve the contract. Did he not read English?

Rod was quick to respond. "Milos trusts Maddy, and so far she has helped his family assimilate into the community quite nicely. Calling her Madushka is his way of showing her affection. It was an interesting exchange, to be sure."

Sebastian sat back, amused at the story, wondering how he could keep Maddy happy enough to return to London and the garden world she had created. He wished he had an interesting project for her. He missed her. After only a few days, he missed her.

Belle and George challenged Sebastian and Helen to a game—a game they had played as young people, right here in the parlour. Josh was pleased to take on his old role at the tally board. The group laughed as he confessed his early training, as the tally man had made him choose a career in banking.

"Great meal, Belle. We'll take care of the washing up; you start the game." Rod stood up with Maddy to clear the table. "I'll drop Maddy at the beach house on my way home. Off you go."

Sebastian walked into the kitchen with the serving bowls. "Maddy, I was hoping to speak with you …"

Maddy turned to Sebastian as Rod walked in, unaware of the exchange. "You prefer to wash or dry?" he asked as he set the plates on the counter. Maddy responded with "Whatever", and the two began their domestic chores, leaving Sebastian to his own thoughts. He looked back as he walked out of the room, thinking how comfortable Maddy and Rod looked standing at the kitchen sink together, laughing and elbowing each other. He felt a pang and realized he was jealous of their easy camaraderie.

The game finally ended, with Sebastian and Helen triumphant champions. George offered one last drink before the evening ended. Helen sat next to Sebastian and touched his hand. "I guess you're not going to rescue me from my banal existence, are you?"

Sebastian smiled at her. "No, I'm in need of rescue myself. You deserve better."

Helen turned to him. "I don't know what I deserve, but unlike your friend Maddy, I would be willing to settle—to be happy with whatever you could offer. You've been my fantasy for years."

Sebastian looked down at his drink, uncomfortable with the conversation.

"Helen, Josh is a good man. He can make you happy. Don't let your fantasies interfere with what's right in front of you. You don't want to lose the chance to be truly happy."

Helen kissed his cheek and walked slowly over to Josh.

Tossing in his childhood bed, unable to turn off the noise in his head, images of Maddy whirling before him along with the hollow sound of his words to Helen and his own lonely existence, Sebastian finally fell asleep, wondering if indeed Maddy would settle for him.

The Rolex

Wednesday night dinner at the club with his cronies, after tennis or handball, was a hallowed tradition. Tonight, Sebastian realized he had heard the sad tales of younger wives running off with personal trainers, the latest must-have Rolexes and jewellery the new wives demanded, the endless hours of spa and salon appointments, the theories of why they were always too tired for sex and how younger children were not as enjoyable as you might think at a certain age, one too many times.

He was bored hearing of the routine lives his friends were living, how unhappy they were with their trophy wives, and how important prenuptial agreements were. He wanted to be at home with the spontaneous mayhem of Maddy and her eclectic collection of new friends. No, on second thought he just wanted to be home with Maddy. He stopped for a moment to consider what he had just envisioned. He wanted to be home. He tried to recall how long it had been since he had wanted to be home—home to see Stephan before bedtime, home to watch the boy sleep in his cot. It was too long ago. Now here he was thinking about home—with Maddy.

He seemed to spend a great deal of time wondering what she was doing; there seemed to be a steady stream of visitors in her entourage. Considering she was new to London, she had a rather robust group of friends. They ate and visited, always with a purpose or cause. She was insatiable; she was interested in everything.

Tweaking his moustache, an elderly gentleman walked by the table, greeting the group with news of the weather. The rain had finally stopped.

Sebastian left the table abruptly, excusing himself by feigning a forgotten commitment, and ran out of the club. He hailed a cab rather than call for Davi and arrived home to find Maddy in the delightful garden world she had created, bidding adieu to Audrey and the older couple next door (what were their names?). It looked as though they had just finished an outdoor meal. He nodded to the visitors and walked with purpose towards Maddy. She was clearing the table, humming and moving to the music as she walked into the apartment.

For an instant he wondered what he would do now that he was nearing her, but the smile on her face as she saw him in the garden filled him with resolve. He was about to ask her to dance when she rushed into his arms.

"Oh Sebastian, you're home. How nice. You missed dinner. Have you eaten?"

He shook his head. "Yes. No. No, thank you." He kissed her softly, and then more urgently when she responded.

Maddy looked up at Sebastian, wide-eyed, surprised by his ardour. Her eyes were sparkling.

How had he not noticed how deep her dimples were before? "Dance with me, Maddy," he whispered.

Sebastian breathed in the smell of her as they danced. She was light in his arms, and he felt heady. Maddy closed her eyes and laid her head on his chest, her heart beating rapidly, her body filling every space against his.

He moved his hand lower on her back and pulled her towards him.

"Maddy, I want you," he whispered in her ear.

Maddy looked up at him, blinking, not sure she had heard him. When she saw the look in his eyes, she felt she would melt. She moved closer to Sebastian, feeling the heat of his body through her dress. Neither knew who groaned first, but they stopped dancing, looked at each other, and kissed a long, hungry kiss: a kiss that said they were more than friends—a kiss that said there was more to come.

As they walked towards the apartment, hand in hand, Maddy looked up at him.

"Are you ready for this?" she asked haltingly, recalling how he had fled once before, afraid to get close.

"I've never been as ready for anything," he whispered with a determined, yet tender, look on his face. "Are you ready for this?"

"It's been a long time; I don't want to disappoint you." Maddy bit the inside of her cheek, looking tentative. She felt she was burning up with fever.

Sebastian stopped, placed his hands on her shoulders, and looked into her eyes. "Shh, it's new for both of us. I can't remember feeling like this. Let's take it slow." His voice was soft and inviting.

He wrapped his arm around her and led her into the apartment; the music followed them, slow and sexy. He laid her on the bed after lifting her dress over her head and gently caressed her; he wondered where the strength and control were coming from, but he knew he wanted to make love to someone very special; there was no need to hurry. Maddy moved with him and lightly unbuttoned his shirt. Her entire being was aching for him, and yet it was delightful. Soon they were lying naked. Sebastian travelled up her stomach with small kisses, breathing on her neck, kissing her ears and her eyes, and then their lips touched—and they could not wait any longer. Sebastian was sure there were fireworks in the room. Maddy was floating in ecstasy.

Sebastian waited for his heart to stop pounding before he spoke. "Ask me for anything …" He was leaning on one arm, smiling down at her. "Anything."

She opened her eyes and blinked several times to reassure herself he was really lying there beside her. "I don't need anything." She smiled lazily. "I feel we should be sharing a cigarette right now."

"No, really, ask me for anything; I'm serious." He traced her cheek, smiling at how soft her skin felt to his touch.

"So am I." She moved her head to his chest. "Oh my, Tin Man, you have a heart; I feel it."

He persisted. "Anything at all. Come on; ask me for anything."

She laughed. "How about … no wrinkles and a firm body?"

"No, anything in my power."

"Anything?"

"Anything." He was emphatic.

"Anything?" she asked playfully.

"Anything."

"Really? Anything?" She was stalling.

"Absolutely. Anything in my power."

She flipped the bedcover over their heads and dove under the covers, kissing his stomach and stroking him.

"Oh, oh my … remember, I'm an old man; I may not be up for this," he gasped.

"Shh," she whispered. "You said anything."

He moaned and closed his eyes, enjoying the sensation.

The second time was more intense, with neither of them hesitating, familiar with each other, reconfirming the passion they had been denying for some time.

Exhausted, they lay side by side, their hands touching. Sebastian looked over at Maddy, smiling. Maddy smiled back, not sure what to do next. Sebastian moved his arm around her and pulled her towards him.

"You could have asked for a Rolex … no, a sports car … no, I think you deserve a villa …"

"Tsk tsk. Oh, silly man, you just don't get it. I have a lovely place to live, I adore you, and I've just had the best sex ever … how does a Rolex trump that?"

"Best sex ever?" He wrapped her in his arms. "Really?"

"Uh huh. I never say anything I don't mean." Maddy sighed and then gasped. "I just realized all the women I meet at your club wear a Rolex … Have you slept with all of them?" She raised her head and looked into his eyes.

Sebastian smiled and shook his head. "No. Stop that. My life has been so simple, so predictable. I set the rules and live by them. Then, without warning, you appear, and you're spontaneous, challenging, and reckless … who's the Tin Man?"

Maddy kissed his chest, snuggled up to him, and whispered something about a wizard before falling asleep in his arms.

Sebastian still didn't know much about her past. She had been in a long relationship with the same man for over twenty years, never marrying—not her choice. Her partner was older, he already had a family, and he wasn't keen on starting over; he was focused on his adventure business, and Maddy worked with him, travelling and arranging tours. Previously she had travelled the globe, searching for film locations. She had been successful at finding just the right houses or settings for films, although not all of them made the big screen. She was vague about her young life and her first career. Things were not going well at home, and something dramatic happened to make her decide to leave. She wouldn't say what happened—only that it would cause a lot of people a great deal of sadness. When she heard the daughter of her old school friend was graduating near London, she bought an air ticket and left, unsure of her future. Maddy left everything behind, hoping she would know what to do about her situation in the coming year.

Her friends were supportive, it seemed, and they were in contact by email, anxious to know when she would be back. Maddy had given herself the year to choose her path, knowing she would not return to the same life—never mentioning the event that prompted her to run away. There was no going back to the predictable, unfulfilling, but comfortable life she had known; there was no plan B. She just wanted to play it out, and a year seemed like a good span of time to decide on her future. She didn't seem to think her leaving was courageous, just necessary. How she would survive financially was a nuisance, not a worry. This was her midlife crisis—no children, no demons in her closet. She was looking for a simpler life, without the bickering and bullying.

Meeting Grace when she arrived in London had made it bearable, and of course now she had the garden apartment and was enjoying making new friends; she had several commitments with the hospital visits and a few projects generated by her quick friendships. Would she last the year? She couldn't say. She had an airline ticket home; that's all she offered.

Wrapped in each other's arms, they explored not only their bodies but also who they were. Sebastian told Maddy he had lived with his aunt Belle for most of his life. He had attended the best schools and studied architectural design, starting his own firm when quite young. His parents had died at sea, during a storm, leaving him an orphan with a small inheritance for education purposes, which Belle had managed. He was involved with city planning groups and international charities. He wasn't comfortable speaking about his life; he felt it was ordinary and not compelling enough to interest her. Maddy felt he was leaving out important details, but she didn't want to push him and stop his story. He wasn't much of a talker; she was pleased to hear him out.

His best friend, Philippe, had been his roommate through boarding school and then at Oxford. They started the business together, working out of London and Paris, successfully building an international reputation. He and Philippe had dated two women who were friends; Claire and Manon were inseparable. After several years, the women had determined it was time to marry and have children, making it easy for the men to agree and marry. Both women had sons within the year. His wife was beautiful but troubled; she was not ready to be the wife of a businessman who left for work each day. Claire supposedly stayed busy with tennis, riding, and partying. She was overly protective of their son and preferred to live with her parents on their estate in France, not enjoying the English or the climate in London. She was a free spirit who needed champagne to exist. Philippe left to manage his family winery in Bordeaux, as his wife preferred to be near her friend. Sebastian remained in London, overseeing the contracts. He bought and sold urban real estate just for the sport of it, realizing he had a talent for finding the right property at the right price, renovating, and selling at a profit.

Returning home from a holiday party with their son Stefan, her friend Manon (Philippe's wife), and his son Jean Louis, the car left the road, exploding in flames. There did not appear to be another car or animal involved in the accident, and the local coroner, a friend of her parents, neglected to report the high level of alcohol in Claire's blood. Sebastian was devastated; he lost his family and his taste for life in one accident. Losing his son was more painful than anything he had experienced. He retreated into his business world, where he was certain he would not hurt another human being or be hurt again. He was an eligible widower, and he did date from time to time, only to appease his hostesses and friends at the club. Maddy watched his face as he slept, hoping she would learn the rest of the story another night. She laid her head on his chest, pressed her body against him, and fell into a deep sleep.

"Good morning. I'm afraid I didn't know you smoked," Sebastian said as he lightly brushed the hair from her eyes. He was propped up on one arm, watching her wake up.

"I don't." She was confused by the question. She stretched and sat up, laughing. "You so need to watch old movies with me." Now Sebastian was confused.

"In the movies, after sex, the couple lie back and have a cigarette, enjoying the moment. After last night, I think I understand why."

Sebastian scratched his head. "Indeed."

"Come on; let's take a shower and get you to work." Maddy playfully pulled back the covers.

"You want me to take a shower with you?" he asked.

"Oh, come on, you can't be shy. Not after last night," Maddy teased, standing before him, naked.

Sebastian hesitated and then laughed. "I guess you're right; why not?"

It was a long shower.

The Classics

"Lambert, how do I get a copy of that film about the Tin Man looking for a heart?"

"Oh, you mean *The Wizard of Oz*. I'll get you the coloured version on DVD. Anything else?"

"What's the film about North Africa during war?" Sebastian was looking out the window at the city below him, his jacket held back by his hands on his hips. He was preoccupied, thinking about the world Maddy challenged him to see and experience.

"*Casablanca*—a classic." Lambert nodded. "Let me just get you the collection of must-see movies. You'll have to watch *Lawrence of Arabia* and, of course, *The Way We Were*; that's a good start." He knew which movies Maddy would want. "By the way, your ten o'clock appointment is waiting in the conference room. The report is on the table for you." Lambert sensed something important had happened; his boss never stared out the window.

"I'll be right there. Thanks." Sebastian was smiling as he turned from the window and walked into the boardroom.

Maddy was humming as she strolled beside Audrey.

"Maddy, you seem different today. What happened? Did something happen?" Audrey asked anxiously. "Stop smiling and tell me what's going on."

"Nothing is going on. I'm just happy. Can't I be happy?"

"Oh, my goodness. You slept with him. You two are sleeping together. It's about time. Does Grace know?"

"Audrey, it's not a big deal."

"I think it is. I'm happy for you, of course. What took so long?"

"We're not teenagers. I don't know what to think right now. I'm happy; isn't that enough?"

Audrey linked her arm in Maddy's and continued walking. This was good news. This meant Maddy might stay longer than a year. Yes, it was good news indeed.

In the Garden

Maddy slowly walked into the garden, turned the lights on, and set her shopping bags down on the kitchen counter. It was good to be home. She looked out at the garden, smiling at the effect of the lights in the trees. She flung her scarf over the sofa and found an upbeat playlist on her tablet. Music filled the apartment. As she was unpacking the groceries, humming, and moving to the music, she saw Sebastian walking towards the patio.

"Oh, what a lovely surprise." She met him, taking his jacket. "You're just in time for dinner."

He smiled at the enthusiastic greeting and held her in a warm embrace. "I just can't seem to get you out of my mind today." He buried his face in her hair. He then moved back, looking at her. Her cheeks were flushed. Was she blushing?

"I thought you might like to go out for dinner. I should have called."

"How nice." She smiled up at him. "Let's eat in, if that suits you. I have the fixings for butter chicken with naan bread. Mango ice cream …" she teased. "Drink?"

Sebastian poured them both a drink and sat on the sofa, looking out at the garden lights. How very comfortable he found it to arrive home and talk about what they were having for dinner. It was a simple pleasure.

He watched her prepare the food, place the dish in the oven, and set the little table outdoors, all the while singing and moving with the music. She kicked off her shoes and joined him on the sofa, curling up to him. He put his arm around her and answered her questions about his day. He had had several meetings scheduled but found it difficult to concentrate. He wanted to call Maddy and ask her about trivial things. He just wanted to be with her, to hold her, to hear her laugh. He hoped he wasn't frightening her.

Maddy kissed his neck and said he was welcome to call anytime. She didn't say she felt that way about him. Several times during the day, she thought about calling him to share silly things or tell him about something she had seen, knowing he was too busy to take the call or be disturbed. She reminded herself he had said "no strings attached". She pointed to the desk and told him she had a file with "stuff" for him. He wasn't sure what that meant, but he promised he would have a look.

"What's on your bucket list, Sebastian?" she asked suddenly.

"Well, I … I'm not sure I have one. If I want to do something, I do it. What's on yours?"

"I want to learn to tango in Argentina. I want to live on the Amalfi Coast in an apartment, not stay in a hotel like a tourist; I want to be a part of the place—speak the language, and cook as they do for at least a few months. I want to see a sunrise on Mount Kilimanjaro and a sunset on the beach in the Maldives so I can experience the neon-blue plankton at night. I want to sing with Rod Stewart or Bruce Springsteen … of course my first choice was Leonard Cohen—too late. I want to surf off the coast of South Africa, and I want to drive on a racetrack. Oh, almost forgot, I also want to go back to Barcelona … I think that's it. For now." She had a faraway look in her eyes.

Sebastian smiled as she finally took a breath. "That seems like quite a list—enough for most people to accomplish in a lifetime. Perhaps we could experience all those things together," he said with conviction. "We can start with Barcelona; I have to be at the design conference next week."

Maddy laughed a throaty laugh and patted his arm. "That would be very cool. Sebastian, in all your travels, what touched you the most?"

He stroked her hand and thought for a moment. "Giza and the pyramids made me want to design and produce things that would last; Petra was beautiful and inspiring. I'd like to take you to Jordan." He paused and looked over at Maddy. She was smiling and encouraging him to go on. "The Great Wall of China was such a monumental feat; I wandered for miles, feeling small and inconsequential. Nothing I would ever design would endure as long or cover as much ground. It was humbling." She nodded, remembering how she had felt walking the wall.

"Have you seen the Taj Mahal?" Maddy asked.

"I haven't had the desire to tackle India; as a Brit, I've always felt we needed to stay away and give them time to forget British rule."

"Oh Sebastian, India is beautiful—the colours, the smells, the noise, the textures, the slums, the sheer number of lovely people, and the chaos; it's wonderful. I loved it. The contrast between caste and modern-day life is so apparent and yet so convergent. I would love to take you there …" She stopped when she realized Sebastian was laughing at her.

"Maddy, with your enthusiasm, you could take me anywhere." He pulled her closer and held her, knowing in his heart he wouldn't be travelling far without her.

Sitting at the little table under the stars, enjoying their meal and each other, the two lovers laughed and talked of things that made them happy, sharing anecdotes and life lessons. After dinner they sat on opposite sides of the sofa, reading, looking up at each other occasionally. When their eyes met, they didn't speak; they stood up and walked to the bed, removing clothing and embracing, unhurried and without hesitation. At some point Sebastian asked Maddy to move into the big house. She was adamant that she would not; this was their place—no history, no memories, theirs alone. Sebastian considered this and decided to bring a toothbrush, a razor, and a fresh change of clothes to the garden apartment. The arrangement felt perfect.

The Market

Maddy and Grace frequently travelled to markets around the city to search out new flavours, new ideas, decor, and teas. Now that Auntie and Uncle were working at the coffee house, Grace had time to get away midday; it was a luxury she had been talked into by her dear friend Maddy.

"How is it you are so special in my life and I've only known you for a few months?" She asked in a sing-song voice as they negotiated the narrow lanes filled with shoppers.

"Kismet" Maddy laughed. "Oh, yes, and great chai." She hugged her friend. Grace and Davi were now inseparable. Thankfully it had worked out for them.

"Maddy, look at those boys. They're beating that old woman; it's disgraceful." Grace was indignant. "No, Maddy, don't get involved. I'm calling the police."

Maddy ran forward and yelled, "Stop! The police are on their way! Stop! Leave her alone!" The gang of young men, coloured, white, and Asian, sneered at her, spit on the ground, pointed their fingers as if shooting guns, and ran down the alley. Several people had passed the group and looked away. Cowering on the ground, an elderly woman was moaning; her sobs were animal-like. She had been kicked and punched, her garb torn, her shopping bags ripped, and a line of fruit was smashed on the steps of the Tube station. It was a pitiful sight, and Maddy was disgusted by the boys. She helped the old woman up and soothingly told her she was safe now. "I am never safe," she cried. "I cannot even buy fresh fruit for my family. I am so afraid."

"What is your name? I am Maddy, and this is Grace."

"I am Leda." The woman responded, looking at the ground.

"Where is your home, Leda?" Maddy asked quietly. "Is it nearby?"

75

"I must take the underground." The woman was shaking with fear.

Maddy looked around the street, saw a taxi approaching, and asked Grace to flag him down. Grace was not familiar with the phrase but did manage to stop the cab.

"Grace, let's take Leda home." They stepped into the cab, and Leda gave the driver her address. She was still shaking and trying to stop the sobbing.

Grace asked to be let off near the bus stop.

"See you tomorrow, Maddy; you're much better at this than I am. I need to get ready for the morning. Hopefully Leda is all right." She blew a kiss and turned to board the bus.

The taxi stopped in front of a Lebanese restaurant with tables on the footway. Several men were drinking espresso and smoking cigarettes. As they stepped out of the cab, a young man ran forward and caught Leda, who was still shaky on her feet.

"Mother, Mother, what has happened? Are you all right? Mother, Mother, can you speak?"

Maddy waited until they were sitting at a table and a glass of water appeared for Leda before she explained what had happened. Leda was still sobbing, but she assured her son she would surely have been killed if Maddy had not stopped the boys. The son was most grateful and anxious to thank Maddy, who argued that she was not a hero, just concerned for his mother. By the time she was able to leave Leda, the crowd had grown, and the story was now epic. Maddy was invited to come back for a meal—no, a lifetime of meals; they insisted. She promised to check in on Leda and waved goodbye. *How can this be stopped?* she wondered. She thought perhaps Sebastian could help.

Maddy was not able to speak with him regarding the assault for several days, so she invited him to lunch at the Lebanese restaurant. He arrived looking very businesslike in a dark suit, pulling his shirt cuffs down and straightening his tie. She was in a kurta with a colourful scarf. It looked as if her lawyer was coming to meet the family. Of course, in this neighbourhood, he would appear to be an Englishman of stature. They sat outdoors and were greeted effusively by the son and then the rest of the family. Food and drink arrived—no menu, just genuine hospitality. Maddy introduced Leda to Sebastian, and she immediately told him her story of the attack, how Maddy had stopped the beating, Maddy returning her home, and how Maddy was important to her family. Leda then went in to prepare another dish. Through the emphatic storytelling, Maddy sat perfectly still, eyes on her water glass.

Sebastian, amused and disturbed by the story, asked why she had brought him here.

"You could have been beaten as well, Maddy; did you think of that?" he asked, looking pained. She was reckless; he had told her this before.

She rolled her eyes and looked around the street. "Everyone has the right to get food for their family without being beaten on an underground ramp. I wanted you to meet the family because I thought you could help me with lobbying for cameras on the steps." She sighed. "It was pointless aggression and I was angry. I was disgusted by those boys and the fact that people just hurried by, pretending not to notice. It's not right." She was speaking in clipped tones. "Grace and I saw the gang beating up a woman; we just acted, unlike all the other people who were going up and down the stairs to the pedestrian walkway."

He took her hand in his and calmly responded. "Let's see what we can do about the cameras, but please call the police the next time you see a gang beating up on anyone … please." His look was stern; he was concerned. In fact, he was secretly pleased she had asked for his help.

She rubbed her forehead and nodded, not wanting to argue, hopeful that he would help her as promised, steadfastly believing the police were too busy and would not have been there in time.

"Let's eat, shall we?" Maddy smiled, hoping to change the subject.

Sebastian had his legal team document the incident, provide descriptions from Grace and Maddy, and convince the transit authorities of the danger. As a result, a commitment was made to install lighting and cameras in high-risk areas in the coming year. Sebastian was now also heralded for his concern within the community, and he was developing a taste for kibbeh, tabbouleh, baba ghanoush, and fattoush.

Occasionally a package would be delivered to his office, the smell of lamb and goat permeating the shared kitchen area. Maddy just laughed and told him they were showing their appreciation with food; it was their currency, and they wanted to repay Sebastian for his good works. Didn't it make for a more interesting office experience?

"Indeed," he muttered.

Breakfast Rules

Maddy watched Sebastian absently sip his coffee as he read the newspaper, fully absorbed in the news of the day. She had prepared breakfast so they could eat together before heading out for the day.

"Sebastian, do you think we're having sex too often … or perhaps not enough?" she asked as though she were conducting a survey.

Sebastian stopped reading and blinked several times, stalling to process the question in his mind. He folded the newspaper and slowly placed it on the table. He looked over at Maddy and saw her wide-eyed expression and realized, in that instant, that she was teasing him.

"I'm ever so sorry for ignoring you when you've taken the time to prepare breakfast and sit with me … it was rude of me. In my defence … I have had breakfast alone for most of my life. It's not an excuse; it's a fact. Am I forgiven?" he asked contritely.

Maddy smiled and touched his hand. "I don't see you all day, so I like to hear what you have planned; it makes me feel somewhat in touch with the real world. I don't want to intrude in your life, but it's a long time until we have cocktails and I just like to imagine you working at various projects throughout the day. That must sound silly to you."

"Not at all. It sounds very comforting and fair. I like the idea of sharing schedules; let's make that our morning ritual." He leaned over and kissed her forehead.

"Thank you," Maddy whispered.

"I've several meetings today at the office with accountants and contract negotiators … I should be home in time for cocktails in the garden by five. You?" He really didn't know what Maddy did during the day.

"I'm at the hospital today; it's my volunteer day. Anything particular you would like for dinner?"

Sebastian leaned over to kiss her cheek. "Anything is fine with me. Surprise me."

As he reached the door, he turned and smiled at Maddy. "By the way, it's not too often; it's just fine. Indeed."

He heard Maddy's laughter as he closed the car door.

"Good morning, Davi. How did we manage before Maddy?"

"It's a mystery, sir … a mystery for sure." Davi smiled into the rear-view mirror, pleased to see his boss starting the day with a smile.

Mentoring

"My mentoring student, Henry, will be expecting me to collect him after his classes today; it's our monthly outing day, and I don't see how I can get there in time. Would you mind meeting him and joining me at the club for dinner?" Sebastian asked Maddy as he tied his tie in the mirror.

"What's a mentoring student?" Maddy asked.

"The school is trying out a new programme—pairing a student who doesn't have parents living in London with a member of the alumni. We are obligated to act like big brothers or business mentors to provide male influence in their lives. I'm not very good at it, I must say." Sebastian shrugged.

"Will Henry be okay with that arrangement?" She asked absently, pouring a cup of tea.

"He's a boy of twelve who is not interested in anything not football-related, and we are obligated to speak French on our visits until his French marks improve; what could possibly go wrong?"

"French? I have to speak proper French with him?" Maddy rolled her eyes.

"Please, he knows the drill, and I will meet you as soon as possible. Thank you … ah, merci." He kissed the top of her head.

He was out the door and out of earshot when she asked, "May I change the programme? Dinner at your club must be boring for a young boy."

"Bonjour, Henri, *je m'appelle* Maddy, I am a friend of Sebastian." Maddy smiled at the boy.

Henry was ready to go when Maddy arrived at the school. He had heard from Sebastian earlier and merely shrugged when she appeared. They walked down the stairs to the street in silence. Maddy stopped and looked at Henry. "So what's your story? Everyone has a story. What's yours, little man?" She swept his hair from his forehead.

"We're supposed to be speaking French. I don't have a story. I'm boring. I'm just a kid." Henry looked away.

"Is it okay if we speak with a French accent until we get to know each other better? I don't want to walk down the street with a drug lord or a convicted psychopath. Maybe you're a budding musician or the next great football star—how do I know?" Maddy shrugged. Henry laughed.

"What kind of friend of Sebastian's are you?" he asked, squinting.

"The kind of friend who agrees to meet a young man she's never met or even heard of until this morning."

"I guess we're stuck with each other then," Henry said with a sigh.

"Exactly, so let's make the most of it. I'm dying for some of those chips. *Un petit* snack before art and dinner?" she asked with a French accent. Henry smiled and nodded. Maybe this wouldn't be so bad after all.

Henry seemed to brighten up as they sat on a bench, conversing in their silly French accents and enjoying their greasy chips wrapped in paper, Maddy asking the questions, Henry responding with as few words as possible.

"I thought you would enjoy seeing some French art since you are a student of the language. Ready to go?" she asked as she started walking towards the gallery, not waiting for an answer.

Henry followed, advising her he had little interest in art.

Sebastian sat in the convention auditorium next to his friend Christian Gerhart, a German banker. He and Christian had worked together for many years on various boards and were now on a standing committee appointed by the city. Christian was a senior financial officer with sun-bleached surfer boy hair that was always too long and messy. He wore Hugo Boss suits and a large aviator watch. The two men were easy in each other's company.

The speaker started and seemed distracted. Sebastian looked at his watch several times before Christian asked if he had another engagement to attend. Sebastian explained he was a mentor or big brother and that tonight was his scheduled outing with dinner at the club. His friend had collected the boy and had messaged him they were going to the gallery to see the French impressionist exhibit before dinner. Sebastian was worried his friend had taken on a superhuman task of taking a young boy to an art exhibit and thought he should be with them to save the day.

Christian suggested they both go, as the incredibly boring speaker could be found on a podcast. (Apparently the first time he gave this talk, he was focused and interesting.)

As they left the auditorium, Christian called for his car, and within minutes the two men walked into the gallery.

Christian sympathized with Sebastian and his concerns, as he had two teenagers who were disdainful of any attempts at cultural, spiritual, or physical enrichment. The boys and their mother preferred to stay in Hamburg rather than London, so Christian was alone much of the time. He was developing a penchant for sailing and female crew.

The two men walked through the gallery looking for a sullen boy and a frustrated woman. When they turned into the large exhibit room, they stopped and stared first at the pair ahead of them and then at each other. Maddy had her hands over Henry's eyes; she was shuffling him to the Monet, speaking in his ear, while Henry was nodding and listening intently.

Maddy asked, "vous etes prete?", to which Henry responded, "Oui, Oui." Maddy moved her hands away, and the boy looked up at the painting with awe and reverence. Maddy asked more questions, and he considered each query with a tilt of his head or a hand gesture to show how the strokes were made. As the men approached the pair, they realized they were hearing an art appreciation class in progress.

Henry saw Sebastian and ran to him, controlling his excitement when he noticed Christian. "Hallo Sebastian, j'aime beaucoup les impressionists," he said shyly. Sebastian introduced Christian, who insisted the learning tour continue, clearly in awe of Maddy. The group moved on to the next canvas, enjoying the exhibit and the introduction to each painting.

When Maddy sent Henry to the coat check for his backpack and coat, she slipped into the gift store. As they walked out of the gallery, Henry asked what was in the bag. Maddy explained it was a gift for a very special friend.

Christian thanked the group for allowing him to participate and exclaimed he had not had so much fun visiting the classics as he had this evening.

Maddy asked if he would like to join them for dinner; she hoped Sebastian wouldn't mind, but she had found a delightful little gem of a restaurant and wanted to give Henry the full French treatment. Christian was thrilled to be asked, as his evening plan was to return to his club alone for dinner. He felt he was imposing, but the invitation was so sincere that he agreed to join them.

Maddy and Audrey had found the perfect venue for their outing—a French restaurant named Chez Henri, after the Chef. Henry was impressed. It was a cosy little bistro, but when Chef Henri saw Maddy and her men, he ran out front in his whites, greeting her with a kiss of the hand and both cheeks. He was introduced to Henry, and the two of them carried on in French for some time. Chef Henri invited them to the chef's table in the kitchen, where they sat and watched him prepare their meal. Young Henry was given a task for each course, and the adults were delighted to see his interest.

There was much laughter and many oohs and aahs over each dish, and many toasts throughout the dinner.

At last, the *Isle de Flotant* arrived with café au lait for the adults and *chocolat* for young Henry. All four guests stumbled out of the restaurant, filled with food, drink, and the knowledge that they had just experienced a special evening.

Christian said good night outside the restaurant and thanked Maddy for an extraordinary experience. He kissed her hand, hopeful they would meet again.

Davi was waiting for them outside the restaurant. When he stopped in front of the school, Sebastian got out of the car to walk Henry into the dorm.

"I almost forgot." Maddy handed the gift bag to Henry.

"This is for your special friend," he said in French.

"You are my special friend," Maddy said with a smile. "Good night, Henry, I hope someday you will welcome me to your own gallery or perhaps your restaurant."

He took the bag shyly and hugged her, turned, and ran up the steps. At the door, he shook hands with Sebastian and blurted out, "J'aime Maddy," his hand on his chest.

Sebastian responded, "Moi aussi," matching the gesture of putting his hand on his chest. "A bientot."

Sebastian skipped down the steps and into the car, whistling. In the car he reached for Maddy's hand, held it in his hands, and then kissed it.

"Thank you, it was a wonderful night, and Henry certainly loved it," he said, feeling very happy and carefree. "Christian also enjoyed the evening; it was lovely of you to include him."

She was pleased. "I'm glad it worked out. He did seem to enjoy our company, didn't he?"

"Indeed."

The next day, a very large basket with flowers, German wines, and chocolates arrived from Deutsche Bank, thanking Maddy for leaving such an "impression". Christian invited Maddy, Sebastian, and Henry to be his guests at the Lipizzaner Stallions event. He also asked if he could be included in their next cultural outing.

The Professor

"Sir, Maddy came to school with me this afternoon, and she was brilliant." Davi could hardly contain himself.

"I can only imagine." Sebastian closed the car door and sat back, mentally exhausted from his dinner meeting. Several times during dinner he had wished he had thought to ask Maddy to come to dinner. She would have filled in the silent gaps easily.

"No sir, she was *more* than brilliant." Davi was clearly excited.

Tired but amused, Sebastian asked what had happened. He loosened his tie.

"Sir, Maddy came to class. The professor was to lecture on family business, but he was rambling, and suddenly Maddy stood up and asked him if he realized who he was speaking to. Sir, you could have heard a pin drop in that hall. He looked stunned and angry. I was worried. He asked Maddy if she would like to address the subject, and she agreed. Sir, I'm telling you, she walked down to the podium, thanked him, and just took over. She asked questions to begin with. Most of the class work in a family business—how did she know that? Everyone was so involved in the discussion that we didn't want to go when the bell sounded. The class gave her a standing ovation, and she was flooded with questions. It was brilliant. I was very proud of her." Davi finally took a breath.

"Indeed." Sebastian was trying to picture the scene in his mind. Yes, he too would have been proud of her. He smiled. "Where is she now?"

"Oh sir, the professor invited her for coffee, like in the movies. I have never seen him so humble." Davi shook his head. "Sir, he assured me he would see Maddy safely home."

Sebastian was smiling, rubbing his forehead, when suddenly he realized he didn't like to hear she had gone off with a strange man.

Stepping out of the car, Sebastian was disappointed to see the garden in darkness. Maddy was still out. Davi parked the car and ran over. "Sir, I am waiting for Maddy in the garden. Would you like tea?"

Sebastian looked at his watch. 11.15 p.m. He shook his head and turned towards the house. "Good night, Davi. We should leave for Plymouth by eight thirty latest, in the morning."

"Yes sir, good night." Davi was still wound up. He turned on the garden lights and ran up to his apartment to make tea.

Sebastian walked into the house and shuddered. The house always felt chilled, not warm and inviting like the garden apartment. He took another look at his phone for emails and checked the appointments for tomorrow. He walked out to the garden, where Davi was drinking tea, his school papers scattered on the table. "I will join you for a drink, but not tea," he announced, holding his scotch glass.

Davi looked up, smiling. His boss was worried. He hoped Maddy would be home soon.

Just after midnight, at the front door, the cabbie waited patiently for the professor to say good night to Maddy.

"If I walked you to the door, would I be invited in for a nightcap?" he asked shyly.

Maddy could sense his anxiety. "No," she said softly. "Not tonight."

"Thank you for that. It means there's hope for another time. May I call you?"

"I'm sure we'll see each other again." She smiled at him. He had been such a gentleman. "I had a wonderful evening. Thank you. Good night, Professor."

"Good night, Maddy." He kissed her hand, turned, and gave her a last look before climbing into the cab.

She waved and walked around to the garden. She was delighted to see Davi and Sebastian sitting on the patio, lights blazing. It was a lovely picture. "What a nice welcome," she said, startling them.

"Oh Maddy, I had to wait for you and be sure you were home safe." Davi jumped up. "Tea?"

Sebastian was sipping on his scotch, watching her. He shook his head, smiling. "I hear you displaced a professor tonight. Bravo."

Maddy blushed. "It all worked out." She hesitated. "I probably shouldn't have interfered."

"No, Maddy, it was brilliant. Was the professor nasty to you?" Davi was excited and concerned.

"He was fine, Davi. He recently lost his wife of forty-two years, and he's not coping very well. I think you'll find him less aggressive and more interested in the group now that he knows who you all are. He's very interesting. His wife was a musician, and before she died, she was given an inheritance—too late to pay for treatments but enough to buy a club in the city. They purchased the building in an auction and have turned it into a wonderful dance club. Sebastian, we must go there one night. It's called Decades. It's really fun."

"I enjoyed your class, Maddy. Thank you. I need to be ready for the morning. I wanted to be sure you got home safe. I'm going. Good night." With a sigh of relief Davi picked up his papers and teacup and hurried away.

Maddy sat down, exhausted.

"Would you like to join us tomorrow?" Sebastian asked. "I have a meeting in Plymouth, but we have time for some exploring in the afternoon."

"Can we have afternoon tea with Devon cream and the works?" Maddy brightened.

He nodded, amused by her quick response.

"Torcross is such a quaint historic seaside town with the best scones ever. I'd love to walk the seawall with you."

"If that's what you'd like to do." He smiled at her enthusiasm. He had no plan of his own.

"Thank you. That's awesome. What time are you rolling out?"

"We planned for 8.30 a.m.—is that good for you?" He was looking forward to spending the time together.

"Perfect. I'd better say good night. It's been quite a day." Maddy stood, touching his shoulder. "Are you going home or snuggling up with me?"

Sebastian leaned back so his cheek brushed her hand. "Good night, Maddy. Get some rest. I'll get the lights." He watched as she walked into the apartment, wondering why he wasn't following her. He had waited up for her to return, and lying beside her was so comforting. He chuckled to himself as he realized Maddy had many friends and he couldn't keep her to himself. He unplugged the lights and walked slowly to the main house. "Old man, you are jealous. What are you going to do about that?" he mumbled to himself.

They had a splendid day on the coast, making the most of the sunshine, walking hand in hand along the seawall, enjoying afternoon tea, chatting with the locals about the war, and watching the sunset from the beach. It was a pleasant excursion. The ride home was quiet as Maddy snuggled into Sebastian's arms. He held her, enjoying the smell of her hair and the warmth of her body against him. It had been some time since he had rolled up his pant legs and walked barefoot in the sand. They arrived home and went straight into the garden apartment, neither wanting the day to end.

The next morning, Sebastian was checking messages at the kitchen counter, coffee mug in hand, when Maddy appeared from the bathroom.

"Is that my shirt?" he asked.

Maddy looked down as if she didn't realize she was wearing a shirt. "Hmm, I just grabbed a cover. I like it; it smells like you. Do you need it?"

"I just wondered why you would be wearing my shirt …" He looked back at his messages.

Maddy unbuttoned the shirt, slipped out of it, and handed it to Sebastian.

He looked up at her naked body walking towards the glass doors. She was going to open the draperies.

"Maddy, no, here, put this on." He ran over to her, wrapping her in the shirt. "There's always someone outside your window. Here, let me cover you."

Maddy looked up at Sebastian with her eyes wide as he buttoned the shirt.

"You do try me, Maddy. I have a full day of meetings, but you just wait until I get home this evening." He was trying not to smile.

Maddy continued to stare up at him. *Damn her.* He really had to get going. As he kissed her, she ran her hands down his chest and behind his back, grabbing his buttocks.

"Maddy, you're killing me," he whispered.

She stepped back, smiling coyly. "Have a nice day."

He picked up his jacket and his phone and walked to the patio. He turned and saw Maddy leaning on the side of the glass partition, one leg bent, one arm up, pushing the glass door wide. He walked back over to the door and kissed her. She looked great in his shirt.

"You taste like coffee," she said, licking her lips.

"You taste like I don't want to go to work," he laughed. "Dinner tonight?"

"I'll see if I can fit you in. 'Way you go. Save the world." She tapped his behind as he turned to go.

He was grinning as he climbed into the car. "What a woman," he said to no one in particular.

November

"Maddy, any plans this evening?" Sebastian was calling from the car, on his way home.

"I'm all yours tonight. What's up?" She sounded out of breath.

"Where are you?" He asked, wondering what she was doing.

"I'm visiting next door. Join us through the garden and we'll have a gin and tonic ready for you." She was laughing.

"Best offer all day. See you shortly." Sebastian looked out the window and hoped they wouldn't be long. He never knew what to say to the neighbours.

As he approached the gate to the next garden, he saw Maddy carrying armloads of wood across the path. "Ah, here you are."

She greeted him and stopped to let him kiss her cheek. "I'm all sweaty." She wrinkled her nose and moved away.

"What are you doing?" he asked as she continued walking with the wood.

"Gordon and Esme had their winter wood delivered today, but the driver dumped it in the middle of the drive; they can't be lifting and carrying wood at their age. I'm almost done. Have a seat on the patio and join them for a drink."

Sebastian waved at the elderly couple, removed his jacket, and proceeded to help Maddy with the wood. Maddy stopped, surprised, removing her work gloves and pushing strands of hair behind her ear.

Sebastian carried an armload of wood and passed her. "Who do you think piled the wood for Belle? Come on; let's get this done." He quickly gathered an armload, and as he turned, Maddy gave him a hug and whispered, "Thank you, it's mighty neighbourly of you to help."

He kissed her on the nose and moved back to the wood. They finished the work quickly and had one drink with a most grateful Gordon and Esme before heading home.

The next day, Gordon and Esme invited Maddy and Sebastian to travel north to their country cottage for a weekend. Gordon was an avid carp and salmon angler, while Esme enjoyed walking; they called their weekend getaway an indulgence. Sebastian was unsure how he would cope with the couple, but Maddy was excited about the road trip. As a compromise, they agreed to meet north, citing impossible scheduling arrangements. Sebastian would drive his beloved MG, so their luggage was limited. Since Maddy had asked about the car, Sebastian felt compelled to drive it whenever possible.

Maddy conferred with Audrey about wardrobe—wellies, a warm jumper, and a rain coat was all she required. Audrey was only too happy to supply everything. Sebastian had all the right kit. He suggested they leave Thursday afternoon so they could stop at a small inn he had heard served excellent meals. Maddy had snacks and music ready for the drive, unsure about the extent of conversation they might have en route. She wasn't sure if Sebastian would want to talk while driving. It was their first road trip alone.

The inn was lovely, with a view of the Loch and easy walking trails. They seemed to be the only couple without a dog. They trekked for an hour before dinner, enjoying the fresh air.

Standing in the pub, Sebastian was looking every inch the country gentleman with a pint in hand. Maddy sat beside him on a stool with a glass of bubbly, looking up at him. Another couple joined them at the bar, asking if they were on their honeymoon. Maddy mischievously responded without answering the question. "Why do you ask?"

"You look so happy together, and we heard you laughing earlier. We just thought you must be newly married. Look around you. Everyone here looks like they can hardly wait to fall asleep alone."

Just then the hostess arrived announcing their table was ready. They moved over to the window table and silently read over the handwritten menu, deciding on two dishes they wanted to try.

Sebastian reached for Maddy's hand and asked her if she was happy. Her eyes were sparkling in the candlelight. She smiled at him and nodded.

"You?" she asked, squeezing his hand.

"Very."

The couple from the bar walked by their table, stopping to invite Maddy and Sebastian for a nightcap.

"Thank you, but this is our first night alone without the children in ages. We started late, and the children are exhausting," Maddy responded.

"Ah, we understand; enjoy your evening." The couple walked away, winking at Sebastian.

Sebastian looked over at Maddy, who was avoiding eye contact. "Well, mother of two, shall we retire?" he asked, reaching for her hand.

"Oh, my gosh, thanks for clarifying; I was trying to recall the name of the third child, just in case they asked." Maddy rolled her eyes.

"What are the children called, and how old are they?" he asked seriously.

"Alexander is sixteen and very serious; Angela is fourteen. She has you wrapped around her little finger." Maddy smiled at Sebastian, and for a moment he felt a wave of sadness, wishing they had met earlier and had a real family. Maddy would have been a wonderful mother, he was sure.

They walked up the stairs to their room holding hands. Before opening the door with the large old-fashioned key, Sebastian pinned her against the wall and kissed her gently, inviting her to spend the night. She threw her arms around his neck, laughing softly. He ran his hands down her back, holding her tight.

Maddy giggled. "Imagine people believing we have children …"

They heard someone coming up the stairs and fumbled with the key, stumbling into the room and landing on the double bed, holding each other, stifling their laughter. Sebastian looked down at Maddy, the moonlight casting a pale light on her smiling face, her eyes dancing, and he was lost—completely lost—in her. They made love, exploring each other, not wanting to rush, eventually falling asleep wrapped in each other's arms.

They woke up with a cacophony of birds outside their window. Maddy stretched and suggested they just stay in bed for the day, which sounded inviting to Sebastian.

An hour later, they were driving north to meet Gordon and Esme, enjoying the wind and the sunshine in the MG with the top down, laughing and stealing glances at each other, holding hands—happy to be together.

The cottage was basic but comfortable, and the couples settled in with a cup of tea, Gordon adding a single-malt scotch to both his and Sebastian's cups. The men walked over to the river, and Esme led the way on the trail, the dog running ahead. The sunshine appeared on and off all day, providing much conversation about the weather at dinner. Esme was delighted to have a walking companion who was willing to hear her concerns about an upcoming fundraiser. It was Esme who had suggested Maddy sit with the chemo patients at the hospital; she felt Maddy would cheer up the patients.

"Gordon says not to fret, everything will come together, but I don't know." Esme confided to Maddy.

"Well, we have a gorgeous day to see what we can sort out," Maddy responded.

And they did.

The men managed to land one appetizer-size fish from the stocked pond, but they had great stories of the ones that got away. Maddy took photos of the sky and the terrain throughout the day, hoping to gift the best shot in a frame to their hosts.

Sitting by the massive hearth, watching the peat burn, the couples enjoyed a nightcap and the silence that comes from being tired and content. The flames cast flickering shadows on their faces, and Maddy smiled, wondering why Sebastian didn't do this more often. He smiled back, deep in his own thoughts, imagining more days like this.

Gordon and Esme were easy hosts, and the time flew by, the conversation light, the weather pleasant enough for outdoor pursuits on the river or on the moors. Maddy was pleased at how compatible Sebastian had been with her friends, his neighbours. They waved goodbye after many hugs, promising to return in the spring for the salmon and to drive carefully.

The ride home was filled with laughter and stories of adventures past and of those to come. Anyone hearing the conversation would think Maddy and Sebastian had lived a long, wonderful life together.

The Bold Move

"Lambert, does the company support the children's hospital?" Maddy asked coyly.

"As a matter of fact, we do. Why do you ask?"

Maddy had to think fast. "Our neighbours are involved with the upcoming fundraiser, and I have an idea that requires amazing individuals with talent. Of course, you came to mind immediately. Interested?"

"I'm intrigued, naturally. Reel me in."

"Excellent. Lunch today. Hospital cafeteria. You are a gem."

Maddy ended the call and smiled at Esme. "It's about to take shape, my dear; don't you worry." Esme was grateful to have Maddy's creative assistance with the programme, as her committee was struggling.

Sebastian was to meet Maddy at the fundraiser later in the evening. As he left that morning, she asked how she would know him. He turned around and shook his head.

"It is customary to have a red rose and a newspaper, you know." Maddy pointed out.

He laughed and kissed her goodbye. "We'll see."

The reception was well under way as Sebastian walked into the ballroom. He saw Lambert hovering, waiting for his arrival. The company table was reserved, and Lambert seemed intent on making sure everything was just so. Sebastian scanned the crowd and saw Maddy holding court with a group of overdressed matrons. He clipped a rose from the table and looked around for a newspaper. A folded programme would have to do.

"Lambert, have you ever seen a bold move?" He asked his skittish assistant.

"Sir?" Lambert was half listening.

"Observe and learn, my good man. One bold move coming up." Sebastian watched Maddy for a moment and then began striding purposefully towards her.

As he approached the group of ladies, he stopped beside Maddy, "Excuse me, you look especially lovely this evening." He caressed her face and kissed her. He had no concept of time, but eventually they separated. Maddy was beaming.

"Come home with me tonight." He was charming. "I'm sorry, ladies; I'm just not very good with small talk." The shocked looks on their faces made him realize he had, in fact, made a bold move. Pleased with himself, he nodded at Maddy, adjusted the rose in his lapel, bowed slightly, and moved away. "I'll get us a drink."

"Well, that was nervy," one of the ladies exclaimed in a shocked voice.

"It was lovely," Maddy beamed, watching Sebastian walk away. She realized the women were still waiting for an explanation. "I told him he wasn't romantic enough … he's really trying."

They all nodded, exchanging looks, eyebrows raised, and continued with their conversation, wondering if that line would work with their husbands.

Seated at the table, appetizers served, Sebastian commented on how jumpy Lambert seemed, surprising himself at noticing. Maddy touched his knee under the table. "You were wonderful earlier—just the right amount of confidence and shock value. Please cut Lambert some slack. He's nervous."

The lights dimmed before he could ask why. The music started, and a lone voice began singing. Suddenly people from various tables joined in, walking deliberately towards the centre of the room. Lambert stood and left the table, singing as he walked away. It was magical; the room was transformed into a live stage, with singers and musicians travelling around, meeting in the centre of the room, and then dispersing, to the music of Stand by You. Maddy was directing the movement of the group with her hand on Sebastian's knee; he felt her hand and wondered if she realized what she was doing. As the song ended, the crowd enthusiastically rose to their feet, applauding the flash mob. No one noticed a very flushed Lambert return to the table. He winked at Maddy and gave her a thumbs up.

Maddy enjoyed the reaction of the attendees, hoping their enthusiasm would carry through to spending in the auction. Lambert was flooded with congratulations from friends and fellow singers.

Esme floated over to the table and hugged Maddy from behind. "Thank you. It was perfect," she whispered. Maddy patted the arms around her neck in response. Esme had been in a dreadful state when she explained that their planned musical was cancelled. Maddy thought a flash mob would be fun and worked with Esme to get the singers from her board and committees, secure the band, and provide choreography. Just two long rehearsals had resulted in the strong group effort tonight.

Sebastian wondered what part Maddy had played in the entertainment but thought it best to wait for her to explain. Lambert would be more than willing to fill him in with the details.

The event was a great success, exceeding the committee goal, netting the children's hospital more than required for the new equipment. Sebastian forced the bidding higher on several items, graciously allowing others to take the items home. Maddy insisted they didn't need a thing, although she was bidding on a bottle of rare single-malt scotch Esme and Gordon had donated. She was thrilled when it was delivered to the table. Sebastian feigned surprise when she presented it to him, having just doubled the previous bid and secured it for her.

It was difficult to leave the building at the end of the evening as many of the attendees waited to thank Maddy and say good night. Sebastian shook hands with Lambert. "Who knew you had such talent?" he said in jest.

Lambert was very serious. "Maddy knew."

They walked to the waiting car, holding hands, Maddy pointing out how beautiful the moon was over the city. Sebastian looked up, wondering if there was anything she didn't notice. She fell asleep in his arms before they left the parking area.

"Hello darling, I'm just on my way to the last meeting of the day. Shall we eat out tonight?" Sebastian was calling from the car.

"Mrs B left us dinner. She said you love her cabbage rolls and strudel. Isn't that sweet?" Maddy was juggling her phone between her ear and her shoulder, searching for the earbuds. She and Audrey were just about to board the train. She mouthed to Audrey "He just called me 'darling'."

Sebastian chuckled. "Mrs B has certainly taken to you. I'm still afraid of her."

"She brought over some shirts, underwear, and socks. You have a drawer now." Maddy was laughing. "She advised me she would continue to make your breakfast when she is here; I don't think she feels I can handle getting you a proper breakfast. She dotes on you, you know." Maddy motioned to the seats.

"Oh dear. I'd rather hear you say you did. See you at home." He added softly, "I missed you today."

"Me too. Ciao." Maddy smiled as she dropped the phone into her pocket.

Audrey made loud kissing noises, fluttering her eyes. "That was rather cute."

Shrugging, Maddy replied, "And surprising. He doesn't phone me very often."

As they settled into their seats, Audrey looked over at Maddy. "You really care about him, don't you?"

Maddy thought for a moment and then slowly responded. "He's easy to be with; he treats me well. It's a good arrangement." Her voice trailed off. "You know, at the club he seems so in control and confident, but he's really an awkward adolescent in other social settings. He has a lovely laugh, and he's kind and generous." Maddy stopped, shaking her head. She had not come to London looking for love; she had come to find herself. She had arrived believing love was elusive and meant for the young; now she knew love had no age limits. It made her giddy.

"Where is this going, Maddy? Are you thinking about what happens when you leave? I need to know you'll be back. You're my friend, and I love having you nearby; you can't just disappear." Audrey sounded concerned.

"I couldn't possibly go back to my old life of pretending to work out all day, lunching with friends who lie about how great their husbands and kids are doing, about how they are so fulfilled … Since I've met you, I've felt alive. Crazy, out of control—but alive. I don't wait for Jeffrey to come home; I'm busy with useful projects and keeping your zany ideas in check. I love it. Now if that's how I feel, imagine how Sebastian must feel …" she turned to look at Maddy. "You know, Maddy, Sebastian is jealous of you. Why are men like that?" Audrey sipped from a bottle of water.

Maddy laughed and looked out the window. "Oh Audrey, men get their first car or motorbike as boys, and they spend hours waxing, polishing, and caressing it, calling it 'her' or 'she'. Eventually they learn about girls, and for a while they treat their girlfriends like their first cars. Then they start to wonder about the other horses on the roundabout and they wander. Of course, some of the pretty horses want a commitment before the ride is over, and that just scares them off the roundabout. Simple fact of life. You must always negotiate free time or the double standard kicks in." Maddy smiled at Audrey. "How does that song go … 'You don't own me …'" They started singing the words to the song, laughing and dancing in their seats. When they ran out of lyrics, Maddy wiped her eyes and in a serious voice assured Audrey Sebastian had no reason to be jealous.

Audrey cleared her throat. "Ahem, Maddy, I have a confession." She looked nervous.

"Do I want to hear this?" Maddy asked, raising an eyebrow, squirming in her seat.

"Maddy, one night we went back to the garden for a drink. I was looking at your potted sprouts, and Sebastian walked into the yard. Of course, he was polite, nodding and giving me his usual frosty one-word greeting, 'Audrey'. I watched him make a beeline towards you, and I caught my breath. He was walking with a purpose. He put his hand on your shoulder and kissed your cheek. You smiled up at him, and honestly, I felt you two were having sex in front of me. It was magical. It was innocent but so sexual. I left, citing a forgotten engagement. You probably didn't even notice."

Maddy blushed.

"On the way home, crossing the boulevard, I called Jeffrey and told him to get home quick, as I had a surprise for him. I was getting out of the shower when he came into the house wondering what was wrong. I grabbed his tie and unbuttoned his shirt, and once he got over the initial shock of me initiating, we had the hottest sex ever—all because of the way you two looked at each other." Audrey stopped, flushed from speaking so fast. "That's what I'm talking about. The way you are with each other … You've got to figure this out—not just for me, but for Sebastian and yourself."

"Can't we just enjoy the time we have? I don't know what will happen when the year is up, but you are my friend, and I'm not going to abandon you, ever." Maddy patted her hand, ending the discussion. "Now, I do like this design for the glass blocks in the shower; what do you think? The conversation shifted to the building project, both women understanding the discussion was not over, just on hold.

Cycles

"Sebastian, you know how you said I could plan the weekend?" Maddy asked as they were finishing breakfast.

"Yes, I do recall offering to let you plan something." He set his coffee cup down slowly, wondering what was coming.

"Great. I booked a cycle tour in Devon, and I rented bicycles, and we'll stay at this lovely little inn, and we should leave Friday night rather than Saturday morning, just in case."

Sebastian considered the plan. "I haven't been on a bicycle for years."

"Well, you know what they say," Maddy teased.

"No, what do they say?" he asked cautiously.

"Whenever anyone says they haven't done something for a long while, people respond by saying, 'It's like riding a bike.' You never forget how to ride a bike. You'll love it. I promise." Maddy stood and wrapped her arms around his neck. "It'll be fun."

"We'll see about that. What's the *just in case*?" he asked, not sure it would be fun at all.

"Oh, if we don't leave Friday, I'm afraid you'll have some work that keeps you here, so we'd better start early and let you ease into the experience. A nice dinner, a good night's sleep, a hearty breakfast, and then off we go."

"Indeed."

They did leave Friday, and they did indeed have a lovely evening at the inn; waking to bright sunshine and a slight breeze on Saturday. They were kitted out and on the trail by 10.00 a.m., enjoying the country roads.

Before lunch, Sebastian stopped at a lookout area to consult the map and give his aching behind a rest. Maddy leaned her bike against the railing and walked over, taking her bike helmet off.

"What's up?" she asked with a smile.

"I just wanted to see where we were and where we were going." He studied the legend.

"Here, I can help you." Maddy took the map and held it up in the air, watching as the breeze buffeted the paper through the air, away from them. She laughed with delight.

"This is where we are. We can go anywhere we like."

"What if we get lost?" Sebastian wanted to be cross with her, but her smile was teasing him to be adventurous.

"If we get lost, at least we'll be lost together. Come on; let's go get lost." She was still laughing.

"Wait a minute." Sebastian sounded stern. Maddy turned to him. She watched as he dismounted and walked towards her.

"If I'm going to get lost with someone, I want to know she is totally committed to the process." Sebastian held her shoulders, leaned down, and touched her lips. Maddy responded with enthusiasm, throwing her arms around his neck; there was no doubt she was committed.

Sebastian stepped back, his thoughts whirling, wishing they were back at the inn.

"Come on; you lead. Take us to lunch." Maddy recovered, her smile daring him to continue. Before she walked to her bike, she tapped his behind. "How's your butt holding out?"

Sebastian laughed, despite himself. No one had ever asked him that before.

After lunch they headed back to the inn, Maddy leading the way; she had an incredible sense of direction, Sebastian noticed.

The weekend was enjoyable, as Maddy had promised. They walked along the shops and the ocean, they had drinks in a quaint seaside pub, and they returned to read by the large window in their lovely little inn room. Their bikes remained parked by the door, a reminder of where they could go.

The Dinner Party

Inevitably, the dreaded invitation came, requesting the presence of Sebastian and a guest to dinner at the home of Deirdre Fontaine's parents. Mr Putnam, a former banker, was a respected member of the club, and an invitation was not to be taken lightly.

Sebastian assured Maddy it was just dinner, with cocktails first and a drink after the meal; they could skip out whenever she felt she had had enough. She took this as a sure sign it would be challenging.

Sebastian was unsure how Deirdre would handle the situation; she was caustic at best. He rationalized he should introduce Maddy to his acquaintances—especially since stories of the incident at the gallery had circulated. This is how men think—just jump in and see how it settles out. What could possibly go wrong?

On the way to dinner, Maddy asked how long Sebastian had been involved with Deirdre. He laughed and assured Maddy he had not been involved at all. They played tennis, and they attended theatre when either needed an escort, but Deirdre was looking for husband number four, and Sebastian didn't need a financial merger or an introduction to London society, so he wasn't a serious contender for a relationship. Deirdre called him when she was in between husbands or affairs. He didn't console or provide solace; he was just a guy with a tux when she needed an escort. It seemed rather cold to Maddy, who valued her friendships above all.

They were greeted in the large foyer by the butler (Maddy almost laughed out loud, thinking, *Who still has a butler?*) and ushered into the library for drinks. Groups of men standing around the room and the women seated on the edges of the big chairs stopped talking and inspected Maddy and Sebastian as they entered the room. Maddy took an exaggerated breath and smiled at Sebastian. He stood, hands clasped behind his back, scanning the room, nodding, and acknowledging waves. He placed his hand on her back to reassure her and then started walking towards their hosts. The greeting was quick, and they moved to a group of men standing by the fireplace. Sebastian introduced her to bankers, CEOs, and a judge, and he then began conversing with a gentleman beside him. Maddy accepted a drink from the tray offered and blinked, hoping she would be transported elsewhere—anywhere but here. This had worked for Jeannie on an old television show called *I Dream of Jeannie.* One of the bankers offered to introduce her to his wife, and off they went. She hoped there would not be a test later; it was impossible for her to remember names and who belonged with whom.

She heard several men discussing American politics and couldn't help but comment on a statement that she felt was ludicrous. The men accepted her light-hearted scolding and welcomed her into the group. They were interested in her thoughts, and soon she was suggesting they were out of touch with the very people who made them wealthy. They laughed and commented on how North Americans always speak their minds. She responded by kidding them about their long, drawn-out formal way of speaking. The conversation was animated, and Sebastian was shooed away when he came to check on how Maddy was doing.

"You could do right by me and ask me to marry you before Mummy and Father ask me to leave this mausoleum again." Deirdre positioned herself next to Sebastian. "I mean, you can only play house for so long with your garden mistress before you see she doesn't fit in, doesn't quite make the grade. And besides, we play tennis and cards, know the same crowd … It would be so easy for you to just make the right decision. We don't even like each other, so there wouldn't be much drama, but everyone would expect it. And we could have a nice life. Father adores you and would offer a very generous dowry." Sebastian tried to move away as Deirdre placed her hand on his chest. He looked over her head towards the fireplace, where Maddy and a group of his crowd were engaged in lively conversation. Maddy had no problem fitting in with his crowd, it seemed. Deirdre followed his gaze and laughed a desperate laugh—a cruel laugh that made Sebastian realize how lucky he was to have found someone less needy.

At that moment, the elderly butler invited everyone into the large dining room. Conversation continued as the group moved towards the table with promises to continue their discussions after dinner. Sebastian breathed a sigh of relief as he moved away from Deirdre.

Maddy wondered how she would get through the dinner. Sebastian was seated across the large table, and she felt vulnerable. She silently named each person for a character from a Jane Austen novel. Sebastian was so far away she would have liked to squeeze his hand right now. No, she would have enjoyed breaking his wrist right now.

Dinner service was formal, with several courses, and Maddy was working hard at prying responses from her immediate table mates when Deirdre, sitting across the table, cleared her throat and asked Maddy in a very condescending voice which designer she was wearing this evening. She said she was unaware who had designed the vestment. *Who says that?* Maddy wondered, collecting her thoughts. She knew this could go very badly. She was a guest in this house, and Deirdre, according to everyone, had a history with Sebastian. She took a deep breath and heard several dinner guests gasp at the clear slight. This seemed to be Deirdre's *modus operandi.*

"Thank you for asking," Maddy responded sweetly. "My kurtas are made by the ladies in a small village near Jaipur, India. My friend is a doctor of textiles, and one of her projects is teaching the women in the village to design and create their own fabric; then they learn to sew and sell their work. As a result, they now support themselves and their children as never before. I wear their work with pride because my purchases are giving hope to a new generation of independent women who will now have the opportunity for a better life. I also feel better knowing the garments aren't coming from a sweatshop." Maddy spoke deliberately and with such passion that everyone at the table stopped to hear her. She knew her face was burning, and yet she could not stop.

"We have been able to build a school, supply sewing machines and looms, purchase ends of fabric from textile mills, and teach courses in dyeing and patterning. It's quite incredible how these forgotten women have rallied and become more fulfilled." She realized she had the attention of the table; Sebastian was gazing at his water glass with a pained look, and Deirdre was defiantly staring back.

"This year we project sales will allow for a water purifier in the village, which is much needed with the lack of rainfall. If you would like a few of these in silk, or a silk scarf, I would be delighted to order them for you." She smiled and folded her hands in her lap, hoping no one would see her hands shaking.

Deirdre raised her eyebrows in surprise. "I just can't see myself trading in my designer frocks for something so simple." She gestured towards Maddy.

Hands up anyone who thought that was condescending, Maddy thought, but she smiled and responded with "I'm sure your designer frocks provide a good living with a fair wage for someone somewhere." She couldn't look at Sebastian, but she felt he must certainly have been angry with her response.

Someone at the table coughed. Everyone was waiting for Deirdre to respond when a small voice asked Maddy if she would speak to the women's auxiliary group at their next luncheon. Mrs Putnam explained her ladies were always interested in fundraising for projects that benefitted women, and this was a fine cause; she suggested perhaps they could arrange a date after dinner. Maddy responded with such delight; there was no doubt the water purification plant would become a reality. The elderly man next to Maddy handed her a cheque for a substantial amount, grabbed her hand, and chuckled. "You've been an interesting dinner companion. Thank you for indulging an old man in conversation. My granddaughters would love to have some colourful scarves like this one. If you need more, call me. Now help me into the cursed library." Deirdre was forgotten as the rest of the table chuckled.

With a quick laugh, their hostess invited the guests for coffee and dessert in the library. As Maddy assisted the elderly gentleman into the room, she looked around for an escape door. She was heading for the powder room when she saw a doorway behind a pillar. She leaned against the cold marble, hidden from the ladies in the hallway. Closing her eyes, she wondered what the repercussions of her response would be. She felt a presence and opened her eyes to find Sebastian staring at her. He looked stern. Tears flooded her eyes. "Just how angry are you?" She sniffled.

He smiled and held her face in his hands "Why would I be angry? I'm sorry I couldn't protect you from what happened, but you were amazing. I think when you go back into that room you will have whatever your little village needs." He kissed her tears and handed her his handkerchief. She laughed at the gesture. Sebastian looked perplexed, holding out the neatly pressed cloth. "It's clean."

"That is so English," she giggled. "I can't imagine blowing my nose and handing it back. Thank you."

He smiled, realizing this had happened before. "Come on, my beautiful Bolshevik; let's get a film theatre or perhaps a bowling alley for your little village."

They walked hand in hand into the library and were immediately surrounded by a group wanting details on the project Maddy was involved in and how they could assist. It was a very productive evening indeed.

Deirdre approached Sebastian, who was watching a passionate Maddy respond to the questions. "Sebastian, my dear man, I know you; it won't be long before you tire of the little charity worker and her sad wardrobe." She smiled and took a sip of her coffee.

"Deirdre," he said, turning to walk away from her, "there's no hope of that."

Dance with Me

"Shall we go to dinner at the club tonight?" Sebastian called as he was heading out the door for his morning meeting. "It's the monthly dinner/dance event. They have an orchestra and a special menu … I thought you might enjoy a night out." He sounded less confident as he described the evening.

"Is it fun?" Maddy asked as she came out with a towel wrapped around her head. She placed her hands on his chest and then around him, under his jacket, looking up at him. "If you think we'll have fun, we should go."

Sebastian smiled at her and moved her arms away reluctantly. "I can't say I wouldn't have more fun right here at home, but I do think you need a night out. Wear something sexy I can easily remove." He kissed her forehead, and with one last glance, he headed for the waiting car. "I should be home in good time. See you then."

Maddy blew him a kiss. "Have a lovely day out there in the big, bad world."

He was grinning as he climbed into the car.

The club tables were filled with groups of four couples when they arrived. The menu was interesting, and the orchestra was engaging, although Maddy would have called them a band. She was wearing a bright red knee-length silk kimono dress she had found in a Chinatown somewhere in the world. She had a pair of ornate chopsticks in her hair and wore gold slippers that matched the gold thread in her dress. The dress had a slit up the leg, making it practical for walking or dancing. Sebastian admired the look and was pleasantly surprised with the red silk tie Maddy produced for him.

After dinner Sebastian chatted with a group of members at the bar while Maddy mingled with the wives and guests. Sebastian watched her work the room, as she called it. Her dress and her smile were so welcoming that she had no problems engaging the usually stodgy crowd in conversation.

"Is this one a throw-away?" The booming voice interrupted Sebastian's vigil. He turned to see a rather robust judge approach the bar. "I'm only asking as a courtesy, my good chap; she seems livelier than your usual." Judge Sidney Barnes continued. "Just wanted to check with you before I make my move, old man." He was enjoying the annoyed look on Sebastian's face. "Seriously, I met your latest fling earlier today, and she was most enjoyable and refreshing. Unfortunately she seems to think you are a perfectly noble fellow." He laughed and hitched up his trousers. The movement was useless, owing to his girth.

"Did she happen to mention our meeting?" Barnes asked cagily. "You know, it was only brief, but she made me feel young again." Barnes chuckled, more to himself than to Sebastian.

Sebastian had yet to speak. He wasn't as disappointed as he was surprised by the comments; Maddy was new to the club, and of course there was speculation about who she was, where she came from, and what their relationship was all about. Before he could respond, Marguerite Stafford appeared at his side, smiling slyly.

"I think I may have underestimated you, my dear Sebastian." She nodded at the barkeep for another drink.

"Oh? How's that, Marguerite?" Sebastian turned away from Sidney Barnes to face her.

"I just met your new friend in the loo, and the wolf pack, your exes, were dissing you with the most unflattering language. Your friend appeared from a stall and introduced herself—which, as you can well imagine, created a deathly silence amongst the witches. Her parting words were, shall we say, memorable. Let me see if I can create the moment for you: 'Oh, and by the way, the sex is …' and here she made the motion of an explosion. It was delightfully entertaining." Marguerite looked around the room, avoiding eye contact. "She may have left the building; she certainly looked as though she had had quite enough."

Sebastian scanned the room for Maddy, concerned that she might have gone. He started to move away when Jason, the barkeep, pushed a tall drink with lime across the bar and motioned towards the garden. Sebastian nodded, murmured, "Thank you", and moved through the maze of tables. As he entered the small garden, he felt a wave of panic. He thought he heard a sob and turned to see Maddy leaning against the wall, obviously upset. He took a deep breath and walked towards her.

"Ah, here you are." He tried to sound light as he extended the drink towards her.

"Just getting some air," she replied in a whisper. "Thanks." She took the drink from his hand and turned away.

"Are you enjoying the evening?" he asked, not knowing what else to say.

"Are these people really your friends?" she asked in a small voice.

Sebastian looked up at the stars, weighing his response. "Not friends in the way you make friends. They are club members, and I know them. I know I am a popular gossip item, and I don't care what they say or think. They may have needed me to make their boyfriends jealous or to escort them, but that's the extent of our so-called friendship." He realized how sad that must have sounded—especially to Maddy, who valued her friendships and worked hard at them.

"Maddy, what happened? Did someone upset you?" He moved forward and decided not to touch her just yet.

"I'm just sad that people have to be that way. I don't understand the cruelty. I'm okay." She shrugged, placed her glass on the ledge, and wiped her eyes.

"Maddy, Belle once told me, when I was quite young, that the best revenge on jealous people is to be happy; it drives them crazy."

"Hmm. What do they have to be jealous about? They seem to have married well, and they have everything they could possibly want. Why are they afraid I'll wreck their happy homes by dancing with their husbands? They don't know anything about me or our relationship … well, except for one small detail. I'm sorry; I just couldn't leave them with the last word. I may have said something embarrassing … sorry." She looked up at Sebastian, her eyes bright. "I guess I'm just as silly as they are." She rubbed her temple.

"I heard you silenced the mob, defending my honour. No secrets in this club, Maddy." Sebastian moved closer and touched her hair. "There will always be talk, especially now. You see, I have a strict set of rules, and suddenly they don't understand how you changed them."

"What rules?" She looked confused.

"My protection rules—never spoken or written, but always obeyed, by me." He held her face in his hands, hoping she wouldn't turn away or run. "I never danced with anyone, never got too close in public, just to be sure there wouldn't be any misunderstanding of my intentions. I never invited anyone to sleep over at my home, ever. If there was an opportunity—and believe me, there were many invitations—to sleep over at someone else's home, I always left before the sun came up; I never stayed to wake up beside anyone." As he spoke, he realized how strange he must sound to the very person he cared about. To her credit, Maddy did not laugh. She just seemed to be digesting his words. "I must have been waiting for you to come along and break my hard and fast rules—throwing caution to the wind."

Maddy smiled. "Indeed."

"Let's dance." He held out his hand.

"You don't dance, remember?" she teased.

"I want to dance with you. My dance instructor tells me that if I close my eyes, hold my partner tight, and pretend no one is watching, it will be magical. Shall we see if that's true?" His hand was still extended, waiting for her to take hold and follow.

"I'd love to dance with you. I imagine it will be very magical." She took his hand, and they walked out onto the dance floor. Time seemed to stop as they held each other and enjoyed the slow music. The band responded with several slow numbers, and the murmurs on the dance floor were noticeable to everyone except the couple, who seemed lost in each other's arms.

"How be we switch partners, old man." Sidney Barnes nudged Sebastian with a loud guffaw.

Sebastian looked over at the man and then looked down at Maddy, who had raised her sleepy eyes from his shoulder. "Not a chance." He smiled and held her tighter, moving them away from the crowd, heedless of the reaction.

"Let's go home," he whispered.

"I've already gone." She motioned towards the door. "Thank you."

Sebastian looked confused.

110

"Thank you for breaking your rule and dancing with me. It was wonderful, and I hope we'll do it again—in public." She smiled and kissed his cheek.

He put his arm protectively over her shoulder, kissed the top of her head, and moved towards the door, feeling lightheaded and liberated. "Let's go home and break the rest of the rules."

They were oblivious to the surprised stares of the members as they left the club. They didn't hear the comments from the women gathered around the punchbowl.

"You know, in all the years I've known Sebastian, I've never seen him like this. Isn't this happening rather quickly for him?"

"It's lovely to see him acting like a teenager. He's not getting any younger, you know."

"None of us are."

"I think after all this time he deserves to be happy, don't you?"

"Why should he be any happier than the rest of us?"

The women laughed and turned back to their cocktails, feeling perhaps just a little jealous.

Decades and Dancing

"What an outrageous outfit," Maria Aeschbach snorted as she watched a woman in a colourful tunic, leggings, and flowing scarf weave her way through the dining room, greeting guests and stopping to chat. In a room of blue suits and black dresses, the woman was quite out of place, in Maria's mind.

Her dinner companions smiled, sensing without turning that Maddy had arrived.

"Where is your friend, Sebastian?" she asked impatiently, drumming her fingers on the table.

"Ah, here she is now." Sebastian stood to kiss Maddy. He was getting used to her late arrivals; 'on time' in her mind meant the moment she stepped into the building; it did not account for her greeting her new acquaintances, making suggestions for dinner, recommending the perfect wine, and asking after spouses and children. Diners wanted to catch her eye and acknowledge they knew her. He usually enjoyed watching her float through the tables; it was as though a window had been thrown open to let a spring breeze in.

Sebastian put his hand on the small of her back, an affectionate gesture, as he kissed her cheek.

Christian stood to greet her. "Maddy, you are a breath of fresh air."

"Thank you. We were sorry to miss you at the show; Henry sends greetings." Maddy smiled back.

"My pleasure. I understand you have another adventure planned for this evening." Christian kissed both her cheeks and held her hands in his.

"*Ya vol*, you are going to love this club. It's called Decades, and every twenty minutes the music changes to another decade, depending on the crowd. I have a booth for us … it will be such fun." Her enthusiasm caused both men to laugh.

"You must be Maria, from Switzerland. Hello, I'm Maddy. I've heard wonderful reports on your work. Welcome to London." Maddy leaned across the table to greet the woman.

Maria nodded from her seat, not acknowledging Maddy's outstretched hand.

"We are trying to complete a report for the National Task Force on Sustainable City Development … we have not ordered yet."

Maria's admonishing was interrupted by Jason, the waiter. "Excuse me, Maddy; Mrs Drake would like your comments on this champagne, ginger, and pomegranate cocktail. She hopes to serve it at her daughter's wedding."

He placed the martini glass down and stood back, awaiting her response. Maddy sipped the drink, commenting on the colour and the fizz, and handed the glass to Sebastian, who sipped without hesitation. To Maria's surprise, Maddy then handed the glass to Christian, who also sampled the drink. Maddy offered the glass to Maria. They had all sipped from the same glass. She shook her head in disbelief.

"Why would you waste perfectly good champagne on a bitter cocktail?" Maddy asked her companions. "Too much ginger for me," Christian replied, nodding.

"Women might like it because of the colour," Sebastian added.

Maddy looked up at Jason. "I suggest you try blood orange. It's not as strong, the colour will be better for a spring wedding, and it will have a wider appeal to both genders."

Jason considered the comments and agreed. "Good idea, Maddy; I'll make one and take it over. Oh, here's your Perrier. Enjoy." As the waiter left the table, Maria, looking flustered, suggested in a loud voice that perhaps someone would like to take their order.

The men looked uncomfortable with her impatience, but Maddy forged ahead.

"Christian, are you seeing lending patterns change with the popularity of crowdfunding?"

Christian, only too happy to lighten the mood, responded, asking Maddy why she had inquired.

"It seems people want to invest in new start-ups. They aren't worried about tax receipts; they just want to be leading-edge. They don't get shares or return, just merchandise or cooking classes in the case of restaurants. It can't be laundered money; it's just mad money people want to invest."

"Are you qualified to speak on this subject?" Maria asked Maddy directly.

"No, that's the beauty of small talk," Maddy responded pleasantly, batting her eyes.

"Maria, it was Maddy who submitted our council date. She was the one responsible for the city funding." Christian proudly announced. "I asked her for a brief or synopsis, which is on page three, if you please."

Maddy stood, touching the shoulders of the men. "I'm going to eat in the bar and let you get your very important work completed. When you're ready to go, please come and collect me."

Sebastian stood. "Maddy, that's not necessary. Please stay and have dinner."

Christian was moving his chair back to rise. Maddy stopped him. "No, really. Maria wants to complete the work, and she's only here for a few days, so you carry on. I'll be fine."

Maddy turned and immediately spoke to the table beside them, smiling and flirting. Maria didn't seem to notice the miserable looks of her dining companions. She carried on with the recommendations they were hoping to present.

Throughout dinner, Sebastian and Christian alternately made excuses to walk by the bar and check on Maddy. She was not alone, as several tables joined her for coffee and after-dinner drinks. Jason had reported to his tables that the "dragon lady" insisted on working over dinner so Maddy had gone to the bar. The laughter from the bar was distracting—especially so for the trio working on the proposal.

At one point, Maria suggested they offer a slate of the top ten solutions. Sebastian pointed out it might be best to stick with three: extreme to the left, extreme to the right, and compromise in the middle. Maria asked if this was a research-driven model or something his new, free-spirited girlfriend had suggested.

Sebastian and Christian laughed out loud, remembering the advice Maddy had given Henry when he was struggling with a presentation. She had explained that in life one should always enter into a negotiation with three proposals: one that is undesirable, one that is desirable, and a third that includes things one must have and things one can give up; one should always give the other person an easy out. The other person will save face and try to compromise with you because you gave something up. Win-Win. Who could argue with that negotiation tactic?

Maddy had also suggested Henry handle the bullies at school by killing them with kindness. Both men had watched the boy accept this advice earnestly, nodding his head and planning his next move. They had both considered how they might use the advice.

They yearned to be in the bar with Maddy, not here being insulted by a woman who had driven Maddy away. Sebastian stood and announced he had had enough and was calling it a day. Christian agreed with his colleague and stood.

"Maddy would want me to ask you to join us at the club, Maria. Will you join us or return to the hotel?" Sebastian asked, nostrils flaring.

"I will return to the hotel. Is there a driver available?" she asked without looking up.

"My driver will take you. We meet at nine in the morning, yes? Good night," Christian said, buttoning his jacket.

The men stopped at the entrance of the bar, watching the crowd around Maddy. She was taking their photos and working with an app to show what they looked like years ago, with hair.

There was an uproar of laughter for each photo; the grown men were all begging to be next. Maddy was sitting in the centre of the large settee, surrounded by wives and staid businessmen, all entertained by the tablet screen.

"Jason, I'll settle Maddy's account." Sebastian waved at the waiter.

"No need, sir. You would be the fourth person who wanted to settle her bill," Jason chuckled.

Maddy looked up and saw Sebastian. "Come on, everyone; let's go. I've sent our playlist, so all our favourites will be spinning on the dance floor tonight."

She held her hand up for someone to pull her up, and several hands fought for the honour.

"What's my song?" Sebastian asked.

"I chose 'Hero' by Enrique Iglesias for you. It's lovely. It's slow. You'll be making it your signature song," she said with confidence.

"What do you have in store for me?" Christian asked.

"They didn't have any oompah, so I chose 'Danke Schon'."

He groaned.

"Just kidding; I chose Santana for you."

As the group started out the door, Maddy noticed Maria at the table alone.

"Excuse me. I'll just be a minute." She touched Sebastian on the arm. He tried to stop her.

Maddy approached Maria and sat down. "Maria, why do you think you have to be so tough?" she asked.

"I work with men in a man's world. They expect it. I expect it." Maria wondered why no one had ever asked her this before. She had rehearsed the response for years.

"Being vulnerable sometimes gets better results," Maddy said in earnest.

"It's a sign of weakness." Maria was forceful.

"Not necessarily; it allows you to control the power. Perhaps if the men you work with believed you were vulnerable, they would adapt. You wouldn't have to follow; you would lead." Maddy smiled. "Are you sure you don't want to come out tonight?"

"No. I wouldn't know how to act."

"We're going dancing. No acting required. You can watch, or you can move. It's your choice."

"Is everything in your world so simple?" Maria asked, softening.

"It wasn't for a long time, but I now choose it to be so."

Maria stared at Maddy, suddenly unsure of herself. "Thank you, Maddy. I don't have many woman friends, but I think you would be a good candidate."

Maddy smiled, left her card, patted Maria's hand, and walked towards her dates, noting the anxious looks on their faces.

"It's all good. Let's go. You two look like you need a distraction." Both men held out their arms for her.

Loud and raucous, walking arm in arm, the group stopped short at the entrance to the club. A well-built Asian man, looking every inch a bouncer, took stock of the group and saw Maddy. "Welcome back, Ms Maddy. The professor is expecting you."

He opened the large wooden door, and a hostess walked them up the stairs to a secondary dance floor surrounded by booths. The group was quiet as they looked around and got their bearings. Sebastian wondered how Maddy knew about about this place.

"Sebastian, here's the professor; he owns the joint." She ran over to a tall older man dressed in a pinstriped suit with a black tie, and they hugged. He seemed very happy to see her and held her hands in his as they spoke.

Suddenly he led her away, and they joined the crowd of dancers. Maddy looked back at the group and shrugged. Couples were dancing, jumping up and rushing to the dance floor as their songs were being played by the DJ.

Maddy had danced with several partners by the time she returned to the booth and sat down. She was flushed and felt warm to the touch. "Are you having fun?" she asked as she leaned into Sebastian.

"I'm waiting to dance with you. You were right about the venue. Everyone seems to be enjoying the music," he yelled back. "Does the professor have a name?"

"I think it's Sam but I can never remember; everyone just calls him the professor." She shrugged. "Come and dance with me," she whispered in his ear, making him shiver.

They reached the dance floor for a fast song. Maddy didn't seem to be slowing down.

"Here's your song." She looked up at him, and at that moment he lost all sense of time and place. There was just Maddy and the music. They were moving together, so close, so in sync. Sebastian whispered to Maddy, "I want you so badly I'm not sure I can wait to get home."

Maddy thought for a moment, grabbed his hand, and led him out to the corridor, where she had seen an open closet. She pushed Sebastian into the room and closed the door behind her. When he realized what was happening, his kisses reflected the urgency he felt. They made love with a passion, fast and furious.

Sebastian stepped back, spent, and then reached out and took Maddy in his arms, kissing her softly. "I have never in my life done that. Wow."

Maddy wasn't sure she could stand on her own. She started giggling. "I feel like a teenager—like a bad teenager. Hmm. Why don't we do these crazy things more often?"

Sebastian smiled at her, thinking his life had taken such a different direction since meeting her. This was not how "good" boys acted. He was officially a "bad" boy. The only thing he was sure of was his love for her. He kissed her forehead. "No, you're reckless. Will anyone miss us, do you think?"

"Let's dance." She opened the door, looking both ways before stepping out into the hallway, through the double doors, and onto the dance floor. She looked radiant.

Thankfully the next song was a slow dance, and they held each other tight. Sebastian realized he wanted to be home, alone with Maddy. He was about to ask her if they could leave when Maddy was whisked away by another colleague. He returned to the booth, stretching out on the leather settee.

"Have you been smoking some good shit?" Christian asked as he sat down.

Sebastian waved his hand and shook his head, surprised by the question.

"You look very mellow, very comfortable—almost foolishly happy. I thought maybe you had taken something." Christian remarked as he finished his beer.

"No, no, but I am foolishly happy." Sebastian was watching Maddy on the dance floor. "I think it's time I took happy home." He stood up, and Christian smiled back at him, nodding.

Sebastian approached Maddy with his jacket over his shoulder, put his arm around her, and asked if he could take her home.

She smiled up at him, eyes sparkling.

"Indeed."

What Came First

Whistling as he walked into the garden, his jacket slung over his shoulder, his tie loose, Sebastian caught a flicker of colour from the corner of his eye and stopped, vigilant for the movement. Before him was a chicken, pecking at the dirt. He stood, frozen in his stance.

"Maddy!" he called out forcefully. "Maddy, sweetheart, come out here." He paused. "Maddy Davis, come out here now." His voice was firm.

Inside, Maddy was pacing the floor. He sounded angry. She tried to stall.

"Maddy ... talk to me." He was almost shouting.

She appeared on the patio, all smiles. "Sebastian, here you are, home ... how lovely." Heading towards him, arms outstretched, she said, "Did I hear you call me sweetheart?"

"Stop, Maddy. Explain this." He pointed to the bird, ignoring her question.

"It looks like a chicken ... how cute," she crooned. "Actually, it is a hen."

"Maddy, there are ordinances against having animals in the city." He was trying to sound logical. "Tell me what's going on. Talk chicken, so to speak." He smirked, surprised at his own joke.

Maddy bit the inside of her cheek, looking very penitent. Just then another chicken joined the gathering on the path.

"Maddy!" he sighed. "How many more?"

"Just two. Oh look, an egg. Perfect for your breakfast."

Sebastian laid his briefcase down, holding his face. He rubbed his eyes, shaking his head, unsure what to do. "Maddy, please, what's going on? Please tell me you haven't taken up farming here in the garden."

"Why don't you sit down right here. Let me get you a drink. Sit, sit. Relax." She started massaging his shoulders, kissing his neck.

"Maddy?"

"They're only here for a day or two. I'm helping a friend. They won't be any trouble; I promise. They'll be gone before you know it. Look how cute they are."

"What's the story?" He knew there had to be a story and it was sure to be compelling.

She walked out to the hens, who were now following her around the path. Taking a deep breath, she started.

"Ray, our regular egg man at the market, had an accident, and his hens were left alone when the ambulance came. The kiosk police were going to take them away, which is bad for Ray. Also they were going to charge him for abandoning the animals—not his fault. Someone had to feed them and care for them overnight, so I brought them home, hoping you would take pleasure in the fresh eggs and the irony of the predicament. Imagine, through no fault of your own, getting a fine for not feeding your hens, and losing them! Anyway, Ray should be out of hospital in a few days. He's given me the truck and the keys to his farm, so it won't be long. He can't recuperate if he's worrying about the animals. The girls shouldn't be any trouble. I'll clean up any mess they make. It's very organic; I promise."

Sebastian walked over to Maddy, held her in his arms, and tenderly lifted her chin. "You're a good friend." He smiled. "Do you think the girls are safe here overnight?"

"They have a lovely little cage, so they should be fine. Help me catch them? You know you called me sweetheart earlier; that means you can't be too upset. Just grab one …"

Sebastian started to laugh. He couldn't stop laughing. "You are too much." He continued laughing, imagining himself chasing the colourful hens throughout the garden.

Maddy watched him with her hands on her hips, wondering what was so funny. The thought of Sebastian crouching over to grab a flapping hen made her smile and then laugh.

After a few attempts, she was able to snatch one of the squawking and flapping hens; she held it out at arm's length and placed the bird in the cage. Sebastian watched in awe as she chased the second hen around a hedge, picked it up, and closed the cage. "Well, that's that," she announced, smoothing her dress and dusting off the feathers.

"Indeed." He smiled.

It was still dark out when Maddy kissed his forehead and pulled the duvet over his shoulders. "Where are you going?" he asked when he opened his eyes.

"Go back to sleep; I set the alarm for you. Don't forget you have a breakfast meeting at the conference this morning. I need to feed Paco and the herd for Ray. Have a nice day." She was gone.

Sebastian climbed into the car and dialled Maddy. "Hi, I left the conference after my presentation. It's Saturday, and I know you always have a list of things we must do or see. Are you free?"

"How nice of you to call. Just about done here. Come out with Davi and have lunch with us. Henry is having a blast." Maddy sounded out of breath.

Davi nodded to acknowledge that he knew where the farm was situated and that he had the lunch basket.

"We'll see you shortly." Sebastian waited for Davi to fill in the blanks.

"Ray is the farmer from the market—the man with the chickens. When he fell, he gave Maddy his keys for the truck and the farmhouse, as well as the chickens, and asked her to look after the animals. Maddy drove out to the country with the professor and found out the horses hadn't been fed, watered, or exercised, so they went out again this morning to get everything ready for Ray. He should be home today. Of course, Maddy knew what to do. Imagine, she just dove right in and took care of those big animals. I was asked to bring the lunch out to the farm, so I have the directions. Maddy will be so pleased to have our help." Davi was chatting away, excited to see the farm.

"Indeed." Sebastian wasn't so sure he wanted to feed animals, but it was a rare sunny day, and he looked forward to seeing Henry and Maddy.

When they drove up the lane, it struck Sebastian that the word "farm" was a liberal translation for such a run-down property. Maddy was riding bareback, looking over her shoulder at the horses following her around the riding ring. Henry was sitting tall in an English saddle, taking instruction from a man clad in riding gear. Davi waved at Henry and turned to point out the professor, who was instructing. Henry waved cautiously, not comfortable on the horse, and the professor nodded to both Davi and Sebastian.

"Sebastian, we've mucked out the stalls; they were bad, and Maddy is so picky. We've fed them, and now we're giving them some exercise." Henry was excited. "The horses like Maddy, not me so much. The professor is teaching me to post. I'm not so good." He dismounted and led his horse into the stable. The professor shook hands with Sebastian and followed Henry. "Maddy should be coming in any time; she just wanted to give them a run. Do you ride?" he asked, keeping an eye on the horses in the ring.

"Not any more. I stopped riding when I was expected to join the fox hunt. I didn't know Maddy could ride."

"I think she had horses in Canada. She was quick to assess what they required, and she got through the chores pretty darn quick. We were just the water boys. It's great of her to help old Ray. He'll be thrilled to see how well-groomed the horses are for a change."

The professor smiled at the improved state of the stables. It occurred to Sebastian he didn't know if the professor had a name. He apologized and asked.

The professor shook hands and introduced himself. "Sam Brown; you won't forget it, given my colour and all." Sebastian laughed and immediately understood why Maddy and Sam Brown were such good friends.

Maddy rode towards them, waving at Sebastian. "You can leave the doors open; they know where to go." She turned around on the horse, one hand behind her; one hand clutching the mane. The horses walked into the stable and found their stalls, as she had directed; the two men closed the stalls behind them. Maddy slipped off the horse, whispering words of encouragement to Paco. She got one last nuzzle before closing the stall and greeting Sebastian with a hug. Her nose was cold as she touched his cheek. She was glowing. He smiled and put his arm around her, holding her close to warm her. He wanted to ask why on earth she was doing this, but he knew she was helping a friend, with a friend—the professor—who seemed to be around a great of the time lately. Henry was struggling with the saddle, and the professor rushed to assist. They each held up a brush, and Maddy nodded, pleased they had remembered to brush the mare.

"Clean up, you two; it's time for lunch. Ray is just arriving home." Maddy walked out to meet the arriving car.

Ray, limping with the aid of a cane, was effusive in his appreciation of what Maddy had done. The hens were laying; the horses were fed, watered, and looking fine. His market friends had reported no loss in business, as Maddy and the professor had carefully arranged the eggs each morning. The truck was washed and fuelled, ready for Ray. He was emotional, shaking his head at the kindness extended.

Sebastian sat back and watched as Davi laid out the luncheon Grace had sent. The group was animated and easy in each other's company. He looked out beyond the bleak farmyard to the rolling hills, washed by the sun, and then back at the table where Maddy was laughing at something Henry was relating, the professor and Ray agreeing with his words, Davi pouring tea with a big smile of belonging on his face. There was a warm feeling in the kitchen of the old farmhouse; Sebastian was reminded of a Currier and Ives image.

When lunch was done, Maddy stood, gathered up the dishes, and announced that Ray should rest. The men washed the dishes and tidied the kitchen while Maddy made sure Ray was comfortable. She left a note with contact information and instructions from the hospital, returning the keys and promising to look in on Ray at the market on Monday. He was expecting his nephew later in the day—someone to stay with him and help with the chores.

As the group piled into the car, Sebastian squeezed Maddy's hand. "You are quite something, Maddy Davis."

Maddy smiled at him. "Aren't we lucky we could help someone when they really needed us?"

"Indeed."

Barcelona, Ole

Barcelona is beautiful, and Maddy did not want to miss a thing. Sebastian was attending a design conference, so they travelled into the city early to catch the Picasso exhibit and study the architecture of Gaudi at the Sagrada Familia and throughout the city. They walked hand in hand, pointing out buildings and stopping for tapas, marvelling at the number of tourists and enjoying their time together. It was refreshing to talk about the art and decide what they liked and what they could pass on. Miro—yes or no? Would you rather collect and enjoy a Picasso or a Miro? They found they had similar tastes in art.

Sebastian left early in the morning for the conference, where he was moderating a panel discussion on the challenges of drones in the city. Maddy left the hotel with him and spent the day exploring, eating breakfast in the market, and taking in the sights. It was exhilarating to be back in the seaside city with so much culture and art around.

On returning to the hotel, Maddy ran the bath, made a cup of tea, gathered the tourist information, and sat in the opulent tub, soaking in the bubbles. "OMG," she murmured, sitting back to relax in the steaming water, enjoying a delightful treat after a full day of walking and touring.

"Maddy, are you here?" Sebastian called as he entered the room, anxious to share his news.

"Yes, I just got in the bath," she called back lazily. "Come in."

He hesitated, not sure on the protocol of the bath. Belle had always suggested that *the bath* was a woman's hallowed experience, not to be disturbed.

"How long will you be?" he asked, standing at the bathroom door.

"I may never come out … it's heavenly. Why don't you join me?"

Sebastian opened the door slowly, peeking in. He smiled when he saw Maddy amidst the bubbles and the steam, her face rosy, having tea and holding a magazine, the lights of the city behind her. He loosened his tie and bent down to kiss her forehead.

"How was your panel discussion?" she asked.

"Controversial, entertaining, and thought-provoking. How was your day?" he asked, sitting on the edge of the marble dais.

"Amazing … no, *muy bueno*," she replied. "Come on in; it's like therapy. Get a drink and join me." She looked up at him and smiled coyly.

Sebastian walked into the room, placed his jacket on a chair, opened the mini bar, chose a drink, kicked his shoes off, and walked back into the bathroom.

"Is there room for me?" he asked.

"Of course." She was laughing at his reluctance to get in the bath. "Just dim the lights so we can see the city."

The bath water was pleasantly warm; it felt good to have her leaning on him. *Why have we not done this before?* he wondered. He made a mental note to install a large bathtub in the apartment.

They talked and searched for familiar buildings in the night sky, Maddy retracing her route for the day and Sebastian adding sites for the next day.

"I almost forgot; we have concert tickets for tomorrow, if you're interested," he whispered in her ear as they were lying back, the bubbles long gone.

"That's nice; are you keen on going?" she asked, wrapping his arms around her.

"I'm easy; I like some of her music," he responded.

She sat up. "Who is it?"

"Adele."

She turned in the water, straddling him, throwing her arms around his neck, and kissing his face. "You are the best." She finally said through the kisses.

He was pleased with her reaction. It was certainly worth the effort to secure the tickets.

The next day, Sebastian left the conference early so they could continue exploring Barcelona. They walked along La Rambla, enjoying the crowds and the market. They strolled down the *Passeig de Gracia* to see the Gaudi apartment building and homes, wanting to take everything in before the concert.

When they finally sat down for Sangria, they found themselves on a pedestrian street looking across at the Sagrada Basilica.

"Gaudi spent so many years of his life designing and planning every detail and he never got to see the finished product. Look at all that scaffolding—it's scheduled to be completed in 2026. We'll have to come back." Maddy was taking in all the intricate details of the building, lost in the story. "We'll have to bring Henry with us."

After several minutes, Sebastian asked Maddy what she was dreaming about.

She smiled back lazily. "I don't need to dream any more; just look at my life." She paused. "Although Gaudi did play a major role in the past."

"I think you can have more than one dream," he said solemnly.

"Hmm." She shrugged. "What's your dream?"

"I may have had a dream or dreams when I was young, but early on, I realized I didn't have the luxury of dreaming any more. I had to make a living, keep busy, and deal with reality." He looked away.

"That sounds so sad. You don't have to sacrifice reality to have a dream." Maddy took his hand. "Being here is on our bucket list, remember?"

"Then tell me about your dreams; I want to know." He squeezed her hand.

"Ah, it's complicated …" she waved her hand to dismiss the subject.

"I'm not going anywhere." He was serious now.

"Sebastian, meeting someone like you was never in my plan. Suddenly, there you were, caring, exciting, willing and able to do things with me … someone without tons of baggage. Someone I could laugh and share silly experiences with. It was a dream, and I was enjoying it." She stopped, looking around at the view before her. "Then one night it all came crashing down, without warning, without knowing what I had done or said. It was just over." She was fighting back tears.

"I went on the Camino to get away and find myself. It took days for me to stop thinking about what I had done wrong … what I might have done differently. I relived every minute of our time together. I cried myself to sleep for several nights." Tears were welling up in her eyes. Sebastian wanted desperately to hold her, but she held up her hand to stop him.

"The day I walked into the town of Astorga, dragging myself up that last hill, I was so tired I had no tears left. I walked around the town with another pilgrim and noticed crowds at the Gaudi structure. I sat on a bench and stared at it but didn't see it. I heard people beside me talking of the beauty and the mastery, and I knew I had to stop feeling sorry for myself and see the world around me. I spent a day there, absorbing the Gaudi structure and the town itself. Finally I took the train on to Sarria, where the final stage of the pilgrimage begins, and I vowed to spend the rest of the walk concentrating on the beauty of the Camino and learning more about the other pilgrims." She wiped her eyes and continued, looking back at the basilica.

"In Santiago de Compostela, I went to the pilgrims' Mass and saw many of my walking companions. We greeted each other as long-lost friends. It was very emotional … a different kind of camaraderie. The next day, I went to Finisterre so I could walk to mile number one. It was magical. On the return to Santiago, I realized I was seeing the route in reverse, not the way you're supposed to travel it." She smiled. "It was a revelation. I thought back to first meeting you and how we had a great time together; no one says how long the dream has to last, just that you find it. I was so caught up in the ending of the dream that I forgot I had lived the dream. Seeing the route in reverse made me humble. I had my dream; now I could only hope for someone to find me and complete their dream."

She looked at Sebastian, tears cascading down her cheek. He looked miserable, wanting more than ever to hold her.

"And then I got off the train in London, and there you were." She smiled. "My head said run, but my heart said, 'Maybe he needs me for his dream.'" She shook her head. "Silly, isn't it?"

Sebastian reached out and took her face in his hands. With a catch in his voice, he said "No, not silly. I was just hopeless. How lucky I am you agreed to stay."

"We couldn't both run. When I saw you, I realized I was getting a second chance at our friendship and if I kept running away, I wouldn't get many more." Maddy smiled, recalling the scene at the train station.

They stared at the basilica for a few minutes more, lost in their own thoughts.

"Maddy, when I wake up beside you and you smile and say good morning, I know I'm not dreaming. I know what we have is real, and I hope the only dreams we have now are dreams for our future. Is that possible?"

"It's a lovely thought," she said, wiping the tears from her face. "We'd better go; we don't want to miss a moment of that concert." She stood up and took his hand.

"Indeed."

On returning to the hotel after the concert, they left the rest of the group at the bar and headed for the lift, laughing and holding each other.

"That was awesome. Thank you." Maddy kissed Sebastian as they rode the car up to their floor. They almost fell out of the lift when the door opened, laughing and groping each other. At their room door stood a woman in a trench coat, looking distressed.

"Ah, here you are … you bastard. I waited all night for you to come to my room … no phone call, not a note; you refuse to answer my text messages." The woman was running her hands through her hair, the coat flapping open to reveal her naked body.

Maddy quickly opened the room door and lightly pushed both Sebastian and the woman into the room, closing the door behind her. "I think you want to discuss this inside."

The woman glared at Sebastian, who was visibly uncomfortable, and then at Maddy. "Who are you?" she slurred. Maddy smiled, removed her jacket and offered the woman a seat on the sofa. Sebastian was quick to intervene. "She won't be staying. This is inappropriate. Elizabeth, you need to go." He opened the room door and waited for her to leave. The woman flung the door closed, swaying, unsteady on her feet.

"You can't be serious, Sebastian. She isn't your intellectual match, she's not rich or famous, she has no credentials, and she's certainly not younger than I am. I don't understand," she whined, running her hand across her face, smearing her eye make-up across her cheek.

Sebastian clenched his fists, his jaw firm. He opened the door and waited for the woman to leave. Slowly and with effort, the woman walked into the hall. Sebastian closed the door and, with determined strides, walked into the bathroom. Maddy had watched the two of them, wondering why the woman was so upset and Sebastian so angry with her. Hearing the sobs, she grabbed the key and walked out into the hall. The woman, Elizabeth, was sitting on the floor, her coat open, her hair matted; she was either too intoxicated to walk or she had just fallen against the wall to weep. Maddy knelt beside her and helped her up, straightening her coat, looking for a room key in her pocket. She slowly walked the woman to her room, using the stairs rather than the lift. She opened the door, settling the woman on the bed, removing the trench coat, and pulled back the covers. "Come on; let's get you some water and wash your face. Your make-up is streaking; you don't want to wake up looking this way."

"Why are you doing this?" The woman seemed to sober up enough to realize what was happening.

"Hmm. Well, according to the programme notes, you are Elizabeth Stonehouse, a well-respected professional in your field. I love your designs incorporating solar panels into the window shutters, and I wouldn't want any of the conference delegates to see you in this state, sitting in the hall, drunk and dishevelled. Come on; let me wash your face."

Hair brushed, teeth cleaned, face washed, alarm set, water beside the bed, Maddy directed Elizabeth into the bed, leaving her a note to call in the morning if she needed something to soothe her headache. Maddy turned the lights off and walked towards the door, not wanting to disturb Elizabeth, hoping she was asleep. As she turned the doorknob, Elizabeth whispered, "Thank you. Don't let him hurt you. You seem nice."

Maddy slipped out of the room and leaned against the door. She took the stairs up to her floor and let herself into the room.

Sebastian was sitting in the dark, anxiously awaiting Maddy's return. He wasn't sure how this would play out. They had left the concert on such a high; how could he know Elizabeth would be drunk and disorderly? He hadn't seen her for a year. He needed to explain to Maddy, but how? How do you explain a convenient coupling to someone you care about?

Maddy walked into the room, dropped the key on the table, and leaned against the door, eyes closed. She had not seen Sebastian sitting across the room. He walked over to her and realized she had been crying. He held her face in his hands, kissing the tears.

"Maddy, let me explain …"

She glanced up at him with a wounded look. "Just kiss me."

Sebastian kissed her cheeks, her eyes, her forehead, her neck, and then her lips. It was impossible not to respond. When he stepped back, he opened his mouth to speak, but Maddy quickly put her finger to his lips. "I don't need to know anything more than that."

Sebastian looked at her with such tenderness in his expression that she buried her face in his chest and threw her arms around him. He held her until he realized she was crying again. He lifted her chin and wiped the tears. "Why are you crying?" he asked in a whisper.

"I don't want you to break my heart. It would be too painful." She was looking up at him with wide eyes.

"Come to bed, Maddy, please. I just want to hold you and make you feel safe in my arms. What you did tonight was very decent and touching. You continue to amaze me." He touched her face, tracing her lips, pulling her towards him.

"Come on; come to bed. Today must surely be over."

The next morning, Sebastian brought Maddy tea in bed, which always seemed to make her smile in appreciation. He found a large gold envelope addressed to Maddy on the floor near the door and brought it back to the bed for her to open. It was an invitation to join the commissioner at his table that evening at the black-tie gala banquet. Sebastian and Maddy had spoken about trying a new restaurant instead, but the invite seemed too important to ignore. Maddy was concerned she didn't have a formal gown but assured Sebastian she would come up with something.

"Indeed" was all he offered as encouragement.

When he left for the meeting, Maddy called Audrey for help. Audrey knew of a young designer who was working for a local theatre company, at a ridiculously low wage, waiting for a break.

Audrey made the connection and arranged for Maddy to visit the theatre and see if any of the gowns could be modified or adjusted for the evening. Maddy met Irena, a beautiful waif of a girl, at the theatre. Together they went through the wardrobe archives, Maddy describing what she wanted, and Irena suggesting what she thought would be best for Maddy. They both gasped when they saw a black-and-white flamenco-style dress with soft pleats rather than ruffles. The dress was so delicate it appeared to be moving on its own; the bolero jacket added a dramatic touch, and Irena offered to do Maddy's hair as well. They had an enjoyable afternoon altering the gown and finding the right accessories.

Sebastian was dressed in his tux, shoes shined and tie just right, anxious to know where Maddy might be, when she called apologizing for the delay. She was on her way; he should go ahead to the cocktail reception, and she would meet him there. He wasn't sure if he should be worried or relieved that Maddy had found a dress; she was resourceful, and as he walked to the lift, he tried to imagine what she might turn up in. The women at the Gala were certainly sporting their finest gowns.

Christian was already in the foyer when he arrived. Christian asked after Maddy and waited with Sebastian for her arrival. The location at the bottom of the long escalator was ideal, as the committee were greeting delegates with a tray of cocktails on arrival.

Maddy looked down into the reception area, hoping to see Sebastian before she called him on his mobile. Christian waved up to her, and she smiled as she walked over to the escalator. Elizabeth Stonehouse also arrived at that precise moment, and both Christian and Sebastian held their breath as they watched the two women greet each other and step onto the escalator together. Christian had seen Elizabeth with Sebastian in past years, and he was concerned as he glanced over at his friend.

"No worries, they met last night;" Sebastian responded, realizing Christian was concerned about a scene.

Maddy and Elizabeth were laughing—an unusual sight, as Elizabeth was always so serious and dark. Sebastian watched the women arrive at the reception, hugging and smiling as they waved to each other. It was only then that he realized how dramatic Maddy looked; she looked like a blonde flamenco dancer with sparkles in her hair and on her cheekbones. Her hair was pulled back tight; her dangling earrings were catching the light as she moved towards him. The dress looked alive; it seemed to be moving on its own. Sebastian was aware that everyone was watching Maddy as she glided across the floor. When Christian nudged his arm, he finally remembered to breathe.

"Sorry to be late; I hope I didn't keep you from visiting with your friends." She leaned forward to kiss his cheek. She smelled so good and looked so lovely he was tempted to grab her hand and run out of the room with her, anxious to be alone with her.

Christian responded first. "Maddy, it was worth the wait. You look exceptionally lovely." Sebastian smiled and continued staring at her. "Shall we find our seats?" He reached for her hand and led her into the candlelit ballroom. "Where did you find this amazing dress?" he asked as they made their way through the room.

"I don't usually buy off the rack; my first roommate was a dress designer and she practised on me. I wore some edgy designs for a lot of years. Oh, and Audrey helps me with her contacts in the theatre. I'm glad you like it."

Just as they were about to take their seats, Sebastian and Christian both holding her chair out, Maddy was approached by an event planner with a headset, clipboard in hand. They had an animated conversation, and when Maddy turned back to the table to sit, she leaned over to whisper in Sebastian's ear. "I was interviewed yesterday on the street. Did you know there was a contest?"

Sebastian cleared his throat and nodded. "I did hear they were trying to capture thoughts of the delegates and companions, but it really didn't register with me. Why?" he asked warily.

Maddy shrugged. "It's probably nothing to worry about."

Now Sebastian was worried. With Maddy, "nothing to worry about" was a prequel to something worrisome.

Further conversation was halted by the opening remarks on the stage. The usual welcomes from dignitaries, the conference chair, and the hosts for next year droned on as Sebastian watched Maddy, who was looking very regal, composed, and serene—totally out of character. Usually she would be fidgeting by this point in the speeches.

The speeches continued. Local students had been invited to follow the delegates and their significant others, to record their experiences in Barcelona. Each team was to submit a feature for judging. The lights were lowered, and a sense of expectation hung over the crowd as the winning short film was presented.

The music started with early morning vistas of Barcelona on all the large screens around the room. Groups of women appeared on the screen, looking shy and uncomfortable but delighted to be interviewed about their stay in the city. Sound bites. More vistas and attractions appeared, and suddenly a clear voice was explaining what one should see and do in such a short time in this amazing city. It was Maddy's voice. The cameraman clearly loved her enthusiasm, her smile and her fluid conversation, her casual switching from English to Spanish and back, as well as her knowledge of the city. The remainder of the feature was Maddy pointing out the sights and flirting with a group of older men on the park bench, dancing flamenco with an elderly couple on the street, tasting local treats at the market and at food trucks, and blowing bubbles with a group of children on the beach. When asked why she enjoyed Barcelona, she looked thoughtful for a second and then smiled engagingly at the camera. "Barcelona is a gem; it may be in Spain, but it's a world of its own." The music faded with a silhouette of Maddy and a man watching the sunset. Applause. Standing ovation.

The mayor approached Maddy with a large bouquet and planted kisses on both of her cheeks. The cameraman captured the scene for the large screens. Maddy was unflappable and humble, looking down at the audience from every screen.

Sebastian looked over at Christian, who was cheering loudly and whistling. He shook his head, shrugged, and pulled out the chair waiting for Maddy to be seated again. He couldn't have been prouder of her. She looked over her shoulder cautiously, not sure what his reaction would be. When he smiled and nodded, she relaxed and flashed a mischievous grin. Her dress was perfect for the evening, and he was pleased to hear the women at the table wondering where she might have found such a smart outfit.

When dinner was finally over, the crowd stood, visiting other tables while waiting for the music to start. Christian advised Sebastian not to leave Maddy alone if he wanted to see her at all during the evening. The commissioner requested that Sebastian and his committee meet guests who were speaking at a future meeting. The circle tightened, and Maddy found herself on the outside of the gathering. She looked around for an exit to the powder room and began walking to the foyer. As she reached the door, she was approached by a distinguished gentleman with an accent. "Are you available for endorsements in other jurisdictions?" he asked as he raised her hand and brushed his lips on the back of it, giving her goosebumps. She smiled, resisting the urge to laugh out loud.

"Do you waltz?" he asked, not taking his eyes off her face.

"Only if I have the right partner." She raised her eyebrows, hoping to discourage him.

"Madame, you are in luck, I am a formidable dancer. Shall we?" He held his arm out for her.

"Oh my, humble and charming." She smiled and took his arm.

"You do realize this isn't a waltz," Maddy whispered.

"It will be when we get to the dance floor. I am Count Orlanski, and the band knows I prefer to waltz," he stated in a matter-of-fact voice.

"What does a count do?" Maddy asked as they walked, his arm cradling her back.

"All manner of affairs." His accent was Eastern European, and Maddy found it very easy to listen to. "Ah, here we are …" His arms were ready to hold her.

Maddy placed her right hand in his and waited for him to place his hand on her back. She realized he was very serious about this dance. She curtsied and held her left hand above his shoulder, waiting for the music to decide how best to hold on for dear life.

The violins started, and Count Orlanski took charge, leading Maddy through a smooth, flowing waltz. It was enjoyable to dance with someone skilled in directing his partner. The music seemed to move from one waltz to another.

Standing by the table, the commissioner stopped talking when the music started, advising the group that the count always delivered a lovely waltz experience for those who were afraid to get up on the dance floor—as he himself was. His wife refused to dance with him when the count was on the dance floor.

Christian looked over at Sebastian with a knowing look that said, "I told you so."

It was an experience watching the count lead Maddy around the floor. Nothing but the music existed for the dancers. The dress was so becoming, the couple dancing so engrossed, that the crowd seemed to be an accessory to the moment.

Sebastian was walking towards the bar when Elizabeth stopped him. "Don't worry; I'm not going to make a scene." She held her hands up as a sign of truce. "Your girl was very decent and kind last night. I'm not sure

I would have done the same for her. I just need to know why her … why not me? Why her? If you wanted more, why didn't you say?"

Sebastian looked over at Maddy dancing and smiled. How could he possibly explain his addiction—his wanting to be with her whenever possible?

"Elizabeth, when you meet someone who is challenging, unpredictable, reckless, fun, clever, fiercely loyal, passionate, and so very, very easy to love, you'll understand." He hesitated, watching the dancers. "She makes me feel alive … excuse me." He turned away, wanting to end the conversation.

"Why didn't we ever get to that point?" She wanted to know; she had to know.

"We had exactly what we were capable of giving or wanting from each other. Surely you realize that?" Sebastian smiled and shrugged. "Good night, Elizabeth. I hope you find someone who makes you feel special." He walked towards the dance floor, concentrating on Maddy and how lovely she looked.

Elizabeth slumped against the concrete column and watched him walk away, out of her life. She laughed out loud, realizing they never had a relationship, never danced or kissed in public, never spoke of anything substantial. He never sent her flowers; he never even sent a Christmas or birthday card. Neither had she. Why did it hurt so much? She shook her head, sighing. She looked around the room and spotted a group of American delegates.

"Okay, it's showtime," she whispered, smoothing her hair and taking a deep breath. "Time to move on."

The count would have danced with Maddy all evening if Sebastian had not cut in, suggesting other women were keen to dance with the count. Maddy smiled at the smooth move, and they danced several slow songs, Sebastian holding her close.

"How many dances before the dress has done its job?" he asked.

Maddy looked up with a questioning glance.

"You look wonderful, and I hate to take you away from all these adoring eyes, but I did wonder when I might get you alone and take it off."

"I've been handing out cards for young Irena; I only have one left, so we can go anytime. I loved wearing this dress. It was fun. I'm returning it tomorrow, but we're not attached or anything. Shall we go?"

"Why don't we keep the dress?" he asked.

"It's a sample, and I'm sure Irena, the seamstress, will want it back." She turned, making the folds flutter.

"If you want the dress, we should buy it. It was made for you," He whispered.

"It's just a dress. It's really a Barcelona dress … I'll remember how I felt in it … how you made me feel wearing it. That's enough." She smiled up at him.

Sebastian led her back to the table to say their farewells, and they left the gala with the large bouquet. He also picked up the last calling card, confident the designer would want Maddy to have that dress, should she change her mind.

Once the flowers had been arranged, Maddy switched the light off and slowly undressed Sebastian. She slipped his jacket off, pulled his tie off, removed his cufflinks, and unbuttoned his shirt, slipping it off, kissing his chest with soft butterfly kisses. She undid the button on his trousers, and as she reached for his zip, Sebastian stopped her, removing her jacket and then her dress. He carried her to the bed and removed the rest of his clothing before moving on top of her. "How do you do that?" he whispered.

"Do what?" she asked between nibbling on his ear.

"How do you manage to make a simple thing so enjoyable, so exciting?" He was kissing her neck, moving down her chest, when she groaned and pulled him up to meet her lips. They kissed with an urgency that surprised them both.

Lying across his chest, spent from an athletic bout of lovemaking, Maddy yawned and snuggled closer. Sebastian stroked her arm but seemed distracted.

"What are you thinking about? I can hear the wheels turning from here," she said quietly.

Sebastian looked over at her. "Hmm, tonight I was forced to answer a question I wasn't prepared for, and I was thinking about what I could or should have said."

"How wonderful is that?" Maddy sat up.

"How so?" he wondered aloud.

"The next time you get asked the same question, you'll know exactly what you want to say. It's like having a dress rehearsal." She moved her head from side to side, raising her eyebrows as if addressing a non-existent crowd, seeking their approval.

Sebastian laughed out loud. "The world always looks better through your eyes." He pulled her close. "What did you say to make Elizabeth laugh tonight?" he asked as she laid her head on his chest. His arm instinctively wrapped around her.

"I just told her she was intimidating to most men and that she needed to be with someone, anyone, who made her laugh. It would make her life better. What do I know?" Maddy sighed. "She's right, you know; I'm not your intellectual peer, I don't have money or fame, and I'm definitely not a sweet young thing."

"Obviously Elizabeth doesn't know you are intellectually challenging, you are rich with friends who would do anything for you, and you never act your age." Sebastian pulled her closer. "Was it difficult to resist the charming count? He was quite taken with you."

"Who needs a count when I already have a handsome prince?" She kissed his chest.

Sebastian grinned and kissed the top of her head. "Indeed. Good night, my beautiful princess."

Maddy was fast asleep.

Painting for Paws

Davi opened the car door for Sebastian and waited for him to be seated. "Sir, just a reminder, we are collecting Master Henry and Maddy on our way home."

"Ah yes, I seem to recall it's 'taco night'." Sebastian smiled.

Henry ran down the stairs of the school and into the car, excited to be spending the evening with Sebastian and Maddy. He had requested tacos when asked what he would most like to eat for dinner. Davi explained they were on their way to collect Maddy at the market, where she was gathering supplies for dinner.

"Maddy said you were going away this weekend Sebastian. Too bad. You're going to miss the fun. We're painting the animal shelter. I get to watch the dogs because they have to go outside." Henry was enthusiastic.

Sebastian looked up from his reading, amused by the enthusiasm in Henry's voice.

"Why are you watching the dogs?" he asked.

"Maddy got leftover paint from a bloke who paints big buildings; everyone is volunteering their time to 'brighten up' the place. This counts towards my volunteer hours at school. My responsibility is to walk the dogs in the yard," Henry offered. "There's Maddy." He leaned forward and pointed over to the curb.

Maddy placed her shopping bags in the boot, slid into the car, and leaned over to kiss Sebastian on the cheek, shooting him a welcoming smile before hugging the excited Henry.

"I am just hearing of your decorating adventure. It sounds like a big job—shall I arrange for a team of painters?" Sebastian asked.

"Heavens, no. The animal shelter is run by volunteers. It will be a labour of love. We have paint and rollers donated, a crew for painting, and offers of food; it's a good way for people to feel they are engaged. But thank you for the offer." She looked away.

"Auntie and Grace will come as soon as they can on Saturday," Davi added.

Maddy's phone rang before she could respond. "Sorry, I have to take this; I've been waiting to hear from the contractor."

"Hi, Maddy here. Hello, Anthony. Thank you for getting back to me. I so appreciate your generosity. That's wonderful. Yes, tomorrow at 5.00 p.m. is just fine. I have rollers and brushes and trays and some dust sheets. Ahh. What a score. Thank you. Ciao."

She was giddy with the news she had received, and Henry was anxious for her to share.

"Not only did Anthony find white paint; he found several half cans of various colours so we can do the splatter wall. Isn't that exciting?"

"Wow, can I do that too?" Henry was keen to splatter paint.

"Everyone can. Let's talk about dinner. When we get home, you take charge of making sure everyone has a drink while I start on our tacos. Fair?"

"Very fair. I love tacos; don't you, Sebastian?" Henry turned in his seat towards Sebastian, who was contemplating whether tacos were, in fact, bona fide dinner food and wondering who "everyone" was; he realized he was frowning. "I'll reserve judgement until I taste them." As soon as he said the words, he knew he sounded boring and stodgy. "I must say I'm looking forward to the experience." He managed a brave smile and was pleased to see both Maddy and Henry smile back at him.

The taco meal was typical Maddy—neighbours and friends at the table, eager to try the make-your-own roll-up or crunchy meal, happy to be included, enjoying Henry's tutorial on how to eat them, laughing at each other as the fillings dropped out on their plates, sharing another new adventure together with their gracious hostess. Sebastian had to admit the tacos were delicious, albeit messy. Any misgivings he had about the evening were soon overcome by the genuine feeling of friendship and camaraderie around the table. Maddy had collected quite a group of friends. He was filled with pride and awe as he watched her include each person in conversation; her ability to create laughter out of awkward moments was a talent.

As the guests were preparing to depart, Maddy wrapped her arms around Sebastian and asked if he would see Henry home while she cleaned up. He closed his eyes, enjoying the feel of her face on his chest, the fragrance in her hair, her arms around him.

"Of course. Great night; everyone enjoyed the tacos, including me. I'll be home soon."

Henry was reluctant to leave the dinner party, although he was rubbing his eyes. He said his goodbyes, hugging Maddy and thanking her for the best dinner ever.

As the car pulled away, Maddy realized how important Henry had become in their lives; they were sad to say farewell after each visit.

In the car, Henry asked Sebastian why he was going away on the weekend. Sebastian explained it was a long-standing tradition for members of his club to go north for a weekend of hunting. When asked if it was fun, Sebastian had to admit it was not. Henry nodded and continued to ask questions. "Won't you miss Maddy? She misses you when you're away. She says you're lovely and you have great character and you make her very happy."

"How is it this comes up in conversation?" Sebastian asked, amused.

"Oh, I had a project for my writing class, and Maddy suggested I get to know you better—you know, you're my mentor and all. Shall I tell you what I'm going to say in class?" Before Sebastian could respond, Henry pulled a piece of paper from his pocket and prepared to read. "If I was looking for a role model, I would want to meet someone who is decent and kind, well-educated but humble, patient and giving, well bred (you know, someone who says please and thank you and holds doors open for ladies) someone who is considerate and neat, not messy in his thinking or actions (like picking up stuff and not leaving a mess). I would want them to have a sense of humour and be balanced (like, interested in more than one thing—ballet, art, culture stuff, as well as sports and such) and that they give of their time to benefit others. I would want them to be a person other people want to be with because they are fun and engaging—I'm not sure what that means, but I think it means they care enough to ask about others. I have been fortunate to meet such a person; my mentor, Sebastian

Walker, has welcomed me into his world. I hope I can learn to be a similar man in the business world someday." Henry took a deep breath. "Jolly good, isn't it?"

Sebastian looked over at the boy and smiled. "It's better than good. Let me assure you I am the fortunate one. You are a pleasure both Maddy and I enjoy."

Henry yawned and then in a serious voice announced he hoped he would meet someone just like Maddy when he was older. She was so good to him.

Sebastian assured him Maddy would be delighted to hear that.

Henry continued talking, telling Sebastian how much he enjoyed having Maddy come for him at school when Sebastian was too busy with work; how Maddy told him he should unclutter his life; how Maddy always knew how to solve a problem by giving him a good solution, a bad solution, and an easy way out; how Maddy always had super ideas on how to do stuff; and so on.

"Are we allowed to tell girls we like them?" Henry wondered aloud.

"It's imperative. Believe me; it's allowed. Here we are; I'll walk you to the door."

On the drive home, Sebastian hummed a tune and found he was smiling at Henry's declaration of his merits … It was good to know he made Maddy happy and that he wasn't messy, although he wondered if "neat" meant something else. He was still chuckling as he walked into the garden apartment.

Sebastian and Davi left the city late afternoon on Friday, hoping to arrive at the lodge in time for the annual pheasant dinner. When Sebastian had completed his calls, he sat back and looked out at the traffic and realized they were not moving.

"Davi, do we really enjoy this trek each year?"

"Sir, every year we say we won't bother next year, but we always go."

"Do you think we would be missed if we didn't show up just this once?"

"No sir, I don't believe it would be an issue."

"Then why are we making this trip when there are walls to paint and dogs to walk and probably better food to eat and maybe even laughter, and we would get to sleep in our own beds?"

"Here's a turnabout. Perfect timing. It's a good decision—a very good decision, sir."

The animal shelter was buzzing with chatter and laughter as Sebastian and Davi approached the front door after 9 p.m. The first coat of paint had been applied, and the volunteers were moving the cages into the yard. They found Maddy in the kennel room with a long roller, painting the ceiling, her face smudged with paint. Davi moved into the next room, looking for Grace. Maddy stopped to rub her nose and roll her shoulders when she looked over and saw Sebastian standing in the door. The look on her face, the joy at seeing him, was the most welcoming invitation to rush in and kiss her. He reached for the roller and began rolling paint where she had left off. She wrapped her arms around him and, without a word, picked up a brush and attacked the corners. It wasn't long before the room was completely white and they were cleaning their brushes, admiring their work.

The volunteers were seated on the floor, sharing a bottle of wine, cans of beer, and sandwiches. Maddy and Sebastian joined them for a short visit, confirming the start time for the morning and thanking everyone for their Herculean efforts. The dogs and cats were settled, and the staff were camping out on cots in the reception area. The ragtag crew looked tired but flushed with pride. Sebastian had to admit the place looked brighter already.

They walked home hand in hand, too tired to make conversation, happy to be together. Leaving their clothes at the door, they fell into bed, Sebastian holding Maddy in his arms. Neither spoke; they were asleep.

Saturday morning the crew returned to see just how the light of day transformed the interior of the shelter. With the second coat of paint applied, the animals well exercised by Henry, and the cleaning up completed, everyone was anxious to hear more about the splatter wall. The cans of assorted paint were placed on the floor in front of the feature wall, and each crew member was given a brush. Each person chose a colour, and one by one they splattered their colour on the wall. Amidst the oohs, ahs, and laughter, the wall began to take shape. Henry commented that it looked as if Monet had painted a garden on the wall. Each person signed his or her name, delighted to be acknowledged. Sebastian invited the group to a proper meal next door at the pub. It was an early night, as everyone was tired. They would meet on Sunday morning to return the cages and do any touch-ups. Anthony, the contractor, had been so taken with the volunteers—especially Claudia, a young, doe-eyed girl who spoke Italian—that he had stayed all weekend to help with the project. He joked he would gladly hire them all for his next job.

Maddy and Sebastian sat out on the garden patio, holding hands, too tired to dance or move indoors.

"Thank you for coming back to work with us. I'm sorry you gave up your hunting weekend, but I loved having you here," Maddy whispered.

"Davi and I both wanted to be here to help you. This was more important. We couldn't abandon you. It was an ambitious venture, I must say, but you managed to get it done. Bravo." He stood up. "Oh my, I'd forgotten how physical painting can be … Let's go to bed. I'm knackered." He held out his hand for her.

"Indeed."

In a Jam

"Hello Sebastian and Christian, thank you both for taking my call. I'll be quick; Henry has a DIY project for school, and his time is limited due to a weekend tournament, so tonight would be the best opportunity for all of you to get together. He would need to be picked up before four o'clock this afternoon. I will have everything you need here at the apartment. Normally I would work on this with him alone, but he needs a report from his co-workers, and I think having you both here would add credibility. Any problems changing your busy schedules to accommodate your mentoring student?" Maddy took a breath and waited.

Christian responded first by laughing heartily. "Not at all, Madam. You make an interesting case for our help. I can move my afternoon around. What's the project, by the way?"

She chuckled. "You'll have to wait for further instructions from your team leader," "Sebastian?"

"Lambert tells me I'm free to go … Christian, shall we pick you up and then gather Henry together?" He paused and then asked, "Will any animals be used in the making of this product?" He was recalling the chickens in the garden.

Christian laughed. "I'm out earlier, so I will come to your office at three. Thank you for including us. You are so good to spend time with Henry. I look forward to the project."

"Indeed," Sebastian agreed.

"Great! Thanks, team. See you later. I just know you're going to have fun."

Both men rang off the call wondering what Maddy had in store for them but pleased to be included in Henry's project.

"I can't tell you; I'm sorry. All will be revealed when we get to our workstation." Henry had been coached by Maddy not to let the cat out of the bag until they were in place, ready to receive his instructions. He was enjoying the suspense and their bribes to know what was in store.

In the apartment, lemonade in hand, the men sat on the sofa and awaited their instructions. Henry had prepared his speech with care, explaining the purpose of the project; he must make something that could be sold and consumed by a potential buyer. He had chosen to make scones and fresh raspberry jam, as opposed to a piece of art or ceramic mug, as people enjoyed eating and he was good at baking. He required assistance with the fresh raspberry jam and had chosen two capable professionals to assist, as the instructions were precise and could easily be followed by amateur apprentices.

Maddy noticed both men taking him very seriously, although they were smiling at his solemn presentation. They exchanged glances at the remark regarding professional assistance, pleased with his choice.

Maddy provided aprons, and Henry began his instructions. The ingredients were laid out on the counter, and the recipe was propped up for easy reference. Henry was patient with his methodology and then asked for his assistants to repeat the sequence. He stressed the importance of consistency and that each element must be perfect.

Soon they were all working quietly at their tasks, Maddy recording the various steps to completion with photos and some video.

"Oh, Great Leader, we have completed our task. Jam is in jars, sealed and awaiting further instruction," Christian announced, clicking his heels together.

"Now we tidy up. We can't leave a mess like this." Henry pointed to the counter and the dirty dishes. The assistants began clearing the counter, smiling at the reprimand.

"My scones are just minutes away from being perfect." Henry announced, looking through the glass on the oven door. "Thank you, Mrs B." he whispered to himself.

Henry lifted his scones from the oven as if the baking tray held precious gems, sniffing the batch with pride. He held the tray and beamed for the photo, requesting another with his assistants, still clad in their aprons.

"Maddy, be so kind as to prepare tea for our tasting," he said in a formal voice, which resulted in much laughter.

Tea was served in the garden. The scones and jam were presented on a tiered serving tray, and a small ramekin of clotted cream appeared as the team admired their handiwork. More photos were taken, and finally Henry announced they could sample their wares.

Nods of approval and exclamations were recorded as the scones and jam were enjoyed. Henry was modest in his final interview, thanking his assistants, his mentors, and, of course, Maddy, for capturing the essence of the project in good taste. They watched the video together before sending it through to the school for marking. There was much laughter, applause, and appreciation for a job well done.

Christian thanked Henry and Maddy for including him in such an auspicious occasion and suggested he treat them to dinner at the Schnitzel House when they were ready for the next course. As they were preparing to leave, Sebastian stopped Maddy and held her hands in his. "Thank you." He kissed her forehead and wondered what else he could possibly say, but her proud smile as she looked over at Henry said everything he might have added.

The restaurant was noisy with accordion music, the clinking of beer glasses, and outbursts of singing at various tables. It was like a mini Oktoberfest, fun and raucous. Henry watched the other tables and insisted they stand and sing *"Ein Prosit."* Sebastian felt very emotional as he realized this little group of Maddy, Henry, and Christian were like a family to him. Maddy looked over and saw his expression change. She leaned into him and whispered, "Aren't we lucky?" He pinched the bridge of his nose and turned to look at her, his eyes moist. "Indeed, we are." The moment passed as Christian rose and sang a drinking song, beer stein in hand. Other tables joined in, and soon the entire restaurant was standing, singing (more like shouting), and raising a glass to good health. Henry was squealing with delight.

Christian and Maddy couldn't resist "Beer Barrel Polka", and when they returned to the table breathless, Henry asked Maddy to teach him the polka. Sebastian smiled as the pair tried to keep up with the more experienced couples on the dance floor. Henry announced it was a great workout and that he was looking forward to Oktoberfest.

Christian stayed to visit with his German friends as Maddy and Sebastian escorted a very tired Henry out to the car.

Henry slept all the way back to the school, lying across Maddy's lap. She stroked his hair and smiled at Sebastian, who reached over and touched her cheek. "It's been quite a day for him," she whispered.

"It's been quite a day for all of us," he replied with a contented sigh.

The Dancing Queen

It was still dark when Sebastian opened his eyes and stretched. The sound of the rain on the outdoor deck was like a drum beat, soft and steady. The patio door was open; he wondered if he should pad across the floor to close it. Maddy was draped over his chest, her hair splayed across his body. His hand instinctively moved her hair from her face. He heard a contented sigh and realized the sound had come from him. This was his favourite part of the day—waking up with Maddy in his arms, the sound of her breathing matching his, no words, no other people or distractions, just the two of them in a warm bed. Maddy purred like a cat and moved her leg, which was already across his legs, farther up his thigh. How could such a simple move make him hunger for her?

He caressed her arm, her face, and in response Maddy moved her hand across his stomach and down, finding him ready for her. She deftly set herself onto him, and soon they were moving in a slow rhythm, with the rain keeping time.

"Good morning. It sounds like the rain has stopped. It's gonna be a great, great day."

Maddy smiled over at Sebastian, who was now propped up on his arm, waiting for her to open her eyes.

"It's always a great day when I wake up like that." He smiled as he moved her hair off her face. "I'll be late tonight. It's Judge Holtby's retirement party. Dinner, drinks, cards, more drinks, stories of his life, more drinks, more cards …" He sighed as he turned over on his back.

"Oh, too bad for you. You're missing the battle of the bands and dancing at Decades. We have a big table. Maybe you could join us later if you get bored with the stories and drinking." Maddy sat up and kissed his forehead.

"I'm already bored with my plans. Can't promise what shape I'll be in, but I'll keep my options open. If Christian knows you have a table, he'll want to leave right after dinner." He laughed and pulled Maddy towards him.

Audrey was giggling uncontrollably at some joke, and Lambert was carrying a tray of shooters to the table when Sebastian and Christian walked into Decades. The professor was proposing a toast to great friends and good music. They threw back the drinks and high-fived each other. All evening the bands had played a mix of lively oldies and current dance music, keeping everyone on the dance floor. Maddy and her friends were taking a well-deserved rest in between sets, toasting each other and laughing at silly jokes. The club was crowded and the lighting constantly changing, providing a festive atmosphere.

"No more for me," Maddy cried. "I haven't had this much to drink in one night, ever. You'll be carrying me home … or better yet, I'll just sleep right here, on this table."

"Here come the bands," Lambert announced, double vision making him see the same band twice. Audrey continued to giggle.

"Yippee. More dance, less drink!" Maddy shouted, arms in the air. The professor caught her as she fell into her seat.

"We'd like to thank you all for making this a great night," said Keith, the lead guitarist. "We wanna slow it down for a song or two, while we wait for the rest of the band to get back up here. We've been lucky enough to be at the club on Wednesday afternoon for some jammin' sessions with other musicians, and we've got to know some cool people. Sam, the professor, is a mighty fine guy; thanks to you, Sam, we can stay together as a band. Maddy here"—he pointed down to the table—"gets us gigs most weeks. Much appreciated. Last week she sat in with us for a sound check, and we got to hear her sing. Maddy, come on up and join us."

The crowd cheered and whistled. Maddy was frozen in her seat. "I couldn't …" she looked at the professor, pleading. "I'm not a singer. I can't do this … help me, please."

The professor leaned closer to Maddy, held her hands in his, and looked into her eyes. "You can do anything. I'll be there with you. Come on; give it a try. Just one song …" He smiled at her encouragingly and helped her up.

At the entrance, Christian and Sebastian watched as Maddy, holding hands with the professor, took the stage and sat on the stool beside him. He leaned over for his guitar and spoke to the drummer.

"Ah, just in time. I'll get us a drink." Christian moved away to the bar. The retirement party had indeed been dull, the judge falling asleep at the dinner table after too many pre-dinner sherries. A few stories later, the judge was taken home and the party dissolved. Christian and Sebastian were delighted to join the Decades party. Sebastian had never seen Maddy drink to the point she was unsteady on her feet. He held his breath as the music filled the room. The professor was beside Maddy, watching her and nodding.

Maddy rubbed her eyes and held her face in her hands, telegraphing how uncomfortable she was with being on stage. Her neck was red and blotchy; he felt he should rescue her—whisk her off the stage and out of the club. The music started, and the crowd was cheering; it seemed to be a popular song. The professor started a Meat Loaf song, and when Maddy joined in, the room was electric. Her voice was sultry and yet strong. She and the professor sang to each other with the crowd joining in. Maddy seemed comfortable, surprising herself and the crowd with a big finish.

"Sheeit, she's really good." Christian was back with a pint in each hand.

"Indeed." Sebastian responded absently, feeling like a proud parent at a school concert.

The crowd joined in on the chorus, and the room was moving from side to side as Sebastian walked towards the stage.

As the song ended, the professor hugged Maddy and she took a shy bow, looking for the stairs. The band started playing a lively song, encouraging Maddy to join in. The professor and Maddy sang a fun duet, which the crowd enjoyed. Maddy danced towards the stairs, and at the end of the song she bowed, her face flushed.

She left the stage and fell into Sebastian's arms. She looked up, not certain it really was Sebastian.

"You were wonderful, Maddy." It sounded like Sebastian, but he wasn't supposed to be here. He kissed her forehead, and she wrapped her arms around him. It felt like Sebastian. She looked up and took a deep breath, focusing on his face. "I'm sorry you had to see that." She mumbled. She then pointed towards the table. "Can we sit for a minute?" Sebastian laughed as he half-dragged, half-carried Maddy to the table. Her friends were standing, cheering, and high-fiving her. Lambert slapped Sebastian on the back. "Glad you could make it, sir."

The room was dark for a second, and then bright spotlights criss-crossed the room. The drummer started a fast beat, the band started playing, and the room was alive with movement.

"Let's dance!" someone shouted, and it seemed everyone was moving.

Sebastian looked at Maddy, expecting her to be nodding off, but she was standing, looking bright-eyed and ready to dance. "Come on; let's go." She reached for his hand, placed his pint on the table, and headed towards an opening on the dance floor. Audrey was beside him, moving her head to the music, Lambert was hip-checking Maddy, arms in the air. Christian appeared and took Audrey's hand, twirling her as they moved forward. Sebastian followed, wishing he'd had more to drink. *This is crazy—absolutely … crazy*, he was thinking as he held Maddy's hand and attempted to move to the music. They were jostled, pushed, and bumped, and yet no one seemed to mind. *Are we too old for this?* he wondered as Maddy fell into his chest, throwing her arms around his neck, forcing him to move with her. *Obviously not*, he decided as he looked over the crowd. All the dancers, including him and Maddy, were enjoying themselves and forgetting about anything other than feeling the music. Not for the first time, he wished he'd known this crazy woman years ago.

Sebastian didn't know all the people at the table, but they clearly knew Maddy and enjoyed her company. Audrey flopped down next to Sebastian and asked if it was time to go yet. "Maddy should be all right. The professor waters her drinks. What a guy. I wish I had a friend like that. You know I love her; we all do. Why am I telling you? You already know." She tried to introduce him to the group at their table, but she was confused by names and affiliations, so he stopped paying attention. When the band played their final number, the dance floor was a close mob. Maddy walked to the table and said goodnight to each person, finally approaching Sebastian and sitting on his lap, one arm over his shoulder. "Is it okay if we go home now? I'm tired. I've had way too much to drink, but wasn't it a great night out?"

"Indeed." He couldn't think of anything else to say to the happy drunk on his knee.

The ride home was slower than usual, as Audrey needed several stops. She apologized profusely, explaining she may have had too much to drink. Maddy slept, wrapped in Sebastian's arms. Davi walked Audrey to the door, ensuring she was safely inside the house. He returned to the car wondering where Maddy and Sebastian had gone. He heard them laughing as they walked across the boulevard.

"Come on, my darling; let's get you to bed."

Maddy stopped walking and looked up at Sebastian with wide eyes. "You just called me 'my darling' …"

"Did I?" Sebastian looked away, trying not to smile. Her drunken behaviour was amusing.

"Yes, you did. I think you like me." Maddy exclaimed.

"What makes you say that?" Sebastian was enjoying her game.

"Shh, it can be our secret. I won't tell anyone. But I think you do like me."

"Is that a good thing?" he asked, smiling back at her. They reached the deck of the garden apartment.

"Unbelievably good. Let me show you how much I like you …" Maddy unbuttoned his shirt, opened the door, pushed his shirt off his shoulders, moved him towards the bed, removed her blouse over her head in one motion, and reached up to kiss him. Sebastian lifted her, and immediately Maddy wrapped her legs around him. Her aggressive behaviour was a turn-on. Sebastian fell onto the bed with Maddy, and soon they were moving in unison.

Maddy stretched and realized she was alone in the bed. She sat up, looked around the apartment, and stumbled into the bathroom. "Oh my God, what have you done?" she asked the image in the mirror. Maddy felt the tears on her cheek and began sobbing heaving sobs of loss. She walked towards the bed, her hands holding back her hair in despair.

"Maddy, are you all right?" Sebastian was standing at the door, holding two takeaway cups in his hands. Maddy ran to him and threw her arms around his neck. "I woke up, and you were gone … I tried to remember what I might have done to upset you or embarrass you, and I couldn't think … I was afraid you were so upset you left …" Maddy barely got the words out between sobs. "I don't know why I felt so alone."

"Oh, my darling Maddy, last night was wonderful. I went out to get your favourite chai so I could wake you up with a treat. I couldn't think of a better way to show you how much I cared for you. Don't cry. Everything is fine. Come back to bed. You must be exhausted … I am." He realized he was still holding the cups over Maddy's head. As he stretched out one arm to set the cup down, Maddy took a step back and wiped her eyes, blinking up at him. Sebastian quickly placed the second cup on the counter and wrapped his arms around her. He held her as if he was afraid to lose her. Maddy clung to the man whom only moments ago she thought she had lost. Neither of them said a word as they slowly moved towards the bed. Hours later they woke, still wrapped in each other's arms, the cold chai on the counter.

The More I
Know You

The car passed the house several times before stopping at the curb. Through the lowered window, a woman tossing her dark curly hair away from her shoulders asked where Sebastian Walker resided. The gardener trimming shrubs shook his head, pointing to his protective headset. The woman was insistent. She stepped out of the car and walked up the drive. In the garden, she spotted Maddy and Esme moving shrubs.

"Hello, hello. Excuse me, is Sebastian Walker at home? He usually meets me, but he isn't answering his phone or returning my calls. Any idea where I can find him?" Her voice was harsh and condescending.

Maddy removed a glove and wiped her forehead, leaving a streak of black earth across her face, and stepped forward. "Perhaps you should try the office; he doesn't work from here." Maddy sneezed and turned back to the shrubs. After tapping her nails on the garden table, the woman huffed and returned to the car. Maddy and Esme exchanged glances but kept on working.

"I have to go soon. Lambert called in a panic asking for a favour." Maddy announced.

"I'm his date tonight with a big American client. I'm to meet them at the Starlight. Do you know it?" Maddy asked, rubbing dirt across her forehead.

Esme assured Maddy she would enjoy the dinner and dance club overlooking the Thames. "Wear something smart ... a little black dress ... You can't go wrong with a little black dress. Do you have one? Shall I lend you a dress and pearls? Come to the house and I'll set you up." Esme was excited to take part in the makeover.

Esme smiled back at Maddy in the mirror, admiring her pearls and the upswept hairdo she had created for Maddy. "You look wonderful, my dear." She sighed wistfully.

Maddy touched the hand on her shoulder and looked up at Esme. "Did you go to the Starlight often?"

Esme sat on the bed, closed her eyes, and nodded. "I know it's hard to imagine that I could be young, attractive, and adventurous, but Gordon was away on business often, and my escape was to go to the Starlight Room and dance." She looked up, and Maddy encouraged her to continue. "I knew Jakub long before we got together. He gave me the pearls. He worked there and eventually bought the place. I heard he was still there." A tear rolled down her cheek. "Thank you for letting me reminisce. I hope you have a lovely time."

Arriving at the Starlight Room, Maddy felt she was entering a bygone era—the big band sound, the waiters in tuxedos with hair slicked back, the trays of colourful cocktails and the coat check girl dressed like a Playboy bunny. The banquette seats were covered in deep red velvet, the tableaus on the wall reminiscent of biblical scenes.

Maddy took a deep breath as she surveyed the room, searching for Lambert. An elderly gentleman, slightly stooped, touched her arm and said he was admiring her pearls. On a hunch Maddy asked if Jakub was still involved in the business. The gentleman considered this for a moment and then, with a sparkle in his eye, advised Maddy he was Jakub.

"I'm delighted to meet you. Esme is my friend; these are her pearls, and this is her dress. For some reason, she insisted I had to wear them here tonight."

"How is she?" he asked softly, his eyes moist.

"She's doing well. Perhaps we could all have lunch together. She would love to see you."

"I'll have to think about that …"

"Don't think for too long, Jakub; enjoy the memories while you can … Please, let me arrange lunch."

Jakub nodded slowly, and suddenly he stood taller and put his arm out to escort Maddy to her table.

Lambert whistled as Maddy approached the table, regal and elegant on the arm of the elderly man. Jakub bowed and left Maddy at the table. Lambert stood and introduced Maddy to Harvey and Ephrom Gold, the father-and-son team from New York City. Drinks were ordered, and the conversation was easy, Maddy asking after New York, theatre, and the company business. Harvey Gold was enjoying her quick wit and fast patter. He asked Maddy to dance, and soon they were spending more time on the dance floor than at the table.

Sebastian and Rachel Gold arrived at the Starlight and were escorted to their table at the window. Rachel made at least two trips to London each year, expecting Sebastian to escort her and take care of her every need. She was demanding, pouty, and high maintenance. She spoke in sexual innuendos. It was a command performance for Sebastian, and he was tiring of her.

Rachel had expressed her disappointment at his lack of attention, and after a full day of meetings Sebastian found it difficult to concentrate on her constant patter. He wondered what was happening at home, at Bellmere. Suddenly Rachel grabbed his arm and, with a look of horror, asked why his gardener was dancing with her father. He almost laughed; her voice was cracking, and she was mortified. He stopped himself as he followed her gaze and saw Maddy and Harvey on the dance floor. She looked amazing. They were clearly enjoying themselves. "My gardener?" he asked, confused.

"Yes, your gardener informed me you didn't work from home." She was patting her chest, upset with the scene.

"What were you doing at my home?" He sounded angry.

"You wouldn't answer my calls. What's a girl to do? I waited for you at the hotel all afternoon. I was wearing my diamond earrings … and nothing more." She was batting her eyelashes and pouting.

"I was in meetings all day. Did you actually go to my house? That seems inappropriate somehow." Sebastian was feeling like he needed to escape.

Rachel announced she was going to the powder room. "Excuse me. Just a quick minute. Be a dear and get us more champagne, won't you."

Sebastian stood and watched her walk away. He left the table and approached Maddy on the dance floor. "Hello, Harvey, good to see you. May I cut in?"

He bowed and placed his hand on Maddy's back. "I'm walking away reluctantly, Maddy. Thank you." Harvey kissed her hand and left them on the floor.

Sebastian found himself staring at Maddy, who was looking up at him with eyes wide. She sneezed as she moved her head to his shoulder. He didn't hear the music; he just held her. She seemed so real after Rachel.

"When did you become the gardener?" he asked playfully, whispering in her ear. Maddy rolled her eyes. "It's a long story." She shrugged and sneezed again. "Sorry; there's a horrible scent on your jacket, and it's making me sneeze." She tossed her head, and all he wanted to do was hold her face in his hands and kiss her.

He moved his hand down her back and pulled her closer—too close to be comfortable. Maddy looked up, her eyes teasing him. He lowered his head, his lips ready to meet hers. Maddy held her breath, anticipating his lips on hers. The spell was broken as Rachel grabbed Sebastian from behind. Maddy moved away, trembling from the near kiss. Rachel wrapped herself around Sebastian, staring up at him, her expression questioning what he was doing.

"Rachel Gold"—he motioned towards Rachel—"is a client of ours from New York City. I believe you have met her father and brother."

Rachel moved closer to Sebastian, rubbing her hands up and down his chest, uninterested in Maddy. Maddy waited for Sebastian to introduce her, but his attention was clearly focused on removing Rachel's hand from his chest.

Maddy turned away, her face burning with embarrassment, and walked towards her table. The walk seemed interminable. Jakub appeared and took her arm. "I don't know what just happened, but you didn't deserve it." He bowed as they reached the table.

Sebastian watched Maddy walk away, on the arm of the older man. Her dinner companions were delighted to have her back. Rachel continued to lean against him. He turned and directed her off the dance floor and towards their table. "Aren't you going to dance with me, Sebastian?" She asked in a little girl voice. "You never dance with me."

"We have a busy day tomorrow; it's time to go." His tone did not offer any compromise. Rachel was visibly upset. She walked out ahead of him, considering making a scene but realizing this was not the time. He would pay for this later.

The lights were out but the door was open. Concerned, Sebastian walked over to the patio and into the apartment. Maddy was asleep, curled up on her side, the bedside lamp on. He smiled as he crept to the bed—careful not to stumble—leaned over, and kissed her forehead. He felt like a parent checking in on his little girl. She looked so peaceful in sleep. He flicked the lamp off and started to back out of the apartment when Maddy sat up in bed, rubbing her eyes. She sneezed. "Sebastian, you're home. Come to bed."

"I'm sorry to wake you. I was trying to be quiet. The door was open. Go back to sleep; I have an early morning meeting, and I didn't want to disturb you. Good night." He was whispering in the dark.

Maddy turned the bedside lamp on. She motioned for him to come and lie beside her.

"I won't sleep if you go—not now. I'm awake." She shrugged and wrapped her arms around her knees. "Come to bed."

He had walked for hours after leaving Rachel at her hotel, finding several bars along the way. His head was spinning from one too many scotches.

"Come and snuggle with me." She stretched. It was inviting, but he could feel the room moving. He stepped back, closer to the door.

"Oh. My. Gosh!" Maddy shook her head, spreading her arms wide. "Here I am, begging the man who sometimes sleeps here to come to bed, and he's walking away. I must seem very pathetic right now." Her voice was quavering. "I never really understood your 'no strings attached' rule, but I guess it means I wait for you every night and you get to decide whether you sleep here, at the main house or where ever." She rubbed her hands over her face. "I'm asking you to come to bed and you've already been. Clearly I misunderstood and I've overstepped."

Sebastian stepped back. He didn't understand what Maddy was talking about.

Maddy shook her head and whispered, "Don't worry; I'll go. No drama, no histrionics. I feel so foolish. Good night." She flicked the lamp switch, closed her eyes, and turned away from Sebastian, who by now had reached the door. Maddy bit her lip, vowing not to shed a tear while he was still in the apartment.

Slowly, Sebastian forced himself to walk back to the house and into his office, where he dozed off in the desk chair. He woke with a jolt, his neck stiff. He was disoriented, and it took several minutes to realize he was fully dressed, sitting at the desk and not lying beside Maddy, where he had wanted to be all evening. He shed his clothes and threw back the covers on the bed—his bed: the bed he had slept in alone for so many years. Sleep would not come as he tossed and turned, trying to find a comfortable position. He needed to hear her breathing beside him; he needed to feel her arm across his chest, her leg across his leg. His pillows didn't smell of her hair.

Finally, it was dawn, and he didn't have to pretend to be sleeping any longer. He showered, dressed, grabbed for a tie, picked up his jacket, and ran down to the garden apartment, hoping to catch her still in bed. He imagined himself slipping under the duvet cloud and holding her, kissing her until she forgave him for being such an eejit.

He opened the door quietly and was disappointed to see the duvet and pillows arranged neatly—no coffee made, no Maddy. The apartment was tidy, almost sterile, everything in its place. He felt a wave of panic when he noticed there was nothing on the bathroom counter. He opened the wardrobe door quickly and was slightly relieved to see her clothes neatly hanging; that must mean she hadn't gone away, hurt. *Why do I keep pushing her away,* he wondered, *when all I want is to be right here, with her?*

Sebastian walked out to the garden, deep in thought. Davi was standing by the car, water and headache tablets in hand, waiting for him. He had forgotten his early meeting. He nodded at Davi and climbed into the car, tie in hand. Davi didn't ask how he was this morning. He didn't have to ask; he could tell it was going to be a quiet ride into the city.

Tear It Down and Build It Up

"Well hello, Maddy. Lambert here, how are you this morning? You were a lifesaver last night. It was such fun having you there. Thank you, a million times."

Maddy moved the phone to her left shoulder, "My pleasure, Lambert; they were such nice people. I hope your day is going well." She was clearing the side counter at the coffee house, having arrived before dawn to have a chai with Grace. They had had little time to visit before customers eager for their morning cuppa began trickling in. Grace had thrown an apron at Maddy, and the two of them handled the morning rush just as they had when they first met.

"Maddy, I took your advice and went to the theatre company auditions, and … I got the part and … I met someone. I was dying to tell you last night." He was whispering into the phone.

"Fantastic! I'm so happy for you. What's more important—the part or the new friend?"

"Oh, the part, of course. The new friend is directing, so I have to be careful."

"Lambert, when you're ready, we'll have tapas and drinks with your new friend … Please be prudent in the meantime." Maddy was pleased for Lambert but concerned he would go all in and mess up a good opportunity.

"Sebastian is still in with the Gold party. He wondered if you were available for lunch at the club today at 1.00 p.m." Lambert suddenly sounded official.

"Oh my, that sounds rather like a summons. It must be dreadfully important," she responded with a British accent.

"Anytime someone gets to spend a lunch hour with you, it's important. He did say 'please'," he drawled.

"I'm heading to the train now, and I won't be back for a few days. Maybe Friday or Monday."

Lambert made a clicking noise and wondered how that would go over with his boss; he was used to having people fall into line. "I'll check and get back; he won't be pleased."

Maddy laughed. "Love ya, Lambert. Why don't you teach him to text message?"

"Then I would never get to talk to you … Ciao."

Maddy laughed. "Ciao, ciao, my friend. Thanks for sharing your good news."

Lambert had guessed correctly. His boss was not pleased to hear Maddy was not available. Where was she? Was she in the city? Where could she have gone? Did she leave any other message? Sebastian grilled Lambert, who was thankful Maddy had not shared any more information. He wanted to protect her privacy, but he could see Sebastian was worried—almost frightened.

"Well, well, well, here you are at the club, having dinner alone for the fourth night in a row. Problems in paradise?" Deirdre sat at the table across from Sebastian. "You know my offer still stands. Father would be so happy if we announced our engagement. You know I'm right about this, Sebastian. We have nothing to lose." Deirdre placed her hand on his. Sebastian closed his eyes and slowly moved his hand away.

"Deirdre, if you want to join me for dinner, as a friend, I will gladly discuss the weather and football results and upcoming events, but please, no more talk about us. We are what we are, and although you are still searching, I have found happiness. My life is with Maddy." He was surprised at how firm his own voice sounded. He looked around the room and then turned to Deirdre. "Shall I order for you?"

Deirdre played with her rings, turning them and pulling at them. She looked up at Sebastian, her eyes moist. "I'm not eating much these days, but I don't want to be alone. Can I just sit with you and drink my woes away?"

Sebastian nodded and felt a wave of pity for Deirdre—the little rich girl who could not find happiness or love. He caught the eye of Jason, the bartender, who had been rather cool to him all week. Perhaps he knew Maddy was gone. When Jason returned with the drinks, Sebastian mentioned Maddy would be home tomorrow, which brought a smile and a polite 'Thank you, sir' from Jason. Maddy was right; having friends was important.

Sebastian was anxiously pacing on the bridge when he saw Maddy walking towards him. She had suggested they meet in the middle of the Millennium Bridge, not at the club, intimating they needed neutral ground. She liked the view of St Paul's Dome from the bridge.

Maddy was curious to know what had prompted the invitation, especially after their last conversation. What could they possibly have to discuss? Working at the coffee house with Grace always had a calming effect on her; she was careful not to mention the incident or what lay ahead to Grace, but she couldn't help thinking her life was about to change. She had not mentioned anything to Belle and George as they walked on the beach, careful they should not have to take sides. Her mind was racing with all the changes that were coming—especially where she would go now. It was clear she was to move out of the lovely garden apartment. She wondered about going home or travelling, which usually brought on a feeling of excitement … but right now, for some reason, she felt sad.

Sebastian was unsure of how best to proceed, especially after that miserable night and his irrational behaviour, yet here she was.

Sebastian watched Maddy approach—a vision in her red raincoat and red boots, her stride confident. She seemed unaware of the heads turning to catch a second glance of her.

"Hello, Maddy." Sebastian moved forward to kiss her cheek. "You look lovely. Thank you for agreeing to meet me."

"I didn't want to say goodbye in an email or text message." Maddy looked away.

Sebastian stared at her in disbelief.

"Goodbye? No, no, no. This is not goodbye." He wanted to shake her and make her see he wanted to apologize and move forward, not out.

Maddy turned to look at him, confused by his words.

"Maddy, before I ask you to forgive me for being such an eejit the other evening, I want to know what you've enjoyed about your stay in London so far. Any highlights—any regrets?" He hoped he sounded nonchalant, although his heart was pounding.

Maddy looked down at her hands. "I'm not sure I can do this right now."

"Please, Maddy, it's important."

Maddy made a face, trying to encapsulate everything she had experienced. "It's difficult—almost impossible—to prioritize, but I did love the garden apartment. I'm so happy to have met Grace and Davi. Audrey and I are working on projects, and Esme has me volunteering at the hospital. Lambert has been a gem, and I can't get enough of Belle and George and my time at the seaside cottage. Henry is lovely, and I've made some wonderful new friends, like the professor." She looked away. "I did so enjoy my time with you—every minute of it."

What she couldn't say, couldn't speak out loud, was "I think my favourite thing was having you come home for dinner, dancing in the garden, just sitting beside you—reading at night or in the rain … it was lovely to say good night and then good morning when I opened my eyes. I adored how you reacted when I said your name; regardless of how thick the report you were reading happened to be or how long you'd been on your laptop, you always took your glasses off and looked at me, waiting to hear what I had to say. It's such a beautiful gesture; I just felt happy. At my age, I wasn't sure I would ever feel like that again."

She shook her head. "Sorry; you were probably looking for something more culturally interesting and deep."

Sebastian smiled. There was hope. He reached over and held her face, fighting with himself to slow down. He kissed her on the lips, willing himself to pull away, not wanting her to move. Sebastian blinked, realizing he had to respond quickly; she had spoken about their time together as though it was in the past.

"Maddy, about the other night … I sat through a long, tedious meeting all day and then dinner with Rachel Gold, who is trying at the best of times. All evening I wished you were there beside me, keeping the conversation alive, as you always do. Several times I almost dozed off. I had no bloody idea what was going on or why a client would go to my house. It was too much … I watched you dancing with others, and I wanted to be with you. You looked amazing. I needed you. I needed to touch you and keep it real; I needed you to laugh and tell her she was crazy, in that nice way you have. I just needed you."

He knew he was speaking quickly, but he couldn't risk having Maddy turn and run before he finished.

"I don't know a lot about relationships, but I do know how much I need to touch you whenever you are near, how I rush home to see you and just be with you, how I can't sleep without you in my arms, and how I need to see you in the morning more than I need coffee … I said 'no strings' so you wouldn't feel obligated to me, but I can't function without you. I want to be the one you say good night and good morning to every day. I don't want to go to dinner meetings without you. I don't want to do anything without you. I don't know how I survived all these years without you; I think I was going through the motions, believing I had a good life. Then I met you, and I realized I wasn't living; I was merely existing." He paused, watching for her smile.

Maddy could feel tears welling up; her heart was beating fast, and she felt faint. She had woken up thinking this was goodbye, but Sebastian was talking about the future.

"Is it possible that you want to be with me? Could you be content sharing your life with me? Can I ask that of you? Please say yes." Another pause. "Please forgive me for hurting you and perhaps damaging the best thing that ever happened to me. I'm not the least bit interested in anyone else. Can you forgive me and consider what I'm asking?"

Maddy shook her head in disbelief. "What? What are you saying?"

She had waited for him every night. She was always pleased to see him; what else could she possibly do?

"Maddy, be my everything," he whispered. He wished she would look at him. He knew he was handling this poorly, but he had thrown his feelings out and was waiting for her to respond—to understand how much he needed her.

Maddy looked over at him and swallowed him up with her eyes. She smiled and touched his cheek.

"I already am, you sweet, silly man." She shook her head, wondering how he could not know.

He sighed, the relief visible in his features. He wasn't sure whether he should laugh, kiss her, or shout out. He gently took her hand away from his cheek, kissed her palm, and held her hand in his. They stood hand in hand on the bridge, oblivious to the traffic, the boats on the Thames slowly moving past them and time itself. Sebastian slowly turned; folded Maddy in his arms; kissed her neck, her forehead, and her eyes; and then teased her lips with his. Maddy moved her arms around his neck and returned his kiss. What a day!

"Maddy, I continually hear that I'm not exciting enough for you, that I won't be able to keep you interested …" Maddy moved back and touched his face.

"I'm sorry I don't tell you enough how wonderful you are—how happy I am to spend time with you. I'll try to be better at that."

Sebastian pulled her closer and buried his face in her hair, delighted with her response.

Lost in their embrace, Sebastian was startled when Maddy threw her head back, laughing, and with a mischievous smile suggested they play hooky for the rest of the day.

"Play hooky?" He looked confused.

"Hooky is when you leave class or your job; I think you call it *skiving off.*"

"I'm sure everyone at the office is hoping I don't return after my growling bear act these past days. I was frantic when I couldn't find you." He held her face in his hands.

"Are you on your way to another adventure?" he asked, aware that Maddy had full days of errands—and come to think of it, he couldn't be sure what else.

She placed her hands on his chest and looked up, smiling. Suddenly she shook her head, turned, and started walking away. Sebastian followed her.

"Did Davi drop you?" he asked, looking around.

"Davi is your driver. I walk or take the Tube when I go out." Maddy was surprised by the question.

"Davi is *our* driver, and you are welcome to make use of his services whenever you like. I'm sorry; I just assumed you would know that." Sebastian realized he had taken so much for granted. Maddy was very independent and always found ways to get around.

"By the way, whatever happened with the Gold Family Development?" she asked, stopping suddenly. Sebastian smiled down at her. "It started badly. Rachel voted against us, naturally, but her father and brother were so taken by you they voted against her. We did get the commission, thanks to you, Maddy, purely because you were so charming the night before. Lambert was ecstatic; he says he has dibs on you for future schmoozing events. How will I break the news to him?"

Maddy laughed. "I'm happy the outcome was positive."

"You're running up quite a large finder's fee, my dear; we may not be able to afford you much longer." Sebastian squeezed her hand, feeling content that all was well. "Oh, by the way, Harvey Gold left several tablets for your hospital charges. He said you needed computers with games and movies. Well done, Maddy."

"How very sweet of him. I must send him a note." Maddy grinned. She seemed lost in thought for a moment. She shook her head and turned, beckoning to Sebastian.

"Come on; it's time you had the best pot pie in London for lunch." Maddy started walking. "I want you to meet my friends."

She wasn't sure how things had just turned around. An hour ago she had been preparing to leave London; now she was holding hands with a man who wanted to include her in every aspect of his life. She shook her head and wondered again if she was too old for this. Sebastian squeezed her hand, as if he knew she was having doubts. She looked up at him, and he offered her a shy, crooked smile. She returned the smile and touched his arm, content to be with him, hoping she would never be too old to find heartache and romance and forgiveness.

The Old Bridge Pub looked out of place in the heart of London, but it was busy with young office clerks and sporty-looking men. Maddy walked into the pub and was greeted by a gruff barman shouting "Cora, come quick; it's the princess of Canada herself."

"Hello, Clifford, how have you been?" He reached over the bar to embrace Maddy, his burly arms lifting her off the barstool.

A flustered pixie-like woman with uncontrollable curls bursting out of a headscarf came from the kitchen, wiping her hands on her apron. When she spotted Maddy, she ran forward to greet them. "Ah, my luv, where have you been?" She was clearly pleased to see Maddy.

"Oh, Cora, my friend Sebastian has not had one of your pies, so we came for lunch."

"Sit, sit, sit. I'll bring out your food. Maddy, the tapas are going so well … Cliffy gets balmy when we have so many in, but he loves it. Don't let him tell you anything else but it's going great. We've had to hire more help. You sit; I'll get your lunch." She hurried off in a flurry of curls and arms, yelling over to the barman, "Get them a drink, why don't you; come on, man."

Maddy looked over at Sebastian, smiling, anxious to see his reaction to the bedlam. He was unsure of what was happening around them, but he knew a pint would be a good start.

Clifford arrived with a pint for Sebastian and a sparkling water for Maddy. "No Frenchie water; this is good English H_2O. Try this lager; it's a local brew." He placed their drinks down gingerly in front of them. He stood over Maddy, arms crossed. "Bloody tapas; too busy to keep up."

Maddy looked up and calmly responded, smiling sweetly, "Clifford, you can control which nights you want to offer the tapas, but if you're busy and it's working, why don't you just embrace the idea and show me the list?"

Clifford walked away grumbling, returning with a card for Maddy. Without looking up, she held out her hand and he placed a pen in her fingers. She crossed out a line, added a few words and looked up at the big bear standing behind her, waiting for her comments. "This is good. Well done. I'll have Jason work it up and drop off the cards … He will need a logo or a photo of the sign. Do you have one?" She returned the pen and placed the card in her bag. Clifford produced a page of logos and leaned on the bar.

"Cora missed you last week. She looks forward to your visit. Don't be a stranger." He walked away to greet a customer at the bar, turning to wink at Maddy. Just as Sebastian thought he might find out what was happening, Cora arrived with steaming pies. "Enjoy, my dears." She looked at Maddy. "Will you come on Thursday?"

"Of course I'll be here, you slave driver. See you then."

"Don't go without a ta-ra, will you?" Cora was already in the kitchen, shouting back.

Maddy turned to Sebastian. "Aren't they adorable? You will love the pot pie; it's the best I've ever had."

In response to his confused look, she added, "I was walking by one day and the owners, Clifford and Cora, were shouting at each other on the street. I stopped and asked if I could help. They laughed and asked if I had any brilliant ideas on how to get more business in the door. They are surrounded by office towers full of millennials. We chatted, and I suggested they have a tapas Thursday happy hour. We chose a few tapas, sent out a notice, and I worked with them the first night, serving and getting feedback. It was hugely successful, and now they offer Tuesday and Thursday night tapas specials. They just needed a break; that's all. They're such characters; the customers love them, as you can see."

Sebastian smiled at her enthusiasm and the ease with which she stepped in to help. It was the best pot pie he had tasted; he had to agree.

Shouting goodbye and ta-ra to Cora, they left the pub after Clifford said he was insulted that Sebastian would think he had to pay—Maddy was family. "Off with you. Come back soon." He winked at them, and Maddy blew him a kiss as they left.

"Shall we take the Tube over to the neighbourhood and walk home from there? It's very pleasant, as you well know," she offered.

Sebastian realized he didn't know. He had never walked in the area. Here he was being introduced to new things in London by a newcomer. It was exciting, and maybe a little frightening. He also realized he didn't know where Maddy had gone when she had left him alone, without word or hope. Perhaps it was best not to know.

The Tube was crowded, with bodies pressing against each other, all looking up, pretending to read the billboard ads, careful not to attract attention or make eye contact. Maddy leaned against Sebastian as the train swayed. It was comforting to know she had agreed to be his … his what? His lady? His constant companion? They really hadn't agreed to any label, but he felt she knew what he was asking. In America, would they be going steady? She looked up at him quizzically. Had he laughed out loud?

The sun was shining on their side of the street as they strolled along, holding hands. Maddy introduced him to the shops on the way home.

She stopped at the flower shop to say hello to Mrs Bing, a small Asian woman with sharp eyes and a tongue to match.

Mrs Bing hugged Maddy, admonishing her for missing mah-jong, then leading her to the refrigerator to see the new colours of gerbera daisies. "I bring in for you … You like big colours." She turned. "Do I know you? Who this?" She was pointing to Sebastian.

"This is my friend Sebastian. You met him in the garden when we played mah-jong. He's lovely." Maddy smiled and wrapped her arm around his waist, looking up at him. "Mrs Bing has the best selection of lasting blooms, and she is a magician with arrangements."

Mrs Bing was beaming and then eyeing Sebastian warily. "What you pick for Maddy?" She asked, testing him.

He looked around and chose orange, pink, and yellow gerbera daisies—the same colours Maddy always had on the table. Mrs Bing was impressed. "Good for you. Here, a blue one too; I wrap." He had never felt bullied in a flower shop before today, but the flowers were lovely. He reached into his pocket to pay for the beautifully wrapped package, but Mrs Bing waved him away. "You be good to Maddy. Go." The women exchanged hugs and whispers as they left the shop.

"Isn't she precious?" Maddy asked, squeezing his hand.

"Indeed." There were no other words.

Every shopkeeper knew Maddy, waving and yelling greetings as they passed. Maddy stopped at Vincenzo's Gelato and suggested they go in. "I don't even know your favourite flavour, and this is the best gelato around." She nodded and smiled. Sebastian smiled back. "I don't even know my favourite flavour, you will recall."

"Buon dia, mi Amore!" she shouted as they walked into the empty shop. Vincenzo appeared, wiping his hands on his apron. On seeing Maddy, he held out his arms and waited for her to reach him. He noticed Sebastian and moved his head back and forth to Maddy and Sebastian, silently asking who she was with today.

"Vincenzo, meet Sebastian. I have assured him you make the best gelato in London, and he doesn't know what flavour he prefers. Can you help him? Let him try some samples." Vincenzo snorted in good humour and walked to the counter.

"You eat all my profits." He tried to sound gruff, but there was no denying he was pleased to see Maddy. After several tastings, it was decided that lemon and chocolate hazelnut were the favourites. Vincenzo handed them both a small dish and moved away from the counter to let Maddy know her contact had made a large order. He was most grateful. Once again Sebastian was told, "Maddy no pay here." They left the shop, gelato dishes in hand, after another hug and promises to return later in the week.

"Your contact?" Sebastian asked as they walked.

"Uh huh. I met a vendor at the market, and his gelato was substandard in comparison, so I suggested he buy from the best, and he did. It worked out for everyone. Now Vincenzo is very busy with a booth at trade shows. He loves it. It makes him happy. But who wouldn't be happy seeing the customers walk away in delight?"

Sebastian was about to say "Indeed" when an elderly man on a bench called to Maddy.

"Maddy, I found a first edition for you. It wasn't easy, but I found it."

"You are an angel, Mr Simpson. Meet my friend Sebastian. He lives near here." She greeted the elderly man with a hug and offered her gelato to him. He shuffled inside, tasting the gelato, calling back with a wave of his spoon, "I'll put the kettle on." She looked over at Sebastian, eyes wide, silently asking if they could stop. Sebastian nodded.

"It seems to be part of the tour. I want to look for a book on Victorian gardens. I heard Lambert say the web search wasn't pleasing the client. You go ahead; I'll browse."

Maddy and Mr Simpson enjoyed a cup of tea in the dusty shop as Sebastian wandered up and down the overflowing aisles. Mr Simpson directed him to a section, and he found several books on the topic.

"Maddy, I hate to ask, but would you mind the store while they do my tests? The hospital says it will only take a day. No one has your love of my books and the importance of keeping the shop open—not even my son." Mr Simpson was pleading.

"Of course; just give me a days' notice so I can free up the time. Thank you for asking me—what an honour." She touched her chest and bowed her head.

Mr Simpson suggested Sebastian look over the books and bring back the ones he didn't need. "I trust that you will take care with them." Sebastian was touched by the gesture, fully aware Mr Simpson thought so highly of Maddy he was willing to let the books out of his shop.

"Thank you."

When Maddy excused herself, taking the tray of teacups back to the makeshift kitchen area, Mr Sullivan stepped closer to Sebastian and in a conspiratorial whisper announced that he was also in love with Maddy.

"I can tell, my dear chap, you care deeply for her, as I do. The first time she came to the shop, I was dusting upstairs. She announced she was just 'looking', and she walked through the aisles, running her fingers across the books. I watched her pick up a book, a classic, and she carefully opened it and inhaled. It was such an intimate act. I thought she had inhaled the words off the page. Then she hugged the book close, and only then did she realize I was watching her from above. She looked at me, still hugging the book, and asked if I was sad when a book left my collection. Imagine her knowing that. Everyone thinks it's just a bookshop, but I cherish every volume. I fell in love with her at that precise moment." He closed his eyes, recalling the day. "But don't worry, my good fellow." He shook his head. "She doesn't look at me the way she looks at you." He chuckled. Sebastian was touched by the older man's confession. Maddy approached, and after more hugs and promises to stop by later in the week, they stepped out.

As they walked, they shared their thoughts on what would make a relationship strong. Sebastian confessed he had no experience in this area, as he had always tried to be aloof and uncommitted. Maddy stopped and stared at him. "Weren't you sad and lonely?" Then she laughed. "I guess people can be together and still be sad and lonely." They walked along, and suddenly Sebastian wanted to know what Maddy expected of him.

"I want you to be honest with me; I hope you only say things you won't regret later, and I hope you never get tired of touching me." She stopped on the footway, surprised at how quickly she had responded.

"I'm in. But if I'm to be completely honest with you, unless it's haddock and chips, I really prefer beef." There was an awkward moment as they laughed, rearranged flowers and books, and kissed. Maddy made a note to stop recommending the fish on the club menu.

Maddy slowed as they passed a small shop, taking in the aroma in the air.

"Smells like vindaloo today … dinner?" She stepped into the doorway. "Hello, Sanjay, what have you today?"

"Ah, Maddy, just putting the Vindaloo chicken out. Have you found a Patel to marry yet? My cousin is available, you know," he teased.

"Not yet, thanks, but I would like you to meet my friend Sebastian."

"Sebastian—such a strong English name. Are your parents Indian?" he asked with a twinkle in his eye. Before he could answer, Sanjay was dishing out a sample for Maddy. "Good?" He waited for a response.

"Amazing. Let's take a dish for Audrey as well." Maddy shared a taste with Sebastian, who had to agree it was delicious.

"Naan or pappadam?" she asked.

"Naan." He was pleased he could contribute to the order.

"Naan all around. Thank you, Sanjay. Please give my regards to your wife and your unmarried cousin." She winked.

Sanjay laughed as he handed the meals over. "No charge today, Maddy; it is part of the dowry. My wife was very happy indeed with her day in the spa. I thank you a thousand times. She is walking better and is most grateful."

"I'm pleased to hear it was a good experience. Namaste." She bowed slightly, hands together.

As they continued to walk along the storefronts, Sebastian was struck by how comfortable this neighbourhood was, how attached Maddy was to the fabric of the area, and how she had made it her own. He stopped her, and as if it had just occurred to him, he realized he must speak with her right now.

"Maddy, where can we sit for a minute? We need to talk."

Twice in one day, she thought better of making a smart remark when she saw the determined look in his eyes.

"Here's a pub; is this okay?" They sat at the wrought-iron table, carefully laying their treasures down. Sebastian returned with a pint and a lemon shandy.

"Maddy, you love this neighbourhood and I'm just discovering it after all these years; I can't believe how insular I've been. You love your garden apartment and the neighbours, and here I am trying to sell the house because you won't live in it with me. I have tried to find another house with a garden, but distance is a factor, and we wouldn't have parking on site, which I know is important to you ... what do I have to do to the house to make it more appealing? Tell me what you would do to make it more acceptable—or should I say more liveable for me ... for us." He took a deep breath and waited to hear her thoughts.

She knew she must tread carefully, but she had thought about it, and before she could stop herself, she blurted out, "Since you ask, I have thought about it. I would tear down the back wall—make it glass. Lower level coming out to the patio, open concept with living area, dining room and kitchen; let me show you." She pulled out a pen and started drawing on the back of the coaster. "I see a living room area with grand piano, a seating area around a fireplace, and more casual seating near the patio ... a long dining room table ideal for entertaining so everyone gets to look out on the garden, a kitchen with a pass-through to hide the mess but convenient for outdoor entertaining." She took a breath.

"Upstairs, move the wall back so the balcony across the front is useable on sunny days. Master bedroom and your office share the fireplace in the wall ... you must have a fireplace and lots of light in your office so when you are working late you won't be so far away. Back bedrooms can stay or become one large suite. Don't forget you have the garden suite already. The entrance door is so lovely, and the stairwell is so ornate; when I first saw the house with Lambert, I wondered why you wouldn't feature the stairs and let people arriving see the garden through the house. Of course, it is your home, and you have memories, and it's probably too expensive, and I'm sorry, but you did ask." She stopped speaking and sat back, her face flushed.

Sebastian sat back and laughed. All these years, I've hated that house, and yet I never thought about changing it or making it brighter. This is brilliant." He reached over, held her face in his hands, and stared into her beautiful blue eyes. He kissed her because there were no words to describe how happy he felt.

"Let's go home. I want to draw this out and have it ready for your approval so you can dream about our new house." He stood up, gathering the books and flowers, and waited for Maddy. He was excited and impatient to start on the plan. Maddy stared at him, enjoying his enthusiasm and yet feeling frightened by his zealous response. It had been quite a day of discovery. She stood up, laughing, reaching for the container of food, and followed him home.

Maddy spoke to Audrey on her mobile. "Audrey, I have dinner for you. Will you join us? You have to take a break sometime."

Audrey was busy sewing the costumes for an upcoming event. "Be a dear and drop it off for me, please; I'm struggling with a seam and don't want to go out of the house. You should see me … I'm a mess."

"I'll be right over."

"Ta. Love ya."

Sebastian deposited his books and the flowers on the table in the garden and immediately went to his office. Maddy walked over to Audrey's, awed by the craftsmanship of the costumes and how talented her friend was. She left dinner on the kitchen counter. "Please don't forget to eat!" she called as she walked out the door, not wanting to disturb the flow of things.

It seemed everyone around her was busy working on a project. She set the table, arranging her flowers and chilling a bottle of white wine. The music was soft in the background, and there were a few weeds to be pulled. She did love the neighbourhood, the garden, and her new life. The man who had made it all possible was upstairs, redesigning his house with her suggestions. Just the thought of it was overwhelming, and she found herself smiling. She was surrounded by people who made her happy. Could she ask for anything more? It didn't seem possible.

Sebastian could not remember taking on a design project with such gusto. He finally completed a blueprint he felt Maddy would approve and printed a copy for her. As he stood and stretched, he realized it was almost midnight. He looked down into the garden, the table set, the lights low. He had worked through dinner. He hurried down to the garden and found Maddy asleep on the sofa. He watched her sleeping for a few minutes before he knelt beside her and kissed her forehead. She stretched catlike and blinked the sleep from her eyes. "Hi, did you eat?" she asked sleepily.

"No, I'm sorry. I got caught up in my work. Did you eat?" he asked tenderly.

She smiled and sat up. "I waited for you. I guess I fell asleep. Are you hungry?"

He shook his head and pulled her up from the sofa.

"Let's go to bed. I so enjoyed the day; now I just want to hold you." He would share the drawings in the morning.

Sebastian woke from a deep sleep, startled by Maddy kissing his face, his neck, his eyes, his forehead, his nose, his lips. He held up his hands to defend himself. "Stop, stop. Maddy. Stop." The more he resisted, the more she kissed him. Laughing, he put his arms around her and turned her over in the bed so he was atop her, holding her hands above her head.

He could hardly contain her as she squirmed under him.

"Sebastian, the drawings are perfect—exactly what I imagined." Maddy was giggling.

He was pleased with her reaction. She had seen the blueprints and renderings he had left on the counter.

"What do you like best?" he asked, still trying to hold her down.

"Everything. I like it all. How about you?" She was trying to sit up, impatient with him.

He sat up and let her go. She sprang from the bed and over to the plans. She had studied them and left salt and pepper shakers where she had questions.

"What did you like best, Sebastian?" she asked, wide-eyed and anxious.

He walked over to the counter slowly, his hand rubbing his chin, contemplating his response. He scratched his head and then, hands on hips, looked over the plans, noting her place marks. He knew he was dragging out his answer and it was killing her.

"The more I worked on the ideas, the more I opened up the space, the more I tried to imagine actually living in the rooms, the more I began to doubt …" He stopped and faced Maddy, who was listening intently, hoping for a positive response.

"Yes?" Maddy was holding her breath.

"I began to doubt my choice of career. You saw it and I didn't until you made me visualize the change." Maddy flew into his arms, almost knocking him over. He held her tightly and then looked into her eyes. "Thank you."

Maddy stepped back, taking his hand and moving over to the plans. "Is it affordable?" she asked, holding her breath.

Sebastian considered how best to respond. "Maddy, if you are willing to let the Regent Street house sell, knowing how much work you and Audrey have done on it, we can turn a handsome profit after expenses and fees. We'll have enough to do the renovations, go out for a celebratory dinner, and throw a very large party in your new home. How about that?" He had not told Maddy there was a bidding war going on for the Regent Street house. Potential buyers were quite taken with the decor and soft colours she and Audrey had chosen. He smiled at her concern over the cost of the project; he would have paid anything to make her happy.

Sebastian left for the office, eager to set the plan in motion. He would give the project to Lambert, who would be ecstatic to work with Maddy and ensure everything was perfect. He felt like a superhero. It felt fine—very fine.

The Accused
and the Judge

The summons to lunch at the club wasn't particularly friendly, so Maddy approached the table with caution. The look on Sebastian's face was stern—serious enough to make her sit before greeting him. "Hi, I feel like I've been called to the headmaster's office. What have I done this time, sir?" she asked, faking an English accent.

"Maddy, I received this envelope in my postbox yesterday, and Sidney Barnes continues to ask me if you've told me about an incident. I thought I should address both matters." He was clearly upset and very businesslike.

"What's in the envelope?" she asked, her curiosity getting the better of her.

"It appears to be a photo of you, taken late at night." He moved the photo across the table.

Maddy wanted to laugh but thought better of it. "Who is it from?" she asked, keeping a straight face.

"I don't know. There's no label or return address."

"Doesn't that tell you something? What a gutless way to start trouble." Now she was angry. "Do you know who this is?" She pointed to the man embracing her in the photo.

"No, I do not." He was tense. "Does it matter?"

Maddy took his hand and half-dragged him into the kitchen. She waved at the small man in whites, and he immediately approached her, arms out in greeting. "Sebastian, meet the chef, Ferdinand, my friend.

"Bom dia Maddy." The chef bowed his head.

"Bom dia Ferdinand. Señor Walker." Maddy moved her hand towards Sebastian.

"Olha, aqui uma foto… *nos somos famosos*—the paparazzi have seen us." She showed him the photo, and he smiled broadly. Then, as if he realized the photo might upset Señor Walker, he waved his hands, motioning to Sebastian. "No, no, no." He gestured to Maddy and himself. "No, no, no."

"It's okay. Obrigado Ferdinand." Maddy laughed and hugged the small man. "What should we eat today?" She spoke slowly. Ferdinand lifted the lid off a pot and let her peer inside. She smiled and gave him a thumbs up before waving and turning to go. "Give my best to Maria." Sebastian nodded to the chef and followed Maddy out to the table.

"Shall I continue?" she asked Sebastian with a steely voice.

He motioned for her to go ahead, his expression telegraphing his confusion.

"Okay, but I want you to know I'm angry. Ferdinand is the chef here, and he speaks little English, as you can see. He was not happy with the purveyor of fish, so I took him to Billingsgate Market one morning where he connected with Portuguese-speaking vendors who can meet his needs and help with the spices he wants. His pregnant wife, Maria, is a much better cook but speaks even less English, so we—Jason, the bartender, and I—meet at their home and try different recipes for the club menu. It's late when I leave, so Ferdinand walks me to the underground stop at the top of his street, and we say goodnight with a hug. It's a cultural thing. Is there anything wrong with that?" She held her chin out in challenging defiance.

"Maddy, you misunderstand my concern. We have a driver; he is available to you, yet here you are on the streets of London, late at night, taking public transport, not even a cab, and someone creepy is following you, taking photos. How can I not be concerned for you and your safety when I see this?" He was quite emphatic, waving his hand and hitting the table to make his points.

Maddy laughed. "I agree it's creepy to have someone take photos of me at night, but really, if taking a cab is going to make you feel better, I will. Will you do something for me?"

"Of course. What can I do?" he asked calmly, relaxing his shoulders.

"You can come to dinner with us; you would love it." She looked at him demurely, batting her eyelashes.

He had to laugh and agree. "I would love to … Perhaps we could pose for a group photo on the stairwell."

His face softened, and he held her hand. "I trust you, Maddy, but you do dangerous things, and I find I can't always protect you from yourself. Understand?"

She smiled back and nodded. "Crisis averted. What was next on your list, sir?"

"Now you're mocking me. We have the incident with the judge. Go." He swept his hand across the table, offering her the floor.

Maddy rolled her eyes. "This town is getting too small for me." She sat back and crossed her arms. "I would prefer to defend myself someplace private, like the garden at home or a park bench, rather than here, if it so please the court."

"Maddy, I'm not judging you. I thought you might like to enlighten me, but I am prepared to hear a lively story which will leave me shaking my head in wonder. Your choice."

"Oh, what the heck. Everyone here already thinks you're scolding me for something I did. It's silly really." She took a deep breath.

"The day of the dance here at the club, I was at the hospital in the morning. I always go to Starbucks before I go in and afterwards so I can walk home with a green tea latte. I innocently buy my drink, sit down for a second to check my phone messages, and I hear two women arguing. One is crying, the other agitated but trying to console the other. I hear your voice saying, 'Don't get involved; walk away', but I ask if everything is okay. The women stop sniffling long enough to tell me their rental car is parked outside on a hill and they can't move it from the parking space as someone has parked very close in front and behind them. They tell me they can't drive a standard and the car rental company will not send anyone to help. Simple solution: I offer to move the car. They gladly give me the keys, point out the car, and sit down to wring their hands even more.

I walk outside and open the car door, and a lovely young constable approaches, advising me I cannot park here. I tell him I did not park here and explain that I am trying to move the car for the Americans inside—who, by the way, do not come out and help me explain their plight. The constable wants to see my driver's licence, which I don't carry here, as I don't drive a car here. He wants to see my identification, which

I don't have because I don't need it for anything. He advises me on several city ordinances, none of which I comprehend or care about. Oh, still no Americans. I ask him if he would mind moving the bloody car and he gets out a book to write me a ticket. You can imagine my frustration at this point. Along comes Judge Barnes with a young lady on his arm. He hears me protesting as the young constable continues to direct me to the enforcement signs. The judge sends his companion into the Starbucks and asks if he can assist. I explain my obvious plight, and he doesn't appear to be listening; he's just eyeing me, funny-like. In the middle of my sad tale, he asks me if I am *your girl*. I really worked hard at not kicking him in the groin, but I smiled and played along. He takes the young constable aside, and suddenly they are all smiles and I am told it's not a problem; I can go. I thank him and ask one more time if we can't move the bloody car, which started the whole affair. He laughs and climbs into the small vehicle, starts it, and hits both cars as he manoeuvres it out of the spot. The young constable places tickets on the other cars and walks away, tipping his helmet thingy at us. The car is now parked at the door. The two Americans run out, get into the car, and drive away—not a word of thanks, not a goodbye, nothing. They just drive away. The judge and I are gobsmacked. We laugh about it, and I say I must leave but I do appreciate his handling of the situation. He asks me if I want to offer a return favour, which I most certainly do not, but I offer to buy him a drink when I next see him at the club. He negotiates a drink and a dance. I had to agree in order to get away. His companion comes out with their drinks, and he winks at me, telling me he knows I will be discreet. I nod and just about forget my now cold latte and book bag. There hasn't really been an opportunity to share this delightful tale with you, mainly because I know you will ask what lesson I learned. I'm sure your advice would be to walk away, not get involved … but you and I know that if it happens again, I will ask if I can help. That's it; that's all."

She shrugged her shoulders, took a deep breath, sipped from her water glass, and waited for his reaction, her hands folded in her lap. She hadn't looked directly at Sebastian throughout the telling of the story, fearing his disapproval. He was staring at her with a crooked smile. Then, to her surprise, he started applauding, clapping his hands together slowly, still smiling. She looked contrite as she watched him, his smile broadening.

Sebastian reached for her hand. "You are amazing." He was shaking his head. "I felt like I was there watching you on the street. I'm not sure I'll ever be able to look at Judge Barnes without asking about his driving skills." He chuckled. "Of course, you are discreet, and you would never mention his young companion …"

"He doesn't know that. But no, I wouldn't. How could I possibly throw any stones?" She looked around the room, rolling her eyes, as if she were waiting for the other guests to respond.

"Well, I've had enough of this place for today. Are you hungry or, shall we just go home?" he asked softly.

Maddy rubbed her forehead. "Let's go home."

"Indeed." As they walked out, Sebastian was still smiling, his hand on the small of her back, protectively. Maddy had agreed to be more careful, but he knew there would be more incidents. Left on her own, she was a magnet for lost souls and moments of distress. That was what made her so special.

The Garden Show

Aunt Belle was anxious to speak with Maddy about the autumn garden show. After sixty years, Belle was stepping down as the grand marshal—a role she first assumed as the princess of the royal ball. It was her event, and of course Sebastian and Maddy would be in attendance to honour her last reigning ball; she insisted. Sebastian was reminded to bring his tuxedo and was instructed to be sure Maddy had an appropriate gown to wear, as she had not previously attended the event. Sebastian knew Maddy had a style—"a look", she called it—and it suited her very well. But this was a traditional royal ball, and there was a formula. She assured him she would be invisible, which worried him. He had visions of her friends supplying a multicoloured sari or belly dancing outfit.

The garden show was popular with Londoners and locals; the landscaping displays were exceptional, and the agenda packed with tours and events. Sebastian and Maddy drove down in the sports car. Since the road trip to Scotland, they had made use of the car most weekends.

"Why don't you drive it? What are you saving it for?" she had asked Sebastian when she first saw the car in the garage. "If it was my car, I'd be looking for places to go every sunny day … top down, of course. Since then he had taken the car whenever he and Maddy were heading out. It was funny how her words had forced him to remember how much he enjoyed driving.

Belle and George had official duties throughout the event, so Sebastian was secured as the driver for George, and Maddy would ensure Belle arrived at the ball on time. There was great secrecy over the gown she would wear, and both men were surprised at her insistence they not see it before the ball.

"I have a feeling those two have hatched a surprise," George chuckled. Sebastian looked worried and nodded, thinking they had been very secretive and collaborative. He sighed and hoped it would sit well with the event committee. Belle had begged Sebastian to please dance this year; it was important to her that he join the president's first dance. He had resisted all these years.

The grand ballroom was just that—grand. The foyer circled the room, and a wide staircase brought guests down into the white-and-gold ballroom. Two hundred guests awaited the start of the ball, dressed in tuxedos, long gowns and gloves, tiaras, and finery. George and Sebastian stood at the bottom of the staircase awaiting their dates, fidgeting and wondering where the women were and when they would arrive. The announcer cleared his throat and waited for silence.

"Ladies and gentlemen," he said in a grand voice, "celebrating sixty years as grand marshal, I present Belle Fletcher, past and present."

There was a gasp in the crowd as they looked up at Belle; a hush fell over the ballroom.

Sebastian closed his eyes. "George, I'm afraid to look."

"You'd best look; it's unbelievable, my boy—unbelievable." George wiped a tear away and started up the steps to greet Belle, who was adorned in a beautiful red gown with a gossamer cape and a tiara. She looked radiant. Beside her, her back turned to the crowd, was Maddy in a mint green velvet hooded cape over a flowered gown. She was a vision: a vision Sebastian had seen before—a vision he remembered from his childhood. This was the dress Belle had worn for her first ball. It was uncanny how the memory flooded over him.

George had taken Belle and Maddy by the arm and escorted them down the final steps. Sebastian took Belle's hand, kissed it, and told her she looked lovely—every inch a queen. She was chuffed and just as pleased with his reaction to Maddy. "It was our secret my boy, and I think she carried it off, don't you?" she whispered in his ear. "Enjoy".

He winked at her and turned to Maddy. "You look …" He paused, seemingly lost for words "You look … delicious."

"Thank you, sir". She removed the hooded cape and stood before him in her gown, looking very vulnerable. The band started a waltz. Sebastian put his hand on the small of her back, held her right hand in his, smiled, and whispered, "Trust me?"

"Indeed," she whispered, her eyes locked on his.

They glided across the floor with such ease, Sebastian leading her round and round the room. Eventually the crowd backed off and watched them take over the floor. The music carried them, and Maddy felt so secure in his arms that she let herself go, unaware the music had stopped. Out of breath and flushed, she clasped her hands to her chin, their eyes still locked on each other.

As the music started for the next dance, an elderly woman approached Sebastian and broke the spell. "Belle looks as beautiful today as she did then. What a masterful idea to have both gowns for her big finale. Sheer genius, your aunt, sheer genius. Lovely Maddy, quite a change from those old sweaters you and George insist on wearing." And she was gone.

Sebastian was swallowed up in a crowd of former schoolmates, and Maddy was surrounded by the ladies who wanted to share their memories of the dress and the day it made its debut.

As they moved away from each other, miserably, Maddy motioned to Sebastian that there was a note in his pocket. He felt his inside pocket and joined the conversation, his mind still on the dance and how perfectly they had moved together.

Maddy could not concentrate on the conversations. Luckily, the women around her did not require a response; they were sharing their thoughts with each other, not necessarily with her. Her mind was still enjoying waltzing in his arms.

Later in the evening, Sebastian pulled out the note. He and George were at the bar, away from the party, enjoying a scotch. He read the note over and over but could not make sense of it. George looked over and smiled. "It's *Maddyspeak*—it's a puzzle. It stands for a phrase or a thing."

Sebastian looked confused, so George continued. "We were discussing forgetting things one day at the café, and Maddy suggested we do these puzzles every day just to keep our minds active. She sends us anagrams, puzzles, word jumbles, or sudoku every day. We call it *Maddyspeak* because some are really hard to figure out, and yet when we do, they are everyday things we say. Let's see … S T L D 4 M … probably ends with 'for me' … .aha! Save … the … last … dance for me. There you go. We were wondering if you could dance, and then tonight you waltzed as if you were born to it. No wonder she wants the last dance as well." He laughed, pleased with himself for solving the puzzle.

"Indeed."

The crowd was starting to wane; shoes were off, feet being rubbed. The garden show was a busy weeklong affair, and the gala was the last hurrah. Tomorrow was a sleep late day, and then the cleanup would begin. The orchestra had gone by 11.00 p.m., and the local band was playing young people's music. Sebastian was recruited to carry instruments and help the musicians clear the pit. He heard the announcement as he was hefting a last case into the lorry. He walked back into the ballroom and suddenly remembered his note. He panicked, looking around. *Where is Maddy?* He had hardly seen her all evening, but she had been a popular dance partner with the locals. They all seemed to have a story in which she was the heroine. Of course, Rod had been very solicitous all evening, as he couldn't help noticing. He was so proud of her; she had plopped herself into their lives, and they loved her. She looked amazing tonight. Where was she? Belle was so pleased she had agreed to wear the gown; those two were fast friends. And George—tonight he had asked Sebastian to sign some papers before he left town; they had something to do with the cottage. Where was she? He looked around helplessly, not wanting to disappoint her. The music ended, and the crowd slowly dispersed. The dance floor was clear, and still no Maddy.

Sebastian ran to the stage and found the band having a drink behind the curtain.

"How much to play one more song? I missed the last dance, and I promised Maddy," he blurted out.

The band members, local boys, had seen the first dance. "You still need a get-lucky-tonight song after that first dance, guv?"

"Indeed".

"Did you say Maddy?" the drummer asked.

"Yes, she gave me a note, and I couldn't get back from loading the orchestra cases in time, so I blew it." He ran his fingers through his hair, defeated.

"Listen, guv, for Maddy we'll play a tune. She hired us. We don't want your money. Get her on the floor; we're cool."

The band stood and clinked their pint glasses. "For Maddy."

Sebastian realized he was holding the pound notes in his fist. "She would want me to get you a pint," he said as he handed the money over, not knowing how much it was. He hoped it was enough. He saluted the band, turned, and started searching for her.

He found her at the entrance, holding her cape, ready to go. She had made sure Belle and George were on their way. The disappointed look in her eyes when she saw him coming towards her made his heart lurch. He pulled her to him and breathlessly asked her to dance. He could see tears welling up in her eyes, and at that moment he would have given anything in his power to make her happy. His feelings for her were so great he felt he was drowning. He put his arm around her and led her into the centre of the dance floor.

He held her tight, and they both laughed when the band started playing "Save the Last Dance for Me". It wouldn't have mattered what song they heard; the two of them swayed to the beat but were lost in their own world. As the number was ending, the band went right into "Meet Me Halfway" and then "You Were Always on My Mind"—a song she had requested at the local pub one night. It was the perfect ending to a wonderful evening. Maddy curtsied for the band and blew them a kiss when they finished playing. "They deserve a big tip for that!" Maddy exclaimed.

"Done." He was pleased to respond.

Sebastian and Maddy walked out clinging to each other, heading for the car. They drove to the cottage, where Sebastian lit the fire while Maddy poured them a nightcap. He took the glass from her hand and pulled her close. "I can't believe you wore that dress tonight … I can't believe I don't want to tear it off you." he whispered playfully.

"It was really important to Belle, and I was honoured to wear it, so you'd better be careful, mister," she teased.

"Maddy, you must know how much I care for you, yes?" His voice was suddenly serious.

"And I for you. Surely it's obvious in the little things I do." Maddy wondered where this conversation was going. "Of course, there's a risk in assuming, isn't there?"

Sebastian looked confused.

"Risk? How do you mean?" he asked.

"When you care about someone, you think the other person knows how you feel; you forget to say the words, and sometimes it can be risky to be first to say how much you care, just in case the other person isn't ready to hear the words or doesn't feel the same." Maddy stopped, not sure how to explain the concept.

"Go on," Sebastian encouraged.

"Sometimes it's risky not to say anything. People move on, never knowing what could have been or that their feelings were reciprocated. Does that make sense?" she looked over at him, frowning.

"Is that what happened to you?" he wondered aloud.

"No, my situation wasn't about the unspoken words; it was about too many spoken words, harsh words, and actions." She looked sad, the memories flooding back.

Sebastian held her face in his hands, looked into her eyes, and kissed her. "Maddy, I tell you how I feel every night when you fall asleep in my arms."

"I'm awake now." She smiled, teasing him and holding his gaze.

He kissed her again, slowly and passionately. "I love you, Maddy."

Maddy threw her arms around his neck and kissed his face. "Thank heavens, Sebastian—me too. Gosh, that sounded nice. I've been so careful not to say anything that would scare you off." She was breathless. Suddenly she moved away. "When did you know?" she asked.

Sebastian thought for a moment and answered slowly. "I'm not sure if it was in the art gallery, or when I saw you on the street, or when you leaned across to whisper in my ear at the ballet, or when I saw you on the platform at the train station … Perhaps it was when I saw you at the Bollywood theatre and Ravi had his hand on your back and you smiled at him—the smile I thought was reserved for me. I realized at that moment that I had never actually been envious of anyone before. I realized I wanted that smile for me … I wanted you." He shook his head and smiled at her. "Don't be angry or disappointed with me, but I had never experienced such a strong feeling before, and it took everything I had to gather the courage to act on the need to be with you. I came home to wait for you; you didn't come home for two days. It was pure agony. That's when I knew for sure I was yours."

"That's beautiful." Maddy kissed his forehead. "If you ever wonder how we're doing, just kiss me."

"Indeed." And he did.

As the sun came up, flooding the back windows with a soft light, they were naked, lying intertwined on the floor in front of the fire, the embers still smouldering, the blanket barely covering them. Their party clothes were neatly hung over the sofa—a reminder of the special night they had shared.

The Cave

When the phone rang, it was late morning and chilly in the cabin, the sun now hiding behind the clouds and the mist rolling in. George was calling to reconfirm his meeting with Sebastian, and Belle was anxious to have Maddy's suggestions on the wedding. It was refreshing to see how excited Belle and George were to be wed at last. A small affair, intimate and simple, was the theme, but so far the planning was anything but. They agreed to meet for lunch at the cafe in the town as they always did. A dress had been ordered, a venue confirmed, meals finalized, and a guest list agreed upon by the time the couples met. George and Sebastian were looking very solemn; Belle and Maddy were hardly able to sit still. Talk of honeymoon destinations and living arrangements kept them engaged and happy to be in each other's company.

Maddy was surprised when Sebastian suggested they stay another night in the cottage, leaving for London later the next day. George was quick to agree it was a brilliant plan.

They walked along the beach in the mist—Maddy in the old jumper and Sebastian in his hunting coat—hand in hand, laughing and exploring the shoreline.

Back in the cottage, sitting by the fire, chilled and windblown, sipping hot chocolate, listening to the sea, they were happy in the moment when suddenly Sebastian cleared his throat and asked exactly what a truant day would look like. Maddy explained it was a shut-in day; you stayed in your underwear or pyjamas, ate in bed, watched old movies, called for takeout, did not answer the phone or open your email … no shower, just pure sloth for a day. Best medicine ever! He looked sceptical but agreed to try it. "How about tomorrow?" He asked with a smile, pulling Maddy closer. "Let's see how we do."

Sebastian woke from a deep sleep, disoriented in the floating king bed amidst the fluffy white duvet. It was quiet and unfamiliar. Maddy did not answer; he sat up and realized it was late morning. He never overslept. "No more scotch before bed," he mumbled as he stumbled over the covers to the bathroom. Looking in the mirror, he saw a reflection of a man he did not recognize. The unshaven, unkempt image smiled back as he brushed his teeth, remembering the rules of the day—no shaving. He walked over to the coffee pot. Bless her heart, she made coffee every morning but didn't drink it herself. "You never know who will drop in and need a strong cuppa first thing in the morning," she said. The little cottage was different somehow—more comfortable and inviting than he remembered.

Barefoot, he trod over to the outdoor deck and looked out at the water, amazed that the view never failed to make him homesick. He saw motion on the beach and watched two people in knit jumpers frolicking on the shore, stopping to pick shells, crouched down to watch a sea critter scurry back into the water. The two people ran, spoke animatedly, and hugged each other, and then one would run off in chase of a gull or the receding water, in pursuit of the perfect treasure. They walked along the beach, the man with his arm over her shoulders. She leaned into his arm; they looked so very content, so at ease with each other. Sebastian recalled an image of two young boys on the beach with a tall man, running, seeking shells for Belle, learning about tides and caves and fish, and skipping rocks. He and Robert had spent hours on this beach with George—happy times, so long ago. He shook his head to clear the image and wished he was the man on the beach with the flighty woman, enjoying the closeness they alone were sharing. He blinked and realized the man on the beach was George and his flighty partner was Maddy. He laughed out loud, grabbed one of the old wool jumpers off the porch, slipped into his wellies, and ran down the stairs to the sand. They saw him and waved, Maddy running towards him, and George plodding along after her. Sebastian met her on the run and swung her around.

"Good morning, sleepyhead," she whispered in his ear as she kissed his face and neck. Her face felt cold on his neck but oh, so good.

"You taste salty," he laughed. "Good morning, George, any treasures for Belle?"

"Aye, she'll be pleased with our foraging." He held out his hand, the shells sparkling in the sun. "Must be off," he said, and he turned to tousle her hair as he had done so many years ago to Sebastian. "Enchanting as always." He bowed, waved, and walked up the path to the town.

As they sauntered back to the cottage, wrapped in each other's arms, Maddy saw the cave entrance in the rocks. She took his hand and started towards it, looking back at him with a mischievous grin. He followed, knowing exactly where she was heading; he had spent hours here, exploring these caves. When they had climbed to the entrance, she stopped, turned, and tentatively eyed Sebastian. He stopped, gasping for breath; it was not an easy climb at this age.

"What's wrong?" he asked with concern.

Maddy looked pained, biting her lip. Stifling a smile, she said, "There appears to be a dress code in this cave; I think you may have to drop the pyjama pants." Sebastian looked down, mortified at his hasty garb. "I, I …" he sputtered. "I ran out to meet you without thinking …"

Her laughter echoed through the cave and out onto the beach. He saw what pleasure she was deriving from his costume and obvious discomfort; what else could he do but join in the laughter, knowing he was a sight. He stepped up on the ledge, held her face in his hands and kissed her, remembering her claim that "the kiss never lies." She responded with such fierceness that they fell into the cave and made love with the waves in the background and the gulls calling.

Wedding Bells

Belle and George were to be married in a fortnight, and there was much to do. Maddy was busy travelling back and forth to the cottage, arranging last-minute details and ensuring both soon-to-be-newlyweds were comfortable with the menu, venue, guest list, and flowers. The honeymoon was discussed; they decided to visit Belleek Castle, on the Atlantic Coast in Ireland—a suitable destination recommended by Maddy, who had enjoyed the food, the grounds, and the suites on an earlier trip. George and Maddy chose a new ring for Belle, although she preferred the ring George had originally given her when they were teenagers. George had protested, wondering how she could settle on the token ring when his love had grown over the years. Maddy thought they were adorable.

Sebastian was asked to stand as best man by George; Maddy convinced Belle it would be prudent if her oldest friend had the honour of bridesmaid or witness, reminding Belle she would see her group of friends more often than Maddy herself and asking her to imagine the talk that would go on if one's best friend was overlooked. Belle agreed but wanted Sebastian to know her first choice was Maddy. "It was her idea we marry after all, you know," Belle had confided. Sebastian assured Belle she was doing the right thing and made a note to thank Maddy for the unselfish gesture. He knew she had struggled with the decision.

The wedding was tasteful and very elegant—a perfect affair for the occasion. Belle was beautiful in a pale blue sheath dress with matching cape; her fascinator was a light blue flower arrangement with a mesh veil. George looked taller in his tuxedo. They made a fine pair. At one point during the reception, Sebastian saw Maddy standing alone, and as he approached, he realized she had tears running down her cheeks. He stopped to kiss her tears and asked what could possibly be wrong.

"These are tears of happiness. I always cry at weddings."

"I hope you don't cry at ours," he said tenderly as he caught the eye of an older gentleman and stepped away. Maddy's eyes opened wide as she watched him usher the crowd to the dining area.

"Indeed," she muttered, adjusting her pashmina and moving towards the crowd.

The professor had helped Maddy find a group of tenors who serenaded the newlyweds and sang their favourites as they danced and wandered, hand in hand, through the crowd. Maddy and Sebastian had hired the group to entertain as their wedding gift to the couple. Maddy pointed out that the couple had accumulated so much stuff that all they really needed was memorable music.

Everyone agreed it was a lovely wedding, long overdue.

The Event Planner

The ladies of the club enjoyed the presentation on the Indian textile project so much that they now included Maddy in their regular meetings. She was invited to speak about her hospital visits the next week, delighted by the generous offers of tablets and games for the patients. It was at one of these meetings that Betty Haversham mentioned her anxiety over the planning of her Sixty fifth wedding anniversary. Maddy suggested a theme party set in the year of the wedding. She described how all the guests should be invited to wear the dresses they had worn post-war; she had seen a gramophone they could use as a prop, and she knew the perfect DJ. The ladies were hesitant, wondering if they could find suitable dresses; but as the discussion continued, the idea took shape, and at the end of lunch an invitation was designed, the guest list finalized, the food agreed upon, and the theme locked in. Audrey would be an asset in securing fashion history for both men and women attending. Cocktails were arranged, reminiscent of the time. For several weeks, the women spoke of little else.

Sebastian paced the room. "Maddy, are you ready to go? We should go." He looked at his watch for the third time. Maddy came out of the washroom, a cape tightly wrapped around her. She was biting the inside of her cheek—a sign she was nervous or unsure. He wondered what the concern might be.

"What if, after all the planning, the women decide not to come in costume?" she asked.

"What difference would it make?" Sebastian wondered, truly confused.

Maddy tried to explain. "Well, in *Bridget Jones's Diary* they change their minds at the last minute, and she's the only one to arrive in costume—awkward."

"Maddy, I'm sure that's not going to happen. Even the men are talking about their ties. By the way, thanks for getting mine. Where did you get these shoes? Let's go; everything will be fine. Why can't I see what you're wearing? Your nails are done; your hair looks great. Let's see your dress."

Maddy slowly opened the cape and dropped it.

Sebastian gasped. "Leave the cape on," he whispered.

Maddy was confused. "What?"

"If anyone sees you in that dress, I won't get to spend a moment with you all night. Keep the cape on."

Maddy laughed. "Belle insisted I wear this dress."

"I remember the dress very well. Belle had the dress made for a trip to the opera with my grandfather. The designer was young and much in demand after she wore it. I was a young boy at the time, but I thought she looked dynamite. You look spectacular in it."

"Belle said she was called 'fetching' when she wore it … you don't mind that she let me wear it?" she asked cautiously.

"No. All I can say is I did not feel like making love to Belle when she wore it."

"Please call her from the car and tell her you remember the dress; she'll be thrilled."

"Do you have anything on under that dress?" Sebastian asked as they walked to the car.

"A gentleman would not ask," Maddy replied, smiling. She was pleased with his reaction and even more pleased that Audrey had sewn clasps in strategic places so the satin dress hung on her body with no risk of falling opening in the wrong place; it was perfect. Audrey had found beige shoes with a strap, forcing Maddy to wear them for a week so they felt comfortable. Audrey also suggested Maddy not eat or drink while wearing the dress, as it was champagne colour and fit like a glove. "You would see the food going down," she said. Audrey also pointed out that a man's hand would slip downward quite easily on the satin.

Maddy held her breath as they walked into the club. The music, the decor, and the guests mirrored the 50's; it was a picture-perfect party. Betty Haversham saw Maddy and Sebastian at the door and rushed over to thank Maddy for the great idea. She was so pleased with the party that she hugged Maddy and then whispered to Sebastian, "I couldn't be happier;

this is perfect. Isn't she clever?" She was gushing. She turned to Sebastian, grabbed him by the arm, and, with a wink, whispered conspiratorially, "I must say I'm glad Reginald didn't see Maddy before he asked me to marry him. I wouldn't have stood a chance against that dress."

"Happy anniversary, Betty. Reginald is a lucky man." Sebastian said the words, but he was thinking, *I'm a lucky man*. He was holding Maddy's hand, and he wasn't letting go.

The evening went well, with the guests enjoying the videos and drinks, the hosts reliving their youth, the music inviting couples to dance, and the speeches entertaining. As Sebastian finally danced with Maddy, he whispered in her ear, "You feel like butter."

Maddy looked up at him and smiled.

At a table near the dance floor, a group of older women were watching the couple. "Sebastian certainly seems completely besotted with that woman," one said.

Another responded, "Well, she has lit a spark in him, hasn't she?"

They watched as Sebastian whispered in Maddy's ear. She looked delighted and kissed him.

"He never behaved like that when he dated our daughters; he was always so proper."

"He wasn't in love with our daughters."

The women sighed, each of them wishing their husbands looked at them the way Sebastian looked at Maddy.

Sebastian asked if Maddy had had offers to arrange future parties. She nodded and told him she had a plan for the upper level of the coffee house. She could hardly wait to speak with Grace. Sebastian placed a finger on her lips. "Maddy, slow down. You're already well into tomorrow, while I have plans for a very long night."

She laughed and whispered, "I bet your plan is much better. When do we start?"

"Can we go now? I'd rather dance with you at home, where everyone isn't watching and thinking I'm a lecherous old man." Maddy smiled back at him and took his hand. He pulled her back towards him and put his arm around her as they walked towards the coatroom.

"Maddy, I saved you a takeaway box. I know you didn't want to eat with that dress on." Jason, the server, held a box tied with ribbon for her. "I've learned so much from you. Details, details, details. Thank you."

"Oh Jason, you are a gem. I enjoyed working with you, and I know you'll have great success with all the new requests. Let me know if I can help. Thank you, what a sweet gesture." She held up the box. "Good night."

"Good night, Maddy. Sir." He nodded to Sebastian.

As they walked into the garden, Sebastian stopped Maddy and held her face in his hands. "Did I mention how beautiful you look tonight?" Maddy blinked and felt tears welling up.

"Thank you," she said softly.

"Maddy, the evening was perfect." Sebastian moved away, taking her cape with him. He found the music he wanted and came towards Maddy with his arms out. "Dance with me."

They moved together, slow and close, in the dark for several songs before moving into the apartment. Maddy held her arms up, and he pulled the dress carefully over her head. She removed her body suit and unbuttoned his shirt. Soon they were moving together, anxious to satisfy each other. They finally fell asleep in each other's arms, content and exhausted.

Giving from the Heart

Maddy walked through the crowd, drink in hand, the smells of expensive perfume enveloping her, the music competing with the superficial chatter of the group: "Darling, you look wonderful. We must get together for lunch." Air kiss, air kiss. "Doesn't she look ghastly in that colour?" "Is that her third husband?" "Surely she could do better." "Whatever was she thinking, taking her trainer shopping?"

The ballroom was brightly lit with sculptures, artists sketching caricatures, mimes, and magicians. White pillars with cascading vines had been placed throughout the room to create an indoor garden. Large screens around the room showed famous gardens and then panned the crowd. The decor was tasteful, the room filled with small cliques; hors d'oeuvres were passed on silver trays. Satellite bars serving champagne and cocktails were scattered throughout.

Maddy exchanged her empty glass for another flute of champagne, catching more titbits as she wandered: "I had hoped for better drinkies with the cheque Ben writes to the charity … oh well, perseverance is expected." "Will you be spending the holidays in France?" "What do you suppose is in this puff pastry?" "Is there no real food?" "The hair replacements are clearly not taking; should we tell him?" "Are there any seats in this mausoleum?" "Let's decide right now how long we have to suffer through this night." "Don't even try to make a reservation at that new Bistro 21; it's months before you get in, and believe me, the portions are so small …"

The orchestra, dressed in white tuxedos, were playing a combination of classical and pop music. A familiar tune filled the air.

Sebastian was deep in conversation with a group of men across the room. He looked particularly handsome in his tuxedo, and Maddy stopped to watch him. He looked up and raised his eyebrows in acknowledgement. Maddy motioned to the dance floor, smiling broadly. Sebastian looked pained and raised his hand behind the back of the man speaking, indicating he was not able to leave for a moment.

Maddy shrugged and turned away, looking through the crowd and wondering how much longer she could endure the evening. She stood beside a pillar and watched the bubbles in her drink. "Surely you can't be bored in the midst of all this pomp and grandeur?" The voice, a thick Irish brogue, was slightly mocking. Maddy turned to see who was addressing her. No one in the room to this point seemed interested in meeting new faces.

"I'm more amused than bored." She smiled at the curly haired man before her.

"You find me amusing?" He laughed and extended his hand. "Michael Riley at your service." He bowed slightly.

"Madison Davis. I don't have a big bank account or oodles of cash, so you don't have to worry about schmoozing me."

"Hmm, now I really want to know you." He held her gaze.

"Then dance with me." Maddy wondered where that came from.

"Oh dear, I'm not the best dancer, but if it makes the lady smile, how can I refuse?" He finished his pint and held his hand out for Maddy, leading her to the dance floor.

They danced and talked, laughing at their missteps and sharing their stories. Soon the orchestra announced they would take a short break, promising to return for more dancing.

Maddy and Michael walked towards the central bar, his hand resting lightly on her shoulder. Sebastian watched them cross the room and headed towards them.

"How will I ever redeem myself for leaving you alone all evening?" he asked Maddy, leaning to kiss her neck.

Maddy turned and had just started to introduce Michael when she noticed the two men were smiling at each other.

"Mick O'Riley, you old poser. How are you?" Sebastian extended his hand.

"Sebastian Walker, you rascal. I might have known you would be here with the freshest, most interesting woman. Life treating you well?" Michael, or Mick, seemed genuinely pleased.

Sebastian turned to Maddy. "Mick and I were at school together. He was a financial wizard then; it's no surprise he's so successful now."

Michael laughed. "Sebastian was the star athlete, excelling at games and academics. We didn't move in the same circles, but we knew each other. He was a rule follower; I was a rogue." Both men seemed anxious to fill Maddy in on their past.

Suddenly the camaraderie faded. Michael stood taller and straightened his jacket. "Here's the Dragon Lady; I'm sure she has something in mind for me."

"Ah, Francis, my dear wife, come and meet Madison, and of course you know Sebastian." He bowed and with a flourish and turned to his friends.

"Francesca Bennett." The tall, slim woman with a cascade of thick, dark hair barely looked at Maddy. "Sebastian, I hope you've written a handsome cheque." She turned, her red lips in a tight line. "Michael, where have you been? I've searched the room for you. Why can't I ever count on you to perform? Ah, there's Crystal Jennings. Go. Make yourself useful." Francesca Bennett moved away without a second glance.

"Madison, it was delightful. I look forward to meeting you again. Thank you." Michael kissed her hand and bowed. "Don't worry about the Dragon Lady; she doesn't like men much."

"I don't think she liked me much either. Are you okay?" Maddy whispered, looking concerned.

"Don't you give it a thought. I'm Irish; we're meant to be resilient." He winked and turned away.

"Sebastian, we really should catch up over a pint." The men shook hands, and a distracted Michael walked away.

Sebastian wrapped his arm around Maddy. "Interesting evening. It was not my intention to abandon you, but I did see you dancing. Quite a coup to get Mick on the dance floor. I'm sure people are talking."

"Sebastian." Maddy looked thoughtful. "I wish … no I can't ask that of you …"

"What's wrong, Maddy? Are you all right?" Sebastian looked over, noting her pained expression.

"It's none of my business, and you can say so."

"Go on," Sebastian encouraged her.

"I know this is a fundraiser. Everyone here can well afford to buy their own drinks, and the object of the evening is to collect cheques, but the director earns a huge salary. I asked Michael—or Mick, whatever his name is. Francis—or Francesca, as she calls herself—is rude and treats people horribly. She expects you all to drop big cheques, but she doesn't contribute to the charity herself. Her address this evening was more about scolding the audience, not about how the money will change lives or make a difference. I hope you will reconsider leaving a cheque tonight. I'll give you a list of charities, managed by passionate volunteers, who need your money to make real change. I probably sound crazy and presumptuous, but if you give to charity, it should be with your heart, not your chequebook. There's no passion in this room." Maddy was pleading with Sebastian. She watched his face for a moment as he processed her words.

"Very well, no cheque tonight. Let's go home. I am so hungry I could even eat a pizza. Shall we?" Sebastian kissed the top of her head, placed his hand on her back, and started to move through the thinning crowd.

Maddy blinked. "Really?"

"Really. Shall we go?"

As they moved away, she looked up at Sebastian, touched by his response. She flung her arms around his neck and hugged him. "Thank you."

Sebastian, caught off guard, wrapped her in his arms, enjoying holding her, wondering why he felt so connected to her and her passion for everything. Maddy looked up at him, her eyes sparkling in the light. He wanted to make her happy, he wanted to take her home, and he wanted to be alone with her. Why hadn't he ever considered what she had pointed out—that tonight a donation was expected but not appreciated?

Michael Riley watched the pair make their way across the ballroom, his expression wistful as he saw them embrace. Damn, they looked so happy. He turned and motioned for another pint. He was the one with the wealth and power, yet here he was, alone at the bar, destined to live a loveless life with Francis while dull and boring Sebastian Walker was going home, and most likely to bed, with a lovely and amusing prize. *Where's the luck of the Irish in that?* He wondered.

December

"The very capable Lambert tells me you were recruited to plan the office Christmas party this year."

"Oh Sebastian, we were talking about how people were out of control at the office party, so I suggested an alternate, and he loved the idea … Are you okay with that? I'm sorry I didn't think to ask you first. We tried to make it early in the season so it doesn't interfere with any religious celebrations. Please tell me you don't mind," she pleaded.

"Maddy, everyone despises planning the annual 'drink yourself silly' party, so if you have an idea on how to improve the event, I'm sure Lambert was ecstatic. Don't tell me; it will be a surprise for me too. By the way, my friend Philippe is coming to town. He's doing a promotion for his wines and has asked us to attend. He's anxious to meet you, and I would like you to know him. Is that all right with you?" He looked over at Maddy.

"Indeed." She laughed as she walked away.

In preparing for the holiday event, Maddy had asked for the breakdown of single vs married employees, the number of children in each family, and where they lived. She mapped out the staff addresses and found a West End hotel with a suitable ballroom for a family party; it was close to the Tube station but also had ample parking. The room had a large dining area with a buffet, enough space for a children's play zone, and a separate reception.

Everyone was invited to a Sunday luncheon in early December. Wine and beer were offered at the reception, toys were wrapped for the younger children and presented by a jolly Santa, and the children were encouraged to share and play with their new-found friends. The animal show was fun and kept the crowd engaged. The finale required the entire management team to hold the large python, creating photo ops and teasing. The corner photo booth was a hit as families and departments posed for photos with hats and feather boas. Henry was a great help with the younger children; he was patient and demonstrated the gift scooter many times over. He was also vigilant of Maddy, ensuring she was never alone. They gave each other nods and winks of encouragement throughout the afternoon.

Sebastian was amazed that each employee shook his hand and thanked him for a wonderful party. "Best party ever!" they exclaimed throughout the day.

"Mr Walker, your new philosophy is wonderful; my husband seems to work less, but he tells me he is more productive, and he gets to see the children. Thank you." One of the wives shook his hand vigorously.

He watched Maddy mingle with the employees, spouses, and children; she was so natural, and to a person they responded to her with hugs, requests for selfies, and hand-holding appreciation. Lambert, the ultimate fusser, was beside himself. He could not contain his delight with the success of the party and kept swooning, hugging himself and twirling to catch the action in all corners of the room.

Grace and Davi attended the party and assured their hosts it was a great success. They were planning to marry in the next year and wondered if Maddy would agree to help plan their wedding. "Try stopping me," she happily agreed. She had already started researching how to merge Hindi and Caribbean into a great celebration.

Home at last, Sebastian was suddenly struck by how festive the little garden patio looked with white lights on the trees. He expected to see skaters with hand warmers glide by him. "This is lovely," he commented. He had often wondered why they gravitated to the private garden and small apartment rather than the main house, but as he looked around, he understood; this was her home. She had made it her own. It was comfortable with glitter, alive with colour, and inviting. The main house was larger but cold in comparison. How silly that they had not moved into the house but rather stayed here. The construction had begun in the upper level, and Sebastian was impatient for the project to be completed so they could share the entire space.

"A penny for your thoughts?" She snuggled up to him on the sofa, kicking off her shoes.

"Hmm. I was just wondering how lucky a person like me would have to be to find someone like you." He kissed the top of her head.

"Today was brilliant. Thank you." He was still in awe of how Maddy had turned the day into such a success.

"I love you," he whispered, but she was fast asleep in his arms.

Let It Snow

Maddy seemed to be the only person in London enjoying the big snowflakes falling from the sky. She was walking to the pub to meet Sebastian and Christian before the theatre, unaware the city was crippled by the unexpected snowfall, with horns blaring, cars sliding, and pedestrians not dressed properly for the weather walking cautiously on the snowy sidewalks. She was embracing the snow after so much rain. Her red beret was covered in snow, her scarf wrapped around her neck several times. Her long jumper and high boots made her look like a catalogue model in a winter wear advertisement.

"Where's Maddy?" Christian asked as he joined Sebastian at the bar.

"She's on her way. Impossible to get a cab, so she's walking over." The two men shook hands and ordered drinks. They had agreed to meet here before heading to an opening night performance.

"Maddy certainly manages to stay busy, doesn't she?" Christian remarked.

"Indeed. There's always a cause—an opportunity to volunteer or help someone out," Sebastian found himself saying with pride.

"I've given her several projects, you know, and I feel bad. I should be providing her with some compensation other than theatre tickets and dinners. She mentioned she missed working. Ah, here she is." Christian waved and laughed as he saw Maddy at the door, covered in snow. "I envy you, Sebastian. We are surrounded by tall, leggy beauties of all ages who try so hard to catch our eye, and yet when Maddy walks into the room, everyone wants to know her. And the shame of it is she wants only you. I would give her anything."

"She doesn't want anything," Sebastian whispered, watching her make her way through the crowd.

Her cheeks were flushed from the cold. As she looked around, catching her breath, a man approached her, inviting her to the table with him and his mates. She smiled and thanked him, letting him know she was meeting friends. She waved back at Christian and started making her way through the crowd towards the upper bar.

"Maddy, is that you?" a voice from the past called out. "Maddy, it's me—Richard. What are you doing here?" Richard worked for a large Canadian advertising firm with offices around the world. Over the years Maddy had worked with him and his team on promotional initiatives. He was familiar with her business and her personal life.

"Richard, so nice to see you. I'm afraid I'm late meeting my friends before the theatre." She pointed towards the bar. "Are you in London for a few days?"

"Maddy, you look wonderful. Are you here alone? What are you doing?" he asked, clearly delighted to see her.

"I ran away from home. I needed a year to think about retirement, and I'm enjoying it so far. I manage to stay busy doing good works and travelling around."

"I need someone on the ground here; are you available to do some promotional work for us? It would be great if you were. Can we get together for lunch? Here's my card." Richard was talking fast, trying to piece together why Maddy was here alone.

She took the card, air-kissed his cheek and promised to be in touch, glancing over at the bar, anxious to move away. Richard looked over at the bar, realizing she was uncomfortable. "Please call me; I'd love to sit with you and hear about your year." He tried to sound jolly.

"I will. Cheers. Richard, it's great to see you. You look well." She waved and walked away.

Christian greeted Maddy with a kiss to both cheeks. "Ah, here you are. You look lovely. I'll get you a drink. The same?" He raised his empty glass to Sebastian.

Sebastian unwound her scarf, brushed snow from her beret, and looked at her longingly before holding her face in his hands and kissing her. "Worth the wait," he whispered in her ear. Her smile was enough to melt any thoughts of snow. She was thinking how sexy he looked while slowly removing her scarf, but the words came out: "You are so getting lucky tonight, mister."

Christian returned with the drinks. "Here we go."

"I just met an old business acquaintance. Canada House is nearby; I'd forgotten this is where the guys hang out. Funny seeing someone from another life …" Maddy shook her head and raised her glass, feeling very much at home with her companions.

The trio finished their drinks, donned their cold-weather gear, and headed for the door. Maddy stopped to introduce Sebastian and Christian to Richard, who was pleased to mention how much he missed working with Maddy.

The production was well-received, and they continued to laugh and tease each other as they enjoyed a light meal afterwards. The snow had stopped, the traffic had slowed, and the streets were slushy with melting snow. "I'll walk; I'm not far from here," Christian announced as he said goodnight.

"Let's catch the Tube and walk from there," Maddy suggested, hoping to be out in the snow longer. "Will your chi-chi shoes handle the snow?" she teased. Sebastian just shrugged, not wanting the evening to end.

As they walked the last few blocks home, Sebastian stopped and turned to Maddy.

She looked up at him, smiling brightly. "Maddy, are you concerned about money? Do you have enough? There's a credit card in the apartment for your expenses; are you using it?" He sounded very serious.

"I'm fine. I have a great underground economy where I do things for people in exchange for other things. It seems to work well. Why? Why are you asking me?"

"Maddy, I want to take care of you; I don't ever want you to be concerned or worried about having enough money, or about getting the things you want or need." He was shaking her shoulders.

"I have a lovely place to live; I don't need anything more … You have been so very generous. I'm fine. Really, I am. I've been concerned about having enough to live on all my life, but here I'm fine. Really. Why are you asking me?" She was aware of his hands on her shoulders.

"We have a driver, and you don't make use of him; you have a credit card for expenses, yet you don't use it. I don't understand why. You earned that apartment; your advice on the building sales netted a handsome profit. It's only right I share that with you. I don't ever want you to worry about money. This isn't your old life; don't bring the old worries with you."

Maddy felt as though she had been slapped. Sebastian felt her recoil and immediately regretted having brought up her old life. He had spent the evening wondering about her need for money, how friendly Richard had been, how time was slipping away, how he hadn't been aware enough of her situation—not working, not earning.

"Maddy, I'm sorry; that was unnecessary. I was out of line. Please, look at me. My life is rich because of you. I just want you to be comfortable in every way. I want to take care of you. Please look at me."

He hadn't meant to hurt her; the tears streaming down her face made him miserable. When she looked up, he brushed the tears away from her cheek.

"I'm sorry," he whispered. He kissed her and was relieved when she responded.

"Just call foul if I ever hurt you by saying the wrong thing or not doing what you expect." Sebastian looked like a schoolboy.

"I don't know why I'm crying. I've always worked and had enough money to do what I want. It's great to work with a budget on renovations and projects but not so great when it's personal and it's only going one way—down. I am comfortable, and I'm doing okay. I've lived on less and struggled through it; I'm okay." She sniffed and brushed her hand across her face. "Let's get home and see how beautiful the garden looks with the snow."

The garden did look magical with the lights sparkling under the snow-covered branches.

That night in bed, Sebastian told Maddy more of his story. Christmas holiday meant all the students vacated the boarding school and a cleaning company arrived to do a thorough sweep of the school. Sebastian and Philippe were the last to be picked up, as they were spending the holidays at the beach with Belle. George called to say Belle had been in a minor mishap on the snowy knoll and he would be there as soon as the roads were reopened. Belle was not hurt, just shaken.

The headmaster invited the boys to dinner that evening. His wife reported the cleaning company had cancelled because of the weather; they would not risk the roads. Philippe suggested he and Sebastian could take the job, as they had to wait anyway. They agreed on a company name—Two Lads Cleaning, or TLC Ltd, and began washing floors, scrubbing toilets and shower rooms, washing walls, stripping beds, laundering sheets and making beds, and scrubbing the kitchen and dining hall. George arrived two days later and assisted with the beds and larger rooms. They slept soundly after their labours. The headmaster was so impressed that he paid the contract rate for the work. George set up their company to accept payment, and they were thrilled with the hefty bank account.

The headmaster suggested they might want to clean out the garage, which housed years of neglected equipment and old vehicles. They found a Triumph motorbike under the tarps, rusting bicycles, and the shell of an old car. George was as excited as the boys and they spent the next two days cleaning and repairing the motorbike. George made a list of parts they would need for the car, and they headed home, just in time for Christmas dinner. Belle wondered why the boys slept through most of the holidays, spending whatever time they were up with George in the garage, taking apart an old car.

The headmaster would never speak of the matter, as the trustees would be apoplectic if they knew they had paid students to do the job. The boys never spoke of it, as they knew their mates would only tease them.

The garage became their study hall. They invited Edwin—the least popular, most brilliant student—to tutor them in the evenings as they worked on the car and motorbike. One evening, a group of boys, including Henry's grandfather and Mick O'Riley, came into the garage after dark, armed with cricket bats. They surrounded the car and threatened to break the windows and destroy the car. The headmaster appeared just as the first bang sounded. He announced that Sebastian, Philippe, and Edwin were repairing the car to work off their detention. He suggested a less desirable detention for the others, sentencing the bullies to cleaning the pot sinks and shower rooms for the rest of term.

TLC was able to retain the holiday cleaning contracts for two more years. George would appear after the boarders had gone and the team took over. They added chopping firewood to their skill set and were delighted to see their account grow. Both boys agreed it was better than running to stay in shape. The headmaster was delighted to have the ancient motorbike and old car out of the garage.

At Oxford, Sebastian and Philippe roomed together and parked their treasures, a Triumph motorbike and the remodelled red car in the yard, under their window. They had little time for outside work but found several elderly clients in the town who needed wood piled, coal bins filled, and odd jobs done. A hearty meal usually accompanied the payment exchange.

Sebastian was complimentary of George and his efforts to help the boys. He continued to assist them by making them invest their earnings in land and buildings. He was their partner, offering to research and fund a third of the chosen projects. The partnership resulted in both men graduating without debt, owning property, and having a clear sense of earning potential and the rewards of hard work. George ensured Belle was comfortable, relieving Sebastian of her care.

Maddy was sure most of the club members would not know how hard Sebastian had worked to earn his present status. Sebastian was sitting up against the pillows as he spoke, Maddy lying across his abdomen. She sat up, held his face, and kissed him tenderly. Sebastian pulled her close and kissed the top of her head. "What was that for?" he whispered.

"For sharing your story with me. Now I know why Belle is so proud of you. I am too. You're my hero."

Sebastian smiled and closed his eyes. He had not told anyone that story and wondered if Philippe had ever shared it with anyone. He wondered if Claire and Manon would have married them if they had known. He slid down into the bed, holding Maddy against him. She was the right person to share with, he felt lighter somehow. She snuggled her head into his chest, and he drifted off to sleep, dreaming of the way she looked coming in out of the snow.

The Friendship Test

After the wine tasting, Philippe invited Maddy and Sebastian to his hotel for a late dinner. Maddy enjoyed watching the two men as they laughed easily. Philippe was charming and very solicitous—eager to welcome her. It was clear to anyone they were best friends, although they didn't see each other as often as they had once.

By the time the main course had been cleared, the party of three appeared to be long-time acquaintances celebrating a reunion.

When Maddy excused herself, feeling the men needed time alone, Philippe congratulated Sebastian on his luck.

"She's lovely, Sebastian. She has a certain *je ne sais quoi t*hat could be dangerous."

"She is dangerous," Sebastian laughed. The old schoolmates raised their glasses in a toast.

The men stood as Maddy returned to the table, smiling at each other.

Maddy caught their smiles and felt she had passed the friendship test. Her cheeks burned as Sebastian put his arm around her shoulders and kissed her forehead. It was meant to reassure her, and Maddy was surprised at how wonderful that gesture made her feel.

The Past Returns

The two women crossed the road, dodging traffic, laughing as they zigzagged between the vehicles. They reached the restaurant door with flushed faces. Richard had invited Maddy to lunch, as promised. Maddy had suggested Audrey would be an asset for the upcoming social media campaign; her contacts in the media would be helpful.

As they approached the table, Richard stood and greeted them. Introductions and qualifications determined, they sat and ordered drinks. Richard touched Maddy's elbow and announced he had a surprise for her. Maddy took a deep breath and tensed as a tall, blonde Viking with a ruddy complexion, trimmed beard, and penetrating hazel eyes appeared before them. Audrey watched as the man slowly walked towards them, determined eyes on Maddy, his demeanour telegraphing his confidence and a sense of ownership.

"Maddy, you look good. Enough of this foolishness. It's time to come home." His voice was firm, as though he was used to giving orders.

"Dag, I don't know what you're doing here, but I do know this isn't the time to be discussing my plans." Maddy was speaking through clenched teeth.

Audrey watched the pair, wondering if Maddy knew anyone who was short and ugly. She was waiting to be introduced.

"Hello, beautiful. I'm Dag Andreson, Maddy's partner. I'm sure she's told you all about me." Audrey felt a chill as he shook her hand. The man certainly had a commanding presence. She realized she was holding her breath, waiting to hear what was going on. She looked over at Maddy, who was now standing and gathering her gloves and hat.

"I'm sorry; I have to go. Richard, there's nothing I can do for you. I'm sorry, Audrey; this was a mistake."

Maddy turned to go, and the scene played out in slow motion. Richard stood, a shocked look on his face, wringing his hands at the surprise gone bad. Dag reached for Maddy, stopping her from leaving the table. Audrey clasped her hands in front of her face, afraid to move. Maddy flinched and walked towards the door. Audrey felt paralyzed.

Dag led Maddy out to the foyer and began speaking, not releasing his grip on her arm. Audrey could only watch as her friend Maddy struggled to free herself from his grip, forced to hear what this man was saying. Audrey looked over at Richard, who was now miserable that his plan had backfired. "I really thought Maddy would want to see him. I guess she was here alone for a reason. What have I done?" He shook his head.

Audrey forced herself to walk towards her friend. She could hear Dag suggesting Maddy should forgive and forget, grow up, and come home with him the next day. He needed her to return and take care of things. He agreed to let her think about it and finally let go of her arm when she promised she would contact him once she'd had an opportunity to consider her options. He persisted, asking her to join him for dinner that evening at their usual hotel.

Maddy shrugged. "Please, Dag, let me go. I'm feeling good about myself. I need time to be alone. Go home. I can't see you at your hotel; we both know that's not the right thing to do. Please let me go." She accepted Audrey's outstretched hand and turned to leave.

"Maddy, it was good for a long time; why throw that away? You're not batting for the other team, are you?" His laugh was cruel; Audrey shuddered. "Think about the comfortable, charmed life you've left behind. Think about the business and all the loose ends you left. Once you've had a moment to think about it, I'm sure you'll decide to come for dinner tonight, stay over, and fly back with me tomorrow. It's the best solution. I've left you alone for long enough - you think you've been clever but I've known where you were hiding out. Your friends miss you; everyone asks for you … Even I miss you. You're nothing but an amusement to these people. You're not one of them; you don't belong here, drinking tea with people who have fake accents. You belong with me. Just get real. You need to come home. Come home for Christmas. Be a good girl and come home. You know where I'm staying. Come to the hotel and stop this silliness." Dag continued to speak in a soothing voice as the women left the restaurant.

The door closed on the sound of his cruel laughter. "Don't make me wait too long …"

Outside, Maddy leaned against the building and closed her eyes, fighting back tears.

"I'm sorry you had to see that … what a performance." Maddy looked defeated.

"Maddy, what was that about? He made me feel uneasy. Are you all right? Let's go and sit somewhere. I need a drink. You?" Audrey looked concerned and flustered.

Maddy smiled. "Let's get you a drink. You deserve it."

In the Pub, Maddy gave Audrey a brief history of her life with Dag. He looked the part of a Viking explorer and had capitalized on that personality by building a wilderness adventure company. He travelled the world with film crews and admirers, documenting his escapades and taking wealthy executives on soft adventure trips. His family ran a wilderness training camp near Toronto. He had swept Maddy off her feet at a conference in Rio de Janeiro, kidnapping her from her own job to accompany him on a three-month South American tour and then a month-long stay in Costa Rica. They returned home and started working together to build the business. Maddy had no home to return to, so she stayed. They worked and travelled together for twenty years, never marrying; his logic was that he already had a family and was not interested in having more children. Dag was used to being in control; he had never been interested in sex or physical contact. Their relationship was based on their work partnership and their love of adventure. Maddy believed his claims that she was the problem in bed. Despite the fact they fought about money, family, and who was right about everything, they had built a successful business. Maddy had turned Dag into a commodity. She planned and took care of all arrangements; Dag wasn't much good at details. Maddy wasn't sure when he started to believe the hype, but he was still invited to speak about his daring and risky adventures. She had such a full life with friends, volunteering, travel, and work projects that she never thought she was unhappy. Returning home early from a conference, she had witnessed something—she wouldn't say what—that made her flee. The graduation in England provided an excuse to leave. She had purchased a ticket and boarded a plane without a plan, running away rather than facing the situation. She had not wanted Dag to find her, and she had been very careful with her friends, not disclosing her whereabouts.

"Surely you aren't thinking about leaving with him, are you?" Audrey asked cautiously.

Maddy shrugged, fighting the tears tracking on her cheeks. "Maybe he's right. Maybe what we had is reality and this … this is just a fantasy. Maybe I'm kidding myself that this, all of this, has any future." She looked so forlorn that Audrey hugged her, surprised at the emotion she felt for Maddy.

"You love Sebastian. I know it; I can see it. You don't love this man. Maddy, consider what you have and what you would be giving up if you left now." Audrey wanted to shake her.

"Oh Audrey, when we're young we're in love with the idea of being in love; then one day we realize the person we were trying to love with all our heart isn't so great and doesn't love us as much or in the same way. Maybe I'm just in love with the idea of being in love again. I was once, a long time ago."

Maddy looked away, shrugging.

"That's ridiculous. I've seen you and Sebastian together; there's no mistaking your feelings for each other. Really, Maddy, come on; think this through."

"Oh gosh, Audrey, you have to go." Maddy wiped her eyes and pointed to the clock tower. "You have an appointment, and Lord knows it's not to be missed." She tried to laugh.

Audrey rolled her eyes. "It's just a hair appointment. Come with me. We'll get matching bobs—my treat. I don't want to leave you alone."

"I'll be fine, Audrey. You go. Shall we take the underground over?"

"Ew, I do not take the underground, thank you very much," Audrey responded haughtily. "Where are you going? You shouldn't be alone. Please, please don't call him. You can't see him alone. I'm afraid he would bully you into something you don't want. You can't go. What would I do without you? Please Maddy, promise me you won't call him. Come with me."

Maddy sniffed and looked at her friend. "I'm going to walk for a little while. I need to think. I'll call you later, when I get back to the apartment.

Don't worry about me. Go, go; if you're late, you'll only get half the colour done … go." Maddy laughed as Audrey hesitated, anxious to make her appointment yet reluctant to leave her friend. It would be weeks if she had to reschedule.

The minute the cab turned the corner, Audrey dialled Lambert. "Where's Sebastian? I need to talk to him right now." No small talk, no greeting, just an urgent appeal.

Lambert, unable to pry information from Audrey, obediently interrupted Sebastian in a team planning meeting, suggesting he take the call in his office.

Audrey was unsure of what she would say until she heard Sebastian on the line.

"Do you care at all about Maddy?" she asked. There was a pause as Sebastian collected his thoughts. He sat down at the desk and stared at the phone.

"Of course I do. What's happened? Is Maddy all right? Has there been an accident? Audrey, why are you calling me?" His voice was getting louder with concern.

"Maddy's past caught up with her today, and if you want her to stay, you'd better cancel dinner at your stodgy club and get to her. Trust me; she needs to know this isn't just a lark. This larger-than-life Viking guy arrived wanting to take her home. Do you understand what I'm saying? Sebastian, I can't tell you how sad it would be for her to return now—return to the life she had."

What exactly would you have me do?" Sebastian was looking out the window, noticing for the first time today that the city was bathed in sunshine, wondering what the view would be like without Maddy in his life.

"Are you seriously asking me what you can do? Get your sorry ass home and take her away, anywhere. Go to a film, go to dinner, go to Amsterdam; you can afford it. Just find her and be a part of her decision. I, unfortunately, do have to go now; I'm late for an appointment. I feel ill. I left her alone, and I don't want her to see this man and go back. Please, Sebastian, if you have any feelings for Maddy, find her and be with her, especially tonight." The line went dead. Sebastian sat in a trance, the receiver still in his hand, images of Maddy bursting through his mind.

"Ahem." Lambert cleared his throat to break the reverie. "Anything I can do to help?" he asked, concerned.

Sebastian realized his assistant was very fond of Maddy; they had formed a tight friendship. He often heard Lambert on the phone laughing with Maddy. Lambert would also miss her if she was gone. So would Grace and Davi. Belle and George would be devastated, and what about the professor? *He would know exactly what to do right now.* Sebastian looked up at the anxious Lambert, his voice firm. "You can find Maddy."

"Where are you?" Lambert was whispering into the phone.

"Let me check." He heard her speaking to someone.

"Excuse me, exactly where am I?"

The voice responded, "Oh Lovey, you're at St James Park, near the duck pond."

"Thank you. Just wanted to be sure. Have a nice day."

"Lambert, I'm in St James Park. Oh, I see the duck pond. Why?"

"Sebastian has been looking for you. You know how these amazing tickets for the hottest shows suddenly become available and how you just have to drop everything so you can go?" Lambert was chatty.

"It's Wednesday; Sebastian has dinner at the club, not to be missed ..." Maddy sounded distracted.

"Maddy, sweetheart, I'm leaving the office now; shall we collect you at the park on our way?" It was Sebastian's voice. He had joined the conversation.

"No thanks. I'll be back at the house soon. I have to deal with something right now. Bye."

Sebastian paced back and forth across the office, wishing she had agreed to ride home with him. What if she was meeting with her past lover or partner or whatever he was and she didn't return home to the garden apartment. He called for the car and hoped Maddy would be waiting in the garden when he arrived.

"Davi, swing by St James Park; let's see if Maddy is by the duck pond." Sebastian found himself playing out various scenarios, with Audrey's warning looming, and suddenly the park was in view and there she was, on a bench, engaged in conversation with an elderly man in a wheelchair. Before he could think of his next move or the best move, he was out of the car, striding towards the bench. Maddy turned, following her companion's gaze, and saw Sebastian, looking anxious, standing behind her.

"Hello Sebastian. Meet Captain Deaks, historian; he has been mesmerizing me with his recollections of the bombing of London and how the city has risen out of the rubble." Maddy stood and brought Sebastian closer. "Captain Deaks, Sebastian Walker. Sebastian is involved with Cityscapes and the redesigning of public areas in large cities. You may have heard of the project. The commission is receiving recognition worldwide." Sebastian blushed at the pride in Maddy's voice.

"Nice to meet you, Sebastian. Maddy Blue-Eyes has been indulging me for long enough. It looks as though you need to be somewhere else, my dear." He smiled at Maddy and gathered his wraps around his legs.

Maddy leaned over and kissed Captain Deaks on the cheek. "Thank you. It was a most enjoyable visit."

"Does he make you happy?" Captain Deaks whispered.

Maddy smiled, nodded, and looked over at Sebastian. "Yes. Yes, he does."

"Well, hold on to that, my Maddy Blue-Eyes. That's really all there is in the end. I must go before my daughter sends out a search party. I'm here most days after lunch. I hope we'll meet again."

Captain Deaks started to roll away, waving at Maddy. He stopped and turned to Sebastian. "Good thing for you I'm in this chair, or I'd give you a run for your money." He winked at Maddy.

"I'm not sure I'd win," Sebastian responded with a laugh. The captain chuckled and carried on down the path.

Sebastian put his arm around Maddy, pulling her close. "I didn't mean to interrupt. Are you ready to come home?"

"It was a fascinating afternoon. I have one more errand to do. I'll take the underground and see you later." Maddy moved away.

"Maddy." She turned back to Sebastian, surprised by the catch in his voice. "Am I losing you?" He hesitated, his eyes taking in the traffic and the movement in the park. "Are we losing you?"

Maddy ran into his arms, burrowing her head in his chest.

Sebastian wrapped his arms around her and kissed the top of her head. Maddy looked up, and their lips met in a long, slow kiss. Maddy gasped and stepped back. She licked her lips, realizing she was more than an amusement; she was connected to this man and this place. She was flushed from the kiss. She had always believed the kiss never lies. Looking up at Sebastian, she knew he felt the same way, and yet he still looked anxious.

"See you at home soon?" he whispered, not sure if that was a question or wishful thinking.

Maddy nodded and turned, walking briskly before her legs buckled from that lingering kiss.

"Are you sure we can't drop you? He called after her hopefully as she walked away.

Maddy waved and forced herself to keep walking, aware that she might fall into his arms if she turned around now.

Sebastian watched her walk away, hoping she was convinced she should stay. He settled into the car, aware that Davi was just as worried. He willed himself to read an article in the latest design magazine and wait for her.

Maddy found herself tumbling through a whirlwind of emotions. She was angry Dag had found her and made her feel exactly as only he could. He was used to being in control and getting what he wanted; he was overpowering and bullish. Maddy shrugged; that was who he was, and he hadn't changed since they first met. She remembered how he had made the city tour bus wait for her when she arrived in Rio; how he had come for her across the beach when she was working with another group at the conference; how he had laughed at her trivial job, scoffing at the need for finding film locations when computers were breaking new ground at the time; how he had called her boss at the agency and quit her job for her because he wanted her to join his Patagonia team; and how he included her in every wilderness trip he was invited to attend. He liked owning her, not necessarily loving her.

She was elated Sebastian had come for her—how could anyone not feel committed after a kiss like that. She replayed Dag's words over and over and felt sad for him. She smiled at how solicitous both Lambert and Sebastian had been, trying to protect her. She guessed Audrey had told them what had happened, and she felt a wave of love for her friend. She decided not to call Dag, not to continue a roundabout discussion with him, not to return with him. She had a few more months of freedom— enough time to choose where she would go and what she would do with her life. Better not to think about whether she was a good enough person to forgive and forget.

As she turned into the driveway, waving at Esme walking the dog, catching the setting sun bouncing off the ivy on the building and over the garden, hearing Mrs B humming with the radio, she breathed in the aroma of a fresh baked pie, and then suddenly there in front of her were Sebastian and Davi, looking anxious, waiting for her to come home. She blinked as she saw Audrey, Grace, Lambert, and the professor on the patio. Her friends had gathered for her. She was home.

Later that evening, after a relaxed dinner with friends, Maddy and Sebastian were comfortably lying on the sofa, in each other's arms, both lost in thought.

"Do you want to talk about what happened today?" Sebastian asked tenderly.

Maddy turned to look into his eyes. "Not really, but I guess I should. If I don't, I'll just keep thinking about it. Thank you for having everyone here for dinner. It was lovely. I felt surrounded by friends. It was so reaffirming—unexpected and wonderful. You know, I was very angry this afternoon; imagine someone surprising you or blindsiding you by inviting your past into your life. But then I realized I do the same thing; I think I'm doing a fine gesture by surprising someone, but maybe it's just meddling. I can learn from this. I'm sure you're silently agreeing." Maddy smiled.

"That's a healthy approach. I know your heart is in the right place and you only want to please, but you might also create some issues for others at times." Sebastian was careful responding, not wanting to break her spirit. "You're a good person, Maddy."

"That's just it. I'm not. Audrey thought Dag was awful, but that's who he is, and most people like his direct approach. He can be intimidating, but today he was self-righteous, and I had to admit I did think he was right about some things. Maybe I am being silly thinking this is real. It's more of a fantasy or a dream—a great dream, but still a dream. Maybe it's payback for not being a good person." Sebastian remained silent, encouraging Maddy to continue. "You know I once killed a baby raccoon just because he was in the henhouse. I didn't even know if a baby raccoon would eat or hurt a chicken, but I killed it. I cried for days, wondering which one of us was more dangerous." Maddy wiped her eyes with the back of her hand. She looked up at Sebastian, expecting him to nod in agreement, but he sat quietly watching her, waiting for more.

"Anyway, it's in the past. I know I gave my poor mother a run for her money. My dad and I were so close she must have felt left out at times. She never said, but I remember the looks she gave me when my dad disagreed with her chosen disciplinary action or how he laughed when I defended myself against her admonishments." Maddy took a deep breath. "I may have done something rash—something I hoped would please you, something I hoped you'd love, but now I'm not so sure." Maddy climbed over him and stood beside the sofa. "Come with me. I might as well get all the surprises out of the way in one day." She waited for him to take her hand. Sebastian was confused, but he took her hand and followed her out of the apartment.

"You'll need your shoes and an open mind," Maddy offered, slipping into her flip-flops.

She led him to the garage door and turned to face him. "Just remember I did this because I care for you and I wanted to make you feel good, especially after I heard your story." Maddy opened the wooden garage door and walked towards a large covered item. Sebastian followed, not sure what to expect.

Maddy flung the cover off, and before them was a highly polished motorcycle—*his* beloved motorcycle—looking as new and shiny as he had imagined it should look when he first found it.

"Merry Christmas—a little early." Maddy sighed as she added the licence sticker she had purchased earlier in the day to the windscreen.

Sebastian was speechless. He walked around the shiny Triumph 3T 350 bike, lovingly touching fenders, handlebars, the large headlight, and the leather seat. He looked up at Maddy, awestruck. Maddy was watching him, hands clasped under her chin, her eyes wide, biting her lip, holding her breath, awaiting his reaction.

"It's running fine. Go ahead and start it. Clifford wanted it to be perfect before you saw it. Are you angry with me? Did you want to leave it the way it was? I couldn't imagine this beautiful bike sitting here, uncared for … please say something." Maddy pleaded.

Sebastian slowly made a tour of the bike, his hand never leaving it. He approached Maddy, a serious look on his face, and met her eyes, contemplating what to say, how to say it, and how to express his absolute love for the gesture and for her.

"How did you do this?" He wanted to know how she could possibly have recreated the vintage motorcycle on her own. He had thought about it for years, but the time commitment and the thought of paying someone else to bring it back to its former glory had always made him put it off. Maddy had done the impossible in just a few months. "How did you find parts and someone with the mechanical ability to work on it?" He couldn't stop staring at the motorbike, which was bathed in the light of a single hanging lantern.

"Clifford has a Triumph, and when I told him what you had, he wanted to see it. He drove me home and literally cried when he saw it in the back of the garage. Before I could ask you if you wanted it restored and running, he offered to come one night a week, when he 'could be alone with her to work in peace'—his words exactly. I helped Cora at the pub, and he came here. The professor and George were able to get parts on the internet, and Mr Simpson found a rendering of what she looked like in her glory. Clifford is quite a talented mechanic, you know." Maddy was racing through without a breath. "Once I saw the progress and how keen everyone was to take on the project, it was too late to ask you. Please tell me you're not angry. I could hardly wait to surprise you … but I know I was meddling, and I should have asked, and you have every right to be upset with me, but you have to admit she looks great."

Sebastian's only defence against her breathless explanation was to kiss her. He hoped the passion in his kiss was transforming itself into the words he could not say. He was thrilled with the work, the thought, and the way Maddy had involved her friends in keeping a secret. *Did Davi know?* he wondered. George would be pleased to see how perfect a job had been done on the old girl.

Sebastian wrapped his arms around Maddy, kissed the top of her head, and whispered into her hair. "Only you could make this happen. I don't know what to say. You must know I'm so very pleased. Thank you, Maddy. It's a lovely surprise, and I can't imagine how hard it was for you to keep this a secret. Thank you."

Maddy sighed. "I'm anxious for you to take her for a spin tomorrow. Let's put her to bed now."

They covered the motorbike and walked hand in hand back to the apartment, Sebastian taking a last look before closing the garage door.

Maddy woke in the night, stretched, and realized she had the bed to herself. She sat up, disoriented, rubbing her eyes. It was dark except for the sliver of light under the garage door. She smiled and resisted the urge to join Sebastian. He had seemed genuinely pleased with the surprise. Maddy fell against the pillows punching the air in victory. She closed her eyes, welcoming sleep.

Sebastian slipped into bed, fitting himself against a warm, sleeping Maddy. The smell of her hair and her body were so familiar to him; he felt he could do or dream anything, if she was beside him. He fell asleep wondering what would have happened if he hadn't found her in St James Park, if she had met with her past and left them. He took a deep breath and nudged the thought out of his mind. He was not going to lose her—not right now.

Discovering the Demons

Maddy made her way through the garden and into the apartment, dropping the heavy grocery bags on the counter. *What a day.* She sighed and walked over to the lamp, switched it on, and jumped back as she saw Sebastian sitting on the sofa, tie loosened, sleeves rolled up, drink in hand.

"Hey, it's Wednesday—didn't you go to the club tonight?" she asked tenderly.

"I came home early to surprise you, but you weren't here." His words were slurred. She wondered how many drinks he had consumed before she arrived. She walked over to him and sat at his feet, leaning her chin on his knees. "Why didn't you call me? We could have had dinner near your office," she asked quietly.

"I expected you would be here; I needed to see you," he said in a hard voice.

"I certainly don't wait here all day on the off chance you will get home early." Her tone was angry but controlled. "Today was a tough day for a good friend," she started.

He cut her off with a cruel sneer. "I had a tough day, but I didn't have a friend to share my woes with because you weren't here."

"Am I to sit here waiting for you, slippers and pipe in hand?" Maddy responded.

Sebastian snorted, not in any shape to carry on a reasonable conversation.

Maddy realized this would only end in hurtful words and tears; she knew the best solution was to get him to sleep it off.

"Sebastian, before you drown in the pity pool, let's get you to bed," she said firmly. "Anything we say now will just leave scars."

"I have plenty of scars …" he sneered drunkenly.

"None from me, so let me get you to bed; you need to sleep this off."

"I can't sleep with you now. Sleeping with you isn't going to make this better." He slurred the words.

"Believe me, buddy, the last thing on my mind is sleeping with you … Now, let's get you to bed."

He struggled against her as she got under his arms and slowly half-dragged, half-pushed him to the bed.

When she had his clothes off, she covered him and lay on top of the duvet, beside him.

"Sebastian, what happened today to make you so sad and melancholy?" she whispered.

"I never got to say goodbye or Merry Christmas or ask him if he liked the toy soldiers. She took that away from me … Why would she do that? Why did she get to decide?" he responded tearfully, closing his eyes.

Maddy suddenly realized he was mourning his dead son. He had told her of the accident and how he had received the call in his office because his wife, Claire, had not wanted him to attend the family party with them. He was called to the hospital but arrived too late. The funeral was near the family estate in Bordeaux. He had not been back to the gravesite since then.

Maddy slowly backed off the bed, careful not to wake him. His breathing was erratic, but thankfully he had passed out. She found her phone and sent Lambert a text message: "*We need 2 tkts to Bordeaux ASAP with car & flowers. Can u arrange plse?*"

She returned to the bed, lying beside him, forgiving him for being so mean; it was the drink and the sorrow. What she could not forgive was his insensitivity to her not being there for him. Why hadn't he called her? She would have had to make a choice. She fell asleep wondering why he never asked about her friend.

Sebastian was in deep water. He was struggling to get up through the churning current, passing glimpses of Claire and little Stefan in the car, in the kitchen, in the nursery reading … Each image was of the little boy waving and smiling at him, calling "Papa!", his mother tight-lipped and pulling him away. He could not get out of the water. Now he saw the car, the tree, the impact of the collision. He was floating above them; he could not protect them from the flames. He was sobbing, still with no way to get air into his lungs. He felt dizzy, and then he saw her. She had a light and a tank with an oxygen mask. He swam towards her, and Maddy gave him air. He woke up rubbing his eyes, his head hurting, not sure where he was. He heard her breathing and felt a pounding, realizing it was his own heart beating in his ears. He tried to lift his head, but it brought on nausea.

Rubbing his eyes and breathing deep, trying to get his bearings, he was able to flip the top end of the bedcover over Maddy. He wondered what damage he had done, closing his eyes and returning to a groggy, dreamless sleep.

The sound of incoming text messages filled the room as Maddy stretched and looked around. Her phone was lost in the covers, demanding attention. Lambert had arranged a private charter for 9.00 a.m. Car and flowers awaited in Bordeaux. Davi was en route with their breakfast. He hoped all was well and sent her a line of Xs and Os.

Time—what time was it? She checked the phone: 7.18 a.m. *Hurry, hurry, get up; get him up and dressed, packed, and ready to go.* She sat up and looked at Sebastian, who was snoring into his pillow. She wanted to touch him and assure him everything would be all right, but the urge to complete the plan was greater.

"Sebastian." She shook him lightly. "Sebastian." She kissed his cheek and he brushed his face. "Please get up. We have to go; we have a big day."

He blinked and saw her face above his, pleading with him to get up. "Maddy, I …" He cleared his throat, wanting to apologize.

"Shh." She put her finger on his lips. "We'll have time to talk later; now I need you to get in the shower, get dressed in your country clothes, and pack an overnight bag. Can you manage that?" She was off the bed, picking up clothes, grabbing a bag, moving too fast for his impaired vision. "Don't forget your passport!" Maddy called from the bathroom. He could hear water running, and she came out with her toothbrush in her mouth, looking for something.

"Sebastian, get up now; shower and get packed—*chop chop*." She clapped her hands, urging him to move. He almost laughed out loud, but his head hurt.

She returned with a tablet and a glass of water. "Take this; it should help your head." He stumbled around the room, trying to remember her orders and wondering why he had to hurry. Had she told him where they were going? He couldn't recall.

Davi dropped them at the corporate park, where a small jet was waiting. On-board they enjoyed some of the treats in the picnic basket Grace had sent for them. They didn't speak. Sebastian snoozed until they had landed and were taxiing in to the small terminal.

"What's happening? Where are we going? What are we doing?" he asked quietly, rubbing his eyes.

"Something you should have done years ago. Come on; do you want to drive, or shall I?"

Maddy was determined to make him face the demon.

"Have you always been so bossy?" he asked with a twinkle in his eye.

She spoke French with the agent, who assured her the GPS was programmed, the flowers were in the car, and the requested map (just in case) was in the glovebox. The airline had also added a bottle of wine, a baguette, cheese, and a flask of coffee. *Bless them*, Maddy thought. With a quick *merci bien* and a wave, they were on the road to the small cemetery near Saint-Émilion. Sebastian drove to the area without consulting either the GPS or the map.

They drove in silence, Maddy unsure of how he would react, Sebastian unsure of how he would deal with what was ahead. His head was clearing, but his hands were still shaking. *Note to self: Do not drink alone all afternoon when you are feeling sorry for yourself.* He almost smiled, but it seemed inappropriate. He determined he must ask what a pity pool was. It occurred to him he should be angry at her for forcing this, but here they were, and he was more apprehensive than angry.

Maddy gave him the flowers, which were beautifully tied with a blue ribbon, and motioned towards the graveyard. She had planned to stay back and read while he paid his respects. He turned to look at the entrance and smiled at the flowers, acknowledging the thoughtful gesture. Then he took her hand, pulled her towards him, and whispered in her ear, "Please come with me … I need you."

She was touched. Holding back a sob, she wiped a tear away and walked through the gate with him.

At the gravesite, Maddy stood back while Sebastian kneeled and placed the flowers in front of the gravestone. He outlined the dates with his fingers, and then the name "Stefan". He brushed away loose strands of grass and gazed at the surrounding headstones. From his pocket he took a miniature battle figure and set it on the grass, where he dug a small hole and buried the soldier. When Maddie realized he was speaking to his son, she turned away, lest her heaving sobs disturb the dialogue.

They sat on the small bench in the cemetery, hesitant to leave, tired and spent from the emotion of the visit.

"Thank you, Maddy." He was holding her hand. "Thank you for bringing me here and saving me from drowning in the pity pool." He smiled sheepishly.

Sebastian looked out at the gravestones and then turned to Maddy, who was deep in thought. She turned her head to him, feeling his eyes on her. He melted at the innocence of her wide eyes and dimples; he reached out and moved the hair away from her eyes, caressing her cheek.

"The last thing in the world I want to do is drive you away. I seem to say I'm sorry quite often. Last night, I'm embarrassed to say, I felt jealous that you were with someone—anyone else but me … How sad is that?" He took her hand in his, bringing it to his lips. "I want to be with you; I want to take care of you; I want you to need me. Is that too much to ask?" He hesitated. "Is it enough?"

Maddy stared at him, feeling an overwhelming urge to tell him she loved him. What was it about this man that touched her so much? She wondered.

"Indeed."

While in France they visited with Philippe at the winery. Sebastian and Philippe were so comfortable with each other they were like brothers. Not only had they roomed together for most of their school years; both had lost parents at an early age. They were similar in many ways: both orphans, both widowed and childless, both wealthy and working too hard. Philippe was delighted Maddy had saved Sebastian from himself.

Sebastian told Philippe he was mentoring Henry, the grandson of a school colleague. Philippe was amazed when he learned who the grandfather was. "He was a bully, Sebastian; he was nasty to us throughout our school years. Why are you mentoring that boy?"

"The headmaster knew we went to school together; obviously he couldn't know about the bullying. Apparently the father committed suicide when the boy was quite young. He and the mother had parted. The grandfather, our former colleague, fled to Australia soon afterward, placing the child in boarding school. How could I refuse?"

"Henry is a lovely little boy; I hope you get to meet him," Maddy added.

Philippe shook his head, raised his glass, and looked out over the vineyard, lost in his own thoughts.

Over lunch Maddy watched the two friends, who were easy in each other's company. She slipped away to visit the village, leaving them to their wine and memories.

It was late afternoon when Sebastian handed Maddy the keys and suggested she drive. She apologized to Philippe for not including him in the gravesite visit.

"Maddy, thank you, but I go most weeks. It was kind of you to bring Sebastian. He has not been back since the funeral. I was lucky; the parents of Manon helped me with the winery, and we remained friendly until they passed. Claire's parents were very bitter and told Sebastian they need not see each other after the funeral. They did leave him a small bursary to be used as a memorial for Claire and Stefan, but they never spoke again. I think Claire left quite a big debt, and it killed her parents; they wouldn't ask Sebastian for help. Maybe they realized their daughter was unhappy not with her husband but with her life." Philippe shrugged, looking into the vineyard.

"Thank you for telling me. He's so private, but I know there are haunting memories." Maddy looked over at Sebastian, who lay asleep in the car.

"Be patient with him, Maddy; you are good for him. He will talk about his life when he is ready." Philippe put his arm around her and led her to the car. "You know, we were so determined to build our business and prove ourselves that we never had time for love; we didn't know what it was. When you are young, you make a life and build your stories together, so when you are older, like us," he pointed to Sebastian and then himself, "You have many stories; some you have forgotten, some you want to forget. Sometimes it is easier to pretend you don't need anyone, and new acquaintances may not appreciate your stories. Comprenez?"

Maddy nodded and leaned over to touch his cheek. "Au revoir," she whispered.

"Non, pas au revoir. A bientot." He smiled and took her hands in his. "Oh, I put a case of drinkable wine in your boot. Drive safe."

The ride to the airport and the flight home were quiet, allowing Maddy time to think about what Philippe had said. How could one ever know what baggage another person carried with him? She looked over at Sebastian, snoring lightly, his head on his shoulder, and wondered if she was the one he would open his heart to someday.

Davi met them at the airport in London, anxious to know how the day had played out.

"It was emotional but a good start towards recovery, I think," Maddy confided.

As Davi parked the car and opened the door, Sebastian stepped out and rubbed his eyes. Maddy collected their bags and laughed when she saw the case of wine. "We can deal with that tomorrow. Good night, Davi."

She moved towards the patio door and noticed Sebastian standing by the car, looking lost. Maddy turned and extended her hand. Sebastian gratefully accepted her hand and followed her into the apartment.

"Good morning, sleepyhead." Maddy softly brushed the hair from his forehead. "How are you feeling this morning?" Sebastian smiled sheepishly and sat up in the bed. "Here's your coffee and something for your head. I must get to the hospital. I promised I would be there for the results. I should be back early afternoon. You know it's Friday night trivia at our little pub, if you're up to it … or not. See you later, alligator."

Sebastian blinked. She was gone before he could tell her how much he appreciated everything she had done, how much he would miss her today, and how much she added to his life. His head hurt but his heart was warm.

Man's Best Friend

"Ah, there's Maddy with Molly," Davi pointed out as they drove into the neighbourhood. Sebastian looked up, removing his glasses. "Sorry?"

"Maddy is walking the dog." Davi responded innocently.

Sebastian sighed before asking, "What dog?" *Do I really want to know?* he wondered.

"The dog from the shelter. It belongs to Esme and Gordon, but they are gone for a visit to the daughter in Cornwall; she doesn't particularly like dogs. Molly is the replacement dog for the Jack Russell they had. She's a beauty—chocolate-brown Labrador. Maddy says she is not only beautiful; she has a nice temperament and is quite intelligent."

"Perhaps we should go back; I should meet the beast." Sebastian was anxious to see Maddy and share the outcome of today's meeting.

Davi was pleased to see the interest on Sebastian's face as he reversed and pulled up beside Maddy.

Maddy waved as Sebastian stepped out of the car. "Meet Molly. Molly, meet Sebastian." She pointed to the dog, who was now wagging her tail and looking back and forth between them. Sebastian kissed Maddy and admired the dog; she was beautiful.

"Are you heading home?" Sebastian asked.

"Yes, let's go this way." Maddy started towards the boulevard. "I can fill you in on the whole story as we walk, if you like."

"There's a whole story?" he asked cautiously.

"Yes, Esme and Gordon—you know, next door—just lost their dog. They really wanted another companion but had to leave to spend the holidays with their daughter in Cornwall, and she doesn't like dogs." She was speaking very fast. "As I went by the shelter today, I realized the animals would be on reduced care over the holidays, as the caregivers need time off. Molly is a rescue dog and has recuperated nicely, given her abusive life. Esme and Gordon loved the photos of her." She looked over at Sebastian before continuing. "I mean, who wouldn't; she's adorable." She smiled and rubbed the dog's ears.

"I was speaking with the school," she continued, "and the headmaster happened to mention Henry would be alone at school for a few days before he was to join the family he usually spends the holidays with … I felt bad and asked if we could take him with us to see B & G." She took a breath. "Henry was excited, naturally, so I picked him up and we went back to the shelter. Of course, he and Molly fell in love at first sight. I thought to myself, 'Wouldn't it be great if Henry had a dog to play with on the beach rather than just walking with us' … so I called B & G and asked if we could bring boy and dog and stay at the cottage. Everything is all clear and good to go." She then said in an aside, "I think they were tickled with the prospect." She took a deep breath.

Sebastian stopped.

"Molly has a cage; it's more like a mobile home, and she won't be here long. She's so sweet, and Henry was thrilled, and I think it's very English to have a dog, so everyone should be fine." She finished with hands on hips, waiting for his response.

"Let me get this straight." Sebastian looked at Maddy and Molly, both of whom were now watching him with interest. "This morning you were still in bed when I left; it was just the two of us. Now eight hours later it's you, me, a young boy, a dog, and a few days away visiting … Is that right? Have I missed anything?"

Maddy bit the inside of her cheek, trying to see the downside in her plan, when she realized he was laughing into his hands.

He finally stopped laughing, looked over at her, and realized she was totally guileless … She was waiting for his approval of her grand scheme. He had so many questions: "How did the school ever agree to let you take Henry out today?", "How did you get approval to take Henry away for a few days?", "Are the neighbours really taking the dog?", "What do you know about taking care of a dog?" She answered each question with a patient response.

It made perfect sense that Henry would have spoken to the headmaster about her, that the headmaster would ask her to chaperone future museum excursions, that the neighbours were anxious to have the dog, that Belle and George would want to see Henry, and that there were many dog walkers on the beach. Maddy had always had a dog and wondered why Sebastian didn't.

Sebastian realized he had been rubbing the dog's ears as they spoke. It was very comfortable walking down a quiet, tree-lined street with one's dog and one's partner. As they walked into the garden, Maddy removed the leash and Molly sat in front of him, waiting for another ear rub. Sebastian sat on the deck, loosened his tie and smiled as Molly lay beside him, tail wagging, her head resting on large paws. He shook his head, petting the dog, "If Maddy likes you, you are in good hands, old girl. Indeed."

'Tis the Season— Christmas

Christmas, a season of raw emotion for many, passed with much laughter as Henry and Molly ran for hours on the beach, chasing driftwood, rolling in the sand, and falling asleep as soon as they ate dinner, Molly lying across Henry on the cot. Belle and George enjoyed the company and were sad to see the makeshift family depart at the end of their stay. Henry's face was windburned, and he was full of chatter on the drive back to London. Sebastian had to admit it had been a fun holiday—perhaps the best holiday ever. All of them were sad to say goodbye when they dropped Henry off at the school. He hugged Sebastian, Maddy, and Molly as if he would never see them again.

On the way home, Sebastian looked over at Maddy, grabbed her hand, and kissed it. "Thank you. It was a wonderful way to spend the holidays."

Maddy smiled back, wondering how Sebastian could live without a dog after the last few days. She was pleased the plan had worked and everyone had enjoyed the time together. George was so patient with Henry; it was lovely to see how they bonded. She closed her eyes, squeezed Sebastian's hand, and revisited the highlights of their time together. When Sebastian looked over at her, she was smiling, deep in her own thoughts.

Sebastian was reluctant to serve Christmas dinner at the mission, not knowing how his involvement would be perceived. Maddy was quick to point out that many of the homeless were addicts who had nothing: no family, no work, no prospects. The only sure thing in their lives was an understanding of how the system worked: if they had money, their dealer would supply. Who in that group did he think would be judging him?

In the end, he was happy to oblige, having no holiday tradition of his own. They ate with a room full of grateful strangers who were thrilled to show off the new gloves and scarves Maddy had collected for gifts. Sebastian was accused of being a "fine English gentleman" (translation: snob) by the other volunteers until he agreed to don an apron and laugh at how domestic he looked. By the time they served pudding, he had been accepted by volunteers, staff, and diners for his genuine interest in the upcoming projects and the complex stories of the homeless. Midway through the evening, he realized there was a warm feeling in the room. Singing carols seemed to meld all the characters into the same mould—human beings holding on to the spirit of the holiday.

Maddy told Sebastian she was proud of how engaged he was, and he had to admit it was a new experience. He thanked her for involving him and asked shyly if she realized she was standing under the mistletoe. She laughed, and they shared a careful kiss, mindful of the applause from the rest of the room.

Since returning from Bordeaux, they had been polite and cautious with each other. Sebastian had desperately wanted to ask about the friend she had been helping, but he felt it was too late to show interest. The getaway with Henry had gone a long way to mending the hurt feelings, and he was enjoying having Molly at his feet. Maddy wanted to believe he needed time to heal and she shouldn't push him. It was Audrey who suggested they were acting weird and needed to get back in their groove.

Leaving the mission, both commented on the possibility of snow, how tired their feet were, and how they could not sleep, as they were on such a high.

Sebastian looked over at Maddy and smiled. "Maddy, I realized tonight that you are addicted to finding trouble and I am addicted to you."

"Why that may be the nicest thing anyone ever said to me, except for the trouble part." Maddy smiled back, taking his hand in hers. "Hot chocolate?"

They walked through the garden, side by side, the trees twinkling with white lights, the windows adorned with apple wreaths. It was a pleasant welcome home. Maddy switched on the Christmas tree lights inside, and the little apartment came alive with brightly wrapped gifts laid out across the room. They were all tied with gold ribbons and big bows.

Sebastian stood perfectly still, only his eyes following the trail of gifts.

"What's this?" he asked cautiously, initially thinking someone had ransacked the room.

"It's Christmas, and these are your gifts. I know we said no gifts, but these are little things I picked up whenever I saw them because they reminded me of you. It's not much, I'm sorry to say, but what could I possibly buy you that would be a surprise?" She was so excited for him to gather up the parcels.

"One at a time … Open your gifts. Merry Christmas."

He was now caught up in her excitement. He was touched by her thoughtful and playful gesture. He hadn't felt like this since he was a young boy. He remembered the year Belle had hidden the gifts; when he returned home from school, he was disappointed to see only one gift under the tree. But on Christmas Day, Belle walked into the room pulling a wagon filled with gifts for him. He felt ashamed and greedy, but after all the wrapping was collected and everything had been opened, he hugged Belle and vowed it was his best Christmas ever. She cried when she opened his gift of a handmade ceramic mug with a crooked heart on it. She said it was the best gift, filled with love and joy. For the next few days, she wept each time she picked the mug up. It was on the top shelf in the kitchen after all these years.

Sebastian had felt very loved then, just as he did now.

He was delighted with his colourful socks; personalized Starbucks gold card; Turkish delight from the market in Covent Gardens; a hand-painted tie; single-malt Scotch from the Highlands; USB sticks with recorded music for relaxing, going to work, and coming home (and one titled "Music if you should ever miss me"); fancy earbuds for his mobile phone; a paisley silk scarf that was exactly what he would have chosen; online newspaper subscriptions (to avoid the black hands); a badger hair shaving brush from Jermyn Street; and a deck of cards with personal services on them (for example, "hugs", "kisses", "shoulder to cry on", "dinner at home", "walk in the park", "museum visit", "breakfast in bed"—a series of creative things they could do together).

He looked up at Maddy sitting cross-legged on the bed, gleeful at his pleasure in opening each package. Didn't she know she was the best gift he had ever received?

"I thought the motorbike was my Christmas gift … but all this … it's wonderful. Thank you." Sebastian walked over to his jacket and produced a small package wrapped in red plaid paper. She blinked in surprise and took the package in both hands.

He leaned over to kiss her forehead, and she looked up at him with eyes wide.

"I thought we weren't exchanging gifts."

"Too late. Open it," he encouraged.

As she lifted the top of the box, she gasped. The diamond tennis bracelet caught the light and seemed to come alive in the velvet container.

"Oh my gosh," she exclaimed breathlessly. "It's beautiful, oh my gosh …"

She noticed an inscription tag and lifted the delicate bracelet towards the light. "A kiss never lies," she read out loud. She closed her eyes, collecting herself; turned to Sebastian, who was now sitting on the bed beside her; threw her arms around his neck, and kissed every part of his face. He was laughing as he fell back on the bed, holding her.

"Shall we try it on?" he asked between kisses. They sat up, and as he helped her with the clasp, he realized he had never given anyone, not even Belle; his wife, Claire; or Stefan a gift that made him feel so happy. She was admiring the bracelet on her wrist, moving her arm out and then touching it close to her face. She leaned over and whispered in his ear, "Thank you, it's perfect."

This was their very own Christmas—a new way to celebrate: visiting the cemetery, taking Henry to the beach, serving at the mission, sharing these gifts, and being thankful for each other. Perhaps the stigma of the season had turned around. They snuggled up to each other on the bed, the steaming cups of hot chocolate long forgotten.

A New Year

Heralding the New Year had been discussed for some weeks. Grace and Davi were celebrating with family, Belle and George were at a soirée, Sebastian had suggested attending the annual fete at the club, and Maddy had suggested they spend the last day of the year alone, at home with Molly, who would be leaving them New Year's Day when Esme and Gordon returned from their holiday. Sebastian received an interesting invitation to attend a New Year's reception at the home of Francesca Bennett and Michael Riley—interesting, as it was the first ever invite from the couple other than the annual fundraiser. Although Maddy was quick to point out how nice it was that the old schoolmates were connecting, Sebastian felt the invite was purely due to Mick O'Riley's fascination with Maddy.

The Bennett–Riley townhouse was modern in decor, very sterile, and magazine-perfect. Sebastian and Maddy were welcomed by Michael at the door. "So glad you could make it. I am in dire need of amusement." He winked at Maddy. "Ah, Walker, good to see you. The bar is straight in on the left." Sebastian offered to refill Mick's glass and nodded to Maddy as he went in search of the drinks.

"I wondered if you would come tonight. I wanted to see you again." Michael leaned into Maddy.

"I thought you wanted to rekindle your friendship with Sebastian." Maddy gazed over the crowd filling the room.

"We were never close. I was always in trouble for one thing or another; he, on the other hand, was always top of class, one of the good boys. He and Frenchie were inseparable. I don't recall even liking him."

"Sebastian is a good person. You've both been successful, and yet you're so different. You have all of this, and yet you seem so unsettled, not very happy. Why is that?" Maddy looked directly into his eyes.

Michael turned his face away from her. "Maybe I haven't found that one thing that makes it all worthwhile … that one person who makes me feel successful."

"Well, it can't be because you don't have offers. At the fundraiser you were surrounded by beautiful women of all ages, just waiting for you to notice them. However, you are married to a very powerful woman, just in case you've forgotten."

Michael laughed and touched Maddy's face. "My marriage is one of convenience; I'm sure you can see that. I do what I like with discretion, and Francis beds her type—which, as you can see, does not include me. It works, but it's not enough."

Maddy was uncomfortable with how close Michael was standing. "Perhaps you need to free yourself and find happiness. There is a someone out there for you, but it isn't someone who has already found happiness with another." Maddy placed her hand on his chest and pushed him away. "Don't destroy someone's happiness just because you can."

Michael moved away, stung by her words.

Maddy realized her words were harsh, so she quickly added, "I hope I get to meet Mick O'Riley someday. He sounds like a fun character."

"He isn't much." Michael responded, looking over the crowd.

Sebastian returned with champagne at that moment. He realized he had interrupted something between them, but when Maddy touched his arm and smiled at him, he relaxed.

"Walker, I never thought I'd be envious of you, but here I am, wondering how you got so lucky. Enjoy the evening. Oh, dear mother of God, here's Francis; she hasn't received your cheque yet."

"That's right." Francesca Bennett appeared beside Sebastian. She wore a colourful caftan with a head scarf and large hoop earrings. Her eyes were lined in black, and her cheeks seemed flushed.

"That's my fault, I'm afraid." Maddy smiled demurely, trying to ease the tension.

"Who are you again?" Francesca stared at Maddy.

"I'm the director of philanthropy at the firm, and I'm slowly making my way through all the charitable requests, annual reports, and good works. It's a rather daunting task." Maddy spoke directly to Francesca.

Sebastian looked over the crowd, amazed at Maddy's quick response. He hoped he wasn't smiling as he turned back to the group.

Francesca waved Maddy off and touched Sebastian's arm. "I'm sure you'll direct your new philanthropy person to make a quick decision."

"She's very thorough," Sebastian responded as Francesca whirled away, leaving only a trace of her perfume behind.

Michael laughed and Maddy realized she had been holding her breath. She looked up at Sebastian, signalling she was ready to go. He threw back his champagne and nodded.

"Well, I must see to our other guests. I'll make an appointment with the director of philanthropy in the new year. I want her to meet someone I used to know." Michael brushed his lips across Maddy's hand, nodded to Sebastian, and walked away. He turned abruptly and with a small bow of his head wished them a happy New Year.

"Let's go home, please. I need to go home," Maddy whispered.

"Indeed. Tell me more about my new director of philanthropy and her role."

Maddy laughed and patted his arm. "Sorry about that; I just didn't think you should have to take any flak because of me. It's not a bad idea though."

The cab ride home was quiet as Sebastian wondered what Mick might have to say to Maddy, and Maddy, curled up bedside Sebastian, wondered why a grown man who had a reputation for being such fun would be a prisoner in an unhappy marriage. Neither spoke, anxious to get home and ring in the New Year.

Lying in bed, wrapped in each other's arms, the countdown to midnight party on the television, they were like teenagers at a slumber party. The champagne was untouched on the bedside table, the truffles still in the box. Sebastian and Maddy were hungry for history … they wanted to know things about each other's past.

"Have you ever wanted to be somewhere else—someone else?" Maddy asked, looking up at him.

Sebastian was pensive, digging deep into his memories. When he spoke, it was in a small voice; Maddy had to strain to hear him. He had never wanted to be somewhere else, but he had wanted to be someone else. As a child at boarding school, the other parents would visit their sons twice a year. Aunt Belle always made an entrance on her visits, and Sebastian was nervous before each occasion. She would arrive with picnic baskets, wearing a large sun hat or carrying a sun umbrella, with a chaise to sit and watch the entertainment. She once brought an elephant to the schoolyard and offered his friends rides. Another time she hired a polo team with horses to teach the boys how to play polo (a great success except for the divots in the lawn). Yet another time she brought a magician to teach them how to do card tricks and illusions. She always brought a large cake and bottles of orange squash—enough for all the boys. He was mortified by her outrageous behaviour. He wanted to be anyone but Sebastian with the crazy aunt.

One day after games, he forgot his jumper on the field and ran out to retrieve it. As he returned to the change room, he heard the boys talking about the weekend visits. He stopped outside the door, afraid to be ridiculed by the boys. He heard them groan about their boring parents coming to inspect their rooms and how they hoped crazy Belle would visit Sebastian with another awesome surprise. Wouldn't it be great if all their parents were like her? "Where is Sebastian?" someone asked. "He's probably ordering the cake," someone responded. "Excellent, let's hope there's cream icing." They all cheered.

Sebastian was so overwhelmed with shame at his mean and ungrateful thoughts of his aunt that he ran back to his room, disappointed in himself, eager to call Aunt Belle and let her know how much he was looking forward to seeing her tomorrow. He did request cream icing, and of course her visit was a huge success. She had a friend with a baby tiger, and the boys were able to hold and feed it. It was a great visit.

Sebastian felt it was his first life lesson: you are who you are, and your family is yours—no apologies necessary. He found it was easier to accept people if he remembered that simple lesson. Belle had also taught him that there would always be people who were jealous of what one was or what one accomplished; the best revenge was to live and be happy.

Maddy thought it was a beautiful story. Before Sebastian could ask Maddy the same question, they heard the countdown to midnight begin.

Ten … nine … eight … seven … six … five … four … three … two … one … Happy New Year! They kissed eagerly, celebrating each other. On the television, the crowds were singing "Auld Lang Syne"; but here in the garden apartment at Bellmere House, only the snoring of a contented dog and two heartbeats drifting to sleep could be heard.

Project Beach House

Maddy spent any available time she had in January at the cottage on the beach. Maddy could no longer keep her project a secret from Sebastian. She explained it would be difficult to tell only a portion of the story when so many pieces of the puzzle were intertwined. Sebastian motioned for Maddy to sit beside him on the rocks and encouraged her to begin.

She told him of her visit to George and Belle after he had left her, when they first met. She had been walking with George on the beach, and he had pointed out his little cottage on the bluff. She was so taken by the cottage: the thatched roof, the wall of glass overlooking the water, the deck and the portico cleverly hidden by the garden. The inside was dusty and damp, needing repair. The layout was perfect, she had agreed, but new furniture and perhaps a loft for a big floating bed would be in order. George had simply told her to go ahead and fix it up so he could rent it. She was thrilled and asked what his budget was. He had no restrictions; he just wanted to have it rented by the summer, whatever it took. Sebastian was so preoccupied with his own work that Maddy had not wanted to bother him with the project.

Maddy met the local contractor and tradesmen; she asked for an estimate and asked about permits. There were major repairs needed, and it seemed impossible the work could be completed within the year, as the permits would take time. Rod and Josh were great resources, introducing local workers to the project.

Since Audrey was bored at home but had a flair for decorating and a wealthy husband who travelled constantly, Maddy had invited her on a day trip to the cottage, and a plan was formulated.

George and Belle began attending council meetings to assist Maddy with the permits required for the development. Maddy had requested statistics and historical data from the council on past developments. She had costs and timelines in line, and she had Mr Karazan and his assets on her side. Rod had assisted with the presentation to the council. It was so complete there were no questions. Several of the council members considered how quickly Maddy had obtained the pedestrian crossing to the beach, how involved Mr Karazan and his family had become in the local scene, and how the promise of controlled growth to the area would bring prosperity and keep out the proposed caravan camp developer. All permits and work orders were approved in the same meeting. George could only shake his head in disbelief.

The next day, Milos Karazan arrived at the beach house with a bottle of champagne for Maddy and a crew of workmen, ready to mend the guardrails on the winding road to the new "estate". Milos toasted Maddy and Audrey, citing that he never forgot a friend; his business was booming due to his initial pedestrian crossing gift. He considered Maddy a fine friend and was ready to ensure she was successful, believing she had given him an opportunity to settle into the community.

Once the work began, Maddy arrived with pizza for lunch so she could speak with the tradesmen. Soon the wives of the workers arrived to see the project and deliver lunches of their own in large baskets. Maddy and Audrey walked the beach with George, asking about the other cottages on the bluff and their owners. The buildings all seemed in need of repair or updating; the owners used their cottages very few weeks each year.

Audrey and Maddy, having peeked into the windows of the cottages, had made lists of the repairs and possible designs for each owner. The tradesmen were offered an incentive to finish George's cottage by early May so they could showcase the work done and book more work.

Of course, the luncheon wives, anxious to have their husbands busy with full-time work, encouraged the men by cleaning and painting and planting flower boxes on the roadway. It was a great effort, and it paid off. Owners of the neighbouring cottages were invited to a reception in George's cottage to see the work and hear of plans for improvements. The gathering was successful, as the other owners saw the possibility of rental revenue and entertaining opportunities for themselves. The idea of increased property value was reinforced by the local rental agency representative, who was thrilled and motivated to increase her commissions. George was delighted with the result, and the women had managed to come in under their own determined budget, largely because of the increased interest of the workmen in the project. Win-win.

Audrey and Maddy would take the early train, choosing furnishings and finishes, and discussing the best colours, flooring options, and accessories. They worked diligently, always walked the beach with George, had lunch with Belle, and returned home on the evening train. It was a labour of love for everyone involved. George was encouraging and proved to be their best salesperson. The women had suggested value-add details for showcasing, and the workmen had responded with fine workmanship, charging the others in the project for the upgrades. George suggested Maddy and Audrey make use of the cottage rather than rent it out; he was anxious to keep them visiting, as it made him feel young to be with them.

Sebastian listened to the story, wondering why Maddy would not have engaged him in the project; his architectural firm and his own expertise would have been helpful. He was proud of what the women had accomplished and realized they had just gone ahead and done it—in Maddy-style, without disturbing anyone else. He smiled, shaking his head, holding her hand in his. He was impressed with the changes to the run-down cottage, having spent time there as a boy. It was now a showplace. *That's my girl*, he thought happily as he stood in the cottage, noticing the fine details.

The Rescue

Just after the New Year, Grace and Maddy found a Wednesday afternoon market with a variety of spices and specialty teas they could mix for chai. As they left the kiosks, bags in hand, they heard a loud crash, glass shattering, and screams from the grassy area adjacent to the car park.

Maddy and Grace ran over to a vehicle now firmly implanted into a light pole. There were children in the back seat beating on the window, screaming. The driver was bent over the steering wheel, and the passenger was draped over the front seat.

The children were huddled together; they were dirty, their clothes a size too small, their faces streaked with tears. Maddy handed the bags to Grace and broke the window with a large rock. She lifted the children out of the window, holding them in her arms. "Are these your parents?" she asked the children.

"No."

"Do you know them? Where do you live?"

The children shook their heads in response. Maddy was confused. "Are you living on the street?"

The ragamuffins nodded.

"What are your names?"

The boy shyly responded. "Jimmy and Jemma. They want to split us up. They were taking us away."

"Where were you going?" Maddy asked in a soothing voice.

"Don't know." Jimmy responded after looking at his sister.

The children were crying now. It seemed strange to Maddy that no one else had come to their rescue. Someone yelled, "The coppers are on the way." Sirens sounded, though there was still no crowd. It was only a matter of time, Maddy thought, before the authorities would come to pick up the children and whisk them away to Children's Services.

Her mind was racing. "If I promise you a nice home and a beautiful mother, will you help me?" They looked at each other and nodded.

"Listen to me; you can stay together in a very nice home if you come with me now so we don't have to talk to the police." They nervously looked around, the police triggering fear. They nodded again.

"Okay, come with me. When I tell you to go to your mother, you run to her and call her Mummy—got it?" They nodded, sniffing. Maddy found her phone and dialled a number. "No questions. Meet me at the West Dover Market as soon as possible. Your children are waiting for you, and they are dirty and scared. Hurry."

She shuttled the children towards Grace, who had called Davi for the car. "Come quickly. There's been an accident. We are fine, but we need you."

Audrey and Davi arrived at the same time, Audrey in a cab. She ran towards Maddy and was surprised to have two filthy little ragamuffins run to her, calling "Mummy!" She hugged them tightly, crying and laughing at the same time.

"Mummy, Jimmy and Jemma are very happy to see you and go home now." Maddy said in a calm voice. "They will need a bath and perhaps delousing. Davi will take you home. Bye bye, my little buttons. Grace, you go too. I'm fine." As they drove away, Maddy saw the confusion in Audrey's eyes. Grace would explain. She turned and looked at the wreck of a car, a late model of junkyard pieces, rusting away, the wheels still turning.

Maddy stayed to answer the police questions. One witness cited her bravery in rescuing the children—where were the children? The ambulance driver gave her a quick check to make sure she had not been injured in the crossfire. She had not noticed the glass cuts on her hands and arms. She tried to avoid the reporter, refusing an interview, saying it was too traumatic to recall and wasn't it lucky no one else was injured. The driver was pronounced dead at the scene, and the female passenger was taken away in the ambulance, her chances of survival slim. The high alcohol content in her system had made her response time slow.

The paramedics sat with Maddy and started taking the glass from her arms with tweezers. The young medic introduced himself as Steve Howe, and soon they were exchanging stories and laughing about late nights in Emergency. Steve was an intern at the Royal Hospital, anxious to be a doctor in a small community where he could settle and start his own practice. He wanted to specialize in heart and lung disease, as his father had passed away without a proper diagnosis.

"What of the children?" he asked, realizing what had happened earlier.

"They have a nice home for the night. They are together, and if there is a God in heaven, everything will work out for them," Maddy replied with optimism.

Steve looked at her and then down at the ground, knowing she had done a good thing but understanding how the system worked. He felt he should have taken them to Children's Services.

"I hope you understand why I sent them away," she appealed to the young doctor. "Audrey and Jeffrey have started the adoption process and are waiting for their baby to arrive. Those kids look like they belong with Audrey. They have the resources and the love to give. You can call on them tomorrow. Here's the number." Maddy wrote out Audrey's number and address. "At least they'll have a bath, good food, and a warm bed. Doesn't every kid deserve to feel safe?" Maddy looked up at Steve with a hopeful smile.

"Okay, I'm not arguing that, but there are laws about kidnapping urchins off the street. I'll see what I can do when Children's Services calls. It would be lovely to think their miserable little lives were going to be better somehow. Next time, though, let us do our jobs, all right?" Steve was trying to be firm, though he couldn't help but feel warmth towards someone who could make such a life-changing decision in a heartbeat, right or wrong.

Maddy shivered, and he placed his jacket over her shoulders.

"Thanks, I'm okay." She smiled gratefully.

"Drop it at the hospital and we'll have tea. I'd like to see you again," he added shyly. "And of course I'd like to know what happens to the children."

Maddy smiled and hugged him. "Indeed." As she walked away, she turned to wave. "Do the right thing, Steve Howe, please."

Lambert, as dramatic as ever, called her, as he had been alerted by Davi of the accident. He pressed for details and inquired as to whether Maddy required medical attention, to which she assured him she certainly did not. Sebastian was in a meeting, and Lambert wanted to have all the facts before announcing the news. He was sure to be frantic when he heard. Maddy was able to convince him she was fine and ended the call. No need to disturb Sebastian at all. She was shaking and just wanted Sebastian here with her, his soothing arms around her. She wanted to go home. She needed a hot bath and time to think.

Audrey had the children bathed and fed by the time Maddy stopped at the house. Friends had delivered children's clothing, and Audrey was waiting for Jeffrey to return home. He had been in the airport departure lounge waiting for his flight when Audrey called to ask him to return home, her voice giddy and nervous. When she ended the call mid-sentence, he rushed home, fearing the worst. She was not answering her phone, and he was in a state of panic when he ran in the door of the house. Maddy was speaking with the buttons ("as cute as buttons," she said of them) when Jeffrey burst through the door, grabbing Audrey in a surprised hug. A very cool and calm Audrey turned and introduced Jimmy and Jemma to their papa.

"Jeffrey, the children will be staying here with us; they have no home to go to and no parents." She waited for a reaction and was thrilled when he stepped forward to shake their little hands and welcome them.

Maddy left them, rushing home to regroup. What had she done? Sebastian would know what to do. Why was she even considering involving Sebastian? He would be very calm right now, but he would also offer the voice of reason. *No, best to leave him out of this.*

She had fallen asleep before Sebastian returned home, He didn't want to disturb her, and it was the next evening before they saw each other. The accident was not mentioned.

Audrey and Jeffrey took to parenthood like fish to water. Jeffrey did ask the expected questions: "Where had they come from?" "Is it possible you can just take street children home without going through the proper channels?" "What if Social Services arrive tomorrow and take them away?" "What made you take these children from the scene?" He had many more questions, but he realized Maddy had been involved and Audrey was enjoying having the urchins in her care. He would deal with the authorities tomorrow; he, too, was enjoying having the children in the house.

Fortunately, Child Services allowed the children to stay, as the preliminary checks had been completed earlier in the adoption process. Steve Howe had given a thorough report on the rescue. Jeffrey's firm had lawyers on retainer, and they were able to start on the necessary paperwork with the authorities within the week. Audrey was amazed at his zeal and wondered when he would go back to work. The buttons behaved as though this had always been their home. They were adorable; no one could fake the love they demonstrated for their parents and their aunt Maddy.

Uncle Sebastian

"Good morning, sunshine, you must have come to bed very late. I fell asleep." Maddy set the coffee mug down on the bedside table and sat on the bed.

Sebastian stretched and smiled. "Whatever time it was, it was worth the welcome."

She leaned over and kissed him lazily.

"Shall we stop in and see the buttons before we head out this morning?" she asked as she hung his jacket and picked up his clothes from the floor. They were heading out to see Belle and George for an overnight visit.

"Who are the buttons?" He furrowed his brow. He couldn't keep up with the procession of new-found friends and acquaintances Maddy collected.

"The children; they are as cute as buttons, so that's what I call them. They are anxious to meet Uncle Sebastian; they can't quite say your name yet."

"What children? Uncle? Maddy, explain."

She bit her lip, recalling that he had not heard the full story of the car accident and the rescue. "Why don't you get ready and we'll skip over there ... I'll fill you in on the way."

"Where are we skipping over to?"

"Sebastian, in good time ... breakfast?"

As they walked across the boulevard, Maddy tried to formulate an executive summary.

"We are going to Audrey and Jeffrey's to meet their children Jimmy and Jemma." She watched his face and continued. "Audrey and Jeffrey are amazing parents. Jeffrey has taken a new job in the company so he doesn't have to travel; they are so happy. Please be nice."

The buttons ran to the door and rushed Maddy; she gathered them up in her arms and kissed their faces. She turned to Sebastian, who was looking uncomfortable and unsure of the situation. "Jimmy, Jemma, meet your uncle Sebastian."

The children stood back, intimidated by the stern look on his face. Jimmy put his hand out to shake Sebastian's hand, and the simple gesture made Sebastian melt. He immediately crouched down and took the offered hand. "Lovely to finally meet you, Jimmy. And this must be Jemma. Hello." His voice was soft as he held his arms out. Jemma tentatively stepped forward, looking at Maddy, who nodded encouragingly, and fell into his arms. Jimmy joined Jemma in the embrace as Audrey and Jeffery appeared in the foyer, holding each other.

"Welcome, Sebastian; I see you've met the moppets. Maddy, they could hardly wait to see you." Jeffery greeted her, air-kissing both cheeks. He then shook hands with Sebastian.

Sebastian stood and noticed how easy Audrey and Jeffery acted with each other and the children, who were now hugging their parents' knees. How radiant Audrey looked. Both Jeffrey and Audrey gave Maddy loving glances. He seemed to be on the outside of a special circle.

Throughout their short visit, the children sat on Maddy's knees, telling her what they had done at the park. They showed her their new toys, modelled their new outfits, and then returned to her lap, pleading for a story, which Maddy was only too happy to provide.

Adult talk involved job changes. Jeffery reported he could hardly get interested in work these days; he hated to leave the family. Audrey was beaming with pride and anxious to share stories of their experiences—new to all of them. They expressed their delight at Maddy's quick thinking and how the legalities were progressing. Sebastian looked confused, so Jeffery suggested they look at the papers in his office. Audrey watched them leave the room and turned to Maddy. "He doesn't know, does he?"

Maddy smiled sadly. "He never asked."

As they drove out of the city, Sebastian waited for Maddy to fill in the blanks. "Please tell me what happened, Maddy. How could you kidnap two children off the street and decide where they would live? Why didn't you tell me about the accident and how the day ended?" He was clearly upset with her.

Maddy looked out the window, fighting back the tears of anger.

"It was awful; those kids were in the car, screaming to get out, and they were scared. *I* was scared. I hoped you would appear and hold me and tell me everything was going to be all right. I was alone, and I had to make a game-time decision. I knew Audrey was lonely and feeling unfulfilled and the children had no home, nowhere to go. They had been separated before, and Jimmy wanted to protect his sister; he wouldn't let go. I just reacted by telling the children I had a lovely home for them where they could be together; all they had to do was call the beautiful lady 'Mummy' when I told them." She was sobbing as she relived the afternoon.

Sebastian pulled over and stopped the car. He ran to her door, lifted her out of the car, and held her, kissing her forehead and her face, wiping her tears.

"I'm so sorry; I'm so very sorry," he said into her hair. "I should have been there for you, but Lambert said everything was fine." He shook his head, upset with himself for not waking her that night, for not holding her and comforting her after the ordeal. How could she not think him insensitive and uncaring? how many other times had he failed her by being unaware?

"You were very brave, and what you did was give four people a chance at a new life. I'm not sure I agree with how you did it, but after seeing that family today, I know you definitely did a good thing. I love you for what you did. I hope the system works and they stay together. I'm so sorry I wasn't there for you." He kissed her tenderly and held her in his arms until she shivered from the cold. "Let's go to the cottage and hide away."

He kissed the top of her head once more, waited for her to settle in, and closed the car door. As he walked around the car, he wiped the tears from his eyes and wished he could be a better person for her.

There's something about a walk on the beach that clears your head, puts your troubles in perspective and makes life bearable again. Is it the salt air; the waves coming in and going out, removing your footprints, depositing tiny treasures and then, just as fast, taking them back out to sea; or is it the soothing sound of the surf and the uncluttered view of the horizon? Maddy sat on the rocks, hugging her knees, pondering the question.

She had come out to watch the sunrise and hadn't moved. She felt frozen in time, incapable of facing the world.

Sebastian was frantic. He engaged George in the search for her. "Where can she be?" he asked George.

"Did you two have a falling out?" George asked, and they walked the beach, searching the cliffs. "I felt Maddy handled the children in a reckless manner, and I may have been a little hard on her," Sebastian confessed.

"What's the downside, Sebastian?" George stopped walking and looked at him. "Lovely Audrey finally has a family, and her man is happy to be home; those children no longer have to go through the foster care system. They couldn't be in better hands, and only Maddy would think so fast and make it happen. I ask you, what's the downside?"

Sebastian shook his head. Why had he ever said a word?

It was after 11 a.m. when they found her on the rocks, alone and vulnerable as the tide rushed in.

Sebastian started up the rocks, but George held him back. "Maddy, can we come up?" he shouted. "Are you okay?"

She was startled by the shouts, looking down on them, aware that some time had passed. She stood up slowly and started down the cliffside towards the two men whose lives seemed intertwined with hers. She paused for a moment; something about the two of the them pacing below seemed strange. She shook off the feeling and continued her descent into the arms of George and Sebastian.

George pulled away as Sebastian wrapped her in his arms, angry that she had created the worry, yet delighted to know she was safe. She seemed to be constantly creating this confusion with his mind; the things she got involved with defied common sense, yet there was always a feeling that she had done right by someone. He felt he must be the one to protect her from herself. Was he up to the task?

"We were so worried about you, baby," he cried into her hair. "Don't ever do that again; don't walk away. I'm glad you're all right." The trio walked back to town along the beach in silence, all feeling relief in their own way, for different reasons.

In the cafe, Maddy looked at the anxious faces of her friends.

"I'm sorry if I worried you; I just lost track of time." She looked down at her hands, afraid she might cry.

"We were ever so worried, Maddy dear. You did give us a fright, but you're safe now, so all is well," Belle said tenderly, patting her hand. Not aware of the upset, Belle brightened and announced that Audrey had sent the cutest family photo.

"Those children are beautiful; with their curly hair and big eyes, they could be Audrey's own. Wasn't it lovely of her to think of us?" She chirped on, not catching the side glances the men exchanged.

Maddy looked away and offered, "Audrey thinks the world of you two. I'm pleased she shared the photo." She looked up and smiled. "The children are amazing, and they are all so happy."

Several locals stopped by to greet Belle and George, nodding to Sebastian, and also to express a kind word to Maddy for the projects she had initiated. One couple offered the opportunity for another community project, and Maddy listened with interest, promising to follow up.

George, who had been very quiet since the beach rescue, cleared his throat and noted, "Maddy, your heart is big, and not everyone understands how pure your motives are. Just remember that, my girl."

He squeezed Maddy's hand and stood up, bowing to Belle. "Come home with me, my bride; it's a good day for a siesta." Belle chuckled in delight, kissed Sebastian and Maddy goodbye, and with a wave floated out with George.

"Would you like to continue walking, or should we go back to the cottage?" Sebastian asked, not sure of the response. He felt inadequate and waited for her direction.

Maddy sat erect, took a deep breath, and suggested they go back to the cottage and light a fire.

He smiled and took her hand.

"Indeed."

The weekend ended too soon. Visits to the worksites to ensure the cottages on the bluff would be ready for summer, time with Belle and George, long walks, and cooking together from recipes on the internet had Maddy and Sebastian leaving for home in a happy mood. Sebastian realized Audrey had little time for the project, so he offered his assistance, which was gratefully accepted.

As they loaded the car to return to the city, Sebastian told Maddy he was already looking forward to the next weekend. He was contemplating a shorter work week and chided himself for not doing this earlier. They sang out loud with the radio on the motorway and dined with Grace and Davi before landing in the garden apartment, delightfully happy to be home. They went straight to bed and held each other tight, waking in the same position.

"I'm not sure I'll be able to concentrate on anything but you today," Sebastian said with conviction as Maddy stretched, smiling at him.

Old Flames

Maddy was arranging lunch with Esme and Jakob, as she had promised. Sebastian was scheduled to attend a seminar in Manchester for the day, so the timing was ideal.

"Maddy, what are you cooking up?" Sebastian asked as she put the phone down. She was humming a tune and drumming her fingernails on the counter.

She smiled. "Oh, just a luncheon with friends."

"Maddy, you're up to something; I can tell. I've seen that look before. What are you doing?"

Maddy walked over to the sofa, shaking her head. "What look? I have a look?"

"You know what I mean. I'm sure when I get home there will be a wonderful story of what magical things took place at this *luncheon*."

Maddy kissed his forehead. "It's just lunch. What could possibly happen?" She crossed her arms and looked out on the garden, lost in her thoughts.

Esme and Maddy arrived at the restaurant, hoping to be early, but Jakob was waiting for them. He looked nervous and so handsome in his suit. Esme played with her pearls, anxious to see her old lover. Maddy sat with them for a cocktail and then left them when her phone rang. She apologized for the interruption, but there were construction details that must be sorted before the workers went home. Esme smiled nervously as

Maddy walked away, promising to be quick. "Please order without me … I'll be back," she whispered as she held her phone on her chest.

When Maddy returned, the two old friends were sipping their coffee, relieved to see her. They were very polite with each other, but Maddy sensed it was time to go.

In the cab, Esme was giddy. "Maddy, that was reaffirming. Thank you."

Maddy smiled and waited for Esme to continue.

"What an emotional adventure. At first I felt young again; it was thrilling to think back on our time together. Then I felt old as I heard of Jakub's life and health, then I felt happy that I had known him at all and then … then I felt elated that I hadn't left Gordon and run off with him." She laughed and touched Maddy's arm. "Does that make sense? I must sound like a foolish old woman to you." Esme sat back, eyes closed, shaking her head.

"Esme, I spoke to Gordon before we came."

"Oh my gosh, Maddy, he didn't know about Jakub," Esme responded, looking shocked.

"Yes, he did. He told me you were the reason he was so successful at the bank; he said you were the most sought-after hostess in banking circles. Without any coaxing from me, he told me about his indiscretions—how you knew but you never said a word. He knew you were seeing someone because you started to change your earrings … Such a little thing. You changed your earrings every day, and he realized you could be happy with someone else. He thought he might lose you, so he took you away on a proper holiday and made a pact with himself never to take you for granted again. He was very forthcoming about the fact that he might have lost you because he was self-centred and driven. He hoped you would come home today knowing in your heart you made the right decision to stay with him." Maddy smiled. "Isn't that lovely?"

Breaking her usual reserve, Esme reached out and cried on Maddy's shoulder. "He knew? He knew. I'm so foolish. All these years I've carried that secret, and he knew."

When Esme sat back, she dabbed her cheeks with her powder puff and composed herself. "I am so lucky, Maddy, and I'm just realizing it now. I've had a wonderful life with a wonderful man, and we are going to grow old together. Do you think it's too late to tell him he's always been the man for me?"

Maddy smiled. "It's never too late."

Maddy was watching an old film when Sebastian walked in. She had tears streaming down her cheeks, the large popcorn bowl on her lap, and a wad of tissues beside her, yet she was smiling up at him. He sat beside her, wiped her tears, and held her. He guessed the luncheon had gone well.

February

"You look *uber* important and more handsome than usual this morning." Maddy brushed lint from Sebastian's lapel.

"Big presentation today. This could be the springboard for bigger and better global coverage. Several options for franchising in North and South America will afford the junior designers some great opportunities." Sebastian checked his shirt cuffs. "If everything goes well, you and I could live in relative comfort for a very long time, and you'll get your tango lessons." Sebastian was in a happy mood as he walked to the door.

"We already live in relative comfort, but my fingers are crossed for you and the tango lessons," Maddy responded, kissing his cheek.

"It may be a late night. Shall I call you if we go out to celebrate?" He looked hopeful.

Maddy shook her head and patted his behind. "I'll be anxious to hear the outcome. Your team will want to celebrate with you. Enjoy the moment."

Sebastian stopped at the car door and looked back at Maddy. Her questions about succession had initiated this process. He had never given any thought to offshore growth or selling or even bringing in partners. He had taken stock of his assets and realized there were no plans in place should he ever wish to retire. He had been annoyed at the question, wondering why Maddy would ask.

However, on reflection, he admitted he needed a plan. Retirement was a reality now that he had someone to grow old with—someone to share his life with. Of course, Maddy had been right to start him thinking this way.

She always seemed to be challenging him. This was not on purpose, but her constant questions seemed to provide guidance in a roundabout way.

Sunshine in England brings everyone outdoors. Maddy was having tea on the patio, wrapped in an afghan, when Sebastian walked over to the garden apartment the next morning.

His steps were measured, and his face looked pained; it must have been quite a night.

Sebastian poured a coffee, eyed the large biscuits on the counter, picked one up, and chewed deliberately. "Hmm. Excellent!" he exclaimed.

"Henry made a batch yesterday; he'll be pleased you like them," Maddy responded, returning to the crossword. She was anxious to hear about his meeting but didn't press—all in good time.

"Henry?" Sebastian asked.

"Yesterday was his day with you; he sent a text message to say he was free earlier because his chemistry master was ill, so I picked him up and we spent the afternoon making his favourite things. We went to the market with Grace, then we had a cooking lesson, and then we came home to bake. He's very good at it. He made biscuits for his classmates."

"Oh, my goodness, I completely forgot. I'm so sorry. I was so absorbed in the meeting it just fell off my radar. Sorry." He looked contrite. His shoulders sagged as he sat down at the table.

"Sebastian, we had a great time together. No worries. Henry was fine; he even baked something for next week. It's a surprise. How did your meeting go?" She stroked his hair.

"Ah, yes, I came by last night, but you were sleeping. I didn't trust myself getting in here without waking you. Everything is signed, sealed, and put to bed, as you say. We may have to do some travelling to open offices … The team was ready and very professional. I was so very proud of how they handled the client presentations." He smiled and held his head in his hands.

"How wonderful. What a lovely legacy. It's okay to feel both happy and sad. It must be exciting and terrifying at the same time." She stood and bent over to hug him.

"Right now I just feel hungover. Oh, by the way, Philippe has invited us to his chalet; let's go skiing, shall we?" He stood up and kissed the top of her head.

The Ski
Trip—France

Philippe met them at the airport and whisked them to the ski shop, where they suited up for the mountains. By late afternoon, they were on skis, enjoying the sunshine and well-groomed runs. Maddy asked if she could acquaint herself with the mountain runs while they tore after each other on the black diamond runs. They agreed to meet in the main chalet at 3.30 p.m.

Heading up the lift, Philippe spotted Maddy skiing perfect turns, nicely carving her way down the mountain. They watched her for a few moments, Sebastian smiling at her reluctance to let him see her ski. He saw a wild snowboarder take a jump and collide with a skier; both ended up lying in a cloud of snow. A rogue ski was making its way across the run. "Oh dear, watch this …" Maddy grabbed the ski and snowploughed over to the jumble of people. "By the time we meet in the chalet, she will be making wedding plans for those two. Mark my words." He laughed, shaking his head.

The chalet was abuzz with weekend skiers and party people. They spotted Maddy sitting by the large mountain-view windows with an older man and his son, who was sporting a plaster cast on his leg. They were having an animated conversation while watching a video on the tablet the younger man was holding. Maddy jumped up when Sebastian touched her shoulder, introducing Mr Marceau and his son Francois. "Francois had an accident on the hill," Mr Marceau explained, "and Madeline was kind enough to stay with him until the ski patrol arrived. He has broken his leg in several places, but he will live."

He paused and bowed his head towards Maddy. "Ah, Philippe, Madeline tells me you produce excellent wine which would complement my restaurant menus. I would be interested in speaking with you about a partnership. Perhaps you will join us for aperitifs this evening at the chateau? My wife will be arriving soon and will need a diversion to take her mind off the accident."

Maddy smiled at the two men before her, eyes wide, waiting for their response.

"Bien sur, monsieur, a quelle temps?"

"Come at 1900, Chateau Bisson. We are just up the mountain, past the ski shop; everyone knows it. I think you can walk up."

"*Enchante.*" He kissed her hand. He picked up the crutches and helped his son up from the sofa. "*Alors, bientot.*" They made their way through the crowd, and both Sebastian and Philippe stared at Maddy.

"Do you know who that man is?" Philippe asked in wonder.

"Uh huh, he told me about his family and his business while we were waiting for you; he didn't want to leave me here alone." She smiled coyly and fluttered her eyes. "I thought you might be interested in meeting him. He had heard of your wines, Philippe, of course. Shall we go back to the chalet? We have to get ready for aperitifs." The men exchanged glances and followed her.

Philippe and Sebastian were donning their coats, discussing how many bottles of wine to bring with them, when Maddy walked into the room wearing a long, colourful jumper, matching hat and scarf, leggings, and high boots. She floated into the conversation, leaving both men speechless. "You look wonderful," Sebastian exclaimed.

"Marvellous outfit, Maddy," Philippe agreed.

"*Merci.* Let's hope Mr Marceau likes it enough to buy your wine. Shall we go?" She walked past the men to the door and pulled it open with wonder.

"Oh look; it's snowing. It's beautiful out; shall we walk?" The men followed her, too stunned to argue or think of anything else to say.

Madame Marceau was charming and jittery about the accident. Not a skier herself, she was distressed that her husband was so cavalier about the injury. Her son stayed in his room, happy to FaceTime his friends and show off his cast.

The cook had left a roast out but had an emergency in another town and would not be back to complete the meal. The storm had forced road closures, and they were, for all intents, snowed in. Madame was beginning to panic. It was too stormy to go out.

Maddy offered to assist, not sure of the protocol of being invited for aperitifs; did one stay for dinner or refuse politely? She was not able to huddle with her men, as they were deep in a conversation about trade barriers and tariffs.

She took Madame by the arm and suggested they see what the kitchen had to offer in the way of fixings. Madame confessed she did not cook and would not be any help. After a quick look through the large pantry, Maddy thought she could prepare something edible. She had Madame set the table and search out candles. They decided to eat in the massive country kitchen rather than the formal dining room. The high ceilings with beams, the wooden slab table set in by a large open fireplace, and the warmth of the range made this a cosy room.

Madame Marceau was eager to light the kitchen with as many candles as possible and to keep the fire going; the effect was magical.

Maddy seared the beef, cut the vegetables and produced a hearty soup, cut the bread, found several blocks of cheese and dates for a platter, and made a simple dessert with yogurt, honey, and pistachio nuts.

Madame invited the gentlemen to join them in the kitchen for a casual dinner. Mr Marceau ("Call me Gerard") mumbled a warning to his guests. "My wife is not a cook; I can only imagine what she has produced. I apologize in advance."

They walked into the candlelit kitchen, and each one of them gasped. The kitchen was warm and inviting, with candles everywhere. The table was set, and Maddy—or Madeline, as her hosts called her—was removing an apron as they approached the table. She was flushed and had flour in her hair. The kitchen was warm, the fire crackling, and the aroma of warm bread filled the room. The total scene simply took their breath away. Madame was very quick to praise Madeline for the bountiful meal, and at such short notice; she was proclaimed a genius.

They drank many bottles of wine, enjoyed a simple but delicious meal, and laughed at each other's stories, and by the time coffee was served, it was clear that the Marceau family now included a newly adopted daughter—Madeline.

The three friends clamoured into the villa, laughing and perhaps a little drunk. The men poured a nightcap, toasting Maddy on a brilliant evening. "Bravo, Madeline."

She bowed and said good night. They agreed to meet for breakfast, joking they would like to meet an Arab sheikh tomorrow on the mountain and asking whether Maddy could arrange an intimate gathering.

Shaking her head, she kissed Philippe on both cheeks and wrapped her arms around Sebastian, who whispered, "I'll try not to wake you; sleep well." She left the room with a wave. "bon reves."

When they were alone, Philippe looked up at Sebastian, who was standing at the hearth. "She is wonderful, my friend."

"Yes, but reckless—very reckless." Sebastian recounted the story of the car accident and her handling of the children, her intervention in the Tube mobbing, her cottage construction deals, and her hand in the marriage of George and Belle.

Philippe laughed; he was delighted the marriage had finally taken place. He had loved Belle as a child, finding her visits to the school so refreshing and avant garde.

Philippe put his drink down, closed his eyes, and then looked over at Sebastian. His accent thick, he said, "My friend, you call it reckless, but let me tell you, every night for almost forty years, I cannot sleep without seeing an image of a busy road, a burning car, and I wonder each time why some reckless person driving by did not stop and try to save our boys." He wiped a tear from his eye, stood, and placed his hand on Sebastian's shoulder. "I'm tired; it's been a hell of a day. Good night."

Sebastian got into the bed and kissed Maddy. She turned towards him, purring, her body warm and inviting. With an urgency that terrified him, he made love to her before falling back, exhausted. She curled up beside him, startling him from his own thoughts. He leaned over and kissed her head, whispering, "How could I love you more?"

Sebastian felt a chill and pulled the duvet up over his head. He reached out for Maddy and sat up suddenly, realizing she was not in bed. His head was throbbing as he walked carefully down the stairs to the kitchen. Maddy had set the table for breakfast and made coffee. She was dressed, and he was sure she would explode from excitement. She rushed over and hugged him, inviting him to join her in making snow angels. He eyed the coffee and, despite her pleading, opted to watch from the window with his coffee in hand. The snowfall had been major; the roads were closed, the ski lifts burdened with snow. There would be no skiing until the village crew could handle the snow removal. Maddy rushed out to the white canvas of snow, waving at Sebastian. She fell backwards and waved her arms and legs and then carefully stood up. He smiled at her enthusiasm and applauded her angel.

He turned as Philippe came down the stairs, groaning, anxious for coffee.

"No skiing today, unfortunately. Ahh, coffee. Where's Maddy? Still sleeping?" he asked, rubbing his temples.

"Come and see what she's creating in the snow." Sebastian moved over to make room for his friend at the window. He was amazed to see several children in the snow with Maddy, angels everywhere.

"Believe it or not, a moment ago there was no one out there." He laughed as he pointed to the scene below. Philippe joined in the laughter, suddenly remembering his hurting head.

"It's universal, the need to make an angel in the fresh snow. Did you do this when you were a boy?" he asked his friend.

"Never. Not enough snow. And when I went skiing, it was to ski. It does look like fun."

"Only a man in love would go out on such a day, with a wine hangover, to make a snow angel," Philippe challenged Sebastian.

"Indeed," Sebastian replied, smiling as he dressed for the outdoors and his first snow angel experience. Philippe merely chuckled and watched from the window.

Big flakes continued to fall throughout the day, forcing the friends to enjoy the fire in the chalet as the ski resort operators coped with the weight of the snow. Maddy was bright and cheery, her companions less so. She sent photos of the two men to Belle, who was delighted to see the friends united. Maddy found old board games, which had the three of them rolling on the floor with laughter at trades in Monopoly; shouts of "cheater" and "mercenary" made them laugh even more. Dinner was a simple affair with whatever could be found in the pantry. They ended the day watching old movies, laughing at Maddy when she cried, the three of them comfortable in each other's company.

Sunday was sunny and clear for an exceptional day of skiing. Maddy had made many friends on the mountain and in the chalet; she was in demand in the singles line at the chairlift. She made conversation with the other skiers, interested in who they were, what they did, where they liked to ski, and best places in the resort area. The men went off to tackle the moguls while Maddy preferred her long, scenic runs.

En route to joining her new friends in the bar at the hotel, Maddy walked through the lobby, her attention directed to a couple at the desk having difficulty with the hotel staff. She heard the Texas drawl getting louder and more forceful. It crossed her mind that Sebastian would advise her to walk away, but the situation was heating up and her legs carried her over to the desk.

"Excuse me; I couldn't help but hear your exchange. I speak English and some French, so perhaps I could assist with translation. I'm Maddy." She held her hand out, more as a truce than a greeting.

"Preston Chase McAllen." A large hand shook hers. "This here is Ms Kaitlin. We are trying to make this bonehead understand there is someone in our room. It's not acceptable, and Ms Kaitlin is upset beyond reason. We can't seem to get through to this guy that there is a problem. Can you fix that?" The big man moved his cigar from the corner of his mouth to his big hand.

Maddy asked for the key and checked with the desk clerk, in French, to ensure they had the right room. She suggested his companion browse the boutique in the lobby while they checked the room.

P. C., as he insisted Maddy call him, agreed this was a good plan. Ms Kaitlin loved shopping.

As they waited for the lift and walked to the room, P. C. informed Maddy he was in oil and cattle; this was a shopping trip, but they had to endure a day in the mountains because of the storm. Ms Kaitlin was anxious to get to Paris to spend his money, he told her with a laugh—a loud, jovial laugh that made his considerable girth jiggle.

At the room door, Maddy knocked, inserted the key, and cautiously walked into the suite, announcing their arrival. The suite was well appointed and vacant. P. C. looked around and stated this was not the same room they had previously walked into. He seemed confused. Maddy checked the room number and pointed out the desk clerk had written the 7 European-style, with a cross. She asked if they perhaps tried 849 rather than 879, which would be so easy to do when deciphering a hastily written number. P. C. was clearly embarrassed. Maddy suggested he run the bath for Ms Kaitlin while Maddy went downstairs to collect his bride. "A warm bath always makes a bad day better," she explained. She suggested perhaps he could visit the minibar and have cocktails ready when she returned. P. C. obliged and set about his tasks as Maddy went down to the lobby to collect Ms Kaitlin, who was agitated for having been kept waiting, her shopping having been completed quickly.

Arriving in the suite, Ms Kaitlin threw her coat on the sofa, asked for a drink, and proceeded to walk around the suite, inspecting the view and the furnishings. P. C. opened the bathroom door and suggested she relax in the bath. He used effusive motions and was clearly on his best behaviour.

Maddy turned to go, wishing them well on the rest of their trip. P. C. offered her US$100 for her troubles, which she refused to take. "I'm glad I could help you get settled. Enjoy your stay. I hear the dining room here is excellent, so you won't even have to leave the hotel this evening." She smiled and closed the door while P. C. was thanking her for saving the day. P. C. was not fond of the French or the language, as he reminded her.

In the lobby, Maddy was approached by the manager of the hotel, Giselle Semil, who thanked her for helping with the American guests. Her front desk clerk had been rattled by the situation and had reported to the manager, detailing how easily Maddy had diffused the situation. "Please be my guest in the dining room this evening," she offered. Maddy thanked her and said she was waiting for her friends to return. Ms Semil assured her a table for three would be available.

"I would love to accept your offer, but only if you will join us and meet my companions." Maddy said, adding, "I'm sure the men are tired of my company."

"That's very kind of you. I am new to the hotel and the area. It would be nice to enjoy a meal with others. Shall we say 2000 hours?"

Maddy was pleased with the plan. Philippe would surely enjoy Giselle; she was petite and foreign looking, smart, and French-speaking—a nice addition to the group. Maddy smiled in delight at her attempt in matchmaking. As she was leaving, Giselle invited her to afternoon tea, a new service in the lounge. Maddy hesitated but realized Giselle needed to talk to someone.

The two women were quick to learn about each other, sharing their stories and enjoying each other's company. They talked about everything from recipes to events to staff issues. Giselle was happy to speak to another woman, she said.

Maddy found the afternoon to be quite pleasant, although at one point she realized she would barely have time for a last run before the men arrived. She hurried out, promising to see her new friend that evening for dinner, men in tow.

The last run of the day is always enjoyable but bittersweet, with tall shadows falling across the slopes as the sun hides behind the mountain. Maddy enjoyed a glorious run, and they all arrived at the chalet at the same time.

"What a day. The conditions were perfect." Sebastian said.

Philippe agreed. "Shall we have a drink before we head home?" he called as he placed his skis in the rack.

"I made a dinner reservation for this evening, and I have a surprise for you two," Maddy added as they made their way into the lounge.

"Great, I couldn't make another decision today. We skied hard." Sebastian held the door for her and kissed her forehead.

They were seated and sipping on a glass of champagne when Giselle joined them, apologizing for her tardiness, explaining she was required in a less pleasant situation.

The men stood, greeting her, appreciating her fine features and precise speech. She welcomed the group and mentioned how wonderful Maddy had been to step in and calm the rather loud Americans earlier in the day. The men gave each other a look and waited to hear what Maddy had done. The story was interrupted by the entrance of a large man and an overdressed young woman. P. C. McAllen saw Maddy immediately and made his way to the table.

"Best advice I ever got, running that bath, Ms Maddy. I feel like a new man." He laughed loudly. "What y'all drinking? Champagne? Waiter, send another bottle over here for my friend." He gestured grandly, the cigar in his stubby fingers.

Maddy introduced P. C. and Ms Kaitlin to her companions, but P. C. wasn't listening; he thanked Maddy again and followed the hostess to his table.

Dinner was pleasant, rich with interesting conversation and stories. Giselle was Algerian, married with two children. Her husband was in Dubai; he had decided he enjoyed life in the Middle East and would not be relocating to France, especially in winter. The children preferred to stay with their father.

P. C., as he insisted being called, asked Maddy to dance the two-step when the band started playing. He was an energetic dancer. Ms Kaitlin didn't like dancing with him; she just liked shopping with him. He was pleased to have such a good partner. As Maddy left the table, Giselle put her hand on Sebastian's arm. He turned to look at her in alarm. "Maddy cannot see the look you give her when she is walking away. It's the look of a man who has found something he doesn't want to lose. She is good for you; she makes you better." Giselle sat back, leaving Sebastian wondering if she had given him a compliment or chastised him. He was happy to have Maddy return to the table.

The maître d' announced the last course, winking at Maddy. Wine was poured, and hand-crafted chocolates were placed on the table. The wine was Philippe's Merlot, and the chocolates were hand-produced in the village. A hint of cherry in the wine with the rich plain chocolate made for a delicious pairing. Maddy offered to introduce the village chocolatier to Philippe, who laughed at the offhand way she found partners and opportunities.

Sebastian and Maddy managed one dance before the band took a break. Giselle was needed at the front desk, so the group said their goodnights and the trio headed back to the chalet, tired and overfed. On the walk home, Maddy, arm in arm between the men, asked Philippe if he would see Giselle again. "Wasn't she beautiful, smart, and elegant?"

Philippe agreed but pointed out that Giselle was more interested in Maddy than in him or Sebastian.

"Well, that's only because she doesn't know you very well yet," Maddy retorted.

"Indeed," both men answered, not daring to exchange a look.

In the morning a package was delivered from the hotel for Maddy. A large box of chocolates with a handwritten note:

> If you ever need anything, call me. I'll take care of it. I have a
> luxury liner in the Mediterranean—use it. P. C. McAllen

Maddy smiled and put the note in her pocket. "How sweet." She was touched. *Poor Preston*, she thought.

Maddy and Sebastian were sad to leave Philippe at the airport, and again promises of more frequent visits were made. As Philippe kissed her on both cheeks, he invited Maddy to come and work with him if she ever tired of London. Sebastian smirked but held her tight as he shook hands with his friend.

The Luck of the Irish

"Maddy Davis. I finally found you. Meet me at my club tomorrow, will you? I want you to meet someone. Let me redeem myself after upsetting you at the New Year's party. My driver will collect you at 1000 a.m.; I've got the address. We'll have lunch." Michael Riley was speaking fast.

"What if I'm busy tomorrow?" Maddy asked.

"Aw, come on, Maddy; I've got a day planned, and you can't let me down—not when I'm apologizing and all. See you tomorrow." He ended the call.

Maddy stared at the phone. What could he have planned? Should she tell Sebastian she was meeting him? Should she even go?

The driver was quite chatty but not Irish; why had she thought he would be Irish? Arriving at the club, he escorted Maddy through the large wooden door into the foyer, where they were greeted by a Greek goddess— the concierge. Her name badge said *Connie.*

"Welcome. Mr Riley has arranged a day in our spa for you. You are to relax and enjoy the services. He will join you later, perhaps for lunch or afternoon tea. Right this way." Connie ushered Maddy into a change room. The driver had disappeared. *No turning back.*

There was a note in the locker addressed to Maddy.

Madison, I owe you a day of pampering and enjoyment. Alas, I am sorry it is not with me but here at the spa. Late lunch on the terrace. Michael

Maddy sat on the bench, wondering what was going on.

"Ms Davis. Ms Madison Davis." A soft voice was calling her. "Ms Davis, I'm ready for you in Salon B. Massage first, manicure, facial, pedicure to follow. We should get started." The voice left the room, and Maddy realized she had a choice; she could enjoy the day or leave and possibly insult her host. She quickly changed and headed to Salon B.

The day was relaxing, and Maddy looked very fresh as she appeared on the terrace. Michael had been informed by the staff she was on her way. He stood as she approached the table, holding her chair.

"Thank you, Michael, it was a lovely day."

"I'm delighted you enjoyed it. I don't get to do nice things for people very often. Usually I'm doing bad things to people: foreclosing their mortgages, breaking their knees … you know what I mean." He smiled, and Maddy realized he really didn't have many friends.

"Well, I'm glad I was on the upside and I get to keep my kneecaps." She laughed.

"Tea? Shall I pour?" He was businesslike.

"Where's your friend?" Maddy looked around.

"I wanted you to meet the real Mickey O'Riley, aka Michael Riley. I'm not the type of person you would associate with, I'm sure. Michael has had to hide Mickey from London society; he wouldn't fit in. He's a gangster. But Michael—he's done well. Married well. Got into this club. Can you believe they let an Irish Catholic into this club? Mickey wouldn't be allowed in—too much baggage. Am I scaring you?" He leaned over the table and touched her hand.

"What makes Mickey so bad? Michael is very successful; surely he doesn't want to forget his roots?"

"He sees opportunity where others see compassion. He makes money on the bad fortune of others. Despicable. His mother is turning in her grave. Bless her soul." He made the sign of the cross and looked upward.

"Yet here he is, at the top of the food chain in London, sipping tea with me on a glorious day. Michael has been good for you. I'm pleased to meet you, Mickey. You have a heart, and you know who you are. You are a survivor … That's all that counts. Scone?" Maddy smiled.

Michael laughed, his head back, his hands in the air. "Finally someone understands me. Let's get out of here. Come on; I want to show you my latest acquisition." He stood and held out his hand.

The acquisition, his latest toy, was a beautiful forty-eight-foot sailing boat on the Thames. Michael was a keen sailor, having grown up by the sea.

"Will you come sailing with me when we have a good day?" he asked. "Right now, we can enjoy the sunshine on deck. I'll be a minute with something to eat. Get a drink from that cabinet over there." He pointed to the bar. "I'll have a lager. Ta."

They sat on the deck, swaying in the wake of the passing boats, eating grilled salmon. If his uncle had not taken him away from his family and enrolled him in the private boarding school he taught at, Mickey O'Riley would have surely done jail time. He learned to survive on the streets rather than go home to his father's beatings. He stole and did gang jobs, working on the docks to earn enough money for his mother and sisters. He dreamed of a life with enough food to eat, nice clothes and money for his mother. It wasn't long before he realized he was lucky; he gambled and won—often. He chose to study accounts, as his maths on the street had to be quick. He didn't want to be cheated by anyone. He carried on at university believing that graduating with a degree meant freedom and earning potential. His knowledge of the dockyards helped him build a solid business.

Soon he was loaning money at high rates to those who could not find financing elsewhere. His collections were sketchy but profitable. Francis Bennett and her family provided stability and class. He didn't love her, but she needed a reasonably good-looking self-made man, and he needed the key to London society. It was a trade—a comfortable trade.

Maddy listened to his story, at times shocked, at times astounded by his drive. He wasn't Mickey O'Riley any more; he was more Michael Riley than he realized. Atoning for his past, he had become a prominent philanthropist.

As the sun hid behind the towers on the Thames, Maddy stood and bade him farewell.

"Thank you for a lovely day, Michael. I hope I do get to sail with you. You're an interesting man, and I think your mother would be proud of you." She leaned over and kissed his cheek. "Goodbye, my friend."

Michael didn't move; he continued to stare out at the water. He didn't want her to go. She was a good listener; perhaps he had said too much. He hoped he would see her again. She was easy to be with. Women were usually keen on what he could offer them, where he could take them, and what he could buy them. They didn't seem content to spend time with him, just sitting and enjoying a meal.

Maddy took the underground home, wondering why Michael had wanted her to have a day at the spa—why he had wanted her to see his sailing boat and have lunch away from the club he obviously regarded as a rung in his ladder of success. As she walked the last blocks home, she concluded he was just lonely. There was a great deal of loneliness in the big city. *Poor Michael.*

Connections

Sebastian leaned against the bar, admiring the way Maddy moved around the room, mingling with the club members. Their schedules had not allowed them to attend many of the monthly events.

A booming voice startled his reverie. "Sebastian, old man, how did you manage to capture that rare bird?"

Derek Benson, the head of the Greater London City Council, was beside him.

Sebastian looked over at the stodgy man, who by now had drunk too many scotches, and wondered what he was talking about.

Benson carried on. "That woman, Maddy, she must be getting tired of you. Are you almost done with her? She seems too feisty for you. You aren't really the type to hold on to someone so long … I'm only asking because I'm a gentleman." He placed his chubby hand on Sebastian's shoulder.

Sebastian gripped the bar to stop himself hitting the man.

Benson laughed. "Don't get so self-righteous. I'm just checking. Also, why the hell am I hearing about your task force from a foreigner instead of yourself?" He was slurring his words.

Sebastian chose to respond to the business question. "The proposal was sent to your office months ago."

"Well, bloody hell, let's fit you in for the next council meeting—last Thursday of the month. Can you be ready to give the proposal to the committee?"

"Certainly. Why the sudden interest?"

"Maddy just chastised me for not being part of the ground-level advisory group. She's right, of course. Her explanation was so concise and compelling that I feel we need to be involved. You would do well to have her present for you; she didn't use the word 'actually' once. She's very passionate in her presentation of the facts. I stopped looking at her legs to listen." Benson laughed at his own statement, leaning over, banging his empty glass on the bar. "Interesting woman. She sails with Michael Riley; she's obviously well connected."

Sebastian scanned the room for Maddy. How could Maddy know so much about the task force? he was careful not to burden her with his work.

Benson tossed his drink back and turned to walk away. "Walker, can you be ready for this month?"

Sebastian nodded, extending his hand. "Thank you."

"Don't thank me; thank your friend." Benson burped into his sleeve and waved.

"Sir." Jason, the bartender, offered a tall glass with lime and nodded towards Maddy, who was now sitting at the table. Sebastian smiled, nodded back, and walked to the table.

"I thought you might like a fresh drink." He placed the glass on the table and touched her shoulder. "Actually, Jason sent it over."

Maddy thanked him and raised her glass to Jason.

Sebastian cleared his throat.

"Maddy, how did you convince Benson to schedule the task force for the council meeting?" he asked carefully.

Maddy looked over at him, biting the inside of her cheek. "I'm sorry; I know you think I'm a bubblehead and I talk too much and I meddle, but Christian sent me a copy of your proposal and asked me for comments. I didn't think to ask you if it was okay to respond. It was tough going, but I think I understand the basics, and that horrible man was coming on to me, so I changed the subject when he told me who he was. Am I not supposed to know anything about it?" She sounded like a robot running out of battery power.

Sebastian leaned back in shock. "Maddy, never would I consider you a bubblehead. You are incredibly bright, and the only reason I haven't spoken to about the task force is that I feel it might bore you. It's not exciting material, as you learned." Sebastian felt helpless.

"But it's what you do. It's important to you. Why wouldn't I want to know what you are working on? That's what people do; they share. It doesn't matter. I'm sorry. I gave my notes to Christian and tried to make it simple." Maddy waved her hand in defeat and looked around the room, not wanting to make eye contact. She always seemed to do the wrong thing.

"We are on the agenda at the next council meeting, thanks to you. I understand you were passionate; I hope you can share that passion with me." He touched her arm lightly. "Thank you."

Maddy looked up and smiled. "I see the possibility for exciting new thinking and opportunities. I listed some. The square in Krakow is a good model for what you want to accomplish ... Sorry, I'm going on." She sat back and clasped her hands as Sebastian laughed and then leaned forward to kiss her cheek.

"I have a gem in my pocket, and instead of embracing you, I'm blowing up the mine searching for the motherlode. What an idiot I am. I promise to talk to you about my work." He held out his hand, silently inviting her to come home.

It crossed his mind to ask her about Michael Riley, but it wasn't important right now.

March

The sounds of her sobs made him run through the garden and into the dark apartment, his heart pounding. "Maddy, what's wrong? Are you hurt? What happened? Why are you sitting alone in the dark?" He felt helpless, catching the outline of her curled up on the sofa, her body heaving from the sobs. He turned on the lamp, dimming it just enough to see her face.

Maddy ran the back of her hand across her eyes, sniffling, realizing she was not alone.

Sebastian knelt beside her, wondering what could possibly have driven her to this state.

He pulled out his handkerchief, wiped her tear-stained cheeks, and then held it over her nose, nodding for her to blow her nose. She giggled and took the cloth from him. It was such a lovely gesture, his habit of always handing her a hankie. Laughing and crying, she looked at his concerned face and knew she had to explain. Leaning forward, she wrapped her arms around his neck and slid down to the floor beside him, feeling comfort in having him there.

"Today was more than I could handle," she confessed, trying to stop the tears from flowing.

"What happened? Tell me. I'm here for you," he whispered as he wiped the tears from her cheek.

Maddy moved away and collected herself before speaking.

"One of my chemo charges passed away this morning, right after his treatment." Her chest was heaving, but she was determined to stop the sobs.

Sebastian moved closer and held her in his arms. "I'm so sorry." He knew she regularly visited the hospital to sit with the chemo patients. Davi had reported she was so positive for the patients, filling the time with small talk, showing movies, challenging them with current events, and reading to them. They looked forward to her visits. "What happened?"

"Liam was a great kid, such a nice young man. This was his fourth session with my group. This morning he had black circles around his eyes, his skin was translucent, and he seemed to have trouble focusing, but the nursing staff didn't seem too concerned."

She stopped to wipe her tears and breathe. "He told us he had three wishes: he wanted to drive a racing car, he wanted to skydive, and he wanted to be kissed by a girl other than his mother before he died. It was really cute, and the older patients joked with him, sharing their last wishes." She smiled as she recalled the light banter.

"Just before the drip was completed, I offered to push the swivel chair through the ward at high speed so he could simulate the racing car feeling. We determined we could hang him from the shower harness so he could experience the feel of falling through the sky or landing with a parachute. He was game to try both, with encouragement from the others, of course." She stopped for a moment. "Then he asked about the kiss. We looked around and took stock, creating lots of laughter and kidding with each other. We could only see male orderlies in the ward, a male cleaner, and a stern-looking matron at the nurse's station. He looked at me with wide eyes and asked if I would be his girl. It was really touching." She smiled, lost in her thoughts and then looked over at Sebastian. He was watching her with such tenderness that she thought she might start crying again.

"Go on." He nodded in encouragement.

"After we joked about the situation, I realized he was serious. He looked so earnest. I leaned over and kissed him on the cheek. It was just an innocent kiss on the cheek."

"You're a great kisser. Was he thrilled?" He was imagining the scene and how poignant it must have been.

"He kept his eyes closed for quite a while. Well, it seemed like a while. He just sat there, smiling, lost in some other world. He didn't say a word. It was weird." She shook her head, as if to erase the memory. "When the nurse came to check on him, he didn't move; he fell over."

"That must have been quite the kiss," Sebastian said lightly.

"Indeed. It was a killer kiss." She sniffed. "There was a flurry of activity, with attendants and stretchers, and through it all it was so quiet in the room. His mother arrived in a fluster, accusing me of turning him against her … It was pretty harsh."

Sebastian rocked her in his arms, whispering in her hair. "You're a good person, Maddy."

Sebastian led her to the bed and threw the duvet over them, fully dressed. Maddy fell asleep in his arms.

After midnight, Sebastian realized he still had his suit on. He gently crept out of the bed, trying not to disturb Maddy. He brushed his teeth, got ready for bed, and noticed the orange file on the desk. Maddy had told him she had a file with things she might forget to tell him. It was labelled in big letters "Stuff for Sebastian." He poured a drink and carried the file over to the sofa.

Maddy had saved cards, news clippings, song lyrics, a progress report on the cottage remodel, and memorabilia from their dinners and outings. Notes from the Texan, Maria, the Marceaus in France, neighbours, and friends had been kept in the file. She had created a hardcover book or album of their first months together. He smiled at the photos of Belle and George, Henry, the buttons, her friends dining and dancing, her memories of their ski trip, afternoon tea, the theatre, the coffee house, and their travels. He felt a tear as he saw the photo of her pilgrim companions in Santiago de Compostela—a month he had thrown away. There were photos of the two of them in the country, at functions, and at home. It was a marvellous collection of memories. He went through the album twice, enjoying the love and thought she had put into the project. He found a proposal labelled "Discussion Paper for a Women's Club", which referred to a club exclusively for women, where they could workout, relax in a spa, work and entertain, stay overnight, and be taken care of by trusted employees, as men did. It was addressed to Maria, and Maddy had placed sticky notes with questions and suggestions on it. He rubbed his eyes, returned the file and climbed into the bed. His mind was racing with the contents of the file, but once he was in bed, Maddy settled into his arms. *How nice it is to provide comfort to another person*, he thought as he drifted off.

When Maddy woke, Sebastian had breakfast ready. He was still in a T-shirt and pyjama bottoms, barefoot. He greeted her with a chai and announced he was staying home for a recovery day. He explained that a recovery day was much like a truant day, but it was for healing rather than sloth. They had movies to watch, crosswords to complete, and lots of junk food. Orders had been issued; they were not to be disturbed.

"That's very sweet of you, but not required. I know how busy you are at work." She hugged him.

"I insist."

"Thank you, Sebastian. I really don't want to be alone. Thank you," she said, burrowing her head into his chest.

"Indeed. You would do the same for me. Actually, you have." Sebastian was looking forward to taking care of her, even if only for a day.

The rain gave up at last, just as dusk approached. Maddy opened the glass door and stepped out on the deck, breathing in the fresh air.

Sebastian walked over to the deck, folding her in his arms. "Are you bored?" he asked.

Maddy turned her face to his. "Absolutely not. It was a splendid day. You?"

He shook his head. "I could get used to spending the day with you. It was nice to be together without the usual cast of thousands."

Maddy laughed and turned to him. "Thank you for today. I've been so selfish, not realizing you also have been through a terrible time. I'm sorry. Today was a healing day for both of us." Maddy sighed and looked out at the garden. "I love the smell of the garden after the rain. It's so, so earthy … so hopeful. I need to feel hopeful."

"When I'm with you, I notice things that passed me by for a lifetime." He kissed her neck. "I also want to touch you, to hold you, to sleep with you," he continued.

Maddy studied his face. "You really are a romantic, despite how hard you fight it."

Sebastian smiled, looking upward. "*Romantic* is not a word most would associate with me; believe me."

"Are you afraid?" Maddy whispered, hoping he wouldn't shut her out.

"Perhaps." Sebastian looked over her head and into space, considering the question. "Perhaps I thought I had my one chance at happiness and when it ended, that was that. It was easier to concentrate on building the business, no distractions." He paused. "Until you happened into my life, and now I welcome the distraction." He felt as though her eyes were pulling him out of the water he had been treading for so long.

Maddy smiled a slow smile, her face transmitting her feelings for him. He felt he had to go on. "When we go out with others, I find myself waiting for you to look over and give me that private smile—the smile that tells everyone else we have a secret. I wait for you to touch my hand or my leg under the table. It's a simple gesture, but it makes me feel you know I'm there, and it's a promise that I'm going home with you." He shook his head and continued. "It's very comforting."

Maddy was touched. She wanted to tell him she felt the same, she wanted to tell him she could hardly wait to see him every evening, and she wanted to tell him she treasured every minute they spent holding each other. She wanted to say so many things, but words seemed inadequate. She held his face in her hands and, closing her eyes, kissed him softly and then more urgently. Sebastian responded to the kiss, pulling her into his arms and pressing his body against hers. *It is true*, he thought. *One can say so much when one says nothing at all.* As they moved into the apartment and across the room to the bed, still holding each other, Sebastian wondered what a romantic person would do to show someone he or she cared. Lambert would know exactly what to do, indeed.

Sunday Morning Experiment

Maddy looked out on the garden terrace and shrugged, realizing the rain was good for the garden but not so good for the soul. She carried the coffee to the bedside table and looked at Sebastian, who was engrossed in a thick report.

"Your coffee is right here." She placed the cup down. "Sebastian, can you help me with something? Please." She stood by the bed, looking down at him. He removed his glasses, marked the page, and looked up at her.

"Certainly, what can I do for you?"

"It's a research project. I'm sure it won't take long." She gave him a sideward glance.

Every instinct told him she was teasing, but he played along. "Fine."

She moved his report and glasses to the sofa, and before he knew what was happening, she straddled him on the bed.

"What am I to do in your research?" he asked with a grin.

In response Maddy held his face and kissed him tenderly, and then more urgently.

He was powerless; his body had a mind of its own. He moved quickly and rolled over her. They made love, moving together slowly, exploring and touching each other as if it were their first time.

Sebastian fell away, breathing deeply, feeling years younger. He looked over at Maddy lying beside him; she was teasing him with her mischievous grin. He turned on his side to watch her. How she had changed his life. He wondered if he could live without her. When she turned her head to him, he felt as though he might drown in her eyes. He touched her cheek and innocently asked how the research was going.

Maddy sat up and looked thoughtful, considering her answer. "It's inconclusive at best. I'm going to need more data. We may have to rethink the method." She stared at him wide-eyed, rubbing her chin.

He smiled back, about to tell her he was happy to be the lab rat in this experiment, but Maddy had already moved under the duvet, her hands behind her head, her expression one of deep thought.

"How many others will be considered in the research?" he asked as he slid under the duvet with her.

"Well, I'm only interested in you, because the results are so ... um, gratifying. I'm not interested in testing anyone else." She looked over at him. "I really wanted to know if the report you were reading was stimulating. It appears to be extremely so. We could market this to people who seem to have lost their mojo. What do you think?" She couldn't keep a straight face.

Sebastian laughed and gathered her in his arms. "Let's leave the report for now and get out of here. What would you like to do in the rain?"

"There's a medieval festival today; you might like the re-enactments. It's not far from here. Come on—beat you to the shower." She was out of bed, daring him to join her.

He laughed and followed her into the shower, shaking his head and wondering what kind of child she must have been. She was crazy, and he liked her that way.

Sailing

"Good morning, sleepyhead. Delivering your tea." Sebastian sat on the edge of the bed, lightly stroking her hair. He was ready to leave for the day.

Maddy stretched and smiled up at him. "You are too good to me … and I love it." She sat up. "What's up today?"

"Just the usual client meeting and reviews on projects. You?" Sebastian enjoyed their morning banter.

"Come sailing with us this afternoon. We're getting pretty good."

"Sailing? I didn't know you had a passion for the sea." Sebastian recalled someone mentioning Maddy had been sailing with Michael.

"Henry needed an athletic credit, and one day of fencing left me bruised and battered. Michael offered to take him sailing, but it's too weird to leave him alone with a stranger, so the school assigned me, believe it or not, as a 'responsible person'," Maddy laughed.

"Why Mick O'Riley, of all people?" Sebastian stood and walked around the room.

"Michael offered when he heard there was a connection with the school. I thought it was a nice gesture. Are you upset with me?" Maddy was confused by the reaction.

"Mick or Michael, whatever you call him, isn't usually helpful unless there's something in it for him. I just don't know what would possess you to go sailing with him. I can't; I won't. I really don't trust him or his motives." There, he had finally said it out loud. He didn't trust Mick O'Riley. Never had, never would. Why was Mick so interested in Maddy?

He turned as he heard a soft voice from the bed. "Do you trust me?"

He closed his eyes and shook his head. That was never in question. "Of course I trust you, Maddy. I trust you with my life."

"Michael has my friendship, but you have everything else." She ran her hands through her hair. "He's a lonely person with few friends, and he has been very generous with Henry. I don't know what happened to make you distrust him so much, but he knows I can only be a friend. You're my guy." Maddy looked so vulnerable sitting in bed against the white pillows, her hair messy, the thin strap of her nightgown off her shoulder. Sebastian felt weak at the knees.

Sebastian picked up his mobile, loosened his tie, and walked towards the bed.

"Daveesh, I have to finish something important before I leave for the office. Let's aim for 9.30 a.m." He dropped the phone, unbuttoned his shirt, tossed the tie on the sofa, stepped out of his shoes, and lunged for Maddy on the bed. She was laughing and kissing him and helping him out of his trousers at the same time. They were playful yet intense as they made love.

Sebastian looked over at Maddy and felt a sudden urge to wrap himself around her and protect her. Maddy was breathing evenly, a smile on her lips, her arms above her head. He propped himself up on one arm and kissed her cheek. He felt the flutter of her eyelashes on his face as she opened her eyes. She moved her arm around his neck, cradling his head on her chest, stroking his hair. "Come sailing with us. Henry would love for you to see how proficient he's become. Please."

"How can I say no to you?" He smiled and threw back the duvet. "Come on; it's time to get up. Quick shower?"

Later that evening, as they sat at dinner with a very tired Henry, Sebastian had to admit he was impressed with the finesse Henry had shown on the boat. He was quick to react to the captain's commands, and he seemed to enjoy being out on the water, the wind in his face. Michael had been a gentleman, different somehow than Sebastian remembered. Both Henry and Michael were vying for Maddy's approval. Well, really, weren't they all?

At the end of the lesson, Mick took Henry down into the cabin to complete his lesson plan.

"Mad, my luv, take us home." Maddy nodded and took the helm as if she were a seasoned sailor. Sebastian sensed camaraderie between them.

It was a pleasant outing, and although Maddy had invited Michael to join them for sushi, he had declined, apologizing as he had a previous engagement. He did seem genuinely disappointed.

As they lay in bed that night, Sebastian stroking her hair, listening to her breathing, he felt he had to say something.

"Maddy, you must think me an awful old fool, but I waited a lifetime for you; I can't lose you to Mick or anyone else. I hope you understand. I'm glad I saw Henry on the boat; you've done wonders with him. He's becoming more confident and attached to you all the time. Thank you." He was whispering in the dark, not sure if she was asleep.

Just One Night

"It's just one night, but I hate to leave you." Sebastian kissed the top of her head as he glanced at his watch.

"You've spoiled me; I hate to sleep alone. Hurry back." Maddy wrapped her arms around him and squeezed.

"Next time we'll both go and spend some time relaxing in Geneva. Is that a possibility?" he asked hopefully.

"Maybe next time. Regards to Maria and Christian."

Sebastian looked back as he walked to the waiting car, smiling as Maddy blew him a kiss. He realized he really didn't want to go without her. He waved reluctantly, capturing her smile in his memory.

Maddy went through the motions of visiting her chemo patients, calling in to see how Esme was feeling, checking in on Audrey, delivering lunch to Mr Simpson at the bookshop, and meeting with the professor to interview a potential entertainment director. She was in no hurry to return home, as Sebastian was away. She ate dinner sitting on the sofa, watching old movies.

Just before midnight, as Sebastian walked into the garden, he heard voices, gunshots and more shouting. Curious, he hurried into the apartment. Maddy was asleep on the sofa, the television keeping her company. He turned off the film and leaned over her, watching her sleep.

He kissed her forehead, her cheek, and her lips. He was rewarded with a sleepy smile.

"Sebastian, you're home. I missed you."

"Me too; I took the late flight. I didn't want you to sleep alone." He whispered in her ear, kissing her neck.

Maddy sat up, throwing her arms around his neck. "How lovely. Thank you. I didn't really want to go to bed without you."

"Come on; let's get some sleep. No more overnights for me unless you join me. New rule."

Maddy stretched and smiled as she sleepily walked over to the bed. He had come home early. Had she willed it, or had he really missed her? No matter, he was here beside her, his arms around her. She felt safe and warm and loved. Who needed anything more?

Just before Sebastian fell into a deep sleep, he realized he had never done anything like this before—rushing home to be with someone. It was a good feeling lying here with someone he cared about—with someone who cared about him. This woman was giving him so many happy moments.

Timing Is Everything

Maddy felt the phone vibrate in her pocket just as the lamb fell asleep in her arms. Trying not to wake the animal, she moved one arm down her side to the phone. "Hello, Maddy here," she said quietly, amid the mayhem.

"Maddy, Sebastian here. I know I promised to take you to dinner, but Maria has flown in for a stopover and we are working on the final proposal. We should have a draft in the next few hours. Any chance you could join us for dinner in town?"

He hoped she wouldn't be disappointed that business was creating a change of plans.

"Why don't you come here and let me prepare dinner. You can work in the dining room until you're ready for cocktails, and then we can eat together in the garden," she offered, distracted by the noise around her.

"That's a nice offer, but I don't want you to prepare dinner for us." He did like the idea of going home rather than eating out.

"No worries. You finish your work, and we'll have a relaxing evening here. It'll be great to see Christian and Maria anyway." Maddy walked to the kitchen door of the main house and motioned to Mrs B., who was packing up baking for the boys.

"If you are absolutely positive, it's a go; everyone would rather sit in your garden than be here at the office. Shall we pick something up on our way?"

"No, no, everything is good. See you soon."

"Maddy … thank you." Sebastian sounded relieved.

Maddy smiled and returned the phone to her pocket. *Oh dear, hopefully everything is in order when they get here.* "Ah, Mrs B, there you are. Sebastian is coming home with his business associates, and they will have to meet in the dining room. Water, coffee, some snacks … is that possible?" She was careful not to demand the setup.

Mrs B waved a hand and indicated it was no problem. She was flushed and enjoying the craziness of the day.

Henry and his classmates had called first thing in the morning, asking Maddy for her assistance. The class trip had been cancelled last minute as insect spraying was taking place and it was not safe for the boys to picnic in the park. The headmaster cleared the suggestion of getting Maddy to help, as he was aware and amused by her creativity and ability to handle any crisis. Maddy called Leda and asked for a cultural learning day with food and stories. When the school bus arrived at 11.00 a.m., Leda and her family had set up tents with large cushions, barbecue cooking areas, and a small enclosure with goats and a lamb. Mrs B had started baking as soon as she heard the group would be arriving. The garden was filled with uniformed schoolboys, tents, Lebanese music, and the aroma of spices. The noise level was high, but it was so positive, and everyone was enjoying the stories, the food, the dancing, and the cultural differences that Maddy was sure the neighbours would not mind. She had invited Audrey and Esme over, and of course Grace stopped in to deliver sausage pies and coffee cake, just in case there were picky eaters.

The little lamb was missing his mother and quieted only when held against Maddy's heartbeat. She was carrying the lamb and laughing with a group of students who wanted to show her their interpretation of belly dancing when she saw Sebastian approach the patio with Maria and Christian in tow. The looks on their faces covered a range of feelings from shock to disbelief to amusement to despair. Another time Maddy would have laughed out loud at how out of place they appeared—adding to the apparent mayhem.

Maddy walked over to Sebastian, thinking fast. "Ah, here you are. I wasn't expecting you for at least an hour or so. Mrs B has you set up in the dining room with refreshments. The boys are leaving soon, so it'll be quiet and tidy in no time. I'll explain later." She tried to move them towards the house, but they were slow to move, taking in the scene before them.

"How nice to see you, Maria." She nodded. "Christian, we're looking forward to your fundraiser. Say hello to Henry before he leaves us, won't you." Maddy caught his eye and smiled back at him.

She could see Sebastian evaluating the tableau before him. He looked at Maddy and the lamb warily. She shook her head and laughed. "No, we can't keep him. He has to go back."

Sebastian tried not to smile, and when Maddy held the lamb out, he backed away. "Please take him for just a minute while I check on the room," she pleaded.

Sebastian held the lamb at arm's length, and immediately the baby started bleating. He looked so uncomfortable, and the lamb was so noisy that the energetic boys turned to see what was happening. Henry ran over to take his photo, laughing and greeting the adults. "Maddy saved the day, and that little lamb knows it."

Maddy returned and relieved Sebastian of the lamb just in time. She handed him a wet cloth to wipe his hands, knowing he would be concerned about holding the animal. He was funny that way.

The adults moved into the dining room, closing out the noise and smell of the garden, still too shocked to speak. The boys were collecting trash and folding blankets under the leadership of the head boy and headmaster. Leda and her family were thrilled with the reaction of the boys and were packing food for them to take back to the school. There was a package for Maddy—enough for several dinners. She hugged the family goodbye and thanked them for being so responsive and providing a wonderful, memorable day for the boys. Leda touched Maddy's face and thanked her for allowing them to talk to the boys. "It will be a better world when young people know who we are and accept that we are all different but so much the same. This was good for my family. The boys were lovely with their questions and their own stories. Thank you, Maddy." Just as they had appeared, they were gone, taking the lamb with them.

The schoolboys moved towards the bus with bags of food and collected trash. They were sunburned and exhausted—but exhilarated as they said their goodbyes to Mrs B and Maddy. Several boys ran over to hug Maddy and thank her for a great day. Henry waited until his classmates had filed by and then slowly walked over to Maddy with a big grin. He wrapped his arms around her and squeezed her.

"Thank you, Maddy. This was the best field trip ever. The chaps are ever so impressed. Maybe next time we could try Indian or Greek."

"Next time?" Sebastian had walked into the garden hoping for an explanation. Maddy and Henry laughed. "We'll see. I'm glad you're pleased with the day. Next time, though, I need more notice." Maddy kissed Henry on the forehead and sent him in the direction of the school bus. Henry nodded at Sebastian and ran over to the bus. He stopped at the door and waved, winking at Maddy.

As the bus backed out of the drive, Maddy waved and sighed. She had hoped to have a minute before having to explain. She turned to Sebastian, put her arms around his neck, and kissed him. He didn't respond immediately; she hadn't expected he would. "I'll explain everything at dinner. Go back to your meeting. It's all good." She reached up and kissed his cheek. "The lamb is gone, if that's what you're worried about."

Sebastian smiled at her, knowing her explanation would leave him feeling humble and stodgy. He looked at her, sunburned, happy, and ready for the next event. He pulled her close and kissed the top of her head. "You may want a shower and change of clothes before dinner—not that the smell of lamb isn't appealing."

She smiled back. "See you for cocktails."

He walked away reluctantly, shaking his head and nodding to Mrs B, who was standing, hands on hips, ready for instructions from Maddy. He almost laughed out loud as he recalled Maria's observation: "This is a crazy place."

Indeed.

Christian, Maria, and Sebastian walked out into the garden, happy to have their draft proposal completed. They were amazed at the transition; a tent with billowing panels; large, soft cushions on the ground; a low table; twinkling lights; and soft music greeted them. They were offered mojitos or sparkling wine as they settled into the comfortable seating. None of the earlier madness was evident.

Maddy floated through the garden with their drinks and appetizers, in a long caftan and sandals. "Welcome to the sultan's tent."

Christian was the first to comment. "Maddy, you look lovely and I feel like I am in another land. How did you manage it?" Maddy exaggerated a bow.

Maria managed only a dry aside: "I expect a camel to walk by any minute." Sebastian embraced Maddy and whispered in her ear. "No camels, right? You are amazing. Thank you."

Dinner was a series of exotic appetizers provided by Leda and her entourage: Moroccan stew, mint tea, and almond biscuits. After dinner, in a relaxed mood, Sebastian asked about the day. Maddy explained how disappointed Henry had been on the phone, as his field trip was cancelled. He told the headmaster Maddy had lots of foreign friends and maybe she could help. Maddy had called Leda and arranged for the boys to learn Lebanese cooking and customs. It had turned into more than she had hoped; the boys embraced all aspects of the day, asking questions and providing stories of their own. They had tried belly dancing, learned simple phrases, and tasted new foods. Henry thought it was a great day. Maddy apologized to the group, explaining that she thought they would arrive well after the party was over. She ended by saying she hoped the distraction didn't hinder their creative process.

Christian assured Maddy it was a wonderful thing she did, and no apology was necessary. They had decided to come to the house right away, as they were not being productive in the office. Once here, they were able to work through the process quickly, anxious to get back out to the garden. Sebastian had to agree. Maria merely shrugged and shook her head in disbelief. Chaos seemed to reign here with construction and schoolboys and animals. Her life seemed very orderly in retrospect.

"Smart boy, that Henry. Imagine how disappointed he would have been if he'd called you or me, Sebastian." Christian laughed and toasted Maddy.

Sebastian was quiet as he recalled his own childhood. Belle and Maddy were alike in so many ways. He was a lucky man. He had to admit he was proud of how Maddy had handled the chaos and then transformed the garden into an oasis for dinner. She never ceased to amaze him with her energy and her refusal to turn down a challenge.

Maddy couldn't help but notice how quiet Sebastian was; she hoped he wasn't angry, but it was possible. She decided he must have been blindsided by the circus in his yard. She bit the inside of her cheek, wondering how to resolve the situation. *In my defence*, she told herself, *this is what Belle would have done, given the circumstances.*

As they said good night to Christian and Maria, joking about counting sheep, Sebastian wrapped his arms around Maddy and held her, enjoying the scent of her. He kissed her neck and heard her groan, encouraging him to continue. Maddy turned to face him, her eyes wide, her lips open. Sebastian felt a wave of love wash over him; how else would he describe this insane feeling that he could not be without this person—that he wanted to keep her in his pocket and never let her go? He kissed her, and soon they were lying together, spent and falling into a deep sleep.

Strangers and the Ambassador

"Good morning." Sebastian looked over at Maddy, who was dressed in a short white dress, a red-and-blue plaid scarf around her neck, and high boots.

"Where are you off to? A Lulu reunion?" He smiled, pleased with his joke.

"Audrey and I have a job today, and this"—she twirled around—"is our uniform ... really. Crazy, isn't it?" She laughed. "We have to help a friend with a group. Not sure what we have to do, but it looks like a nice day, and if you don't mind dropping us off, it would be great." She put her arms around him and smiled.

"Come on, then; let's go. You don't want to be late for your big job in the city." Sebastian tried to look serious.

"Maddy, is there any possible way you could join us this evening at the Dorchester? There was a miscommunication about the number of tickets we held, and it appears we have another seat at the Ambassadors' Ball. I know you had a busy day, and I'm sure you're wondering why I would ask you with such short notice, but if there is any way you could manage, we'd love to have you join us. I hope to see you. Cocktails at 6 p.m., dinner at 7 p.m. Main ballroom, the Dorchester." Sebastian sighed as he left the message. He hadn't heard from Maddy all day; her assignment must have been all-consuming for her not to call him back or be in touch.

She was probably wondering what to wear. He felt his phone vibrate. Ah, thankfully it was Maddy.

"Hello, sweetheart. Any possibility we'll see you at 7.00 p.m.?" He realized he was whispering into the phone.

"Hi. Got your message. I'll try. I had a kick-ass day, but I'll try to make it on time. Meet you in the foyer? Gotta go; here's my train."

He smiled as he realized she had sent him an air kiss. He shook his head and returned to the meeting.

Christian and Sebastian, handsome in their tuxedos, waited in the foyer, hopeful that Maddy would arrive on time. The Japanese delegation was ushered in by a colleague who stopped for introductions. The Asian gentlemen were excited about their day; they'd had a fabulous guide who took them on a "kick-ass" tour of London—not the usual boring city tour. Sebastian smiled, realizing Maddy had used the same term to describe her day.

Maddy ran through the lobby of the Dorchester, following the signs for the function. She flung open the door to the foyer and stepped inside, out of breath, hoping to see Sebastian. She turned quickly and body checked a well-dressed, grey-haired man with an entourage. "Oh, I'm sorry. Is this the right room for the ambassador's ball?" she asked, not sure why she was whispering.

"It appears to be." He smiled back.

"Am I late?" she asked hopefully.

"Not if you walk in before me." He had an amused look on his face.

"Oh dear, you must be the ambassador. You don't seem pompous." Maddy smiled as the security team surrounded them. The ambassador laughed a throaty laugh—a laugh he didn't get to use much any more. Maddy held out her hand and dropped one of her shoes.

The ambassador wondered why she would be carrying them, but as they both bent down to retrieve the shoes, the security team stepped forward. The ambassador held up his hand. "It's fine, gentlemen. Really, it's fine."

"I'm Madison Davis; you can call me Maddy. Is it Mr Ambassador or sir or …?" she smiled.

"I'm Dermot Matthews; you can call me Dermot when we're alone."

"Sorry, I don't know the protocol for these things. There are so many rules ..." Maddy rolled her eyes. "Good luck with your address this evening. Everyone will be anxious to know if you really care or if you're here to deliver the standard 'happy to be here' message." She turned to go.

"Maddy, will you let me know what you think of my remarks later this evening? I'd be interested in your comments."

"Least I can do. Good luck." She started walking away, waving at Sebastian and Christian, who were exchanging amused glances.

"Maddy?" The ambassador and his party were still at the door, waiting to be escorted into the ballroom.

Maddy turned and saw the ambassador, Dermot, holding her shoe in his hand. She laughed and walked back to the door. "We could share towel monograms, perhaps, but not shoes. Thank you." She leaned on his arm to adjust the strap of the high-heeled slingbacks, realizing they each had a shoe in their hand, making the security team uneasy. She clicked her heels, smiled, shrugged, and started towards the men at the bar.

As she approached the men, Christian nudged Sebastian again. "She never lets you down, does she?" Both men were enjoying watching Maddy in her long white tunic over flared black pants, her hair pulled tight into a single braid—simple and yet more elegant than most of the women in the room. They could hear the women behind them wondering who she was:

"Is she the wife of the ambassador?"

"No, his wife has gone back to America."

"Is she a presenter?"

"Perhaps she is with the conference organizers."

"Wish I could wear something so simple yet so elegant."

Before Maddy reached her date, she was intercepted by Percy Blake, the man who had hired Audrey and Maddy to take his clients on city tours. "Ms Davis, I understand you went rogue on the tour today." Percy was obviously upset. "Not a good thing." He was shaking his head.

"Before you scold me, perhaps you should know the group had been to London previously and they weren't keen to see the same old stops. They spent a lot of money on Carnaby Street, they walked across Abbey Road, and they had high tea at the Savoy and then spent more money in the shops on Germain Street. I don't see the downside. I have your unused vouchers right here." Maddy handed him an envelope, staring back at him in defiance. I had photos framed; they will be delivered here shortly, so the group has a takeaway that will mean something. Not everyone aspires to look at jewels on a crown."

"Fine, granted, the group was delighted with their day. How much are you out? Will fifty pounds cover your expenses? I'd like to call you again for other groups." Percy was desperately trying to salvage this relationship.

"Fine, but don't call me if you don't want me to improvise." Maddy started to walk away.

"Ms Davis." Percy stepped forward, leaning into Maddy. "Just in case you don't hear this from anyone else, you look bloody good; you look hot." Maddy blushed and looked around; surely no one else had heard. Percy was gone. She collected herself and started to walk.

The waiter stepped in front of Maddy, offering a glass of Prosecco. "I'm going to need a lot of these tonight … here's twenty pounds. If you could be so kind, just keep them coming—a splash of Prosecco in Perrier water, all night. Is that possible?" Maddy asked.

Certainly, Madame. I will be sure your glass is never empty." The waiter nodded.

Sebastian reached for her hand, kissed her cheek, and whispered, "I'm so glad you made it. You look amazing. I just want to take you home."

Maddy laughed, head back, and then with her hand on his cheek, she whispered "You'd better feed me first; I'm starving."

Christian brushed her cheeks in greeting. "My dear Maddy, you have the most eclectic wardrobe, but you wear it so well. Stunning. Cheers." They were toasting each other when Mr Kobayashi caught Maddy's eye.

"Maddy-San." He bowed and took her hand. "It is lovely to see you here."

Maddy looked surprised. "Mr K., are you following me? How nice to see you again so soon. May I introduce …" She turned to her companions.

"We have met wonderful man and banker earlier. You must join us." Mr Kobayashi pointed to his delegation, bowing and smiling at Maddy. She was just about to elaborate when Mr Kobayashi, very keen to tell the story, explained that Maddy had been a most delightful guide, offering a "kick-ass tour", which he and his party were fortunate enough to enjoy. They had heard about "a wonderful man" from Maddy during the tour and guessed Sebastian was that man.

"Mr Kobayashi, Mr Gerhard is with the bank, and his company prospectus identifies a desire to increase offshore or foreign investment in areas of sustainable development. You two may want to connect." Maddy smiled at Christian.

Christian shook his head and whispered to Sebastian, "That means two people read the prospectus—Maddy and me. Amazing."

"Come, the ambassador is arriving, and we will enjoy each other's company this evening?" Mr Kobayashi directed the group towards the darkened room with his arm. When he saw Sebastian and Christian nod, he put his arm through Maddy's and began walking into the ballroom. Sebastian and Christian followed, exchanging amused glances. As they were strolling towards the table, Maddy tapped Mr Kobayashi on the arm and asked him to remind her of a parcel she was expecting to be delivered at the hotel later in the evening. "I simply ran out of time, but I must pass it on to you."

Mr Kobayashi nodded as he pulled the chair for Maddy. Sebastian was seated next to her with Mr Kobayashi on her right. The stage lit up, and the proceedings began. Maddy was happy to be sitting down. She looked around the table at her group and her friends and wondered at how small her world was getting. It was a comforting thought.

After the formal part of the programme, Maddy walked out to the lobby to check on her parcel. As she re-entered the ballroom, she was stopped by a team of men in dark suits who were wearing radio earbuds. "Ms Davis, please follow us; the ambassador would like to see you. Right this way." There was no option, as they were flanking her, directing her. They climbed the stairs to the mezzanine level and left her. She placed her package on the floor and looked around.

"I was hoping you would dance with me." The ambassador was standing in the shadows.

"You must be a really bad dancer." Maddy smiled, looking around the bare room.

He laughed. "That may be true. Unfortunately, there's a protocol, believe it or not—an order of whom I should dance with before I get to ask whom I want to dance with. This is my rebellion move. May I have this dance and perhaps the next?" He held out his hand.

Maddy was amused by the move, and yet something in his voice sounded so lonely she walked towards him and took his hand.

"My pleasure." She waited for him to hold her. As they danced, Maddy realized he was indeed a very good partner. "You must come to my friend's club; it's called Decades, and it's fun. You can get a private room for all your friends."

"I don't have any friends," he said over her head.

"Nonsense, I'm your friend. I'll invite you out with my crowd. I know it's hard when you first arrive, but there are so many lovely people here … I'll include you in my next get-together. Not one controversial person in the lot." She smiled up at him.

Maddy was watching his face when he leaned over her and whispered, "Maddy, if you want to leave after two songs, you'd better stop looking at me with those bedroom eyes." Maddy smiled a broad smile—a mischievous smile. She shrugged and closed her eyes, inhaling his aftershave. She couldn't help but think they were both too old to flirt.

The song ended, and neither moved away.

"One more?" He raised his eyebrows.

Maddy nodded.

"How long have you been here? How long will you be here?" he asked.

"I gave myself a year. It's almost over." She sighed.

"Glad to have met you, Maddy Davis. I hope you will remember to include me."

The music ended, and the orchestra conductor announced they would take a short break.

The ambassador bowed and thanked Maddy for the dance.

Maddy nodded and picked up her package. As she walked away, she heard her name.

Turning, a curious look on her face, she waited.

"You didn't tell me what you thought of my address."

Maddy hesitated, considering her response. She looked up, smiling. "I believed you."

She touched her heart and turned to go. She turned back quickly. "Oh, by the way, they don't say 'period' here; they say 'full stop'. Just thought you might like to know." And she was gone.

As she entered the ballroom, flanked by the security team, she stopped and insisted she would be fine on her own. Sebastian walked towards her, a look of concern on his face. He was pleased to leave the conversation at the bar. When he reached Maddy, he took the package from her and placed his hand on her back. He seemed preoccupied, but they reached the table before Maddy could ask him what was bothering him. She opened the kraft paper and presented the first package to Mr Kobayashi. Maddy bowed as she ceremoniously handed each one of the men a wrapped offering. Maddy was quick to add that this was not a gift, so they would not lose face without a reciprocal gift; this was a souvenir—a reminder of the fun they had had during their time together. There was much discussion about whether they should open the packages now or later. Maddy laughed and said she couldn't wait to see their reactions. Like excited children exercising great control, they carefully removed the wrapping. Maddy could not have wished for a better reaction to the plaques. They each held up their photos of them crossing Abbey Road, oohing and ahhing and expressing much pleasure at the sentiment.

Sebastian watched the interaction of bows and appreciation with a pang—of what he wasn't sure, but his heart fluttered as he witnessed the sheer joy of being with Maddy. His head was still reeling from the comments at the bar. "How are you keeping your lady interested, Sebastian? Women like to trade up, you know. Take it from me; I've had several of them love me until someone more exciting came along. I see the ambassadors' men have taken your lady out of the room. Trading up—fact of life. Good progress on the committee. Well done." As the man staggered away, Sebastian realized he was holding his glass a little too tight. Then he saw Maddy return to the ballroom. He walked towards her, anxious to be alone with her and yet suspicious of what the ambassador would want with her.

Maddy touched his arm and asked if they could leave. "Are you done with all your official duties for tonight?"

He stood up and touched her back to direct her out of the room and into the car. Davi opened the car door and asked how the evening had gone. "Splendid," Sebastian responded absent-mindedly. Maddy leaned against Sebastian, as she always did, her shoes off, her feet up on the seat. His mind was spinning.

"Are you not capable of just sitting quietly in a vehicle?" he snapped at Maddy. Looking out the car window as they drove away, he was aware she had moved over to the other side of the car. He squinted, rubbing his temples, reprimanding himself. Why had he said that? *Trading up … more exciting … women trade up … fact of life.* The words kept repeating themselves.

"Sir, Maddy has left the vehicle." Davi spoke softly, but there was an implied urgency to his statement.

Sebastian sat up, looking around him. He opened the car door and saw Maddy walking, shoes in hand, across the bridge. "Maddy, come back; get in the car. I'm sorry; I don't know what just happened. I'm sorry."

He ran to catch her. "Maddy, please stop. I'm so sorry. It's been a long day and I couldn't find you and Fraser Wells was going on about women trading up because we're not exciting enough, and I realized that could be true; I'm not that exciting. I'm sorry; I had no right or reason to snap at you. Please stop." He caught up to her and tried to stand in her way.

"No, no, you don't get to say whatever you want or do the things you do to hurt me and then say sorry. I keep forgiving you, and you just keep hurting me. Do you see a pattern here? Let me go. I need to be alone."

"No, no, you don't. You need to come home with me. I know I hurt you; I don't even know how I do most times, but please, come home. I am so sorry."

"You should go back to your old life, be with your own kind. Elizabeth and Deirdre and the rest of the proper crowd probably sit ramrod straight in a car, have just the right dress for every occasion, and know what to say or what to do all the time. I don't. Go and be happy with them." Maddy was crying, hurt by his words. Hadn't she rushed around London finding something to wear, soliciting help from Audrey, wearing those uncomfortable shoes, just to please him? Why wasn't it ever enough? *Who cares how a person sits in a car … darn it all!*

"Maddy, I love how you always sit beside me. Last week we flagged a cab, and Christian laughed at me when he got in. My arm was up on the back of the seat. He reminded me you weren't with us and he certainly wasn't going to snuggle up beside me." He waited, hoping she would find the humour in the recollection.

"I was reacting to the comments, not you."

He moved closer, holding out his handkerchief. "I don't want a stiff, proper life—not now, not now that I've met you. If I thought for one moment you would like to have a dress for every occasion, I'd hire the best designers in London and get you a room full of gowns in every colour. But that's not you. You don't have to worry about saying the wrong thing to anyone; they just want to be with you. They love you for your honesty. I love you for everything. You looked so striking, walking into the room with your own look, your own style; you just radiated self-confidence. How could a mere ambassador not be taken by you? How could I let ridiculous comments ruin a perfect evening when you worked so hard all day and then made such an effort to be there for me? How could I not feel proud of the reaction from your tour group? Please Maddy, come home. I am so sorry." Sebastian seemed to run out of steam. Maddy kept walking backwards, away from him.

"I'll just pick you up and carry you to the car." He tried to sound stern.

"You'll have a heart attack, silly." She sniffed and wiped her eyes with the handkerchief. She dropped a shoe and kept walking.

"You'll have to live with the knowledge that you could have prevented it." He held his hand out for her. "Listen, you can administer any punishment you like; just get in the car."

Maddy hesitated. She did love him; he was such a complex man, but just a man—a man who didn't realize how much she cared, regardless of her actions. She looked up at his face and was angry at herself for wanting to forgive him and just go home.

"I just want someone to love me for who I am. You go back to your perfect life, your perfect friends, your perfect manners. I need some time to think about what I want to do. Let me have some time." Maddy had been slowly moving away, walking backwards. She turned and kept walking.

"Fine. I'll give you time. Where will you go?" Sebastian shouted after her. "Should we drop you at the embassy?"

Before he realized what was happening, Maddy had thrown a shoe at him. In disbelief, he realized the shoe had caught his cheek. Maddy was running across the bridge.

"Maddy, you can't walk around London barefoot; please come home." he cried.

Maddy disappeared into the night, feeling a sense of freedom. Sebastian pounded the car with both hands in frustration.

Davi collected the shoes and waited to hear where they were going.

As the car arrived at the garden, Sebastian finally spoke. "Daveesh, where would she go? It's late; there are no trains to the seaside at this hour. Where might she be for the night?" The images of Maddy wouldn't leave him. "Davi, does Grace have a bathtub?"

Davi considered his reply, knowing in his heart she would be at the coffee house, sipping tea with Grace. "That's a good, strong possibility, sir; yes indeed. Shall we make our way there?"

"I'll change and get her some clothes and shoes, and yes, let's go. If by chance she isn't there, I'll bring the car back myself."

Grace opened the door cautiously, wondering who would be pounding and ringing the bell so impatiently at this late hour. Sebastian burst through the door, Davi in tow.

"Is she here? Did Maddy come here? Where is she? It's imperative that I see her, Grace; where is she?" Sebastian wanted to shake the answer out of her. He saw Grace nervously look down the hall, considering her options. He strode down the hall and opened the first door. Maddy was in the bath, the steam rising from the tub.

Maddy sat up, opened her eyes, and blinked. "What on earth are you doing?" She sat up and reached for a towel.

"We need to talk. It won't wait for morning. I can't sleep without you, and I don't like this being apart … Talk to me, please."

Maddy looked up at Sebastian, her arms across her breasts. "I feel a little vulnerable—somewhat exposed right now."

"Of course." Sebastian moved towards the door. Maddy sunk into the tub, her head under the water, enjoying the warmth. Now that he was gone, she had time to think about what he had said and how she had reacted.

Suddenly something touched her leg. She sat up quickly, opening her eyes to see a naked Sebastian standing over her, getting into the bath. She had an uncontrollable desire to giggle, or even laugh, at the silliness of the scene before her.

"What are you doing?" she asked in disbelief, realizing she was crying.

"I'm just levelling the playing field—isn't that the expression? I understand you are angry with me, and you have every right to be, but …"

Grace opened the door of the bathroom and stopped when she saw Maddy and Sebastian in her bathtub, staring at her. "I'll get more towels." It was a statement, not a reaction. She closed the door and leaned against the door sash, trying to digest what she had just witnessed. Grace chuckled to herself, proclaiming life with Maddy was never boring. She shook her head and went for the towels.

"Davi and I are going to bed; we have an early morning, Maddy, I'll see you at 6 a.m. sharp. The lads can go home and change in the morning, but I need you. Remember that Auntie is away. The sofa is ready. Good night."

"Good night, Grace … and thank you." Maddy smiled, looking at the bathroom door, considering how strange this must all seem to Grace. Come to think of it, this was bizarre. She turned to Sebastian, who was clearly uncomfortable in the tub, and touched his face. He had a large bruise under his left eye. Maddy looked down at her hands, recalling the instant she threw the shoes.

Sebastian cleared his throat and asked Maddy to look at him.

"I can't; I may laugh at the situation."

"Please, Maddy, look at me." He reached over and touched her chin.

Maddy looked up at him. Sebastian fought the desire to pull her close; he was a slave to her wide-eyed gaze.

"Maddy, you stepped into my world and shattered the glass dome protecting me from life. You made me tentative with all the broken glass around me; there's nothing in my past that can guide me through the debris you left behind. I need you to help me navigate through the shards of glass. I wasn't a good husband or father; now I want to protect you and yet give you the freedom you need for your friends and your passions. You are so passionate about everything; it's frightening to someone like me. Take me with you, and I promise I can make all your dreams come true. Don't give up on me. I need you more than you'll ever need me, and I will fight for you because what we have is worth fighting for. Hopefully you know I care and I want you in my life, and I'm sorry for being such an ass." Sebastian looked away and then back at Maddy. "How can I possibly explain the sheer enjoyment of seeing and knowing another human being—you?" he whispered.

"I want to be with you, you alone. I'm not interested in anyone else.

You leave me for long periods of time when we go out; you go to the bar, and I'm on my own …" Maddy looked down at the bubbles.

Sebastian smiled. "When I'm at the bar I get to watch you and adore you from afar."

"I'd rather be near you. It's strange introducing myself as your friend."

"You're much more than my friend, Maddy; you're my future. I'll stop now. Is this the part where you forgive me and we kiss and make up?"

Maddy put her finger over his lips. "No more words, Sebastian. Let's get some sleep."

Maddy stepped out of the tub, wrapped herself in a towel, and extended her hand to Sebastian, who was struggling to stand in the tub. "Don't fall, for goodness' sake. Here, let me help you." Maddy offered a towel and draped it over his chest. Sebastian pulled her to him, letting the towel fall. He touched her cheek with a gentle stroke and then kissed her, his lips hungry for her, his mouth covering hers. Maddy gasped at the power of the kiss, moving her arms around his neck, not wanting to let go. They gathered their scattered clothes and padded up the stairs to the lonely sofa bed situated in the middle of the former dance hall, anxious to be in each other's arms. The moonlight through the large windows reflected against the mirrored walls, casting shadows across the room.

Sebastian closed his eyes, comforted by the scent of Maddy, and her body moulded into his, her breathing even. "Good night, my love. I do love you just the way you are. Marry me," he whispered to the woman sleeping in his arms before he closed his eyes.

The smell of coffee woke them.

Sebastian groaned and looked down at Maddy appeared peaceful in his arms, the moonlight on her cheek. She stretched and, with a quick kiss, leapt out of the bed.

"Good morning. You stay in bed. I can't let Grace down after last night." Maddy was scrambling to find her clothes on the floor.

"Maddy, what can I do to redeem myself? Give me a horrible task or ask me for anything or make me do something you know I hate, just so you'll believe I'm truly sorry. I was completely irrational, and I don't know how to fix this." He looked over at her, his face lined with concern.

Maddy watched him for a moment, contemplating her response. "I want to be angry with you, but you climbed into the bath with me—that was crazy. I can't be angry with a crazy person." She sat on the bed. "Why can't you understand or accept that I care for you and you are the only one that can hurt me."

Sebastian smiled. "I guess it's true; we only hurt the ones we love. Oh, we need to get Grace a better sofa." He stood up, grimacing. "I should go; you are being summoned. Dinner tonight?" He held her in his arms, waiting for her response.

"Dinner tonight." Maddy nodded, smiling at him. "You brought me a change of clothes; how can I refuse?" They walked hand in hand down the stairs into the coffee house.

Grace offered Sebastian coffee and gave Maddy a hug as she placed an apron over her head and headed for the baking area. Davi was whistling as he removed a tray of baking from the oven and the first customers came through the door. It was just another day.

Sebastian arranged to meet Maddy after the lunchtime rush. The new menu was well received, and the kitchen was busy. Maddy climbed into the MG with a picnic basket and a blanket. "Sunshine in the afternoon demands a picnic," she proclaimed.

They drove towards Windsor, stopping on a country road lined with trees.

"Maddy, are we good?" Sebastian asked, wanting to be reassured.

"Sebastian, we have so little time I don't want to spend a moment being angry or second-guessing my feelings. I just want to cherish the time I do have with you, and I don't care what others have to say or what they think. What's important is that you know I care about you." She caressed his face, wondering if the bruise was as painful as it looked.

"Fair enough. Maddy, I asked you to marry me last night. I'm asking again. Marry me. All the idle chatter will cease, and we can stop calling each other friends, partners, or whatever the words are."

Maddy looked up at him. "You know I have to go back and get my affairs in order. It's not a good idea right now. But thank you for asking." She kissed his chest.

"You won't marry me, and you won't give me penance to serve ... How can I possibly feel good about myself?" he asked, feigning hurt.

"Okay, let me see … The next time we get together with friends, we'll invite the ambassador. He doesn't have any friends here, and it never hurts to have your patron on your side. How's that for penance?"

"Oh, you drive a hard bargain, and I will hate seeing him with you, but if that's what it takes for you to forgive me for my absolutely unwarranted behaviour, I'll do my best—for you."

"Thank you." Maddy hugged him. After a moment, she whispered, "Sebastian, there isn't anyone else in the world I want to marry."

Sebastian closed his eyes, kissed the top of her head and thought that was as close to yes as he was going to hear right now.

Turn It Over

"Sebastian, this parcel arrived for you this morning. Shall I open it or leave it on your desk?" Lambert asked, anxious to know what was in the package.

"Who is it from?" Sebastian asked absently, not looking up.

"Some novelty gift house in the city."

"Open it; I know you're dying to see what it is."

Lambert opened the package with gusto. "Oh, it's a snow globe. You know, the kind of globe you turn upside down to watch the snow fall." Lambert turned the ball over several times. "It's got a woman on a pedestal; she's leaning over to help a man get up off some broken glass ... The little figurines could be you and Maddy. How strange. Shall I take it away?"

Sebastian looked up, slowly processing what Lambert was describing.

"On the desk is fine, thank you." He wanted to hold the snow globe and study it himself.

As Lambert walked away, Sebastian picked up the globe, a smile spreading across his face. There was a note attached to the felt on the base:

Come with me. It's not easy but I'm trying. M.

He folded the note and placed it in his credit card wallet. He turned the globe again, watching the snow fall on Maddy saving him from the shattered glass. He didn't realize he was laughing out loud until Lambert appeared, looking concerned. He placed the globe on his desk, where he could easily see it as he worked.

"I want to do something unexpected. What do you think Maddy would like to do for the weekend, Lambert? Something I could surprise her with. Grand, but not too grand."

"She was talking about walking the Cinque Terre in Northern Italy. Easy walk … You could do it without training."

Sebastian nodded and punched the speed dial on his phone.

"I would like to take you for a walk. Are you able to free up a few days?" He smiled. "It's a surprise. I want to surprise you. Just let me surprise you."

Sebastian looked out over the city, pleased with the suggestion. He turned and gave Lambert a thumbs up. "How soon can you get us there?"

Lambert backed away from the office door, excited to begin the arrangements for trains and hotels. *When did the boss become such a romantic?* he wondered. Maddy would be pleased with the trip to Italy; he was sure of that.

Delicious meals, fine weather, the walk across the well-travelled path to each of the five towns on the coast rewarding them with brilliant sunsets, the passion at the end of the day, the absolute delight in having Maddy to himself, four days of laughter and thought-provoking conversation— Sebastian would always have fond memories of their Cinque Terre getaway. Maddy cried in his arms at the sheer beauty of the vistas and his lovely surprise. She said it was a brilliant idea.

He was getting quite comfortable in this new role as a hero to his fair maiden.

The Benefit

Maddy stifled a yawn at the table. They had agreed to attend the black-tie fundraiser to support Christian and his charity. The room was decorated with ice sculptures and blue lights; the tables had ice-carved bouquets with coloured ribbons, and the silent auction items were in the foyer. It was visually formidable, but boring. Maddy caught Sebastian's eye as he was leaning over, listening to the banker on his right. She stood and announced she was going to check on her bids. "Shall I check on items for anyone else?" she asked as she touched Sebastian on the shoulder. The other guests at the table shook their heads or waved their hands, no thanks.

Maddy whispered into Sebastian's ear, "I'll meet you at the cloakroom in five. Oh, by the way, I'm not wearing panties." She walked away, smiling sweetly as Sebastian turned his head as if it were on a swivel. He reached for his water glass, surprised at his trembling hands.

"How is Maddy's father?" the woman on his left asked Sebastian. He looked confused. She continued. "I see Maddy at the hospital with an elderly gentleman, and they look so comfortable together, laughing and carrying on; I just assumed it was her father."

Sebastian thought she must be confusing Maddy with someone else. "Maddy does visit with the chemo patients, sitting with them during treatments. She seems to enjoy the patients." He was fidgeting, checking his watch.

"Yes, I know. I'm the nurse on the floor. My patients call her 'our Diamond Girl'." Sebastian looked confused. "She arrives with such bright colours, her eyes are sparkling, and she has the lucky diamond bracelet. She lets the patients wear the bracelet during treatments; they all believe it has magical powers." She paused as she noticed Sebastian look at his watch again. "It's not usual for women to like other women—especially when their husbands are interested—but there's something about Maddy that makes women want to be her friend. It's funny, isn't it?" She laughed. Sebastian was about to say "Indeed", but the woman carried on. "Maddy lost one of her boys a fortnight ago; I think it hit her hard." She shook her head.

"Yes, she was quite devastated," he added, paying attention.

"Liam was so in love with her. He didn't respond to anyone but her. It was tragic, but I believe he would have gladly passed on rather than give up his sessions with Maddy," she said quietly. "How do you keep up with her?" she asked, trying to change the subject and lighten the mood.

"I'm not sure I do," he chuckled. He looked at his watch once more.

"I'm sorry; I have to make a call." He touched the women's hand. "Pardon me."

Several minutes later, Sebastian walked into the cloakroom, where Maddy was waiting with a devilish grin on her face. She took his hand and led him into the staff washroom, locking the door behind them. "I have always wanted to do that …" she giggled, clapping her hands in delight. "I wasn't sure you would even come."

"I wasn't sure myself." He was rubbing his thighs. "Maddy, it's reckless and dangerous and insane." Sebastian was clearly uncomfortable. "Is this an experiment of some kind?"

Maddy laughed. "If it was an experiment, I could have asked anyone in that room, but you—only you—are the object of my affection, and I'm tired of always doing the right thing. I can't wait for exciting things to happen to me. Life is too short. I was bored, I looked over and saw you sitting there looking like a matinee idol, and I just wanted to see if real life was as exciting as the movies. I didn't mean to upset you, but there was an element of excitement." She looked contrite. "I'm sorry."

"I'm going back to the table; please join me." He opened the door and waited.

Maddy was sitting on the vanity. "I need a moment."

"Indeed." Sebastian hesitated and then walked out.

Maddy leaned against the mirror and closed her eyes, smiling at the sheer craziness and exhilaration of waiting to see if he would meet her. Liam died so young; he never had this feeling. She realized she was crying and laughing at the same time. She was sad, and yet it was enough just to think about what might have been.

The door opened abruptly, the lock clicked, and as Maddy opened her eyes, startled, Sebastian was in front of her, his face intent. He lifted her dress, moved his hands up her thighs, and gasped. "You really don't have …" he whispered. He kissed Maddy as he shed his trousers, moving into her, one arm on her back, the other holding her head away from the mirror. Maddy had no time to respond, but her body was moving with his, and it was delightful. She couldn't control the moans or the sense of urgency only those who think they may get caught are capable of, but she found herself thinking, *Wow, what a great way to have sex.*

Sebastian held her, shaking, breathing hard. "You okay?" he asked.

When Maddy caught her breath, she held his face, kissing him gently. Sebastian was smiling as he dressed himself. "Now we're both reckless." Maddy laughed, stood, and straightened his tie. "I'll see you at the table. We can't leave together."

"Indeed."

Sebastian turned to look at her, wondering how he was going to sit at the table without smiling foolishly for the rest of the evening. How his staid life had changed. He managed one more kiss before she pushed him towards the door.

"Sebastian, I hope you are bidding on many things you do not need." Christian greeted him just as he walked into the ballroom. "Drink?"

Sebastian accepted the pint of beer. "Cheers. Will you reach your goal this evening?" He asked, hoping he sounded interested.

"My good man, what are you smoking?" Christian asked. "I want some. You seem too happy for this world. I've told you this before, my friend."

Sebastian laughed. *Who wouldn't feel happy after what just happened?*

"Where's Maddy?" Christian asked, looking around the room.

"I believe she's checking on her bids," he answered, searching the crowd, hoping to find her.

"Ah, yes, there she is." Christian pointed across the room. "She's excellent at driving the bids up, making everyone think someone else wants the item badly. Who could say no to Maddy? She has many talents, your Maddy, many talents."

"Indeed," Sebastian responded, watching her float back to the table. "Indeed."

April

"Sebastian?" Maddy came out of the bathroom, wrapping the towel around her head like a turban.

He looked up from his reading, removing his glasses. "Hmm?" He watched her approach.

"You remember Preston, P. C., the man from Texas we met when we were skiing in France."

"Ah yes, the larger-than-life man with the shopaholic girlfriend," he responded with an attempt at a heavy drawl.

Maddy rolled her eyes at his accent. "Yes, that's him. He's in London for a few days this week, and he wanted to have dinner with us."

"Dinner with you, more than likely." Sebastian smiled. "He didn't even acknowledge the rest of us. He probably thought I was your valet."

"Silly, you just intimidate him with your good manners and proper speech. Anyway, I thought it would be nice to have him here for a Texas barbecue, since he's been travelling for some time. He's alone; Ms Kaitlin left him in Paris. Oh, I think you mentioned Maria was coming to town, so why not have them both here? It's a great time to have the ambassador here too." Maddy was talking fast—a sure sign she already had a plan in mind. Sebastian had learned to wait for the rest of the story.

"It's also your night with Henry, and he would love to try making the biscuits."

"Biscuits?" Sebastian asked.

"They're really more like scones." She held her hand up. "Of course we'll invite Christian as well; he can take care of the beer, and you can all come from work."

"What if they're not available?" he asked.

Maddy stopped pacing, turned around, and stared at Sebastian, surprised. "It never occurred to me people wouldn't want to come." She was biting the inside of her cheek.

"Come here." Sebastian patted the bed beside him. "Of course everyone will want to come to your barbecue. Well, maybe not Maria, but everyone else, I'm sure." Trying to sound supportive, he added, "What can I do to help?"

"You can procure a beautiful bottle of Kentucky bourbon." She was back on track. "Imagine how pleased Preston will be with you when you offer him a drink. It'll be fun; you'll see."

"Indeed." He kissed her forehead and headed to the shower.

Maria accepted the invitation with reservation. Christian was delighted to be invited; he wasn't sure he could handle yet another working dinner with Maria. The ambassador was formal in his acceptance, although secretly pleased to be included. Henry arrived early and worked with Mrs B in the main house kitchen, preparing biscuits and fruit pies for dessert. The weather was perfect for a barbecue; the garden tables had cowboy hats filled with salsa and nacho chips, country music was playing, and the barbecue had glowing red coals, ready for the steaks. Grace and Davi had gladly taken on the catering job. Audrey had secured the barbecue and accessories. It was perfect, Sebastian had to admit. The guests arrived laden with beer, flowers, and chocolates. Preston and Maria were soon engaged in a deep argument about world politics. Sebastian, Christian, and Dermot entered a discussion about Brexit. The professor arrived with his guitar and Lambert. Soon there was a comfortable patter across the room, with Henry joining the conversation and Maddy ensuring that everyone was included.

Preston had been touched with the offer of bourbon, and he wiped a tear away when he realized Ms Maddy had arranged a perfect Texas barbecue just for him, complete with biscuits. "I do declare, Ms Maddy, you've made me homesick. You are a treasure." Everyone drank to that, glasses clinking. "Ms Maddy, here, is the best kind of friend, and I appreciate that." Preston raised his glass.

"You are so right, my friend. I was just glad to be a part of the production." Christian raised his glass, laughing.

"What production?" Maria asked, sounding critical.

"Shall I tell the tale, sir?" Christian stood and bowed to Preston, who nodded his head and his cigar simultaneously.

Maddy interjected, "Perhaps another time?" She wasn't sure how Sebastian would react. He shrugged and gave Christian a nod to continue.

Christian cleared his throat and launched into the story. "I hope I can do it justice in the telling. Preston"—he turned and acknowledged the Texan—"called Maddy for assistance with a delicate matter involving a boat he had obtained in a poker game. It turned out to be a luxury liner in the Mediterranean. Maddy found the boat online and had it appraised, but she also noted that the owner, Signor Sorento, and his family were much photographed on the boat last season. Preston is not a sailor, but he did want to purchase pastureland in Texas—which, by the way, is very affordable since the drought. Maddy set up a meeting with Signor Sorento at the coffee house. Preston and I, the banker, greeted him and waited for our counsel to arrive. Davi was wonderful as her driver, stopping in front, opening the door, and standing in wait for her. Maddy breezed in, asking if the Signor would like a cappuccino or Pellegrino water, uttering a few words of Italian. As you can imagine, Signor Sorento is now captivated with our counsel, staring at Maddy, unaware we are in the room." He paused for effect, noticing Maddy squirming and looking uncomfortable.

"Maddy gets right down to business, asking both men if they realize how painful the gambling debt would be if their families knew of it. She then folds her hands and asks the Italian what he has chosen to do; his options are to transfer the money with Deutsche Bank or provide the cash—euros or dollars. He hesitates for a moment only, then opens his case and sets the bills on the table. Maddy motions for me to remove the money, hands him the transfer papers for the yacht—which, by the way, Preston has not ever signed to take ownership. She stands and extends her hand. Signor Sorento kisses her hand and asks for her business card. As cool as a cucumber, is that what you say?" Christian hesitated. "Maddy tells him she works solely for Mr McAllen, Preston here, and that if he needs to contact her, he can do so through her employer." Christian stopped to take a drink. His audience was waiting for the end of the story. Maddy covered her face with her hands.

"Signor Sorento follows Maddy to the door, almost chasing her, as she quickly shakes hands with me and then Preston. She motions outside, saying her driver is waiting. He grabs her hand and asks if she will come to Milan. It was beautiful when she turned to him and said she would love to have a reason to return to such a beautiful city. I tell you, I almost wanted to take her there myself." There was laughter from the group.

"Signor Sorento is now beside himself. He tells her he is a prisoner to her eyes and will design a collection called 'Azules', just for her. She was so gracious, Sebastian; it was a Grace Kelly move. She turns and smiles and touches his face; we are holding our breath. We couldn't hear what she said, but he followed her out, and of course Davi had the car door open for her. She was in the car, and he was still talking to her. What did he ask you, Maddy? What did he want?" Christian looked at Maddy. "We were inside, desperate to know."

She looked around her and sighed, realizing she had to complete the story.

"He wanted to know why I wore the dress I was wearing and what I liked in a garment. Then, as I got into the car, he said he would have paid more, asking why we hadn't asked for more. I was shaking, I just wanted to drive away, but I had to respond. You can't ever think of clever things when you are in the frying pan, but I remembered a phrase I had heard in a play once: *"Onore di sopra del denaro"*—honour above money. Davi was wonderful; he closed the door, and off we went without a backward glance. Anyway, everyone got what they wanted in the end, so it worked out okay." Maddy sighed. "Am I right?"

"You could have been arrested for pretending to be a lawyer." Maria stated in a flat voice. "What if he's Mafia?" She shook her head. "It was irresponsible."

Preston laughed, his body shaking. "No, Maddy wasn't my lawyer or legal counsel; she was just 'my counsel', and she was wonderful." He raised his glass to Maddy.

"The best part of the story—Maddy doesn't know this either," Christian continued. "The very best part, after Maddy leaves, Signor Sorento approaches us with a package; he says, 'Signor Preston, your counsel must be very expensive,' to which Preston replies ..." He paused and motioned for Preston to fill in.

"Sure, but she's worth every penny," he responded in a booming voice. The group laughed.

Christian continued. "Sorento hands us a package telling us to be sure she gets to Milan for his collection in the fall. This package contains 10,000 euros for Maddy. In all my years in the banking business, I have not seen a negotiation like this." Christian shook his head.

"I can't believe you would take on this danger and then laugh about it." Maria was stern.

"Oh, Maria, Signor Sorento is a somewhat famous designer, the boat was his, and no one wants a record or paper trail of their bad poker debts. Preston got his pastureland. The family gets another summer on the boat. I think Maddy had a good plan." Christian held his arms wide apart, as if looking for approval from the group.

"I could use a creative negotiator in my office," the ambassador laughed.

"What will you do with the money, Maddy?" Maria asked.

"We knew she wouldn't take the money, so we invested it for her. I believe her nest egg is doing quite well." Preston laughed loudly, patting Christian on the back.

"All I can say is, thank you, Ms Maddy; I am forever grateful to you." Preston McAllen stood, walked over to Maddy, and kissed her hand. They exchanged smiles and winks, and the evening continued with coffee and apple pie. The professor and the ambassador knew several American ballads, and the group sang along to their favourites.

Grace and Davi offered to take Henry back to school, as he was nodding off and Grace had an early start. Davi was becoming a proficient baker and enjoyed assisting Grace with the morning rush. He had confessed to Maddy the kitchen might not be big enough for all of them, as Auntie and Uncle were enjoying their involvement.

At one point during the evening, Dermot asked for directions to the WC. Maddy showed him into the garden apartment and pointed the way. "What's the arrangement here?" he asked.

"I live here. The big house is being renovated. I'm so lucky to have a garden," Maddy responded, clearing the counter as she spoke. When she looked up, she realized Dermot was watching her. "Does this mean we're destined to be just friends? He asked, hoping he was wrong.

"We can be great friends." Maddy smiled back at him. "I'm leaving soon. I have no idea how things will settle out, but I treasure my friendships regardless."

At that moment, the professor walked into the apartment carrying two platters and a bowl. Maddy quickly made room on the counter and thanked him. He looked at Maddy and then over at Dermot. "Everything all right?"

Maddy touched his arm and nodded. "Don't bother; I can clear things later. I'd rather hear you play your guitar than worry about this. Let's enjoy the garden."

The evening air was pleasant, and the guests reluctant to leave, moved by the haunting Spanish melodies the professor had begun to strum.

Sebastian stood behind Maddy, swaying with her. "Great party, as usual. Well done."

Maddy reached up and touched his face. It had been a lovely evening; Henry was so proud of his baking, Maria seemed to soften around Preston, the men discussed investments in Europe, and Sebastian had merely closed his eyes and shaken his head on hearing the yacht story. The ambassador and the professor made plans to meet, Maddy suggesting the ambassador join an early jam session with his saxophone. As he said good night, Dermot kissed Maddy's hand and thanked her for a truly American experience. Preston gave Maddy a bear hug and offered to drive Maria to her hotel. It had been a good night indeed.

Friends Looking Out for Friends

"Maddy, join me for lunch. I'd like to talk to you about an upcoming event."

"When?" Maddy looked both ways, crossed the busy street, and waited for the response.

"Now. I'm on my way to the Savoy. Can you meet me?"

"Sorry, lovely invite, but I'm just meeting up with friends at the Old Bridge Pub. Why don't you join us there? Your Secret Squirrel guy can park the car in the side lane." Maddy waved at Audrey across the bridge.

"Well, that might work. If that's the only way I'm going to see you, I'll be right there. Are you sure it won't upset your plans?"

"No, not at all. We'll wait for you. See you soon."

"Who's that?" Audrey asked as she hugged Maddy.

"Just a new friend. He's American. He seems lonely. I don't think he has many friends here. Be nice. Here's the professor. Sebastian is picking up the cake; he may be late."

The professor greeted the women and suggested they get their table.

"We're waiting for a friend of Maddy's—some American." Audrey looked around.

"Here's Christian; his driver wears a hat, so he's easy to pick out in traffic."

A black SUV with dark windows and bonnet flags turned the corner. Maddy waved.

"Just who is this guy?" Audrey asked as the door opened and a handsome man approached the group. He kissed Maddy on both cheeks, holding her hands in his. *Perhaps a little too familiar*, Audrey thought. He shook hands with Christian and the professor and bowed when introduced to Audrey.

"Great we could all get time together. Let's get in and start with a drink; Sebastian will be here any minute," Maddy suggested.

The group walked into the pub, and Clifford swept Maddy off her feet in a bear hug. "Here's my girl. Your table is ready in the side room," he said. "Cora, Cora, come and see!" he shouted at the kitchen door.

Cora came rushing out of the kitchen, wiping her hands on her apron. "What is it? I'm busy. Well, saints alive, Maddy, hallo." She reached up to embrace Maddy.

"Hello, my friend. We came to have the best pot pies in London. How are you, Cora?"

"Go and sit; I'll get your lunch. Where's your other handsome man?" Cora looked at the group and laughed a loud, throaty laugh. With her curls spilling out of the kerchief, her cheeks flushed, a wooden spatula in her hands, Cora looked like a life-sized apple dumpling doll.

"Coming soon. We'll see you before we leave." Maddy hugged her friend and walked towards the private room, group in tow.

Clifford delivered drinks to the table, offering a selection of Old Bridge Pub specialties and sparkling water for Maddy. The group settled in and caught up on news, what was happening in their lives, and plans for the weekend. The professor had chosen a new early band at a recent audition and was sharing the demo on his tablet. Maddy leaned over the table to see the band; as she moved across the table, her hair fell from behind her ear and covered her cheek. Dermot reached up and slowly brushed her hair back behind her ear. Maddy quickly turned to him, smiling a thank you, intent on watching the band on the screen. The professor and Audrey exchanged glances, raising eyebrows, feeling the gesture was perhaps a little too familiar.

Just then Sebastian arrived, taking the seat next to Maddy. He touched her leg to let her know he was beside her. Maddy sat back in her chair, looking over at him, eyebrows raised in question. Sebastian nodded and, moving her hair from her neck, kissed her softly, whispering "Cake in the kitchen, package at the bar. My work is done."

"You will be rewarded soon enough, my little captain of industry," Maddy whispered back.

Sebastian laughed and apologized to the group. The conversation continued across the table.

Dermot left the room to have a few puffs of his vape machine. He watched the table of friends from the doorway and was surprised to see the professor approach him.

"Don't mess with her. She's happy. She chose him, and she's happy. She'll be leaving soon, and we all want her to come back. I'm telling you this like a big brother." He spoke softly but firmly.

"Perhaps she would enjoy what I can offer. Perhaps she would be happier." Dermot watched Maddy, distracted.

"Listen; she doesn't do so well with rules or fishbowl living. She will be the best friend you've ever had if you accept that she has made her choice. I think you know what I'm saying." The professor patted Dermot on the back and returned to the table.

The lights went out, and Maddy entered the room with a cake, candles blazing. The group started singing: "Happy birthday to you, happy birthday to you, happy birthday dear Sam, happy birthday to you." Whistles, applause, and whoops followed.

The professor looked at Maddy and shook his head. "How did you know?" He smiled shyly at his friend. The cake was a turntable; it was a work of art.

"I read your licence on the wall; it renews on your birthday. The cake was created by Grace, of course. It has all your favourite desserts in it."

"Audrey, will you play Mother and cut this beautiful cake. But first, Maddy, take a photo." The professor was touched by the gesture; he wasn't sure his hands would be steady enough to cut the cake.

"Oh, I almost forgot. Happy Birthday, my dear friend. We hope you enjoy it." Maddy handed him a large gift bag containing a tissue paper eruption.

"Maddy, the cake and the thought were ample. Thank you." He couldn't remember the last time he had celebrated a birthday with cake and friends. He slowly made his way through the tissue paper and pulled out an album cover. He looked up at Maddy in awe. "Where in the world did you find an original John Coltrane vinyl?"

"Mr Simpson helped me find it. Please tell me you don't already have it." Maddy was leaning over Sebastian.

"No, it's wonderful. I can't wait to listen to it. I can't wait for you all to hear it. Thank you." He walked over to Maddy and kissed her cheek, shook hands with Sebastian, and returned to his seat to admire his new album.

"This cake is uber amazing; eat up." Audrey was licking her fingers. The group ate in silence, nodding at the delicious flavours and textures of the cake. Once coffee arrived, the conversation was light and easy, the group calling on the professor for a few words.

Christian looked at his watch. "Ach, I have to run. Sebastian, if you are going to the same meeting, you can ride with me."

"Thanks, that works." Sebastian stood up, nodding to the professor, saying his goodbyes before kissing Maddy.

"You two have to choose the painting for the main room, over the fireplace. I can't choose the samples without the go-ahead on the art. Please, today." Audrey was firm.

"I can meet you after this meeting. Say 4:30 p.m.?" Sebastian looked at Maddy.

Maddy shrugged. "Fine. I may just head that way now."

"I'm late for a rehearsal. Maddy, will you sit in on the interview tomorrow?" the professor asked as he packed up his album. "Can't tell you how chuffed I am to get this." He smiled at Maddy.

"I'm glad you like it. See you tomorrow." She looked up, and he kissed her forehead as he headed out.

"Sweetie, this was fun. Must go. I must pick up football uniforms and then collect the children. Please let me know your choice." Audrey hugged Maddy and looked across the table. "Nice to meet you, Dermot." She squeezed Maddy's shoulder and picked up a takeaway container with cake for the buttons.

"I can certainly take you to the gallery. It would be my pleasure." Dermot gave Maddy a charming smile.

"I should say goodbye to Clifford and Cora. Are you in a hurry to get going?"

"I can wait. I'm a patient man. Take your time." He sat down and checked his phone for messages.

Maddy disappeared into the kitchen, and after many hugs and assurances she would return from Canada and come directly to the pub, she was ready to go.

"I wondered if you would help me with hosting an event at the embassy this summer, Maddy," Dermot said as they drove towards the gallery.

"Won't your staff be touchy about that?"

"I was hoping you would be the hostess."

"Dermot, that's sweet, but I'm not American, and people might think it strange. I would. If there's something I can do behind the scenes, I'd be happy to. When is the event?"

"July fourth."

"That's a major celebration. I'll be gone by then. Thanks for thinking I could help. Here we are. Thanks for the ride. It was nice of you to join us for lunch. See how easy it is to go from no friends to a great group?" Maddy realized the car door was locked and she would have to wait for the driver.

"Would you like me to come in with you?" Dermot asked hopefully.

"If you have time, you could certainly offer an opinion." She smiled, remembering he was lonely.

"We'll step out on this side, closest to the door. Here, give me your hand." Dermot held out his hand as the door opened, and he was cleared to proceed.

They walked into the gallery, Maddy realizing they were still holding hands. "Which canvases are you choosing from? he asked, enjoying having her hand in his.

"May I help you with a particular piece? My name is Zoe." The willowy attendant spoke breathlessly.

"We are to see the two musical pieces Audrey chose. Are they hanging together?" Maddy asked.

"Not at the moment, I'm afraid. Right this way." She directed them to the side room.

"This is the abstract." Zoe pointed to a rich canvas with striking shades of brown, red, and orange. It was possible to see the musicians in the brush strokes. "The Votland is over this way."

The second canvas was brighter with definite characters.

"Not so easy to choose, is it?" Maddy looked at Dermot, feeling uncomfortable holding his hand.

"Could you move these two to a white wall? We need to see them side by side." He spoke with authority, and the attendant nodded. Several young men appeared in a matter of moments to move the large canvases to the next room. Maddy and Dermot walked through the gallery as they waited. Suddenly a flash blinded them, and a photographer was asking the ambassador who his companion was. Maddy stood still in the middle of the room as Dermot was whisked out by his bodyguards, the reporter escorted to the door. The gallery attendant locked the front door and suggested Maddy move into the back room. Sitting on a bench in the back room, Maddy realized she was shaking. It had happened so fast. Not a word was spoken; she was left in the gallery alone. She dialled Sebastian on his mobile, and as soon as she heard his voice, she started talking.

"Sebastian, hi, this is Maddy. I'm at the gallery. A crazy thing just happened. I need you." Suddenly she realized she had been talking to his voicemail. She dropped the phone in her pocket and watched the team hang the canvases.

Sebastian felt his phone vibrate. He looked down and saw Maddy's face on his screen. He placed the earbud in his ear and listened to the message. All he heard was "crazy thing just happened. I need you." He looked around the table, realizing this group was not going to save the world today, caught Christian's eye, and motioned he had to leave.

Christian followed Sebastian into the hall, concerned there was an emergency.

"I have to go. She needs me." And he was gone.

Sebastian spoke to Maddy on his way to the gallery, assuring her he would be there soon. He pounded on the glass door several times before someone came to let him in. The attendant directed him to the back room, explaining the unusual circumstances as they fast-walked to the room. He found Maddy lying on an upholstered bench in front of two large canvases. He touched her shoulder and she bolted up, throwing her arms around him. "You're here," she whispered into his neck.

"Of course, I came right away; you needed me." He held her tight, feeling like a hero. She needed him. She had called because she needed him. "Which painting have you decided on?" he finally asked, looking back and forth at the choices before him.

"Which one makes you want to make love to me?"

"Everything in this gallery. But if we only get to choose one, at least the musicians aren't staring at us in the abstract." He smiled at her.

"Sold." Maddy sighed.

A dozen yellow roses were delivered to the garden apartment the next morning. The card read "Apologies. A friend?"

Making Scents of Your Life

"Sebastian, Maddy did me a big favour; I need to get her a gift to show my appreciation. What perfume does she like?" Christian asked as they walked into the meeting room.

"She doesn't wear perfume," Sebastian answered, surprised at his quick response.

"Seriously, she always smells so good. Isn't that a funny thing to notice about someone?" Christian laughed. "With my wife, any sin can be forgiven with a bottle of expensive perfume."

"Maddy definitely doesn't have any perfume, but you're right; she does smell good." Sebastian settled into his seat, thoughts of Maddy swirling in his mind. "I asked her what perfume I could bring her back from our last meeting, and she was adamant that she didn't wear it. Limits gift buying somewhat." He looked over the crowd, adjusting his shirt cuffs, uncomfortable with the conversation.

"Well, what would you suggest as a thank-you gift? It was a huge favour, and I have to do something," Christian pressed.

"Take her to afternoon tea; she adores going to traditional afternoon tea. You might like it yourself," Sebastian laughed.

Christian smiled and nodded. "Sounds good … You British are so traditional. I will ask her to tea. Don't spoil my surprise." He mimed holding a teacup, little finger in the air, and pretended to take a sip of tea.

"You'll do just fine," Sebastian assured him.

He wondered what favour Maddy had done for Christian, but the speaker began his address and he gave his attention to the subject matter.

Arriving home later in the day, Sebastian was pleased to see Maddy in the garden, surrounded by baskets of herbs. She was positioning the potted plants to create a walkway. Esme and Audrey were studying the hand-drawn diagram and seemed to be in a heated discussion over the placement. Maddy stood up among the plants, hands on hips, laughing at the two women. "Enough, you two; let's call it a day and see how we make out in the morning. Anyone ready for a cold drink?"

The women smiled at each other and agreed a drink was exactly what was needed.

Maddy wiped her forehead, leaving a streak of dirt. She looked up and saw Sebastian approaching, smiling at her. *Why do I always feel so happy to see him?* she wondered. He kissed her cheek and wiped her forehead.

"You're just in time for cocktails. Join us." Maddy took his hand and led him towards the deck, where the ladies had arranged the table with drinks, olives, figs, and assorted nuts.

After a few drinks, the ladies bade farewell and left Sebastian and Maddy alone on the deck, enjoying the late-day sun.

"Maddy, Christian asked me what perfume you favoured, and I was at a loss to come up with a fragrance. I wondered how I wouldn't know something so basic. Do you have a favourite?"

"No. It's a long, involved story, but I don't wear perfume." Maddy seemed lost in thought.

Sebastian pulled her close and wrapped his arm around her. "I want to hear. Tell me. I know so little about your life. Please tell me."

Maddy closed her eyes. "I've never talked about it. It's personal, and I would feel like I was betraying my parents."

"How could I not want to hear after that statement? I'm sorry I can't meet your parents, but I would like to hear about your life."

"You'll have to be patient, because it's a saga."

"I have time," Sebastian said softly.

"Okay, but remember that you asked if it drones on … I haven't thought about this for a long time. It's complicated." Maddy sighed. "I had a perfect childhood with two loving parents, lots of friends, a stable home life, and lots of travel with my parents. When I was twelve, my mother lost a child—a boy—in childbirth. You can imagine the pain and anguish they went through, having lost a son. I know it was painful for you too.

My mother retreated to her room, and my father said we had to treat her tenderly because losing a child is the worst thing that could happen to anyone." Maddy stopped for a moment. Sebastian ran his hands through her hair—a gesture of encouragement.

"My father had to travel for his job, and whenever he had to go overseas, he took me with him. I think he was worried about me being alone with my mother. It was fantastic. He would leave for his meetings in the morning, leaving me with my budget, a map, and instructions: 'Don't waste your time. Get a feel for the place, learn nuances of the language, and let me know your favourite thing about the city when I get back. Oh, and chances are we will have dinner with a client, so let's get some nice chocolates for the host. People can be allergic to flowers, but everyone loves chocolates.'" She smiled and shook her head. "Imagine letting a twelve-year-old girl loose in the city … It just wouldn't happen today."

Sebastian tried to imagine a young Maddy wandering the streets of major cities. For some reason, it didn't shock hm.

"The doorman was usually a good resource for chocolates and pointing me in the right direction for a treat. In Paris, Monsieur Basile would collect the chocolates for me and send me to the Cafe de la Paix for *chocolat* and croissants. One day I was enjoying my morning ritual, dipping my croissant in my hot chocolate, when the little dog at the next table came over and stared at me. The owner was an older man with white hair and a blue beret perched on an angle. He looked like a painter. I offered the dog a piece of my croissant, and the dog just stared, so I dipped the croissant in the chocolate and held it out. He eagerly lapped it up, and that made me laugh. We carried on for a few more bites, and suddenly the man stood, called for Napolean—honestly 'Fifi' would have been a better name—and they left, Napolean stopping once to look back at me.

The waiter placed another cup of chocolate and a large croissant on my table with great flourish. I shook my head; my budget for the day wouldn't allow me to have two treats.

The waiter bowed and explained it was a gift from Napolean and Monsieur.

That night at dinner with the Boursalin family, I told the story when asked what exciting things happened to me during the day. Monsieur Boursalin laughed and said he thought it was the first of many croissants

I would be offered in my lifetime. Madame Boursalin was not so pleased; she chided my father for leaving me alone all day." Maddy looked down at her hands. "Monsieur Boursalin was very helpful later in my life, when I needed sites in Paris and environs. He was like a mentor to me … and then more. Madame never really warmed up to me." She shrugged.

"Anyway, when we got home, I sat with my mother and told her of my adventures, as I always did. She would ask me what I learned and if I realized how lucky I was to have had the experience. I know she didn't agree with my father taking me with him. I thought she would enjoy the story of the croissant and Napolean, but she got very serious and told me that I had to be careful what I said to others, as it's human nature for them to judge you when you tell them personal things. She made me repeat the sentiment several times; I guess it stuck with me." Maddy squirmed but continued.

"In Moscow my father hired a young lady to be my guide. Vlada and I became very close after four different visits. She always called me her *little Western sister*. We stayed in touch for years, and when I needed a site for a documentary in Eastern Europe, I hired her; she was so resourceful and well-connected. I was pleased to meet her children and take them for ice cream in the park as she had done with me. When we sat down, she started sobbing, weeping into her hands. The children asked her why she was so sad, especially after being so happy a moment earlier. She stopped crying and told them she was overwhelmed that her beautiful children were able to meet her little Western sister." Maddy wiped a tear from her eye. "It was lovely."

Another sigh and Maddy continued. "You know my father always said Moscow was a fishing trip, but he didn't have a fishing rod, and we never went near the water; it was years before I had the courage to ask him about it.

"My father seemed to travel more than ever when I was in high school, and my mother was concerned that I was missing too much school. They argued about it a lot. I missed travelling with my father, but I also had lots of friends and activities at school, so we compromised—only one trip each quarter.

"My father would bring my mother a bottle of perfume every Christmas. The bottles were beautiful, but my mother never opened one—she just lined them up on a high shelf in her bathroom, untouched. It seemed ungrateful, but we were still being 'nice' to her, so we didn't comment or suggest it was weird.

"We got word that my father had passed away while on the road. His secretary, Ruth, arranged the funeral, presumably because my mother was too fragile to deal with the details. At the funeral, there were two women who looked like clones of my mother in her younger years. They both approached me and asked me questions about school and my life, as if they knew me. They both smelled wonderful. I remember the smell surrounding them even now. It wasn't until years later that I realized my father still loved my mother (despite her shutting him out of her life) but had affairs with his secretary and this other woman. They had bought my clothes and gifts for many years; that's how they knew all about my life." Maddy reflected on this for a moment.

"After the funeral, my mother went into the bathroom and knocked all the perfume off the shelf; it was a mess of glass and expensive liquid. The smell was unbearable. I had to cover my nose and mouth. My mother seemed quite at peace as she walked away from the mess. I was shocked. She turned and pointed at the broken glass and told me this was the 'scent of betrayal'. It took me hours to clean up the ruins. I'm not sure the cloying smell ever left the bathroom. Since that day, I have never even looked at a perfume bottle or had any desire to wear perfume. When I stand beside someone wearing a strong scent, I wonder if they chose it or if it is the scent of betrayal. How sad is that?" Maddy looked away, lost in her thoughts.

Sebastian held her tighter and kissed the top of her head. "Thank you," he whispered. He had so many questions, but he knew one thing: he would never betray her.

Several hours later, Sebastian realized Maddy was not beside him in bed. He sat up, his heart racing, concerned that the telling of her story had uncovered memories she wanted to keep locked away. He blinked to adjust to the darkness and saw Maddy sitting on the floor in front of the fireplace, a blanket wrapped around her. She was hugging her knees and staring into the flames. He padded over to her, anxious to know if she was all right.

"Maddy, may I join you?" he asked tenderly.

She looked up and smiled, opening the blanket, offering him a seat beside her.

"Can't sleep?" he asked when he was settled in.

"No, the perfume question brought back too many memories, and I can't shut them out." She looked over at him, her smile more sad than happy.

"Would you like to tell me? There's so much about you I don't know. Maybe if you talk about the past, it will stop haunting you." He was speaking softly and slowly, aware that he himself had locked many memories inside until he met Maddy.

"Hmm. I don't know where to begin ... How do you make sense of something when you're older that seemed so natural when you were young?" She laughed, mostly to herself.

"What happened after the perfume was cleaned up?" Sebastian encouraged.

"Ah, a good place to start. I called the Boursalin home to let them know about my father, but they already knew. Mr Boursalin asked me to come to Paris so we could celebrate the life of my father in a way that paid homage to a great friend. 'Come alone,' he said."

Maddy paused and took a deep breath.

"He met me at the airport, and we went to the Cafe de la Paix for lunch, the opera, and then dinner. He had booked a hotel for me, and I was pleased to see my friend Basile at the hotel again. I didn't see Madame Boursalin, and we didn't mention her or my mother for the entire time we spent walking around Paris, visiting the Louvre, the university, galleries, and lovely restaurants. It was really grand."

Maddy shifted and turned to look at Sebastian. Her eyes were bright.

"When I returned home, my mother had sold the apartment and moved to an assisted living home; I moved on campus and so looked forward to being at university with other young people. I thought everyone had travelled to Europe and spoke a few languages; I was wrong. The students I met lived at home in little houses with fences; they had never been on an aeroplane, and they were politically savvy—interested in the rallies and protests, not history and places. I was the freak. I realized it was better to just be one of the guys and not talk about my life, ever. Everyone had grown up with friends who knew their parents, their neighbours, their life stories ... It was great to be included in everyone else's family gatherings and celebrations."

She smiled as memories flooded back.

"Before I graduated, I had a job as an intern working for my friend's father at a film location company. They had offices in Toronto, Vancouver, Manhattan, and Los Angeles. It was majorly exciting, and suddenly my talents were put to practical use. I was sent to Europe to photograph old homes and buildings we could recreate in the studio for period pieces. My first trip was to Paris. I left before the crew so I could spend some time alone enjoying the city. I went straight to the Cafe de la Paix and ordered *chocolat* and a croissant. As I was opening the city map to plan my day, someone kissed my cheek. I was startled, but it was Monsieur Boursalin. He said he had been passing by, as he did every day at this time, and was surprised to see me at my table—we always called it my table. He was visibly hurt that I had not called, and in retrospect, it was mean-spirited and selfish of me to want some time alone, after all the hospitality he had shown."

Maddy sighed and then smiled.

"We sat for hours, walked for hours, talked for hours, and had couscous in a little Algerian restaurant near the university. We walked back to the hotel and he—now Paul, not Monsieur Boursalin—advised me we were going to have a wonderful day touring old homes and historic sites beginning at 9 a.m." Maddy pointed to an imaginary watch on her wrist.

"The next morning, a car was waiting, and we did indeed find lovely old homes and sites for the crew. We also had a hair appointment for a styling. He confessed he would not want people to see him with a student when I was now a professional. We laughed a lot, and then I found myself in a boutique trying on clothes I could never afford. Paul sat on a red velour sofa, legs crossed, sipping champagne, chatting with a clerk who ordered several outfits to be brought to the change room. It seems silly now, but at the time it was ... heady. Apparently I needed a proper gown for the opera and a few things to wear to receptions in the coming week. New hair, new clothes, new experiences—but I was still me." Maddy shrugged.

"Paul was very charming to the crew when they arrived at the hotel, inviting them to join us for cocktails in the lounge, and telling them where to get the best deals on meals and where to go for entertainment.

He explained he and my father were great friends and he was required by the laws of friendship to accompany me to the reception at the Louvre that evening and to the ballet the next evening. They were so charmed and so pleased with the photos I had scouted out they insisted I go and report back. We completed our work before deadline, so Paul arranged for us to visit Versailles. Of course they loved it. According to the crew, when we got back, I was a 'rock star' with friends in high places."

Maddy cleared her throat.

"When I had a location anywhere in Europe, I would meet Paul, and we would 'do the town', as he called it. He was so attentive and so comfortable to be with. He always had a surprise for me in each city—a special bakery in Prague, a new shop in Budapest, a new play to see in Oslo, a cruise in Helsinki … He never seemed to tire of my visits."

Maddy looked away and stared at the fire for a few minutes. "I don't even remember when we became lovers … It just happened."

"There was an atelier in Paris, near the Sorbonne, which was my home away from home. I mentioned that I enjoyed making my own bed and doing laundry when I was home, as life on the road wasn't real any more. Paul gave me the key, and we never really discussed whether he went there without me, but it always smelled like Chanel No. 5 when I arrived … I would drop my bag and open the large window panels wide, enjoying the sounds of the city and the smell of auto fumes wafting in from the street. Why didn't I ever think that wasn't normal?" Maddy smiled at the thought. "You know, Paul never called me Maddy or Madison; he always called me Mirage." She moved her cheek to her shoulder, recalling his touch.

"Anyway, my boss asked me to find an old train and get some photos. Paul booked the Orient Express to Bucharest; sadly, they weren't going to Constantinople (Istanbul) any more …" Maddy laughed. "When my boss heard I was going on the Orient Express for my holiday, he was more excited than I was. He said every photo would be worth big bucks— instead of getting an expense cheque." She looked over at Sebastian and then back at the fire.

"Are you tired? Shall I stop?"

"Not at all. Keep going. I've never been on the Orient Express … was it grand?" He encouraged.

"Yes, very … it was old world, shabby beautiful—but very proper. I remember the dining car being almost intimidating. Somewhere along the journey, I realized it was a strange relationship, but it was comfortable and undemanding. It was sad arriving in Bucharest; it was sad leaving the train. It was … It was exciting, but the hotel room seemed too large after the train. We did journey on into Istanbul, just for the fun of it." Maddy rubbed her face with her hands, afraid to look over at Sebastian, considering what he must think of her.

"My life was moving so fast. Europe was eventually replaced with South American locations: deserts, mountains, remote areas perfect for filming science fiction movies and remaking westerns. I was in South America for most of the year. I really didn't have a life other than driving long hours and finding the most desolate but wondrous places on earth. It was difficult to stay in touch with Paul, as phone service was limited. I missed the history lessons and the insider notes on local customs; there were no local guides with the knowledge Paul had shared. He was my Google and *Wikipedia* source before they existed.

"When Paul passed away, I went to the funeral, and suddenly it occurred to me that I wasn't sad or remorseful … I felt I'd lost someone important and the time we spent together was wonderful. We never spoke about his wife, his home; we never spoke about love or being together more than my schedule allowed. I never had to deal with office romances, because everyone knew I had a 'boyfriend' in Paris. My friends from school were getting married; I can't tell you how many weddings I went to. They started having kids, and life changed. I couldn't relate to their lives, and they certainly weren't ready to hear about mine. It all seems so surreal as I say it out loud. I guess that's why I never felt I could talk about those years …" Silence.

Maddy wiped a tear away and continued. "Madame Boursalin looked very old and withered, standing by the coffin in the church; the sunlight streaming in through the windows wasn't bathing her in soft light. Isn't that an awful memory? I paid my respects and turned to leave, and Madame followed me out.

"'Ah, ma pauvre petite Madison. He loved you like a daughter—a daughter we never had. He knew your father and I were lovers for many years; your wonderful father needed comfort since your mother was such a cold fish. Your father and I argued about you many times. I thought he was too liberal with you. Paul always agreed with your father. You are so like your lovely father. You have his free spirit. I can't have you in my life; it would be too painful.' She turned to go back into the church. 'It's a shame Paul didn't make provisions for you in his will; he left you nothing. Au revoir, Madison.'"

Maddy heard Sebastian gasp.

"I suppose I deserved a virtual slap, but as she walked away, I almost burst out laughing. He left me with so much; what else could he possibly have made provisions for? He gave me the keys to Europe and his friendship. He was my mentor and my lover; he taught me so many things …" She sighed as she remembered. *Always have a favourite something. Always choose where you want to eat or go next—never say you don't know; that's for shallow people. Read the reviews and know everything that is happening wherever you are. Speak first; don't wait for anyone to find you. Don't ever go to a man's room; he will come for you … So many life lessons.*

"Suddenly, as I was running down the steps, I wondered whether our friendship was based on revenge against my father or whether Paul really had been the person who changed my life and helped me grow up. I guess I'll never know if he really cared for me." Maddy sighed and looked over at Sebastian, not sure if she should smile or hide her face.

Sebastian wrapped his arms around her and pulled her close.

"He loved you, Maddy; of that I'm sure."

"You know, I never cried for Paul. I thought I should be sad and mournful, but instead I went to dinner at Les Deux Magots, a Paris institution, to pay homage to my friend and mentor. I almost cried when I was presented with the bill." She smiled at the memory.

"I'm sorry if knowing more about me makes you uneasy or distant, but it felt pretty good to tell someone after all this time," Maddy confessed.

"Thank you for sharing what must have been a heady time for a young woman; I can't imagine anyone else living through it." Sebastian had so many questions.

"At the time, it felt like a door had closed on another part of my life, and then, almost immediately, I met Dag." She shook her head.

"How did you meet?" Sebastian wasn't sure if she would continue with the story.

"We were both at a conference in Rio de Janeiro, and he was speaking about adventure travel in the wilds. We seemed to be thrown together for most of the events. He thought my job was ludicrous. I thought his life was fascinating.

On the last day of the conference, I was late arriving to the beach event. We were to build a sand castle of the future on Copacabana Beach. I was sent to a group, and we had started planning our entry when we saw a man striding towards us on the beach. He seemed as if he had a mission, and we all watched him, curious as to what he was looking for with such determination. He stopped in front of us, hands on hips, announcing there had been a fatal error and we had something that belonged to his group. We looked at each other, unsure of what that could possibly be. He took my hand and pulled me up, wiped the sand from my bottom, and started to walk away. He turned around and motioned that I should follow. Then he told the group that I was part of his team. 'Thank you. Carry on.' Of course, we all laughed and thought it was a grand move, but he took my hand, and we returned to his sand castle. We never discussed it again.

"At the end of the conference, he asked if I would join the team travelling the Carretera Austral, which would be leaving from Puerto Montt in Chile the next day. The media person had cancelled because of a high fever. If I wanted to journal the journey, I was in. It sounded like a good idea at the time. I wasn't sure I could get time off from my job, so Dag called my office and told my boss I was quitting my job. I joined the group, and we left early the next morning. We stayed on after the most spectacular trip ever—Ruta 7 through Patagonia is exceptional—and we ventured over to Bolivia and the Road of Death ... again, another crew, another journaling job. It was a wonderful experience, and the fact that I got a pay cheque was a bonus!" Maddy rubbed her neck and then rubbed her eyes. She looked over at Sebastian, contemplating whether to continue. He smiled encouragement, so she carried on.

"We spent months in South America finding rivers and deserts, living in tents, covered in dust. It was great fun. We were surrounded by crews with cameras, crews with safety equipment, local guides, and government officials who wanted the tourists to come. We were packing up and thinking about home when we got an invite to visit Costa Rica and see what they were doing with sustainable tourism. It was a new idea, and they needed to tell their story." Maddy laughed.

"We flew into San Jose and drove to the Arenal Volcano area; a hotel bed never looked so good. We spent a month seeing every nook and cranny in Costa Rica. I was getting paid for my writing, but I also seemed better at dealing with locals than Dag; he was too impatient and too absorbed in his work to be civil to the people trying to help us. We flew back to Toronto—reluctantly on my part; there didn't seem to be any discussion on whether we would go direct to the wilderness ranch and settle in. I liked the lifestyle and saw the opportunities to build a business. Dag had a dream, and he was a good guide, but he wasn't so good at the organization part. We worked together on setting up tours, guiding, and researching new adventures. His family lived nearby, and they were happy to have him home. They were just a little younger than I was, so I thought we would get along fine.

"Maybe my limited experience with family life made me try too hard—our best times were when we were away, trying to create a saleable tour, working out the details and building trust with the locals. I was busy with marketing, taking bookings, and handling the travel arrangements for each tour. Dag and I had a place to live, a dog, lots of contacts, and many trade shows to attend. He was always invited to speak at various events, and he insisted we travel together. It was difficult making local friends while living out of town on the ranch, but I eventually got involved in fundraising for charities and met some great people. Dag didn't like me to be away from the ranch for too long; he needed to know where I was and what I was doing all the time. I don't remember when it stopped being cute and became loathsome." Maddy looked up, a pained look on her face.

"Enough ... I don't need to rehash life with Dag. I'm here because I finally had the courage to run away. I'll deal with the consequences soon enough. I hope you realize how much I trust you to tell you about the past. It wasn't easy. Let's go to bed."

Sebastian held Maddy and listened to her breathing on his chest. She had fallen asleep as soon as they were under the duvet. It was quite a story, but it explained her need to explore and see everything, to accept people as they were, to expect her kindness to be returned … *How can I compete with the ghosts of the past?* he wondered.

He fell asleep with visions in his mind of Maddy walking down the corridor of the Orient Express, touching the wood trim with her hand, appreciating every detail; her lover was behind her, his hand on her back, anxious to be alone with her. He saw her waking up in a tent, overlooking the mountains, stretching; anxious to meet the new day … He saw her running towards him …

He woke with a start and sat up in the bed. Where was Maddy? His heart was pounding in his ears. He heard the bathroom door open and felt her pull the covers. He lay back as her body moulded itself to him, her head on his chest. He moved his arm around her and kissed the top of her head.

"Did I wake you?" she asked softly.

"No, sweetheart, go back to sleep."

"Sebastian, are you okay with knowing about my past?" She was making circles on his chest.

"We all have a past, Maddy. It's how we got here. At this point in my life, I can't expect to meet anyone with a blank slate. I wonder if you could see a future with someone like me."

"Someone like you?" Maddy was thoughtful. "No."

His heart stopped; he felt as if he were falling from a high cliff over dangerous water.

"I don't want someone *like* you in my future … I just want you." She kissed his chest.

Sebastian groaned and held her tight. "That's good, because I'm not going anywhere. Good night."

Tennis, Anyone?

"We've been invited to the Annual Featherstone Tennis Tournament this weekend. It's a grand tradition, and the hosts always win, but it is fun, and you'll enjoy the estate, I'm sure," Sebastian announced at breakfast as he was reading the headlines on his laptop.

Maddy waited for more details, but none were forthcoming.

"We'll leave early Saturday morning and stay overnight. You'll need a tennis outfit and something casual for dinner. Ah, look at the time. See you tonight." He leaned over and kissed the back of her neck as he left the garden apartment.

Maddy sat at the table and chuckled, wondering if that was an invitation or command performance. "Good thing I'm free this weekend," she said out loud to the garden.

"Audrey, any chance I can borrow a racquet and your tennis court for an hour or so?" she asked as she walked into the house. Audrey laughed and pointed to the court outside the window. "Be my guest; you'll be the first on the court this summer. Do you need an outfit? I have a collection of fab club dresses that I used for an ad shoot. Let's get you dressed and warmed up."

Maddy hugged her friend and explained how the weekend had come about.

"Imagine making an announcement like that and expecting someone to be ready to go …" She wasn't sure if she should be pleased or angry. "After Italy, how can I be upset about a silly tennis tournament? Really, I should be pleased Sebastian wants me to go with him. Shouldn't I?"

"The estate is beautiful, but the tournament is so contrived. Still, it's a good experience, and I'm sure you'll enjoy the *old English establishment*."

Audrey was trying to make light of the situation, surprised at the way it had been presented. "You know, your perfect Sebastian is one of the original snobs; that's the only thing that makes sense. This is his club crowd. Don't confuse a walk in Italy with a command performance. Are you sure you want to go?"

Maddy shrugged. "I should serve a few and hit some balls, just in case. I've been advised the hosts always win. Thanks, Audrey, the outfit is killer … I'll be sure to give you a full report." She headed to the court. "Here goes nothing."

The Featherstone Estate was impressive; not so much beautiful as grandiose, perhaps a little tired. After lunch on the terrace, the teams were determined, and Maddy was paired with Roger Blakely, a very tanned and fit older man. Sebastian was paired with his usual partner, Deirdre. The rules were reviewed: "Best of seven games per set, with the best record for each team posted. The trophies will be awarded at dinner this evening. Play fair. Enjoy the day."

Roger introduced himself as Maddy's partner and immediately apologized. He said he was very rich and considered to be entertaining company, but he wasn't a very good player. He hoped Maddy would not be too disappointed having him as a partner. He was so genuine in his concern she laughed it off, reminding him they were here to have fun. He assured her that was not the case.

She excused herself and headed for the ladies' change room. As she was changing, Maddy could hear the ladies discussing the teams and confirming how often the hosts had won the day. They laughed at the pairing of poor old Roger and Sebastian's friend, hoping they would be finished with their matches in time to watch them be pulverized by the hosts. They also commented on Sebastian and Deirdre, together as usual, and how well they played.

Maddy sat on the bench and listened to the chatter, her jaw set, her mind made up. If it was entertainment they wanted, let the show begin.

The first group was over when Maddy walked out to their assigned court. She and Roger warmed up and waited for their game to begin. It seemed a long wait, but finally they were on the court. The first serve was easily returned and Maddy could see Roger was a tentative player at best.

The hosts won the first game 40–15. A crowd was beginning to gather, as their match was one of the last on the courts. Maddy noticed that the hostess directed the out-of-play balls straight at Roger, with force. Her partner was coming undone after just one game.

Maddy walked up to the net and faced Roger. "Okay, we don't have to take this lying down. When I yell 'duck', you duck; get out of the way and hope for the best. Deal?" Roger nodded and seemed to come alive, moving side to side on the court.

Maddy bounced the ball twice and served as hard a serve as she could muster. Point.

The hostess moved back, rattled. 15–love. Second serve, just as powerful. 30–love.

Roger was bouncing on his toes, afraid to look back at his partner.

Sebastian and Deirdre lost their game on the centre court and were directed to the end court. "Sebastian, you are going to want to see this, you devil; why didn't you say?"

Sebastian shook hands with the winning couple at the net, leaving Deirdre there chatting as he walked over to the last court. He had just taken a drink from his water bottle when he saw Maddy serve, and water jetted out of his mouth. He hadn't known she could play tennis like that. He was mesmerized with the force of her game. Roger was along for the ride, clearly. He heard the others describe her 'killer backhand', her steely returns, and her wide coverage of the court. She was playing like a pro, returning balls with a fierce spin, retrieving low bounces with a swat, and forcing her competitors to make silly mistakes and look flustered.

Roger ducked when ordered, and the hosts, unused to losing, were terrible bad sports, waiting for Maddy to walk back before hitting her with the out-of-play balls. She didn't seem to mind; she was focused on winning the game.

"The score is 5–1; do you wish to continue playing?" the scorekeeper asked.

Roger nodded enthusiastically. Maddy nodded as well, but the hosts turned and walked off the court, sending the dead balls across the net, refusing to shake hands. The crowd applauded. Roger swung Maddy around, ecstatic at the win. Friends had gathered and forced the hosts to return to the court to shake hands at the net. Lavina Featherstone was flushed and speechless, barely able to go through the motions, while her husband James was quietly enthusiastic about the outcome. He congratulated Roger and Maddy and invited Maddy to play singles at his club; he wanted another chance to return her serve.

The crowd had moved to the terrace for the post-tourney gin and tonic. Roger hurried away to relive the game with his cronies. Maddy slowly walked over to the bench to gather her things and place the racquet in the case.

"You enjoyed that, didn't you?" She turned to see Sebastian leaning against the referee chair, his arms crossed, and one leg bent, crossed at the ankle.

She shrugged, not sure if the look on his face was amusement or anger. She bit the side of her cheek and waited, wondering what was next. "I was provoked," she responded, chin up in defiance.

"I didn't know you could play like that. You never said."

"You never asked. No one did. Your friends were sure we would provide a good laugh at the end of the day. I might have played a different game, but it wasn't fair to Roger, and they were bad sports," Maddy said passionately.

"Oh, Maddy …" He shrugged.

"Don't 'Maddy' me. I'm angry." She was shaking her finger at him.

Sebastian looked up at the terrace crowd and back at Maddy. "You know they must think I set them up."

"You should go and be with your snobby friends if that's what worries you." She turned away in disgust.

"Why are you so angry with me?" He asked, clearly perplexed at her reaction.

"You seem more worried about what your friends think than how I might be feeling …"

"Maddy, you won the tournament. Isn't that cause for celebration?" he asked.

"What do you want from me?" He was searching—his arms out in front of him.

"How about a little respect?" she retorted.

Sebastian was quiet for a moment, thinking about what Maddy had said and trying to find a way to turn this around. He didn't want to fall out with her; she should be celebrating her win, after all.

He touched her cheek, lifted her chin, and looked into her eyes. "I can do that. I'm sorry, but in my defence, you excel at everything you do, and every day I hear about some hidden talent you have or something you've done in another life. I should not have assumed you played tennis at all, but you didn't say you preferred not to play either. Forgive me?" he asked tenderly, bending to meet her lips with his.

Maddy placed a hand on his chest, hoping he would know she was still angry. Suddenly she realized she was responding to his kiss; it was comforting to feel his arms around her, his strength and his support. How could she be angry with a victory?

Sebastian took a deep breath, pleased to know he was forgiven. He stepped back and, with a quick look at the terrace, said, "We may never be invited back, you know."

"Is that important?" Maddy asked, her eyes wide.

He laughed that velvet laugh that came from the core. "No, not really, not any more; although I do want to play tennis with you when you're not provoked. Could you teach me that spin?"

"I haven't played for so long. Today I played such a reckless game. I took so many chances. It could have gone either way, you know." She was afraid to look at him.

Before he could respond, Roger walked out to the court with glasses of champagne. "Maddy, great game. We'll have to share the trophy. I can't believe it! Wow." He was on a high.

"Roger, you deserve it. You keep the trophy." She put her arm around Sebastian. "I already have one." She smiled up at him, not knowing how he would react. To her surprise and delight, he smiled and kissed the top of her head.

"Come on; let's have a drink and take the flak. It may not be pretty."

"Whatever happened to 'Keep a stiff upper lip' and all that?"

"Not in tennis, baby, not in tennis." He directed her to the terrace.

As they walked into the group, he realized he didn't care what they thought; they had forced Maddy to respond in the only way she knew how. She played to win. He had mistakenly taken her for granted, and once again she had knocked him for a loop. He felt proud of her and knew he cared more for her than his old lifestyle and the facade of friendship.

Maddy bravely faced the false smiles and congratulations, anxious to tell Audrey how the day unfolded. Dinner was long and tedious as the mix of sun and too many drinks turned the group into a groping, sad lot. Sebastian never left her side, his arm protectively around her. Maddy was longing for a hot bath; muscles she hadn't used for some time were screaming at her. Getting old—hell, being old—required more warming up, it seemed.

It's Never Enough

Henry rushed into the garden apartment, his coat trailing him like a cape.

"Maddy, I got invited to the regatta as crew—isn't that the best?" He was breathless.

Maddy waited for his usual hug and smiled at his excitement. Michael had asked if it would be appropriate, and the headmaster had no concerns; how could she say no? It would be good experience for Henry.

"Great news. I bet Sebastian was pleased." She was winded by his bear hug.

Sebastian walked in carrying the backpack, smiling at the excited boy.

"Where's Myles? I thought you were bringing Myles with you today." Maddy looked through the glass into the garden.

"I don't want Myles to come," Henry whined. "This is my day with you and Sebastian."

"Well, that's fine, but his parents always invite you away for the summer and school holidays. His father seemed happy to have you, so I thought we should include Myles in our outings." Maddy was patient. Sebastian poured a cup of coffee and waited to hear what Henry had to say.

"Myles has his own family. His father is mean. We can't laugh or talk at the dinner table; we're supposed to be 'seen and not heard'. He never comes to the school to see Myles, and I don't know why you always need to have other people around. Why can't you just do things with Sebastian and me? Don't you like us? Aren't we charming enough for you? Maybe—"

Sebastian cleared his throat and touched Henry on the shoulder. "Henry. A word?" He pointed to the door. Henry stopped his tirade and turned in frustration, stomping out to the garden.

Maddy blinked. What had just happened? Was she neglecting the two of them? She truly believed Henry would have more fun if his mate was with him. They were best friends, after all. She felt the tears on her cheek and realized she was crying. She looked around the room, blinking back the tears. *What now? I know; I'll make tea. That's what the British do, isn't it?* She was muttering to herself when Henry appeared before her, his hanky in hand.

"Maddy, I'm really sorry. I don't want to share you and Sebastian with everyone else. All the other kids have family; I have you. Don't cry. Are those the chocolate biscuits we baked on Wednesday? Let's have one, all right?" He handed her the hanky and carefully chose a large biscuit from the platter. The issue was over, in Henry's mind.

Maddy smiled at the hanky, patted her eyes, and handed it back. Henry looked distracted, not sure what to do with it now. He looked over at Sebastian, who motioned he should return it to his pocket.

"Are we ready to see Greenwich?" She tried to sound cheerful.

"Oh dear, Davi hasn't been there, so he asked if he could drive and hang out with us today. Shall I tell him no?"

Henry took a bite of his biscuit, shaking his head. "Davi should come with us. He can drive, and we can see it together. I'd better wash up."

Maddy looked over at Sebastian, raising her eyebrows in question. "Ready to go?"

Sebastian slowly walked over to Maddy, wrapped her in his arms, and kissed the top of her head. "Ready for whatever adventure you have in mind for us."

"Me and Davi … Sorry … Davi and I are going over to the pavilion for ice cream. Coming?" Henry stood in front of the park bench they had just landed on. "You go ahead; I'm too stuffed from lunch. Sebastian?" She looked over to see Sebastian getting ready to lie across the bench, setting his head on her lap. Henry ran off to catch Davi.

Shading his eyes with his hand, Sebastian turned his head up to Maddy. "I learned something new today."

"You mean just how bad my attempt at parenting really is? How my expectations are unreal?" Maddy was still stinging.

"Not at all." Sebastian sat up and took her hands in his. "I was humbled by a young man, a mere schoolboy, who verbalized what I was thinking.

It happened again when I was trying to explain why we have to accept the terms." Sebastian touched her face and stroked her cheek gently. "You see, both Henry and I have been selfish about your time; we rely on you for entertainment and encouragement and caring. Neither of us have many friends; we're loners. You, on the other hand, need friends around you all the time. You have enough love and caring for everyone. But it's your network, your group of friends, that allows us to see special concerts, take piano lessons, go sailing, and have backyard parties at a moment's notice. We just need to be better at letting you know how much we appreciate what you do for us. Fair enough?" He moved his arm around her shoulders.

Maddy felt tears welling up, so she blinked several times. No more tears. They were having such a wonderful time here. She looked over at Henry and Davi strolling back towards them, licking their cones and laughing at something they had shared. Smiling, she turned to Sebastian, her heart full of love. She laid her head on his shoulder and whispered, "Thank you."

Sebastian kissed the top of her head. He smiled as he watched Henry and Davi approach, excited with their choices.

"Maddy, try this flavour combo—it's to die for." Henry offered his cone with a flourish.

The group arrived home tired and sunburned, giddy from their time together. Davi was so appreciative to have been included in the day. Henry exclaimed it was the best day ever, and Sebastian was ready for a quiet night. Maddy made popcorn, and they all fell asleep watching a film about saving a zoo.

Fashion Forward

"See you at the fitting tomorrow." Christian winked as he left the meeting. Sebastian looked up from his notes, wondering what fitting he was referring to. He checked his phone agenda and called Lambert. "Do I have a fitting tomorrow?"

"Well, yes ... have you spoken with Maddy? I wasn't sure you had agreed ..." Lambert was evasive.

Sebastian rubbed the bridge of his nose. "Lambert, you'd better tell me what I'm doing; enough of the code-speak."

"Perhaps you should speak with Maddy first; I'm not too sure of the details."

"Lambert." Sebastian rarely used the forceful *I am the boss* tone.

Lambert hesitated and quickly did a pro/con analysis in his head. Pro: it was a fundraiser; he and Christian were joining the professor and Michael on the runway; and Henry, Audrey, and the children were involved as well. Con: Maddy had not yet asked Sebastian to be one of the models; she was afraid he might say no—especially since the last outfit was to be a wedding gown.

Lambert decided his friend Maddy needed help with consent from Sebastian; he cleared his throat and plunged in.

"Maddy has arranged a fashion show for the annual hospital tea. She met a designer and, well ... that's a long story. We, all her friends, are modelling outfits in the fashion show next week. Maddy is to wear the final gown, and she wanted you to wear the morning suit and walk with her. She's worried you might not want to participate, so she's procrastinating. It's kind of important, you know; she has put so much into it. I'm sure she'll ask you tonight. It's not like her to be so tentative." Lambert sighed. "There, now you know. I hope I haven't spoken out of turn."

"Indeed." Sebastian ended the call.

He found Maddy in the garden, sitting at the table with her laptop, typing furiously.

The table was covered with cutout dolls—men, women, and children; there were several outfits for each cutout. "This looks interesting. Working on a project?" He bent over to kiss her neck.

"It's the hospital fundraiser; we're doing a fashion show for the tea. Just to change it up a bit, you know. It's always a tea, so we thought the fashion show would be fun. We've sold out, and we've already done better than previous years." Maddy turned and looked up at him. "I was hoping to ask you a favour."

Sebastian moved a box from the chair and sat down across from her. "Go ahead. What can I do to help?"

"Well, it's more than a favour. It's a …" Maddy was squirming on her chair. "I met this designer at a market, and I really liked her style— very simple and elegant. I asked her to help us with some costumes and, well, it's a long story. She was hoping to start a retail business, so Audrey and I helped her find a location and suggested some other lines and … anyway, here we are featuring her retail shop in our fashion show. Isn't that wonderful?" Maddy took a deep breath.

Sebastian sat back. "And you need me to …"

"Well, the last outfit is a dress I sketched for Jacqueline, that's her name, and she made it. She wants to end the show with it, but the finale really needs a couple. It would be perfect if accompanied by a tall man in a morning suit … a tall, handsome man. Jacqueline wants to sell it as a wedding dress. I don't want to walk down the runway with anyone but you. I've been afraid to ask you because you'll know a lot of the crowd attending, and you might find that weird …"

"I'm happy to do it. What shall we do about dinner?" Sebastian stood.

Maddy blinked and looked up at him. "What?"

"I'm happy to walk down the aisle with you. Heaven knows I've asked you to marry me several times. I'll consider this a dress rehearsal." He shrugged.

Maddy stood up quickly, knocking her chair back, and threw her arms around his neck.

"Thank you. I was so worried. I didn't know how you would react … Thank you." She kissed him, feeling light-headed. The finale would be perfect—absolutely perfect.

Sebastian realized his desire to please Maddy was greater than any reservations he may have had about the show. Here he was, once again, a hero. Indeed.

The luncheon had been sold out for some time; the crowd was anxious to see a new designer, and the models were giddy. The young designer, Jacqueline, was heady with the prospects. Maddy had done such a wonderful job of welcoming the guests and introducing not only the need for new hospital equipment in the ever-changing world of technology but also the promise of hope for the future in both fronts—health and fashion. It was brilliant how she wove the need for new equipment and new clothing together. As the first models walked out to the positive cheers and exclamations of a delighted gathering, Jacqueline looked over at Maddy and mouthed a thank you.

Maddy was to appear in the gown at the end of the show. Sebastian had walked out to the end of the runway, looking very distinguished, with Jimmy and Jemma beside him. The buttons had been through several costume changes, so they were feeling familiar with the music and lights; the scene was a photographers' dream. When Maddy appeared in the striking pearl-white gown, there was a hush in the room. Sebastian watched her walk slowly towards him, his eyes blinded by the spotlights. She was floating down the long runway, her eyes on Sebastian. The large white hat perched at a saucy angle on her head blocked out the spotlight, and Sebastian finally saw her face. Her cheeks were flushed, her smile for him alone, and her eyes were sparkling, and before he realized what he was doing, he stepped forward and kissed her, much to the delight of the crowd and Jacqueline, who had not scripted the move. The applause and whistles were deafening; both Jimmy and Jemma covered their ears.

Maddy turned to reveal the back of the dress, and Sebastian moved to her side, taking her arm and whispering in her ear, "Marry me right now. You look divine."

She smiled and leaned into his arm as they walked back to meet the rest of the models, who were carefully arranged on the staging for a final photo. As Maddy and Sebastian settled into their places, Jimmy and Jemma in front of them, Jacqueline appeared and took a selfie with the group. There was much laughter and applause at the gesture. The standing ovation seemed endless.

Jacqueline was overwhelmed with the orders she received from the show. As the outfits were returned and make-up removed, the models enjoyed a reception with champagne and strawberries Michael Riley had arranged for them. Audrey had juice boxes for the buttons, who were permitted to sit on the edge of the stage, feet swinging. Maddy thanked her friends for their amazing poise and cooperation, hugged Jacqueline and wished her the best with her career, winked at the buttons for being the very best little models ever, and asked for a round of applause for the professor, who had provided the music—guitar, piano, and saxophone. She stated her appreciation for the flowers and champagne Michael had supplied and finally presented a very healthy cheque to Esme for the hospital.

Sebastian stood at the back of the room, watching Maddy and her friends relive the show, laughing easily at their lack of experience having been overcome by unbridled enthusiasm. He had been nervous, but seeing Maddy in that dress had made him realize he would do anything for her; he would never forget the look on her face just before he kissed her.

"Man oh man, wasn't that a rush? My first modelling job. Ha ha ha." Christian appeared at his side, his glass raised in a toast. "What next?"

"Indeed."

Still Boring After All These Years

Sebastian walked into the club and immediately scanned the room for Maddy. His meeting had run late, so they had agreed to meet in the city. He was disappointed, as he always enjoyed the ride in with Maddy beside him, telling him about her day and asking for highlights of his day. It was a simple yet comforting ritual.

He felt a hand on his neck as someone whispered in his ear, "Long time no see, lover."

He turned to see Veronica Wainwright. Ronnie, as she liked to be called, had left London several years ago in the heat of a much-publicized scandal involving a lord and drugs. Sebastian had accompanied Ronnie to several functions and events in the day, but she had complained he was too boring for her, and they had lost contact. The years had not been kind to Ronnie; he noticed her thick make-up and lifeless eyes.

"What brings you back to London, Ronnie?" he asked, removing her hand and stepping back.

"Mummy and Daddy separated and sold the villa in Barbados, so I'm forced to look for a new sponsor or husband or sugar daddy. Interested?" she asked in a mock coquettish manner.

"Fortunately for me, I recovered from your dismissal and have a wonderful life with a lovely woman, whom I'm sure you'll meet any minute now." He smiled with the confidence of a man who has found his place in the world.

Ronnie laughed. "Sebastian, lover, let's let bygones be bygones and have a drink." She touched his face and moved her body against him. "You wouldn't let an old friend and lover drink alone, would you?"

Sebastian moved back, creating distance between them. He was uncomfortable with her behaviour. Where was Maddy? He felt her presence before he saw her.

"Hi, sorry I missed you when you arrived. Isn't the band splendid?" Maddy kissed his cheek and looked over at Ronnie, who was now angry at Sebastian for pushing her away.

Maddy held her hand out. "Hello, I'm Maddy."

Ronnie smirked. "We're not going to be friends."

"Too bad; I'm a great friend," Maddy responded, and she looked up at Sebastian with a pleasant smile. "I like this song …"

"Maddy, this is Veronica Wainwright; we knew each other years ago. Ronnie is just returning to London after a few years in the Caribbean." Sebastian wanted to move away before Ronnie had more to say.

"Let's dance, shall we?" Sebastian placed his arm on the small of Maddy's back and started to move away.

"You don't dance," Ronnie spat out.

"Ah, I finally found the right partner." Sebastian looked tenderly at Maddy.

"Deirdre tells me you two continue to play tennis and she had a most enjoyable lunch with you just last week. I didn't realize you were still so close. I also heard …"

Sebastian stopped for a moment and then turned towards Ronnie, his jaw set.

"Ronnie, you haven't changed at all; you're still the spoiled rich girl who needs to cause trouble to be happy. We've all grown up. Look around you—same crowd, same club. People are happy and carrying on with their lives. Pouting isn't attractive, and being mean-spirited is infinitely worse than being boring. Excuse us."

On the dance floor, Maddy waited for Sebastian to say something. She hadn't heard him speak so frankly to another person, and she thought it best not to ask what had happened. She looked up at him and smiled, hoping to let him know she was supportive.

"How many more of these old girlfriends am I going to have rescue you from?" she asked playfully.

"I'm sorry about that Maddy. It was uncomfortable, to say the least. Ronnie left London years ago, and her final farewell, right here at the club, was to announce how boring we all were. I believe all of London breathed a sigh of relief when she left." Sebastian looked over to the door, where Ronnie was clinging to another old friend.

Maddy followed his gaze. "She doesn't seem very happy. She seems lonely."

Sebastian sighed and kissed Maddy on the cheek. "Trust you to find something positive to say. Why do women of a certain age seem so aggressive and desperate?"

"They don't want to be alone. They want to be with someone—sometimes anyone. It's different for men. You can be single and alone, but there are always women who want to take care of you. Women don't have as many options—especially if they aren't financially secure. It's sad really …" Maddy placed her head on his shoulder.

Sebastian held Maddy close as he thought about what she had said.

"Maddy, when you get old, if you're alone it will be because you choose to be alone. I plan on being with you until the end."

Maddy threw her arms around his neck and kissed him. "You are looking anything but boring right now."

"Indeed." He held her tight and buried his face in her hair.

And Then the Sky Fell

"Lambert, I can't reach Sebastian. I really must speak with him right now. Do you know when he'll be free?" Maddy was frantic on the phone.

"Mad, you sound awful. Are you crying? Where are you? Come here; come to the office and I'll make you a nice cup of tea, settle you into the boss's office. He's with a client group—shouldn't be too much longer. He's rolling the pen; he only rolls the pen when he's ready to sign. Maddy, come up here. You're better here than on the phone. Maddy?"

"You're right. I'm only a few blocks away. Oh, Lambert, it's just awful. I can't even think right now…"

"Just get here. It's going to be fine. You'll see." Lambert spoke tenderly to his friend.

Maddy rushed into the office, searching for Lambert; he would calm her—he and his infernal cup of tea … Where was Sebastian? Lambert, intercepting, guided her to the office, where tea was waiting. Maddy could hear Sebastian wishing his clients a safe journey home, looking forward to working with them, blah, blah, blah … He sounded so calm and self-assured. How could he be, knowing what she was about to spill?

Sebastian was on his way to his office, loosening his tie, checking the time. He gave a wave to the team in the boardroom. "Good work, Joseph; you were well prepared. You deserve the opportunity. Go home; we'll finish tomorrow. Go celebrate." He sounded fatherly.

As he turned, he saw Lambert signalling that he should go straight to his office. Another time he might have laughed at the facial expressions, but something about the urgency of the gestures made him walk quickly into his office. Maddy was pacing across the window, the magnificent view unnoticed, which was not like her. She was upset—so upset she didn't hear him close the door.

"Maddy, are you all right?" He moved towards her, attempting to stop her pacing.

"Oh, Sebastian, you're here. I've just had the worst news. Epic bad news." She wiped the tears from her cheek.

Sebastian gently held her shoulders and forced her to look at him. "Tell me what's happened." His voice was so calm.

Maddy took a deep breath and started speaking, her voice escalating. "The headmaster called to say Henry's grandfather was ill and the family wants him to leave the school and fly to Australia immediately. He hasn't completed the year, his exams are coming up, he doesn't know these people, he can't just leave, and he has a trust for school, you know; they can't just take him away. Don't you see? We'll lose him. If he goes to Australia, we'll lose him." She was crying into his shoulder.

"He was never ours, Maddy. He should see his grandfather, regardless of the family dynamics. We need to do whatever we can to make this happen. He'll come back if it isn't meant to work." His voice was soft and calming.

Maddy moved away and shook her head. "How can you be so calm and reasoned when you know we may never see him again? Why aren't you angry at the unfairness of it all? Why aren't you throwing something or clenching your fists? How can you be so damn perfect all the time?" She cried into her hands.

Sebastian wrapped his arms around her and waited for her sobs to subside.

"Maddy, you came here because you needed me to be calm and reasoned. Of course I'm upset about the news. His family may genuinely want to see him before the old man passes on. We can't fall apart now; we have to be strong and let Henry know he can come home anytime he wants to." He lifted her chin, wishing he could stop her tears.

"Who is letting him know?"

Maddy sniffled. "The headmaster asked if we could be there this afternoon. He felt Henry would need some encouragement." She smiled as he handed her his handkerchief. She wiped her eyes and looked up at

Sebastian. "I'm sorry. I just felt so helpless, and I did need your calm resolve to understand what was happening. I always do. Thank you."

Sebastian heard her words but felt lost in her blue eyes. He was angry; he was disappointed. He had hoped to talk to Maddy about guardianship; he was sad, as he knew how close Maddy and Henry had become. But right now, he knew he must be strong for Maddy and for Henry; it was expected. He held Maddy in his arms and looked out over the city. "Right, shall we go?"

Sitting in the headmaster's office, Sebastian was flooded by old memories of sitting here in these very velvet chairs, looking at the wooden panels and books, the heavy draperies censoring any light from the outside world, waiting for a lecture from the headmaster. He hadn't been there for many disciplinary interviews, but there had been times he dreaded being called into this office.

The headmaster and Maddy had developed an easy friendship; Sebastian smiled at her total lack of respect for his position.

"Maddy, I must say, I'm surprised at your composure. I thought you would take this to heart." The headmaster was tender, like an old uncle.

"I was a mess earlier, but Sebastian always grounds me." She smiled at Sebastian and took his hand in hers.

"Henry has written several essays for his terms; I must say I'm impressed with his new-found passion in history, music, and art." The headmaster looked over at Maddy. "I know your methods are somewhat unorthodox, but the results speak for themselves. May I ask how you managed to get Henry so interested in the Greek wars?"

Maddy squirmed in her seat. *Where to begin …*

Sebastian cleared his throat and raised his eyebrows, encouraging her to respond.

"Henry told me he was struggling with history because he couldn't see it. I wanted to buy Sebastian a set of toy soldiers—that's another story— and Mr Simpson directed me to his old landlady, who had an attic full of toys from God knows when. She was happy to have me clean out her attic in exchange for some special favours." Maddy waved her hands. The special favours included chocolate and sweets the elderly woman was denied by her children, but that was a secret deal, adding nothing to the story.

"I happened to take the box of toy soldiers to the mission with me; it was our night to serve dinner for the homeless. I think Henry needs to see the other side of life; not everyone dines at the club. He and I serve on Mondays. He has developed quite a talent for cooking and small talk." Maddy ignored the shocked look on the headmaster's face, not daring to look over at Sebastian for his reaction.

"Anyway, the box was a great curiosity for the men, and when they found the soldiers, they insisted Henry should see the re-enactment of certain battles on the tables. He was keen and read the passages aloud on how the forces were positioned. Mr Bowles, one of the regulars, read history at Cambridge and was quite knowledgeable about the battles and strategies. It was difficult to tear Henry away and return him to the school that night, so the men promised to continue their battle studies the next week. They also offered to paint and repair the set. Isn't that wonderful?" Maddy challenged the headmaster with a winning smile. She stood and walked around the room, running her fingers over the books, turning the large globe, waiting for a response. Silence ensued, so she continued.

"Not all learning happens in the classroom. I really want Henry to max out his potential—be aware of the world around him and yet be thankful for what he has. Is that wrong?" Maddy asked, challenging the headmaster. She was still unsure how Sebastian was reacting to this.

"The results would argue that our methods are outdated, but we should have been informed you were introducing Henry to certain segments of life in London—for safety reasons, of course." The headmaster was trying not to smile.

Sebastian raised his eyebrows when Maddy replied with almost an apology. "You're right, Sebastian is always telling me I'm reckless, but I would never do anything to put Henry in danger. The men at the mission, the East Side Shelter, are harmless; they may use colourful language, and they don't smell so good, but they are careful around Henry, and I assure you they will be quite sad to hear he is leaving. He shares what he learns with them, and they have great discussions. Mr Bowles is forcing him to think strategically before responding. It's delightful. I wish you would join us sometime."

"Yes, that would be interesting." The headmaster rubbed his chin, contemplating the sheer madness of the idea. "How did you manage to get Mr Riley involved? He has donated a rather large sum of money for a sailing programme."

"Oh, how fantastic. Great news. Michael has been so patient and diligent with Henry; if the school benefits from the programme, it's only because Henry was so enthusiastic. Those two will miss each other." Maddy crossed her arms, her expression wistful.

"Ah, here's Master Henry now. Come in, young man." The headmaster waved Henry into the room.

Henry nodded at the headmaster and approached Sebastian to shake hands. "Sir." He followed Sebastian's gaze and ran to Maddy, embracing her.

Maddy wrapped her arms around him, resting her chin on his head. "How was the history essay?" she asked.

Henry broke away, winked, and gave her a thumbs up. They both laughed.

The headmaster was very gentle as he explained the situation to Henry, assuring him there was always a place for him at the school and that he would be given a passing mark for the term. Henry was to fly to Melbourne on Friday morning. He would complete his classes tomorrow and have a day with Sebastian and Maddy before his flight.

Tears he could not control fell on his cheeks as Henry listened to the news and realized any protest would be wasted. Maddy touched his shoulder; he knew she was trying to make him feel better, but he was suddenly angry: angry at Maddy for letting the headmaster send him away—angry that she wasn't fighting for him to stay. He raised his shoulders, taking deep breaths, hoping to shrug her hand away.

Sebastian saw the conflict on his face and spoke softly, leaning forward in his chair. "Henry, Maddy and I are very upset with the news, but your grandfather has every right to want to see you before he passes. You have family in Australia, and it would be wrong of us to keep you from them. You know we are here if you ever want to come back; you will always be welcome in our home."

Henry nodded, slowly stood, and wiped his eyes with the back of his hand. "I should go." He wondered if this was punishment for being so selfish about his time with Maddy and Sebastian.

"I'll be here to collect you for sailing tomorrow after your last class.

You'll stay the night with us, if that's okay. Mrs B and the professor will want to see you. We'll have tacos." Maddy tried to sound light-hearted.

Henry nodded and left the room, his head down and his body language signalling resignation.

"We'll have his things ready for you tomorrow. He won't have much without his school uniform." The headmaster sounded defeated. He had seen many students expelled or forced to leave the school over the years, but today he felt old and tired. He wasn't just losing a student; he was losing contact with an exciting dervish—Maddy had certainly added some colour to the term. He would miss her. Sebastian probably wouldn't want to jump back into the mentorship programme immediately; it had been a great experiment. He ran his hand over his balding head and wondered how the trio would make out.

"Thank you," Maddy whispered, breaking his reverie. "Your job can't be easy. I'm going to miss your disciplinary lectures, headmaster."

"I'm hopeful you will join my advisory council, Maddy. They need shaking up, and I need you to keep challenging me. Perhaps we could look at alternative learning. Sebastian, I do not know how you cope."

"I don't usually ask." Sebastian smiled and shook hands with the headmaster.

As they left the office, Sebastian placed his arm around Maddy, hoping to show his solidarity and love for her. They didn't speak as they drove home, Maddy resting her head on his shoulder, her legs folded under her on the seat. Davi didn't speak; he knew the news wasn't good. He would wait.

"Michael."

"Hello, princess. Are we still on for a sail today? The weather is fine, and the wind is promising." Michael Riley was always pleased when Maddy called.

"Yes, we're okay for today, but Henry has to leave; his family in Australia wants him to come home before the grandfather dies. I'm having a little party for him tonight. Will you come?" Maddy's voice cracked.

"Ah, Maddy. Where are you now?" Michael sounded concerned. "I'll come for you right now."

"I'm okay. He needs clothes and travel things, and I want to get his favourite foods for dinner. I'll see you later. I just wanted you to know before we arrived on board," Maddy sighed.

"Have lunch with me. I'm coming to you now. Where are you?" Michael insisted.

Maddy had to admit Michael was a charming lunch companion. He knew Henry's family history and kept Maddy in stitches with his recollections of the antics of Henry's grandfather. "He'll be back, Maddy; you'll see." Michael touched her hand, loving the smoothness of her skin. He fought the desire to touch her face.

"Oh gosh, I'd better go and collect Henry. He'll be late for his sailing lesson, and the captain will be feisty." Maddy laughed as she stood and collected her packages.

Michael, the captain, feigned shock. "Come; my driver is outside."

"Thank you, Michael. Thank you for lunch and for your friendship with Henry. I can't tell you how important you are to both of us." She leaned over and kissed his cheek.

A flustered Michael Riley followed her out of the restaurant.

The send-off for Henry was a festive affair with his favourite foods, his friends, and laughter as the group shared stories of their time with Henry. Any sadness was replaced by the genuine feelings everyone had for the boy. Henry fell asleep at the table as the adults continued to plan for his return.

Davi nervously looked in his rear-view mirror, his three passengers sat quietly, holding hands, not daring to speak or create a reason for tears. The ride to the airport seemed to take forever. Davi shook hands with Henry as they gathered his luggage.

"Take care of Maddy, will you?" Henry whispered to Davi, who nodded solemnly.

"Shall we start this Australian Adventure?" Sebastian asked, not wanting to prolong the goodbyes. He wondered if Henry would indeed be fine with strangers, but then again, he and Maddy had been strangers themselves once.

Maddy grabbed the backpack and took Henry's hand, moving towards the departure lounge. She was handling this well, and yet, he wished he could kiss away the sadness from her eyes, assure her everything would be all right, Henry would be back soon.

Last minute instructions, declarations of love, and promises to keep in touch kept them occupied until the final call for the flight. Sebastian held Maddy as they waved so long. Maddy refused to say goodbye. Henry was brave until he was settled in his seat, seatbelt fastened, and the aircraft door closed. His shoulders heaved, and the tears flowed down his cheeks and onto his jumper. He roughly brushed his arm across his face, hoping for one last look at Maddy and Sebastian. Eventually the tears subsided, and he slept, dreaming of how wonderful his return would be.

In the car, Maddy rested her head against Sebastian's shoulder; she felt warm and safe sitting next to him, his arm around her, holding her close. She was determined not to cry, as she herself would soon be leaving him. She sat up quickly. "Let's do something crazy. Let's go to Paris for an overnight. Right now."

Sebastian smiled, aware she was trying to brighten the day. He also wondered if returning to Paris would bring back old memories for Maddy.

"What would we do there?" he asked, grinning at her.

"Let's have dinner at the Eiffel Tower. 58 Tour Eiffel is lovely on a clear night. We can make the nine o'clock seating. My treat. Sebastian?" Her eyes were bright, her cheeks flushed; he would have said yes to any suggestion to see her like this. "I want to go to Paris with you."

"Davi, you'd best turn this car around. We have a flight to catch." He looked out at the traffic. "It's definitely my treat."

"Yes, sir. My pleasure." Davi smiled as he watched for an opening in the traffic. Maddy always found a way to make a sad day hopeful. Thankfully Grace wasn't this spontaneous.

They caught the next flight to Paris, holding hands as they rushed through the airport with no luggage and no plan. By the time they landed at Charles De Gaulle Airport, Lambert had arranged a driver, booked a hotel, and confirmed a dinner reservation at 58 Tour Eiffel. He was giddy just thinking about someone running off to Paris at a moment's notice.

Sebastian insisted on a shopping trip—a fresh shirt for him, an outfit for Maddy. Buying a new shirt had never been such fun. They returned to the hotel hand in hand, dropped their shopping, and fell on the large, white duvet; it was like falling into a marshmallow cloud. They slowly undressed each other and made love with the urgency of young lovers. It was as though all the feelings for Henry and his leaving had been bottled up, anxious to be shared.

Sebastian walked into the room from the bathroom, adjusting the knot in his tie, whistling "Le Marseillaise", and noticed Maddy bouncing on the bed.

"Hello, aren't you supposed to be getting ready for dinner?" He smiled as he watched her land in the cloud of covers.

"Sebastian, come here." She wrapped her arms around his neck. "I just had this great revelation. Here I am in Paris, in a beautiful hotel; I've just made love with a handsome man, and I'm going to dinner at the Eiffel Tower … it's every girl's fantasy. Thank you." She kissed his face with butterfly kisses and then met his lips.

Sebastian responded, thinking most men would consider making love to a beautiful woman in Paris a fantasy as well. Visions of a young Maddy, in love, in Paris, had crossed his mind, but her joy at being here with him was so intoxicating he knew this was their moment.

"Get dressed; I'm hungry." He tapped her on the behind, sorry to break the embrace. He found his shoes under the bed and sat on the delicate flower-patterned chair, waiting for Maddy. As he reflected on the day, he couldn't help but wonder how dull his life had been before she came along. He had never done anything like this; it would have seemed irresponsible to the old Sebastian. But he liked it—the new Sebastian liked it.

"Audrey, it was wonderful. We just went to the airport, caught a flight, and spent the night in Paris. I don't remember what we ate, but the lights of Paris and the music and the late-night walk back to the hotel were amazing. I think it was the most romantic thing I have ever experienced. You absolutely must do it!"

"Maddy, you're crazy. Of course it was romantic—it was Paris. Jeffrey would never consider leaving the children; nor would I, come to think of it. We find it romantic when the kiddos are curled up with us on the settee. Of course, I want to know every detail. Come on over. We must do a yoga class first; the new weird yoga instructor chap is coming over, but after that …"

Explosive News

Michael held the door open for Maddy, his umbrella blown out, his trousers soaked. Maddy had not been able to control her laughter when they had been splashed by the lorry as they waited to cross the street. Michael had sworn and shaken his fist at the driver as the wave of water washed over them. Maddy had started laughing, after a sharp intake of breath registered how cold her wet clothes felt against her body. Her laughter made him angry and then he realized how futile it was to be angry. He shook his head as a gust turned his umbrella inside out, leaving them exposed in the downpour.

As they entered the vestibule Michael pulled Maddy aside and pinned her to the wall.

"You always make me laugh. Why are we not lovers?" Michael was serious.

"Lovers are fickle, friends are forever—and we are great friends. Let's have lunch, friend." Maddy laughed, realizing they were soaked to the bone.

"Maddy, run away with me. Let's go somewhere warm and sail away our days." He looked serious enough for Maddy to stop laughing. She blinked as the water ran down her face.

"Michael, what are you doing?" She sensed he was agitated. His face was flushed, and his grip on her shoulders was starting to worry her.

"Maddy, I need to get away. I don't know how much time I have. I haven't told a soul; do you understand? I haven't told anyone. I just want to be happy for what time I have left."

"Oh, Michael, you're scaring me. Are you all right? What's wrong? You know I can't just run away; I'm going back to Canada soon. I need to settle my past and embrace my future. Can't you do that too? Please tell me what I can do to help you." Maddy was starting to panic.

"Nothing can be done, Maddy, it's too late. I just want a chance to be happy for a little while." He sighed.

"Michael, you have the resources; can't we beat this, whatever it is?" Maddy was pleading. "What about going away with Francis? What about going back to Ireland—to your roots?"

Michael laughed out loud, his head back, his face contorted. He dropped his hands and stood before her, looking like a madman. Then, just as suddenly, he stood tall and took her hand in his. "We'd better get into the warmth and dry off by the electric fire. Don't want you to catch your death." He seemed amused by his choice of words and laughed once again.

The pub was warm and inviting, and as they ate their lunch, they talked of world events, weather, and how much they missed Henry. The rain was over when they walked outdoors, the mood lighter.

"Madwoman, you always make me laugh and feel better about everything. Maybe in my next life I'll meet you first." He kissed her cheek gently and hailed a cab for her. "Stay dry, my muse." He waved as the cab drove away. Maddy waved back from the cab, hoping he was all right.

The sunshine on her face made her squint as she walked out of the hospital. She smiled, enjoying the warmth of the sun and the fresh air. The morning had been tiring, as the chemo group was getting smaller and more anxious about their futures. Maddy felt drained from forced cheerfulness.

"Maddy." She started as someone touched her arm. She shook her head and opened her eyes to find Sebastian in front of her.

"Sorry; I didn't mean to startle you." Sebastian motioned to a table at the coffee shop. He had preordered her chai and a coffee for himself.

"Maddy." His face was tight, and he seemed unsure of something.

Maddy smiled at him. "What's wrong, Sebastian? Are you okay?" Now she was concerned.

He cleared his throat. "Maddy, there's been an accident …"

Her heart skipped a beat. "Oh my gosh. Belle or George?"

"No, Maddy, last night there was an explosion at the wharf. Mick O'Riley … Michael Riley was on the boat; the cameras caught him arriving earlier. They have found his clothes, his shoes, and his watch.

They think they may have his phone and some other personal effects …" Sebastian touched her hand. "They haven't found him; so far, no body. The explosion was set up by a professional. The police believe it may be a hit. I wanted to tell you before you heard the news bulletins."

Maddy was biting her lip, her eyes filled with tears; her throat felt constricted. Her mind was racing. Flashes of her conversation with Michael were confusing her, and here was Sebastian, watching her reaction, offering his handkerchief.

Maddy wiped her eyes, took a deep breath, and looked at Sebastian.

"So there's still a chance they may find him?" she asked hopefully, a catch in her voice.

"It's a possibility—a slim one, but a possibility nonetheless." Sebastian was trying to console her.

"Thank you for coming to tell me. I know you must be busy. I'll be fine if you want to return to the office." She leaned forward and kissed his cheek, and then she sat back, tears welling up in her eyes once again.

"Francesca rang me this morning. She believes you may know something. Be prepared for the authorities to seek you out for questioning." He was clearly disturbed by the situation and the call from Francesca.

"What could I possibly tell them? Michael is my friend, and of course I want to hear he walked away and he's fine. I'll just wait. I'm sure he's fine." Maddy looked off into the distance, and Sebastian felt helpless watching her struggle with her emotions. If only he knew what to do. She looked fragile, and although he had never cared for Mick or Michael, he would be supportive and catch her when she fell.

Several days later Maddy was questioned, and her responses were recorded. She had nothing to add to the investigation, and she was told she could leave the country as booked. There was no word on Michael—dead or alive. Maddy believed, in her heart, he was sitting in the sun or sailing in some remote part of the world, laughing at the drama of it all. She hoped with all her might he was raising a pint and toasting his own brilliance.

June

Maddy was scheduled to fly home at the end of the month. Bellmere House was now fully under construction, with scaffolding and dust curtains over the back wall of the house. Audrey was handling the interior while Lambert supervised the contract workers and the landscapers. Both were excited with the project. Maddy and Sebastian had decided to leave the project in their hands, moving into the new house together on completion. Sebastian had insisted on waiting for Maddy to return before moving in.

The coffee house was also getting a facelift. Audrey had chosen soft colours with a mocha trim, so Maddy and Grace were painting walls and trim. The effect was stunning. It was a labour of love with the promise of a great meal when the job was done. The women expected Sebastian and Davi to arrive in time for dinner.

Grace confided in Maddy that the coffee house building was available for purchase. The owner of the building had returned to his native land and did not expect to be back in London without legal conflicts. He offered Grace first right of refusal and was waiting for an answer. The second floor of the building had been a dance studio at one time and was ideal for banquets or large parties. Grace was apprehensive; she would love to own the building, but the mortgage was too much for her to carry. If the building sold, she was unsure the new owner would want her to stay. The apartment on the third floor was comfortable, and Grace hated to leave it, but the whole affair was worrying her; she was up against the wall with the deadline.

Before they could talk further, the door opened and whistles filled the room. The men were audibly complimentary of the new look. Sebastian had purchased a painting for the wall as a gift. He and Davi hung the art and stood back to admire the effect. The footway cafe scene was perfect; it was the first work of art Maddy had shown him in the gallery when they met. Maddy threw her arms around his neck. "What a wonderful gesture."

"You said I would like it …" He smiled back, feeling very pleased with himself. "I felt I should buy something from the artist at the gallery that changed my life."

"Indeed." She smiled, remembering the first time she had seen him.

As usual, dinner with Grace was amazing—it was also bittersweet, given how few occasions they would have left to share. There were toasts and recollections of the adventures Maddy had been involved in during the last year. Davi shared stories. Grace could not stop laughing at the bathtub story. There were sober reminiscences of Leda and the buttons. She had truly touched their lives.

"Take me home, lover boy; it's getting too sad here." She cuddled up to Sebastian. He looked so at ease with his sleeves rolled up and his shirt buttons undone … he was always so perfect; it was refreshing to see him like this; Maddy told him so on the way home, and he was pleased that she still found him attractive.

"You're not just attractive; you're devilishly handsome and so very adorable," she said as she rubbed his chest.

"If that's true, kiss me," he said softly.

"With pleasure," she responded between teasing his lips with hers.

"Indeed."

"Sebastian, if you knew a friend needed your help, financially, and you could help, would you?" she asked him as they sat on the patio after breakfast.

He stopped reading the hefty report and looked at her, removing his glasses. "What do you mean? What kind of help? Is someone in trouble? I'm going to need more information."

"Grace has the opportunity to buy the building but doesn't have the means, and I would hate for her to lose her business or the location. I feel I have to do something."

"Why don't we buy the building?" he offered, just like that. And so they did. Maddy negotiated a very good price with the exiled developer; Sebastian signed the purchase agreement, naming Maddy and himself as partners. It was all done within the week. Sebastian was pleased she had asked for his help, and Maddy was delighted he was willing to help Grace; Grace was ecstatic with her new landlords and the opportunity to keep her business. As Maddy said, it was win-win.

Futures

"Please, can we not talk about what will happen or how we'll deal with things after next week?" Maddy asked. "It's going to be difficult enough to get on that plane; I don't want the time to end before the aeroplane door closes."

"We have to have some plan or I'll go crazy not knowing how you are or when I'll see you again, if ever … I need some direction from you." He was pleading.

"Okay, fine, but not tonight. Tonight our friends will be with us at the coffee house, and I want only happy memories to take away. Fair?" She hugged him, her arms around him and her heart doing cartwheels.

"Fair enough. But just for the record, these people are *your* friends; they just tolerate me because you like me."

"They know I love you … and by association, they love you too. No, that's not true; you have been very kind and generous to all of us, and people don't forget that."

"Have fun tonight. I'll be here for the after party." He kissed the top of her head. He was dying inside. How was he going to get along without her? How was he supposed to carry on as if she hadn't parachuted into his life? How could he go back to his staid and ordered life? He hadn't believed he was boring until he met her. Maddy had said she loved him. It was enough to get him through the evening.

Sebastian smiled as he watched the crowd. He was recalling the night they had spent in this very room, the moonlight on Maddy as she slept, her hair still wet from the bath. It seemed a lifetime had passed since that night.

The second floor of the coffee house was suddenly awash with twinkle lights and brightly clad eclectic characters: Ray (chicken man); Leda and her Lebanese friends; Audrey and Jeffery; Grace and Davi; Uncle and Auntie; Belle and George; the professor; Christian; several construction crew members and wives; Ambassador Matthews; Chef Ferdinand and his wife Elda; Cliff and Cora (in their finest, they were unrecognizable); acquaintances from the mission and the local corner shop; the older couple from next door (why did he never remember their names); a few coffee house regulars; Philippe, who had flown in; and, of course, Lambert, who was there with his new love. Mr Simpson, from the bookshop, arrived with a book wrapped in brown paper, which he insisted on presenting directly to Maddy. A young medic, Dr Steve Howe, approached Maddy on arrival and was immediately ushered to Audrey and the buttons.

The children were told they could stay for one hour only before going to bed in the apartment. Maddy introduced them to Philippe, who was charming and delighted with their French.

"Bonjour," Jimmy said, proudly holding out his hand.

Jemma held out her hand and said, "*Enchante*," as Philippe kissed the back of her little hand.

"They are quite sweet," he said to Sebastian, smiling at them hiding behind Maddy. "Why are they called buttons?"

Sebastian replied with a straight face, "Well, they are as cute as buttons. That's what Maddy calls them; that's what they answer to."

"I see," Philippe laughed, confused but enchanted by the two curly heads and their attachment to Maddy.

Moments later, Maddy approached the men with Jemma in tow. "Excuse me, gentlemen, sorry to interrupt, but it appears you forget that Jemma is a big girl now," she said very seriously. Both men, to their credit, looked solemn, nodding in agreement. Maddy crouched down beside Jemma and motioned for the men to do the same. They exchanged glances of amusement but crouched as well. Jemma approached Sebastian, air-kissed both cheeks, and then turned to Philippe and air-kissed both cheeks. She curtsied and ran off giggling.

"Thank you. She thought it was unfair that you kissed everyone but her," Maddy told them in a conspiring voice as she stood up. Both men looked up, amused, realizing they could now stand.

"Are you teaching them French, Maddy?" Philippe asked, but she had turned and disappeared into the group.

"Yes, she is. Maddy feels the children need to learn at least two languages," Sebastian responded.

"Why two languages?" Philippe was curious.

"She tells me it's because beauty fades." They both chuckled, lost in their own interpretation of the statement.

Sebastian was tending the bar as he watched Maddy mingle with trays of food. Everyone had brought dishes; it was a decadent feast. There were speeches and well wishes and lovely sentiments all evening. She belonged to them; they were all going to miss her terribly. She made it through the evening without crying, not wanting to waste a moment with tears.

Mr Simpson approached Maddy, a sad look on his face. "My dear, I shall miss you terribly. Please write me and get back before you forget what I look like."

"I could never forget you, Mr Simpson. You inspire me to surround myself with things and people I love. So far, so good." She smiled as she looked around the room. She put her head on his shoulder.

"Oh my, excuse an old man for being so distracted. I have a postcard for you. It came to the shop a few days ago … no return address and not much of a message, but I'm sure you'll understand it. Ah, here it is." He handed her a postcard of a beach scene with no indication of where it might be. Before turning it over, she smiled at Mr Simpson and said her goodbyes.

The address on the postcard was printed by hand. The stamp was faded, undecipherable.

The message was sparse:

> Mad, miss you and your laugh. All good.
> You were right. Travel safe. Love

Maddy smiled and placed the postcard in her pocket. "Thank you, Michael," she whispered, feeling both relieved and sad.

As the crowd thinned, a core group remained. Jeffery chided Sebastian at the bar for letting Maddy leave. "How can you be so foolish, man, just letting her go like that?" He was about to continue when Sebastian gratefully spied the professor, guitar in hand. "Excuse me; it's time for some entertainment." Sebastian approached the professor and asked if he could play some of Maddy's favourites from the jam sessions.

Belle and George were delighted to be included. They enjoyed the children and Maddy's friends, as well as hearing the stories and sharing their own stories of Maddy. They were staying with Audrey, as was Philippe, because of the construction. On arrival, Belle was confused as to why they would abandon the beautiful big house for such cramped living quarters, but as they sat in the garden for tea, perusing the plans, she agreed the setting was most pleasant. George, of course, just smiled. *This was more Maddy*, he thought.

The plans for the house were on display in the room, and everyone was anxious for the upcoming unveiling. Throughout the evening, nods of approval, thumbs ups, and genuine interest were expressed; there didn't seem to be any question that Maddy would return to live in the renovated house.

Maddy gently covered the sleeping children with a blanket, wishing Henry had been here with them tonight. Dr Howe had spoken with Audrey and Jeffrey, his news on the adoption process encouraging. He smiled as he watched Maddy with her strange entourage, wondering how she had factored in each of their lives.

Soon it was just Philippe and Sebastian at the bar, watching Maddy as she cleared glasses and closed the large windows. She smiled up at them, flushed from the goodbyes. Philippe seemed content to sip his drink and take in the soft music, enjoying the warm feeling in the room.

"What a lovely group of people. It was a very easy evening. You must have done something right to deserve this, my friend." He toasted Sebastian.

Sebastian raised his glass and looked over at Maddy.

"Indeed."

Sebastian handed Maddy a small package when they arrived at the garden apartment. She carefully opened the wrapping to find a lace handkerchief with embroidery in each corner. She read "Maddy", "Sebastian", "Henry", and "London". She lovingly touched the names and felt a tear roll down her cheek.

"Thank you. What a wonderfully thoughtful gift." She rushed to Sebastian, wrapped her arms around him, and buried her head in his chest. He held her tight. There were no words to describe the feeling of loss to come.

Sebastian had asked if he should travel with Maddy, or if he could help her in any way. She was quick to dissuade him; he would not help the negotiations.

"Maddy, if you are worried about having enough money to live on, I can easily take care of that. Tell me what everything you have is worth, and I'll set up a bank account for you in that amount. Just leave it all there. You don't have to worry about anything. You know I will take care of you," he said tenderly, suggesting she stay and not go back.

"Thank you. That's lovely, but I've worked hard and made sacrifices for over twenty years, and my foolish pride makes me want to know it had some value. I know it's difficult for you to understand, but I've put up with a lot, and I am ready to move on. I need to know I'm worth something. Please let me resolve this on my own."

"How long is reasonable?" he asked tentatively.

"For you to change your mind about how you feel? Is that what you mean?"

"No, Maddy, how long should I wait before I come for you?" He held her face in his hands.

"Please let me deal with everything; the sale of assets, changes to insurance, and such should take a month or two. Can you wait?" Maddy looked hopeful.

"What if you return to the ranch and everything has changed for the better? What happens then?" He sounded anxious. He was struggling with thoughts of Maddy returning to find a man who would change for her, as he had. The what-ifs loomed, and he felt helpless to discuss or even imagine how hard he would fight to have her back. Was he foolish to let her go at all? What would he do if she called to say she wasn't coming back? He was falling into a deep, dark hole.

In response, Maddy kissed him; it was a kiss that held a promise.

Farewell

The last week in London was hectic with making visits to the markets; exploring new exhibits; cheering on the buttons at their after-school football matches; poring over house plans with Lambert and Audrey; and ensuring Lambert, Davi, and Mrs B had adequate notes on caring for Sebastian in her absence. Sebastian arrived home early for long dinners and walks, surprising Maddy with picnics and afternoon teas. They attended a an Association football match—a first for Maddy. Sebastian was delighted by her reaction to his surprise jaunts. They enjoyed stargazing and dancing on the patio before retiring, content to lie in each other's arms until they fell asleep. Neither spoke of the flight date, neither wanting to break the spell of their time together.

Sebastian preferred driving to the beach when visiting with Belle and George, and although Maddy missed the train rides, she did enjoy the drive. The MG transformed Sebastian into a younger, more carefree version of himself. Both looked forward to their time with the older couple, who were so happy and vibrant. Marriage looked good on them. Each visit included a walk on the beach and an overnight in the lovely little cottage. Maddy was always sad to drive away.

"Sebastian, please try to see Belle and George at least once a week when I'm away. They really miss you," Maddy pleaded.

"I should have time with you gone; there won't be so many distractions." He smiled.

He dodged the cushion she threw at his head.

There was barely time to sit with Grace, and Maddy missed her already. They spoke on the phone as they were running errands, and Davi carried treats home for Maddy most nights. They talked of the wedding plans—laughing at how they would mesh East Indian and Caribbean cultures for a celebration and how renovations were going on the second floor of the coffee house. They had produced a business plan and were seeing healthy bookings for weddings and parties. Audrey, bless her heart, had taken the project on with gusto. She was balancing her work on the house renovation, the coffee house, and her little family, and she looked born to the role. What a time of change in everyone's life.

"My last sleep," Maddy playfully teased as they sat in the garden. She stood up and draped her arms over his shoulders, kissing the back of his neck. "Sebastian, I'm going to miss you so much."

He didn't speak—he *couldn't* speak. His heart was racing; he was having a difficult time breathing. He held her hands in his for a moment and then pulled her around and onto his lap.

"Please don't come to the airport tomorrow," she pleaded. "I don't think I could handle saying goodbye in an airport."

No words could say what he wanted to express. Frightened he would say the wrong thing, he nodded, holding her tight.

"Indeed" was all she heard as he buried his head in her hair.

The next morning, Sebastian watched the car as it drove away. Standing alone on the cobblestones, he realized this was what Maddy would have felt like when he left her on the walkway to her small bedsit. It seemed it was just yesterday. What a fool he had been to hurt her and lose a month of being together, for such a selfish reason. He was going to make it up to her. He turned and felt disoriented. He hesitated for a moment and then walked back to the garden apartment. The house was a construction site; soon it would be completed.

"Hurry back, Maddy; I need you to make this a home," he mumbled, feeling miserable. He looked around the garden and sat on the patio, face to the sun, wishing with all his might she was already back beside him. He slowly walked into the apartment, scanning the bookshelf for the file Maddy had once left for him. He smiled as he found a much thicker binder bearing his name. Maddy had continued to compile mementos and photos just for him. He sat down and slowly turned the pages, knowing he would return to find solace in the memories until Maddy was back here with him.

Several times, while standing in line at the airline counter, Maddy had the urge to turn around and run for the doors. At check-in she was advised she had been upgraded to business class with lounge privileges. She smiled and silently thanked Lambert.

She found a quiet seat in the lounge, and while sipping her tea she scrolled through the photos on her North American phone, wondering what welcome she could expect.

Maddy walked onto the aircraft, found her seat, and settled in. Across the aisle, an elderly gentleman wearing a blue blazer and ascot asked her if she was returning home or leaving home—an innocent conversation starter. Maddy looked over, blinked as if she hadn't previously given this any thought, and burst into tears.

August

Forty-one days later

In her dream, she was walking slowly towards the edge of a giant abyss, looking back over her shoulder, hoping to be rescued before it was too late. She heard a phone ringing in the distance. She continued walking, and the phone continued to ring, interrupting her dream of being saved before she fell. Suddenly she sat up; the phone was ringing. It was 3:30 a.m.—never a good time to receive a call. She shook her head to clear the dream away and tentatively answered. "Hello." Her voice was heavy from sleep.

There was silence on the other end for a moment, and then her heart skipped a beat.

"Maddy, George has been taken to hospital, and the doctor is not optimistic about his recovery; please come home." His voice was controlled and soft. "I'm sorry to wake you, but I thought you'd want to know."

She threw her legs over the side of the bed, fully awake and alert. "Yes, yes, of course. How is Belle?"

"As expected, she's delirious; she called here to see what you advised. We all miss you."

Maddy was afraid she might cry. Her mind was racing. "Please be sure to bring Belle the blue afghan on the settee in the sunroom; she believes it's her lucky cover, and she will have forgotten to collect it."

"Of course. Shall I have Lambert confirm your travel arrangements?" He was in business mode now. How she missed his calm, reassuring voice.

"Thank you. I can be at the airport this afternoon." She was taking stock of what she would need to pack. "Oh, shall I call Robert?"

"You get here; I'll call Robert."

"Sebastian"—her voice quavered—"how will I know you?"

He hesitated. "I'll be the one with the red rose. I can't wait to see you, Maddy."

"Indeed," she said softly, not knowing if he heard her. The call was over.

Lambert had arranged for her to fly business class from Toronto to London that afternoon. She boarded the flight, and memories of her time in London washed over her. She tried to sleep on the flight, knowing there wouldn't be much time for rest when she arrived. Her return to Canada had been a series of visits with friends and tense moments at the ranch, confirming her desire to move on. She sold most of her belongings or gave them away. She had taken a drive that proved to be less than calming—another adventure … and she was alive.

There were a few more business details to be finalized, but she had moved out and was ready to start a new life. The call just hurried the process along. Maddy had been in contact with Grace and Audrey, leaving a weekly message for Sebastian on his phone, which he did not respond to. She would soon learn he refused to carry the phone while she was away, resisting the urge to speak with her at least once an hour. Hearing his voice again felt so fine; she was nervous, wondering how they would react to each other. Her feelings for Sebastian had only grown stronger; she wondered how he would feel.

Excited and anxious to arrive before George lost consciousness, she closed her eyes and willed the aircraft to make haste.

In London, Sebastian was anxious for the time to pass as he waited for the plane to arrive. He had not shared his thoughts with anyone and now had time to reflect on the walkabout, as Maddy would call it. He had been thinking about Maddy on a sunny day a fortnight after she left, and after several attempts to concentrate on a building report, he'd left the office and walked the same route they had taken not so long ago. He stopped at the Old Bridge Pub for a pint and a beef pie, happy to be recognized as Maddy's beau. He took the underground to the neighbourhood and visited with Mrs Bing at the flower shop, the gelato man, and Mr Sanjay, assuring them all Maddy would be home soon. Mr Sanjay produced a takeaway bag. "Maddy would want you to eat."

Mr Simpson offered tea and proclaimed he had found the perfect piano for their home. "It was rented by the Beijing Student Choir and returned with two ivory keys cracked, impossible to match or repair. Maddy would love it; to her it would be perfect in that it had a story—a history of sorts—and no one wants to take it damaged." Sebastian almost choked on his tea when he learned of the deal Mr Simpson had made on the baby grand. "You're right; Maddy will love it. She can't resist a bargain." He laughed and shook his head.

Sebastian headed for the garden apartment, carrying the food and flowers. As he neared the garden, he heard Maddy's laugh. Was she back? His heart raced and his senses were sharpened when he realized Audrey was speaking to her on the computer. He stopped at the corner, not meaning to eavesdrop but not confident enough to walk into their conversation. He leaned against the wall, listening, happy to hear her voice and their familiar banter.

"Audrey, did the chair arrive?"

"It's wonderful. Where ever did you find it without me? It's perfect for the dining room. Does Sebastian know you got it?"

"No, don't tell. It's a surprise. I saw it online and bid on it—I had to sell my stand-up paddleboard to buy it, but they promised to deliver it to your house that same week. It looks like a chair Henry VIII would have dined in, doesn't it?" She laughed, and the sound made his knees weak.

"Audrey, you have to ask Sebastian about the fireplace for the dining room and the sitting room; they should match, but because the chair is so huge, we really shouldn't have a hearth at all in the dining room. It will be difficult to ask him to choose and not show him the chair, but do your best."

"Right. What about the piano? Bloody hard to find a black or white baby grand within your budget. The saxophone and fiddle are here … compliments of the professor. Are you sure you want them on the wall?"

"Great, they should look awesome on the blocks, with the spotlights. Please check with Mr Simpson; he seemed to indicate he had a lead on the perfect piano."

"He's creepy, Maddy, but for you I'll call. Let me see your car again … why don't you bring it over?"

"It's not right-hand drive, and it's time to sell it anyway. I'm taking one last ride before it goes; you can have the money for the piano."

"When are you coming home? We miss you. The buttons have a lifetime of what you call fridge art waiting."

"Just a few more legal transfers; the lawyers are getting rich on the paperwork alone. I'm almost done. Did I tell you Preston came to visit?"

"What, the Texan? That's just too crazy. Why? How did that go?"

"Oh Audrey, it was pure Preston—he flew in by helicopter. I was riding on the ridge, and I saw him circle. I have to say I held my breath when he stepped out, hoping Sebastian was with him. It took me a minute to realize it was a crazy thought and to remember to breathe. Anyway, we took the horses out for the afternoon and had dinner over a campfire. It was really nice."

"Why did he come to see you? I didn't realize you were so close."

"He calls a lot. He brought the package. It's a long story; I'll tell you when I see you."

Audrey laughed. "No way … I have all the time in the world. I'm waiting for the delivery, and I've got time. Come on; it would be cruel not to tell me. What package?"

"You remember the boat situation and how we met the Italian designer Sorento? He said he was inspired to call his fall collection Azules, remember?"

"Vaguely … I can't always keep your escapades top of mind. Go on; did he do it?"

"Apparently he did. I would never have believed it. It's such a throwaway line—you know, 'I want to capture your eyes, you are my muse'." She spoke the line with an Italian accent.

"Ah, no, sweetie, it's not a throwaway line, and it doesn't happen every day. Go on."

"The collection is being shown in Milan in October, and Preston wanted to know how many tickets I needed."

"Oh my God, Maddy; how many did you get?"

"One for me," Maddy said slowly, "one for Sebastian, and one for …

By the way, the sun on the mountains is gorgeous right now. Um, I also got one for … you, of course."

"Bravo, Maddy!" Audrey was clearly excited.

"Preston will take his daughter, who is a huge fan of this guy, and her husband, so we should have a *bellissimo* time in Milan. He left a huge box. Audrey, it was like opening a fairy princess gift. The dress is a lovely blue—very simple with a slit pocket for my phone, just as I requested. The scarf, earrings, and evening bag are just so elegant, and the shoes are perfect. Everything fits, if I don't ever eat again. It's very cool."

"I would say so. I miss you, crazy lady. Nothing like that happens when you're not here."

"Audrey, I have to go. My phone is getting low, and there's a campervan coming down this mountain so fast I'm not sure he can stop to make the turn. Oh dear … wouldn't you know it—a transport truck is rounding the corner … not looking good … Give my love to everyone … Oh dear God …" An explosion sounded, and Audrey was frantically calling Maddy.

Sebastian ran into the courtyard to find Audrey pacing in front of her computer, sobbing in her hands, calling Maddy's name.

"Audrey, are you all right? I could hear your screams out on the driveway."

He grabbed her shoulders and tried to steady her. He felt as anxious as she was but couldn't let her know he had heard the explosion as well. His mind was filled with mixed emotions, having heard her voice, thinking she would be home soon, and then the sound of the crash. He wanted to know Maddy was safe. They both stared at the screen, smoke clouds obscuring the view. Sounds of panic—crying, screams, and shouts for 911—rang out. "Someone dial 911! Get an ambulance!" a man's voice shouted.

Maddy did not return to the phone before the screen went black, leaving her friends wondering what happened and how she had fared.

"Oh, Sebastian, I was talking to Maddy, and she saw an accident about to happen. What if she's hurt and lying there alone, without someone to look after her? I should have ended the call earlier, but I miss her so much, and I just wanted to keep talking to her." She was sobbing into Sebastian's shoulder.

Audrey, she's a survivor. I'm sure she'll be fine. As soon as she is able, you know she'll call you back." He tried to sound calm and convincing. He was shaking, experiencing what Maddy would call *worried* sick.

"Here, sit down; I have lunch. Let's eat and have a drink. We'll wait to hear from her, all right?" *Who is this calm, reasoned person?* he wondered as his heart skipped a beat.

They ate in silence. The delivery lorry arrived, creating a diversion, and they were occupied for at least an hour with the order and placement. Audrey arranged for Jeffrey to collect the children, not wanting to leave the garden or Sebastian.

"Why didn't you take her calls?" Audrey asked, looking up cautiously.

Sebastian ran his hand through his hair. "I tried calling Maddy right after she left, and I got a message; it was too painful. I threw the phone across the room, and there it sits. It occurred to me just now that she may have left her UK phone here, but I promised her I would give her time … It's been difficult … really difficult."

Audrey touched his hand and nodded.

"You are a good friend, Audrey. You must know how much we both appreciate the care and effort you have put into the house. Thank you." Sebastian spoke softly.

"She's become my best friend; I love her, and I miss her. You must miss her too." She stopped to blow her nose. "Please, please, please let her be all right." She looked upward to the sky.

Sebastian wasn't sure how to respond, but Audrey continued. "Before I met Maddy, I was so focused on my dead-end life; I really didn't care about anyone else … She always says you can complement others or give them praise without reducing who you are. She's so right. Jeffrey and I would have coffee in the morning, no conversation, and then one day I told him he looked sharp. I asked if he had an important meeting, and he looked up from his paper, smiled at me, and asked me what we were doing for dinner. It seems small, but it was the start of our being civil to each other. I learned so much from Maddy, and of course, she gave me the greatest gift of all—I love those children." Audrey was drying her eyes and blowing her nose as Sebastian nodded encouragement, thinking back to all the times Maddy won over the hardest cases by just being pleasant and starting a conversation.

"I'm sorry, Sebastian; I can't stop talking." He smiled, encouraging her to continue. "You know it's my fault she was there so long. I wanted to keep talking to her. If I had just stopped talking and let her go, she would have been gone from the scene and she'd be safe right now." Audrey shook her head in grief.

"No, Audrey, Maddy would have returned to the scene if she thought she could help. She's a magnet for mishaps of any kind; you know that," Sebastian reassured Audrey.

Audrey sniffed and stared out at the garden. "She has a way of asking for something and then listening to people until they run out of steam, then she cocks her head, touches her heart, and apologizes that her simple request was so stressful. Construction workers and providers of all sorts would instantly look down and literally fall over themselves trying to complete the task as she asked. That's a talent." Audrey laughed and shook her head. They sat in silence for a moment, lost in their individual memories.

Sebastian cleared his throat. "By the way, Audrey, I spoke with Mr Simpson today; he said he found the perfect piano. He said Maddy would love it; it's not *perfect* perfect, but perfect for her. Do you understand that?" He looked confused and yet happy.

"I wouldn't have understood it last year, but now I do," she laughed. "While we're waiting, let's choose the fireplace. Here are the options; you may want them to be the same, since you'll see them both in the open room."

It was three hours later when they heard from Maddy. Audrey answered in tears, begging to know Maddy was safe. Maddy reported details of the accident in a clipped, need-to-know fashion: "Only one dead—the dog, four people badly burned and injured, two vehicles written off, traffic just beginning to move. My car is a write-off, and I have a few burns from pulling the family out of the vehicle. Just some little cuts from the glass. No big deal. My phone died, but I thought you'd be worried, so I borrowed a phone—didn't want to leave you hanging. I've been invited out to dinner with the firefighters … It's like having my very own Chippendale crew … very cool. Preston is sending a chopper; he has dealt with the insurance and is getting me a loaner car. That's enough excitement for one day. I'm so tired. Talk later. Love ya. Hugs for the buttons—and Sebastian. Bye."

Audrey and Sebastian hugged each other, and both wiped their eyes. "That's my girl. It will take an evening to hear the whole story, I'm sure. Go home, Audrey; all's well with the world." Suddenly he wanted to be alone with his thoughts of Maddy; she was alive and safe.

Audrey wasn't sure she should leave Sebastian, but she wanted to be home, hugging the children, thankful everyone was all right. She looked back to wave at Sebastian, but he was sitting with his head in his hands, processing the news.

Sebastian didn't hear Audrey leave. He realized how empty his life had been after hearing Maddy's voice. She would be back soon.

Heathrow was hectic as Maddy walked swiftly through passport control, her luggage in tow. She stepped out of the airport and into the sunlight, shading her eyes. She saw the car and her handsome hero leaning on the grill, holding a rose. How was she to know he had paced back and forth for the last twenty minutes? It took every ounce of strength to walk towards him rather than run wildly through the crowd on the footway. When he saw her, he stood tall and started walking towards her slowly, and then faster; then both were running. When they connected, it was electric; he lifted her, and for a moment they were the only people in the world. They kissed a long, magical kiss laced with urgency and tenderness. He looked at Maddy, who was dressed in a bright cape and matching hat, her blue eyes shining like diamonds in the sun, her smile just as he remembered it. He gasped and held her face in his hands. He was totally 100 per cent over the top, unabashedly in love with her.

A whistle blew, and the concierge suggested they move on from the loading area. They headed to the car, laughing, holding hands. "Nice car. Is it a rental?" she asked as she ran her hand down the side of the bonnet.

"It's yours." He held out the keys. "It's a welcome-home present. Better than an umbrella, I thought." He was pleased she had noticed.

"I can't deal with this right now; you drive. It is beautiful." She held her hands up in front of her as she circled the car, admiring the lines.

"Don't ask if we can afford it ... It's a gift." He was smiling. He couldn't stop smiling.

He watched her breathe in the smell of new leather, and for some reason the sight of her enjoying the car made him want to reach out and touch her. He had missed her so much.

Maddy watched him driving, changing gears and checking his mirrors as he manoeuvred into the traffic. He shot glances at her and reached for her hand. They drove in silence for many miles, smiling and touching, content to be in each other's company.

"Maddy, I can't tell you how many times I drove to the airport to fly over and see you." He shook his head. "I knew you needed time, and I was afraid of what would unfold if I pushed you. It's so good to see you." He kissed her hand.

"Every day, I saw something I wanted to share with you; I would hear a song and wonder if we had danced to it, I made notes of places I wanted to see with you … I missed you too."

She looked out at the countryside, which seemed so familiar, and yet it was as if she was seeing it for the first time. "Tell me about George."

"It's his heart; there's nothing they can do for him now. Belle told me you had been with him at his hospital appointments for the last few months. He really treasured the time with you. Why didn't you tell me?" he asked, unable to disguise the hurt he felt.

"You were busy, and I didn't want to worry you. You know, you never asked what I did all day or where I went—unless, of course, there was a brawl or an accident." She smiled, touching his face.

"I think I missed a lot."

"Indeed."

Belle welcomed Maddy with a hug, sobbing and holding her as if she couldn't stand on her own. "I'm so happy to see you, my dearest." She said through her tears. "George will want time with you. He's not doing so well … Whatever will I do without him?" She was fragile, so Maddy handed her over to Sebastian, who took over holding her up.

"Belle, why don't we have some tea?" He was moving her to the hallway. He nodded to Maddy, giving her time alone with her friend.

Maddy was shocked to see George lying in the bed, connected to machines, sallow and so thin. She took his hand in hers, whispering "You're giving everyone quite a scare, my friend." He tried to move his lips, pressing her hand. "George, let's get you out of here, this is no place for you to hang out." She saw tears fall on the bedsheets and realized they were hers. "Come on, handsome; we have many miles yet to walk on the beach. Can you hear me?" Again he pressed her hand. Leaning over him she said softly, "George, we also have unfinished business. There's something bothering me; I think we need to sort it out before it's too late. Please …"

She stood up quickly as Belle and Sebastian entered the room.

She smiled at them and wiped her eyes.

"Belle, come with me to the chapel for a moment." She almost laughed out loud when Sebastian offered her his handkerchief. It was such a natural move, and yet it made Maddy smile.

Belle kissed Sebastian and leaned over George to caress his forehead and lightly touch his cheek before she took Maddy's arm. They walked into the little chapel, Belle sitting and Maddy kneeling. "Shall we pray for him?" Maddy asked.

"I've been doing nothing but since he fell," Belle responded, lost in her thoughts.

After a moment, Maddy sat beside her and took her hand. "Belle, George may not ever leave this hospital; you do know that?" Belle nodded, her eyes downcast. "When George came into London for his medical tests, I went with him to the hospital; did he tell you what the doctors reported?"

Belle nodded, looking away. "He said you were marvellous to him." She sounded frail.

"I wanted to be sure he wasn't scared or afraid to face the news. You know I love you both so much; you're very special to me." Belle smiled and touched her face. "Belle, I think you and George have kept a secret for so long you're not even aware of the repercussions to anyone else. Am I right?" Belle fell forward in the seat, and Maddy reached for her before she slipped off the bench seat, holding her tight. "Belle, if we were to take a blood test now, would it answer my question?"

Belle began to sob, as if years of tears were welling up in her chest. Maddy held her tighter, letting her cry it out. "Why, Belle, why?"

Belle wiped her eyes with the offered handkerchief and started her story. When she was done, she closed her eyes, spent. Maddy moved so Belle was lying on the pew, her head in Maddy's lap. Maddy stroked her hair and shoulders as she drifted off to sleep.

Her legs were beginning to tingle when Sebastian came in, looking anxious and wondering if the women were all right.

George had just fallen asleep, and the matron advised it was wise to let him rest.

Sebastian knelt in the next pew, leaning over to see Belle breathing evenly. He helped move her so Maddy could slip out. He placed her blue afghan around her shoulders.

Maddy took Sebastian by the hand and sat on the bench at the back of the chapel.

"Sweetheart, have you ever wondered about your parents—how convenient it was that they were swept away at sea?" she asked tenderly. He turned his head, his nostrils flaring. "I think you know what happened. It doesn't matter why, but you have so little time left to share with them, I think you need to acknowledge the reality." He pulled his hand away. "Sebastian, please, I think it's important for your future."

"Leave it alone, Maddy; it's not important at all any more". He paced back and forth in front of her.

"I really think it is," she said softly. "Let me help you understand." Maddy continued, recounting the story she had been told, trying desperately to keep any emotion from her voice.

"Things were so different in the 1940s. Appearances were everything. The war had ended, and there were many young widows trying to make lives for themselves. George and Belle were so in love, they spent every hour together. George bought Belle a ring after the night they spent in the cave; they had been out on the beach, and a storm drove them into the cave. The tide came in, and they were forced to stay overnight. It was the first time for them; they were afraid of your grandparents, so they didn't say a word to anyone. When it was evident Belle was with child, your grandparents sent Belle, her friend Janet (the woman who eventually married George), and Serena, your alleged mother, away to Italy for the summer, where Janet fell in love with a local scoundrel, leaving her pregnant and alone as well. Belle had the baby—a beautiful boy. She and the baby stayed in Italy at the family holiday villa until your grandparents could agree on a plan. Serena had married a wealthy captain of industry in exchange for a portion of the family business. They lived abroad and had no children or ties to the community, so before she and her husband left on a sea voyage, she returned home with the baby and left the boy with Belle. She could hardly be expected to take a toddler on a long journey at sea." Maddy paused and touched his arm.

"Serena and her husband were lost at sea in a storm—that part is true. Once news reached Britain, it was clear you were an orphan." Maddy took a deep breath and continued. Sebastian would not look at her.

"Belle was forbidden to see George when they returned from Italy. Janet had a son, Roberto, and your grandparents arranged for her to marry George so Belle would not be tempted. George wanted to protect Belle; he loved her so much, so he went along with the charade, accepting Robert as his own son and entering into a hopeless relationship with a woman he detested. Both Belle and George were denied the life they wanted and longed for. Belle married the local minister, an older man who offered stability. Their marriage was amiable but childless, so Belle doted on you. Father Fletcher died shortly afterwards, leaving Belle a young widow. George was forlorn; he could not fathom life without his true love, Belle. He and Janet were unhappy from the beginning—he pining for Belle, and she hating her situation and knowing she would never love him. The child, Robert, was her only focus. She protected him, smothered him, and drove him to leave town as soon as he was able to escape her. Janet died soon after he left; she fell from the cliffs. They said it was an accident, but George knew she couldn't live without Robert, her only reminder of a first, but abandoned, love. It breaks my heart to know they wasted so many years being apart." Maddy stopped for a moment, watching his face, looking over at Belle.

"Belle and George treated you and Robert as their own, which you were. There seems to be a time when they realized it was too late to correct the past. You were settled and financially secure, and they had their friendship; Robert found a partner and moved to America to start a new life with a story of a life that didn't include this town or any of you." Maddy told the story as she had heard it from Belle. Sebastian sat expressionless, not interrupting or reacting.

"Your grandparents forbade Belle to marry George, threatening to cut off her inheritance. The shipwreck story was accepted—being an orphan was a far better fate than being born out of wedlock … Do you see why they kept the secret?" Maddy asked tentatively.

"So my life has been a lie. I don't even know who I am." Sebastian shrugged, concentrating on a point on the floor.

"Yes you do. Who stayed up with you all night when you had a nightmare or a fever? Who taught you how to fish and skip a stone on the water? Who cared for you and showed you right from wrong? Who helped you set up your business? Who calls you every week to see how you are? Have you seen the patient card in the door?" Maddy pointed to the chart on the wall.

He slowly walked over to the patient card and looked back at Maddy. It read "George Walker Montgomery".

"How did you know?" he asked.

"You and George stand the same way, your gestures are the same, and you both say "indeed" as if it's a complete sentence. Belle loves you; she touches you and looks at you as only a mother would. The garden show dress and her insistence that I wear it—it was almost macabre. Belle said you hugged her and told her she was so beautiful in it you wished she was your mother. It was a bond for her, and she kept that dress all those years, just for you. Shall I go on?"

He closed his eyes and sat beside her, head down, the weight of the world on his shoulders.

Maddy put her arm around him. "I was with George at the hospital the day you came home so upset I wasn't at the apartment. He had several tests, and he was so worried, so scared. His condition is hereditary. You need to have the tests. You need to know."

He looked at her as if seeing her for the first time. "Right now I need to be with him."

Maddy nodded. They stood, looking at each other. She took his face in her hands, reached up, and kissed him. "Indeed, you do."

Later, watching Belle and Sebastian sit by the bed, holding hands and talking, laughing and crying, Maddy felt a great relief that they were united at last. Through the glass she saw the tender gestures and the raw love they shared. She wondered how lovely their lives might have been if they had been allowed to be a family all those years.

Maddy turned from the window, tossing her cape over her shoulders. She bent to collect her hat and her bag and started for the door, destination unknown.

"Maddy, where are you going?" Sebastian was walking towards her in the corridor, looking alarmed. "Please come in and join us. You brought us together, and you are as much a part of this family as anyone." He held out his hand.

Maddy faltered, biting her lip. "You have so much time to make up for ..." She tried not to cry.

"Maddy, George loves you like a daughter, Belle has grown to depend on you, and I finally have you back—I hope. Please make us all happy and marry me." Sebastian knelt on one knee in front of her. "Please make me the happiest man on earth and marry me."

Maddy wanted to run away, and yet she felt she was destined to be with him. She looked back and forth between Sebastian and the hospital room, not daring to breathe.

"Maddy, please, I need you; we need you. Please, George has to know I did the right thing and made you a part of our family."

"Sebastian, you need time to digest all of this ..." Maddy needed time.

"Maddy, we're lost souls who have found each other. We have a chance to be happy, very happy, especially now that we know everything there is to know about each other. Please, Maddy, marry me." He was still kneeling in front of her.

Her heart was racing, and her eyes were swimming in tears. "Yes, yes. Oh yes, Sebastian, of course I'll marry you." She was laughing and crying. "But right now you need to concentrate on your parents—on all that lost time. Don't worry; I'll be here for you." She spoke in a whisper, looking towards the room where his parents were embracing the truth, finally.

He jumped up and folded her into his arms, kissing her face and hair and finally her lips.

He grabbed her hand and rushed her into the hospital room. "She said yes!" he called out gleefully.

Belle clapped her hands and then hugged Maddy; George blinked his eyes and squeezed her hand. His eyes travelled to Belle, and she nodded, taking off her ring and handing it to Sebastian. "Maddy and George spent so many afternoons looking for the perfect ring for me; please, I want you to have it. It's a lovely ring, but I prefer the first ring George gave me so long ago" She held up her hand with the simple band on it. She leaned over and took George's ring off his finger and handed it to Sebastian. "These would be yours someday; please wear them now, and we'll always be with you," Belle said tenderly.

Maddy and Sebastian looked at each other, touched by the words and the gesture.

"Where will you go for your honeymoon?" Belle raised her eyebrows in question.

Maddy looked at Sebastian, who shrugged and motioned for Maddy to decide.

"I would love to go to Italy and find the villa you were born in." Maddy felt Sebastian needed to complete the story of his life.

Belle responded first. "We've never gone back simply because George wasn't a part of that time." She gave George a loving look and squeezed his hand. "The contessa is still alive. She loved you, Sebastian; you were the son she never had. We travelled to the villa every year when I was a child." She paused, reminiscing in her mind. "Shall I contact the contessa and see if she will accept guests?"

Maddy nodded enthusiastically after giving Sebastian a questioning look. He merely shrugged in defeat.

The oxygen machine was beeping loudly, and George was moving his head on the pillow. Almost immediately, a nurse appeared to make an adjustment. "I hope you aren't creating any excitement in here," she warned. The three of them laughed.

"Maddy, do you want a big wedding with all the trappings?" Sebastian asked when they were ushered out of the room.

"No ... not at all," Maddy replied, surprised by the question.

"Could we get married here? Would that be all right for you?" he asked. "George and Belle, my ... my parents"—he relished the words—"would be present, and Philippe is arriving shortly, so we would have a witness. We can have a formal ceremony later, if you want." He waited for her response.

"Perfect." She smiled back. "Perfect to have George and Belle here." She shot a glance at the hospital bed. "Except for wishing Henry were here, I truly don't need anything more than this."

Sebastian looked at her and thought his heart might burst. He was marrying Maddy, and they would have a wonderful life; at long last he felt complete. Only then did he remember the diamond ring in his pocket. He had spent considerable time choosing the perfect ring for Maddy—simple and elegant; practical and unique.

Maddy drove to the cottage, stopping en route at Belle's to gather the offered cape and flowers from the garden. She could hardly wait to see the view of the seashore, smell the sea, and hear the waves crashing. The memories of walking with George along the seashore flooded over her, overwhelming her with grief. She sat on the deck, tears flowing, wrapped in a blanket. She very quickly fell asleep.

At the hospital, Sebastian was busy organizing the vicar, the music, and champagne. He watched Belle and George through the window; they were holding hands, Belle tenderly combing his hair with her fingers, George smiling at her with such love in his eyes. Sebastian caught his breath; a vision of him and Maddy in the years to come, looking just like this, made him smile. Had he ever imagined he would feel this complete? He had a family, a past, and now a future. Where was Maddy? He panicked. What if she had changed her mind and realized she wanted more? He called her phone—no answer. He called again. He didn't want to alarm Belle, so he moved away from the window. He knew she would sense his worry. Small beads of perspiration appeared on his forehead. Another call—no answer.

Philippe arrived, apologizing for his tardiness, citing car rental issues and delays on the motorway. He stopped talking, sensing something had changed. Sebastian calmly filled him in on the news. The story of Belle and George brought tears to his eyes.

"Ah, my friend, what wonderful news. After all these years, he can rest in peace knowing you are happy; and you know the truth. Belle must be relieved." He embraced his friend. "What is wrong? Should you not be elated?"

"I asked Maddy to marry me here, with you as our witness, so Belle and George could be here. She agreed." He stopped to clear his throat and contemplate his next message. "She hasn't returned. I can't reach her on the phone … I don't know what to think. I don't want to leave the hospital; I should be here with … my parents." He stopped, realizing he had chosen "parents" rather than naming Belle and George. He looked over at the hospital room window, turned towards the long hallway, and then returned his gaze to Philippe. "Perhaps she's had time to think about it and has decided it's not such a great offer." His eyes mirrored a deep sadness.

"I'm sure that's not true. She'll be back. Let me greet Belle and George, and then I will help you find her. She loves you; you and I both know that." Philippe turned and opened the door to the room, effusively greeting the elderly couple.

Sebastian watched his friend embrace his parents; it was so easy to see them as parents now. Where was Maddy? He leaned against the wall, eyes closed; her face filled the darkness. He saw her smiling at him as she walked into the club, opening her eyes as she woke up beside him, and floating into the ballroom in Barcelona in the black-and-white dress. He saw her wide-eyed wonder as she pointed out the constellations, her arrival at the ambassador's ball, her teasing grin as she tied his tie, and her face streaked with tears as he left her so long ago. He opened his eyes and shook his head, trying to get his bearings. Philippe was engaged in animated conversation with Belle and George. He dialled Maddy again—no answer. He walked the length of the hallway, feeling lost and anxious.

Philippe suggested tea, the British panacea. Sebastian smiled despite himself. They walked to the cafeteria in silence.

Maddy rushed into the hospital, flowers in hand, her face flushed. She had fallen asleep and woken with a start, shivering from the late afternoon breeze on the deck. A quick shower warmed her, and she dressed hastily, donning the Azules light blue linen dress and Belle's hooded cape. She laughed out loud as she realized she had not given any thought to what she would wear to her own wedding.

Sebastian was not in the room with Belle and George, and for a moment Maddy thought he might have changed his mind. He had seemed disoriented when he asked her. Had she imagined the proposal? She turned away from the window, not sure what to do. She slowly walked down the hallway towards the chapel. No Sebastian. She turned and started towards the exit, tears welling in her eyes.

"Maddy, Maddy is that you?" Sebastian called as he and Philippe turned into the hallway.

She turned slowly, her eyes bright. At the sight of Sebastian running towards her, she smiled the smile he was waiting for—It first spread across her mouth, tentatively; then her cheeks, flushed and dimpled; and then her eyes, sparkling. It was the smile he would always run towards.

They met in an embrace, both talking at the same time.

"I thought you had changed your mind."

"I was losing my mind waiting for you to get back. I thought you had changed your mind." They both shook their heads. "Not at all."

"No. I fell asleep. I'm sorry."

"You're here now; that's all that matters. I love you."

"Me too."

"Here's Philippe. Everything is set. Let's get married."

"Indeed."

In the hospital room, they gathered, standing by the bed so George could see. Belle had chosen the readings with care, incorporating the love she and George felt for both Maddy and Sebastian. The music was soft in the background. The vicar was delighted to be involved in the occasion, despite a reminder they needed to see to the proper paperwork as soon as possible. When the vicar asked if anyone had any reason these two people could not be joined in matrimony, there were smiles all around—no objections.

Sebastian had prepared his vows thoughtfully, thanking Maddy for making his life so full. He held her hand and promised to love her, to protect and care for her as best he could—or as much as she would let him—and to always treasure her as the best part of his life.

Maddy threw her arms around his neck, and they kissed.

The vicar cleared his throat. "We're not done here." His face was red as he looked over at Maddy. "Maddy, have you prepared something?"

Maddy locked eyes with her lover. "Sebastian, come grow old with me. The best is yet to be." Sebastian smiled, as he realized he hadn't given her much time to prepare, and yet here she was quoting Wordsworth; it was the perfect sentiment for their future.

They exchanged the rings, and when the vicar pronounced them man and wife, they looked into each other's eyes, wanting to cherish this moment that would start a new chapter in their lives. The vicar cleared his throat once again and announced they could now kiss. Everyone in the small room laughed as Maddy and Sebastian continued to look into each other's eyes. Their expressions of love for each other showed all the anticipation and desire they felt for the future.

"I love you," Sebastian whispered.

"Just kiss me," Maddy replied, a mischievous smile lighting up her face.

He held her tight. "Indeed."

Philippe popped the cork and poured the champagne. They drank to happiness and to George and to friends and to family and to all the tomorrows they would share.

It was the most perfect wedding day Maddy could have imagined.

Just hours later, George took his last breath, surrounded by his loving family.

George had many friends, and his funeral was well attended. Belle and Sebastian, his family, greeted the many mourners. Throughout the wake, Sebastian scoured the room, looking for Maddy. She was the glue keeping his life together; she had brought him back to life and then found his family. In her mind, life could have no loose ends. She was floating through the room, greeting people, touching their arms, and listening to their stories of George, and every now and then he found her crying around a corner. When the last mourner had paid his respects and they were alone in the large room, the three people who loved George most said their goodbyes.

Difficult as it was to believe life could go on, Belle was adamant that George would be upset if she grieved too long. He had left her with several tracts of forested lands. She had no financial worries. Her friends were anxious to play bridge, and regular card parties resumed within the fortnight. She didn't care to stay in the house without George, preferring to move into the manor home, where her friends were installed. It was a sad move, and Sebastian suggested they keep the house for a while, just in case she changed her mind. Belle reminded Sebastian it was his house, after all.

George had left many of his holdings to Sebastian, the two of them having been involved in every purchase and sale since George had initially given his advice to the boys at college. They had become partners when they realized they thought alike and enjoyed the time together. Maddy tried to imagine how different their lives would have been if only they had sorted out their secrets so many years ago.

Robert was unable to attend the funeral but was pleased to have the acreage in Scotland. He and his partner, Xavier, hoped to build a bed and breakfast in retirement. He was pleased the truth had not hurt anyone, and he promised to visit Belle when he was next in the UK. He was very open to Maddy, letting her know Sebastian had been like a brother to him and he wished them well.

The biggest surprise was the cottage. George had transferred the title to Maddy six months prior, with assistance from Sebastian. He wanted her to enjoy it for her lifetime and had arranged for taxes and repairs in a fund. In the cottage, they found a book with notes from George. In it were his thoughts, aspirations, declarations of love, poems, fond memories, and regrets. One page was dedicated to Maddy, the daughter he had always wished for. She was touched by his words and his joy at their walks and talks together. He had left a page for Sebastian as well, including codes and passwords, a plea to care for Belle, and a reminder that happiness could easily escape those who did not take risks.

Return to Bellmere

Sebastian and Maddy were finally arriving home to the garden apartment Maddy had missed. Both were anxious to be home; the last few days had been taxing with family matters: Maddy's return, the reconciliation with Belle and George, the wedding, and the funeral. They had barely had time to get over the jet lag and the euphoria of being married.

As they drove onto the avenue, Maddy felt a pang of happiness spread through her thoughts; this seemed like home. After only a year, this *was* her home. She wanted to jump out of the car and run up and down the quiet boulevard, shouting for her friends to come out.

Sebastian parked the car at the front door, opened the car door for Maddy, and took her hand. "Welcome, Mrs Walker, to our new home."

Maddy smiled up at him, giddy at his formal behaviour.

He led her around the house to the garden, sensing her confusion. As they turned the corner into the garden, the lights shining brightly, she caught her breath. In the garden, champagne glasses in hand, were her friends—their friends.

"Surprise!" they shouted, raising their glasses. Maddy turned to Sebastian and hugged him, thanking him for the wonderful homecoming. He held her tight and whispered into her hair, "I wanted your return to be a happy occasion."

"Hey, you two, you have time for that later. We missed you, Maddy; we need hugs!" Audrey stepped forward, arms out.

Maddy greeted each of her friends, quickly catching up and realizing how much she had missed them in her life. Suddenly Sebastian clapped his hands and asked for attention. Friends gathered around, everyone waiting to hear what he had to say.

"Thank you all for being here tonight. I wanted Maddy to be with those she loved tonight. Oh, I forgot the most important thing of all. May I introduce you to Mrs Madison Davis-Walker, my wife." He paused. "She finally said yes." He reached for Maddy's hand and slipped the diamond ring on her finger. He had been carrying the ring in his pocket for months. Maddy gasped and threw her arms around his neck.

There was laughter, applause, and shouts of congratulations.

"Tonight we return to our new home, so please indulge me for a moment; this is the first time we will see the result of our dream home, and it's only fitting that you should all be here with us to share our new beginning. Maddy conceived the plan; I only drew it out. Thanks to Lambert and Audrey, the plan came to life. They handled every detail and the decorating. Please join us for dinner in our new home." The dust cloth dropped and was whisked away. The curtains slowly opened on the glass structure, unveiling a softly candlelit dining room with a long table, food arranged on the sideboards. As the curtains continued to open and the windows moved to the side, the sounds of a piano filled the space. The fires were lit in both fireplaces, giving the room a warm glow. There were gasps and whistles and a murmur of approval as the house was unveiled to the garden. Maddy was holding her breath, taking it all in. She felt Sebastian's arms around her, holding her from running into the house and touching everything, running her hands over the welcoming furniture and artwork. She turned in his arms and held his face in her hands. "It's better than I imagined. Thank you." They kissed and realized their friends were applauding. Laughing, they gave each other one last look and then gestured for the crowd to move into the dining room.

Maddy rubbed her eyes, hoping this wasn't a dream. She watched her friends enter the house and admire the seating areas, the art, and the flow of the main floor. It was truly a house built for entertaining. She found Audrey fussing with the throw cushions. "Audrey, it's beautiful. Thank you." They embraced, rocking back and forth.

"I remembered everything you loved about the cottage and tried to bring it here; we can exchange any of the art pieces you don't care for, and we can add anything else you want. I really hope you like how it turned out; it was a labour of love, Maddy."

"I don't like it; I love it. You are so special. I just want to walk around and be here."

"Sebastian hasn't been allowed in, so it really is your new home." Audrey patted her on the back and gently led her into the dining room, where everyone was seated.

Maddy sat at the end of the table, affording her guests the garden view. Sebastian looked comfortable in his large antique chair at the head of the table, offering wine, passing platters of food, and accepting the praises of his tablemates. He looked very much at home. The conversation was light and easy, the room offering a perfect setting for the outpouring of friendship.

Sebastian was pouring a glass of wine and enjoying the interaction of their guests when he looked over at Maddy. She was laughing with Grace and Lambert. He stopped to watch her, her eyes so alive and attentive to the matter at hand. At that moment, Maddy turned her head and caught sight of him. She slowly turned back to make eye contact, smiling shyly, transmitting all the love in her heart for him, her friends, the room, and the evening. She placed her hand on her heart and mouthed the words *"I love you."* Sebastian was so taken by the gesture and the tender way she looked at him that he sat down, overwhelmed by a wave of pure love.

When he looked up, Maddy was already engaged in animated conversation with Mr Simpson and Leda. The professor was sitting on the arm of her chair, one arm draped over her shoulder. It was a wonderful picture. The ambience of the room and the happy chatter made him realize this was his future. This is what he had missed for so many years.

When the guests left them, waving goodbye and weaving along the front drive, Maddy and Sebastian walked through the house, hand in hand. They were delighted with the house—their house, their home. They fell asleep exhausted but happy to be together at last in their own bed.

Sebastian woke suddenly, realizing Maddy was not beside him. He sat up in a panic and looked around, calling her name. As his eyes adjusted to the dark, he saw the outline of her body out on the balcony. She was standing at the railing, looking at the garden, her hair blowing around her face, the afghan tight on her shoulders. He watched her for a moment and then joined her, careful not to frighten her. He slipped his arms around her, and she snuggled into him. "Isn't it glorious?" she whispered.

"Come with me." He took her hand and led her down the stairs.

At the front door, he stopped, took her face in his hands, and whispered, "I almost forgot." He opened the door with a flourish, ushered Maddy out, and stood with her at the entrance. "Welcome home, Mrs Walker." He scooped her up in his arms and carried her across the threshold, delighting in her laughter.

He took her hand, and together they walked into the centre seating room. He found the remote, and the fire came to life. They sat in the dark, the flames licking their faces and warming them. "It feels like home, doesn't it, Maddy?" he asked softly.

She turned to look at him, tears streaming down her cheeks. "Indeed."

Sitting up in bed the next morning, Maddy looked over at Sebastian, engrossed in the morning news. "Sebastian?" she had been wondering how to approach him on the subject.

He looked over, giving her his full attention, removing his glasses. "Yes, my dear wife, what is it?" He was enjoying the word "wife".

"Have you given any thought to what we might give Grace and Davi for a wedding present?"

"No, I knew you'd have a perfectly awesome gift in mind," he threw back.

"Now you're mocking me. It's not like they need a salad spinner or toaster oven. I wondered if we shouldn't give them some ownership in the coffee house building. They really have nothing to start their life together, and they work so hard … It would be a perfect venue for their own wedding."

"That's a good thought. As partners in the building, we can sign a portion of the mortgage over, if you want to let it go, or we can offer shares. You decide. I'll get the paperwork done before we leave," he said, picking up his glasses.

"Anything else?"

She was grinning like a Cheshire cat.

He placed the laptop and his glasses on the bedside table, turning to catch Maddy as she pounced across the bed. He was ready for her.

The coffee house was transforming into a popular meeting place, and the buttons had a busy schedule with after-school activities—Audrey and Jeffery had successfully completed the adoption process, and Lambert had been promoted to vice president, taking on new projects with gusto. It was time to take a honeymoon.

Sebastian left the decision to Maddy. She was conspiratorial with Belle, and he thought perhaps he should have suggested a mainstream destination instead. Maddy was still convinced there was a need to visit the villa in Italy where he had been born. She insisted it was necessary to close the circle on his roots. He was not convinced. Belle was hesitant, for some reason, which only made Maddy more diligent. In the end they were invited to the villa by the contessa, Belle's childhood friend. Arrangements were made for flights and car rental. Maddy was bursting with excitement; Sebastian was reticent.

Christian had hoped Henry would be back for the wedding or at least the dinner to surprise Maddy, but although Henry was miserable in Australia, his relatives were holding on to him. It was believed he would be free to go when the grandfather passed away—there was no reason to keep him if there was no money forthcoming. The trust fund was designed to keep him in school, not in the care of the relatives. Maddy was hopeful he would be home soon. Christian and Sebastian had applied for joint guardianship through the school, offering to continue mentoring. The procedure was painstakingly slow.

Maddy suggested Mrs B would be the perfect hostess for a bed and breakfast operation. Sebastian laughed out loud when Maddy pointed out that Belle's house was ideal. Mrs B was pleased to have Maddy home; there would be much entertaining now. She would be busy enough in the kitchen at Bellmere, thank you very much.

The Honeymoon

Sebastian leaned back in his seat, his arm around a sleeping Maddy. He marvelled at how she could fall asleep as soon as her head hit his chest. He closed his eyes and wondered what they would find at the villa. He woke Maddy as they landed and they proceeded through the airport to the car rental, her excitement infectious. Maddy asked if she could drive, feeling more comfortable with the left-hand drive car. They meandered through the countryside, arriving at the villa in the afternoon sun.

The villa had seen better days, but the garden was magnificently cared for and ornate. They were greeted by the housekeeper before they reached the door.

"Sebastian?" An elderly woman, gathering herbs in a basket, came forward. "I am Allegra. My English no good. I know your mama as a child. You born here." She pointed to the corner window. "Welcome. I go to tell the contessa you here." Maddy nudged Sebastian, raising her eyebrows and giving him the "told you so" look. He grinned, bowed, and ushered her past him to the door.

The contessa invited them to tea in her chambers, a dark and closed-up sickroom. After awkward introductions, Maddy offered to open the draperies so the contessa could see the beautiful gardens. The contessa was surprised to hear the gardens were in any condition; she had not looked out for some time.

Maddy placed her sunglasses on the contessa's face. "Trust me; you will need these," she said as she drew back the heavy velvet draperies, sneezing from the dust. She struggled with the stiff latch, opening the balcony doors. A warm breeze enveloped the room, spreading the scent of the garden.

As Sebastian made small talk with the contessa, Maddy found a wheelchair and lined the seat with blankets she found in a cupboard. She wheeled the chair into the room, brightly announcing that the chariot was ready for take-off. Sebastian lifted the contessa into the chair, patiently ignoring her instructions and complaints. The old woman cried with delight when she saw the colourful, frothy picture in front of her. "Lorenzo, the dear soul, he always worked such magic in the garden. He is a master of flowers and landscape, is he not?" She held her face in her hands and cried. "We must have a garden party. I have not seen the people from the village, except for Father Dominic, for some time. We must celebrate your return to the village, Sebastian. Maddy, perhaps you could organize a festa for us." Sebastian was quick to agree that Maddy was the best person to accomplish whatever the contessa dreamed. He was amazed at how easily the two women had found common ground. "Maddy, seek out Father Dominic; he is the best person to give you any assistance. Sebastian and I have much to talk about." The contessa waved Maddy out of the room.

Maddy walked into the old stone church, looking for Father Dominic. She was directed to the confessional. She opened the door, knelt by the screen, and waited, rubbing the dust off the grillwork. The grate moved, and a tired voice spoke in Italian. Maddy leaned forward, whispering. "Hi. Father, I'm Maddy; we are visiting the contessa, and I need your help. She adores you. I don't think I have any sins to confess. Does anyone in this wonderful little village sin? I mean, it doesn't seem like a place a sinner would live … You must be so bored. What's the worst thing you've heard? Should we lock the car doors? Am I supposed to call you Padre?"

"Do you wish to confess?" the voice asked in clipped English.

"Sorry, not really. I just want to talk to you. Well, actually, it's imperative that I speak with you. It's very dusty in here. You might to want to air this space out." She ran her finger across the wooden grate.

"Make an appointment after the Mass. This is the time for confession."

Maddy pushed the door open and peered out.

"There's not a soul waiting, but okay, when can I meet you?"

"After the Mass."

"Oh, will that be a long Mass or a short Mass?" No response was forthcoming, just a sigh. "Did you want to give me any prayers or something to say?"

"Recite a Hail Mary for your impertinence."

"Father, could you help me out here? I haven't said a Hail Mary for a while … No problem with the Lord's Prayer, but I admit I am rusty on the Hail Mary"

"Perhaps you could Google it."

The grate closed, and Maddy left the enclosure feeling dismissed. There was no queue, so she wondered why Father Dominic would be so grouchy. She sat in the last pew, watching the elderly churchgoers arrive and take their places. They seemed intent on praying in the middle of the day. Maddy settled in to wait for Father Dominic.

Maddy watched Father Dominic solemnly conduct his service for a few parishioners. He was tanned and fit; his greying temples were the only indication he was not a young man. His face looked chiselled, like a stone sculpture. He was tall and stooped, as though he were permanently speaking to a shorter person. His voice was melodic—very easy to listen to, even in another language.

As Maddy was watching his every move, he too was watching her, wondering why she would be in the village and how she was related to the contessa. He had been amused with her conversation in the confessional; it seemed a long time since anyone had spoken to him with so little reverence.

While the choir of three sang the hymn, he followed her wide-eyed gaze taking in every square inch of the church: the faded wall murals, the stained-glass windows, and the altars, and then she ran her hands along the wood pews, smiling at their worn smoothness. He found he was holding his breath, waiting for her to smile again, somehow waiting for her approval of his little parish church. He tried to concentrate on the service, disturbed by the stranger in their midst. She looked so peaceful, her eyes sparkling as though she had a secret she would later share. He shook his head as the altar boy coughed and dutifully completed his service.

Maddy walked out of the church with Lorenzo, deep in conversation, speaking with her hands more than in her limited Italian. Father Dominic took her hand and welcomed her to the church.

"Hi, we met earlier." Maddy pointed towards the back of the church.

"Yes, I know." He smiled, crossing his arms.

"Father, the contessa assures me you are the best person to assist me with planning a garden party for the village. Lorenzo has the gardens looking *supremo*, and I've been charged with getting everyone out next Sunday—after church, of course. What do you say? Oh, by the way, I'm Maddy Davis. Well, Davis-Walker now." She was talking fast, and Father Dominic realized saying no was not an option.

"How can I help the contessa, Maddy Davis-Walker?" he asked with a slight bow of his head.

She smiled readily, citing the need for tables, chairs, and minor tasks he would be required to perform. He laughed, partly because he was pleased to be included, partly because she spoke with such certainty. "Your biggest task is to invite everyone. I would think you know everyone here, right?" She paused, eyebrows raised.

"Si," he replied.

Maddy laughed out loud. "Sebastian would say "indeed" in that same tone."

Father Dominic looked confused, so Maddy hooked her arm in his and guided him towards the villa. "Please have lunch with us and meet Sebastian."

Maddy knew everything about Father Dominic by the time they reached the kitchen of the villa.

Sebastian and Father Dominic quickly agreed that Maddy had things well under way; they understood their roles and decided choosing the wine was a safe task. Maddy had invited Philippe to the party, hoping he and Sebastian could visit local vineyards and take on the bar. Father Dominic was pleased to offer his services as a vineyard guide.

After a long, leisurely lunch of bread, cheese, prosciutto, melon, grapes, and olives in the garden, Father Dominic excused himself to visit the contessa. Sebastian closed his eyes for a moment, feeling very relaxed and content. Maddy had found a faded hammock in the cellar and was having Lorenzo hang it in the shade of the tall trees.

Loud voices woke Sebastian from his reverie. The scene before him was comical; several older men with hats in hand were speaking loudly to each other, while Maddy, with hands on hips, was holding her ground and pointing to what she wanted done. When she held up her hands in frustration and reached for the hammock, the men stopped speaking and fought to hang it for her. When it was up securely, they pointed to the hammock so Maddy could test it. She tentatively lay back as they waited. She moved her arm above her head and closed her eyes, adjusting her body in a comfortable position. When she opened her eyes and sat up exclaiming it was perfect, smiling and giving each man a personal "*grazie*", the men beamed, and Sebastian knew they were her slaves for life.

"Sebastian, come and try out your hammock; it's lovely in the shade." She motioned to him. She turned to the men and announced it was time for a siesta. They slowly backed out of the garden, snickering, shyly waving ciao. Sebastian wondered how he would ever get Maddy to leave this place; she seemed to be quite comfortable, and this was only their first day.

Father Dom, as Maddy called him, was a regular visitor at the villa who proficiently secured tables, chairs, platters of home-baked goods, and anything else Maddy required. He and Sebastian played cards and visited wineries, buying copious quantities of local wine. Maddy was pleased a friendship developed between the two men, as Philippe's arrival was delayed. He would arrive for the weekend with her friend Giselle and cases of champagne. Sebastian decided to surprise Maddy with the news, knowing she would be thrilled to see Giselle again.

"Sebastian, do you think Father Dom did something bad in his youth?" she asked as they were enjoying a glass of Prosecco in the garden.

"Why do you ask?" It seemed a strange question, but he knew better than to dismiss it.

"Well, he seems so intelligent and worldly … Why would he want to devote his life to the Church, especially here?"

"Maddy, he made a choice to serve God; he has a simple life, and he seems happy. He has an old Ducati, you know. Don't you go digging into the poor man's past; just accept him as he is—a friend."

Maddy smiled back and raised her hand. "I promise. But it is strange, don't you think? Everyone has a story." She closed her eyes and let the afternoon sun warm her face. Sebastian smiled at her, hoping Father Dom was indeed just a happy priest.

The contessa was enjoying daily reports from Maddy on the party details. They had developed an easy friendship. The contessa was unable to resist the enthusiasm her new friend brought to each visit. Maddy ventured into the past, asking questions about Belle and the birth of the baby. She was given free rein to visit the cellar and the attic storage, her interest piqued by the signs and files hidden away. One evening she invited Sebastian to come up to the attic with her; she wanted to share her findings with him. He followed her up, not sure he wanted to know what she had found.

"Sebastian, look at this; I found old correspondence on this embossed stationery. The villa was called Villa Contessa, and the family ran it as a tourist home. There are records of Belle and her family staying here for years. Look; here are some photos of the gardens and the family who owned the vineyard. Did you realize there was a vineyard? Look at this; it's a photo of Belle with you and the contessa." She knelt beside Sebastian with the photo album.

"This was your grandparent's summer holiday home for years. When the contessa's parents died, they stopped taking guests and seemed to work hard at botching the winemaking enterprise. The contessa married a man who wanted to live like a rich man without putting any effort into the upkeep. He died several years into the marriage, an alcoholic. She never recovered; she hardly left the villa, and the locals started calling her the contessa because she lived in the Villa Contessa and they never saw her. Isn't that a wonderful story?" She looked up at him with bright eyes. Sebastian was touched by her need to uncover the details surrounding his birth, and her relentless desire to complete the story. He leaned over and kissed the top of her head.

This was not the honeymoon he had envisioned, but he had to admit he was enjoying the experience, the locals, and being with Maddy.

"Sebastian, I have a confession." She was biting the inside of her cheek—not always a good sign. He nodded, encouraging her to continue. "There's more to this garden party than just having a few people over." She paused and looked around the dusty attic.

"Go on."

"The contessa is quite ill. She doesn't have much time left, you know. We have a deal; my job is to ensure she sees all the people she once knew— some are friends, some are people she has wronged over the years. You see, the contessa doesn't have any children or heirs, and she always maintained that your birth here gave you a right to the villa."

Sebastian started to protest, but Maddy touched his arm.

"The lawyers have cautioned her that if she leaves the villa to you, it would be contested and it would take years to settle, at which time you would probably walk away—which is the intent, of course." She took a deep breath. "If the villa were sold before she died, there would be no such contest or legal recourse. So I bought it." There, she had said it.

"You bought it? How is that possible?" he sputtered.

"I wanted you to have your birthplace, and the more research I did, the more I found. There are acres of vineyards lying dormant, this building, the gardens, an artesian well, and olive groves. It's massive, and it's so beautiful."

"But how could you possibly afford to buy this?" he asked, closing his eyes, worried Maddy might be in over her head. "Just the legal fees would be staggering."

"The contessa and I worked out a deal. I—well, we—have to take care of her burial arrangements, and I—that is, we—have to deliver a kick-ass garden party in exchange for the money I had in my pocket that day. I had 120 euros, so she lent me the money from her account to buy the decrepit property in total. The proviso is that I—sorry, we—cannot sell it until after she dies, if we don't want to keep it. She lives here until I—we—bury her and we decide what we—ah, that is, what you—want to do with the property. I still have a bank account in my name in Canada, so it was sold to a foreign investor. There are tax issues, but the lawyer has taken most of the onerous clauses out of the equation, and the deal was final just this morning.

"You know we never married in a civil service, so the transaction is valid, as in the eyes of the Italian law we are not married. The contessa insisted everything be done before the party. I wasn't allowed to discuss the sale or the deal with anyone, including you, as a condition of sale. Now you are my tenant, and you will have signing authority on her accounts as her legal heir. The banker will be here with the legal paperwork tomorrow morning. You will have to pay rent, which should empty the accounts in the next three months, ensuring there is no estate to disperse after her death. I'm sorry I couldn't discuss this with you; it was killing me. The contessa thought you might be too proud to take the villa. She says you are like your grandfather." She let out a long breath. "That's it. Are you upset with me?" She looked over at Sebastian with wide, questioning eyes. "I just knew there was more to the story … never mind. First things first … aren't you delighted?"

Sebastian needed a moment to digest the news. One thing was certain; he was madly in love with this woman who continually surprised him with her passion and schemes. The villa would be theirs because she had forced him to confront the past. The contessa believed in Maddy enough to leave the future in her hands, the villagers had accepted Maddy as their own, Father Dom had become a good friend, and they were comfortable here. This was on the bucket list, wasn't it? He couldn't speak.

"How would you react if you were me and this unfolded in front of you?" He was confused; the news was too much to digest.

Maddy looked around the room and then locked her eyes with his.

"I would throw my arms around you and kiss you with all the love in my heart. I would be so pleased you wanted me to connect my past and my future. I would be ecstatic that someone cared enough to make this crazy scheme happen, and I would be thrilled to receive such a wonderful wedding present from the person I loved. Then I would take you to bed, hold you tight, and dream of a wonderful future and how I was going to revive the vineyard." She stopped speaking, her eyes brimming with tears, her arms wrapped around her shoulders. "You?"

Maddy was patiently waiting for his response. He reached for her and looked into her eyes. Slowly and with all the desire and passion he felt, he kissed her. No words could say what the kiss would say. Maddy was giggling in between kisses. He stopped to look at her, holding her face in his hands. Tears of happiness were streaming down her face. "Indeed."

As they lay in each other's arms in their canopied bed in the villa that was now theirs, Maddy asked Sebastian why he had asked her how she would react.

"You always see the bright side of every situation; you always seem to have the perfect response, and I have never experienced anything like this. Before I met you, my life was simple and uncomplicated. I'm just not equipped to respond to these grand gestures. I needed confirmation— perhaps reassurance. As usual, you provided the best take on it." He kissed the top of her head. "As usual, you were able to articulate what I was feeling, better than I could."

He smiled as he realized she was asleep in his arms. "And my beautiful wife, it appears I get to marry you again."

The garden party was framed by the bluest of skies, a bright sun, and a steady stream of guests. The contessa sat between Father Dom and Sebastian and greeted each arrival, sometimes with familiarity, occasionally looking at Father Dom for an introduction.

The men in the village set up tables, anxious to have Maddy approve of their placement. The women delivered platters of cannoli and other treats to add to the ample food displayed on the bright-coloured cloths Maddy had found in her search. Local musicians were scattered throughout the garden, allowing everyone to enjoy the afternoon. Giselle and Philippe started the dancing, which continued well into the evening. Maddy was thrilled to see her friend Giselle. The two women embraced and then launched into nonstop conversation, catching up on their separate lives. Sebastian and Philippe had walked the vineyard to assess the viability of salvaging the vines. Both were pleased to report it was possible.

The contessa looked radiant in a long gown, a jewelled tiara in her thinning hair. Maddy had given strict instructions to her bodyguards, Sebastian and Father Dom. If she tired, they were to escort her into the house to rest. After asking how she was doing several times, the contessa admonished the men, saying she was enjoying the party and asking if they could please be quiet. They exchanged glances and shrugged, feeling like scolded schoolboys.

All afternoon the villagers came by to speak with the contessa, some wagging fingers at her, some kneeling beside her and clasping her hands, some kissing her cheek, and others bowing their heads with their hats in their hands. It was a receiving line, and it seemed all those in attendance wanted an audience with the contessa. Maddy stopped by for the occasional selfie with the contessa, who beamed and posed for each photo.

As the sun settled on the horizon, there was still food to be enjoyed, wine to be shared, dancing to be done, and garden paths to explore. The garden walls reverberated with the sound of laughter from friends and neighbours gathered.

"Maddy has done a marvellous job of engaging the village," Father Dom remarked as he handed Sebastian a glass of wine.

"Just one of her many talents. She can be very persuasive … but she does good things." Sebastian smiled, searching for her in the crowd.

"I don't imagine many people say no to her, do they?" Father Dom was also scanning the faces to see where she might be. They both sighted her dancing with an elderly man, laughing as another elderly man waited for his turn. Both men were enjoying her playful behaviour on the stone dance floor when the contessa nudged them.

"Where is Maddy?" she snapped. "I want to speak with Maddy." Sebastian immediately went to fetch Maddy, sorry to take her away from the adoring crowd.

"The contessa would like to see you, beautiful," he whispered in her ear. Maddy bowed to the men and pointed to their wives on the chairs, winking.

"Ah, here you are, Maddy. Come; I must go up." The contessa suddenly looked quite old and frail. Maddy was attentive, covering her in the blankets and moving the chair slowly towards the door. Inside the bedroom, Maddy helped the contessa into her dressing gown, careful to remove the tiara only after a last look in the mirror. Tears were softly falling on her cheeks. The contessa looked away.

"Oh, my dear, did you stay too long? Are you tired? Did you not enjoy the party?" Maddy asked, hoping she had not expected too much of the older woman.

"Oh no, it was wonderful. I never imagined such a regal affair. Thank you, my dear girl. You have been so kind to me. I know I am doing the right thing, and I know you will love this place as much as I have—perhaps even more. Please take care of the villa and Sebastian, Maddy." The contessa was crying, her tears mixing with her make-up, streaking her face.

"I promise. Why are you so upset?" Maddy knelt beside the regal woman in the chair.

"Sebastian was promised to me. I lost him as a boy. Belle was my friend until she realized I was to have the boy. Her parents were so angry she would not leave him here with me. He could have grown up here, happy as a lark." The contessa was sobbing.

"He had a good life; Belle loved him so much. George was amazing; I wish you could have met him. You would have been happy for them. I'm sorry it took so long to bring him back," Maddy said soothingly, her arm around the contessa. "Let's get you settled. Sleep and we'll talk in the morning. You must be reeling with the noise, the faces, and the conversation. You were amazing, dear contessa. You were truly a contessa, holding court in the lovely garden." Maddy kissed the top of her head, smiling at the elderly woman in the mirror. The contessa reached for her hand, patting it, smiling back weakly. She looked up at Maddy, her eyes tearing. "It's time to sleep; I am tired—so very tired. Maddy, this is yours now." She handed Maddy the tiara.

"It's still yours, Contessa," Maddy said softly.

"No, it's truly yours, you have taken over as the contessa, and I want you to have it. My lawyer knows it's yours, and I don't want anyone else to touch it but you. It will bring you good harvest and many years of laughter, but only if you wear it." The contessa smiled in the mirror. Maddy placed the tiara on her head and helped her benefactor into the bed, covering her gently and ensuring she was comfortable before turning the lights out and leaving the contessa to dream of her beloved villa and the many conversations at the garden party.

The music and the wine were intoxicating; the villagers were still dancing when Maddy and Sebastian slipped away to their suite.

During the night, Sebastian opened his eyes and felt the bed for Maddy. Panic set in when she wasn't beside him. He tried to sit up and felt her head on his abdomen. She was sleeping across the bed, one leg out of the duvet, spread-eagle. His heart stopped pounding, and he lay back on the pillow, not wanting to wake her but desperately wanting to hold her in his arms. Maddy stirred, so he pulled her up onto his chest. She snuggled into his arms, and soon he heard her soft purrs. He fell asleep matching her breathing.

The guests at the villa were busy moving tables and clearing up when Maddy came downstairs the next morning. She had checked in on the contessa, ensuring she was awake and comfortable in her room before she joined the group. Allegra was singing as she prepared breakfast, and Sebastian was setting the table in the garden. Father Dom was directing the placement of what was to go and what would stay. The group finally sat down to enjoy a leisurely feast. Maddy sat back, enjoying the banter, the sun, the food, and the fresh air. She looked over at Sebastian, who was seated at the head of the table, laughing at something Giselle and Philippe were discussing. He was tanned and easy with life at the villa; she couldn't help but think he looked handsome and "*to the manor born*." She chortled as she smiled and watched him.

"Sorry, did you say something?" Father Dom asked, his hand touching her arm. Maddy turned to see Father Dom looking at her anxiously, as if he had misheard or missed her comment.

"No, Father, I'm just enjoying this wonderful life, the food, and my friends." She smiled at his concern. "Shall I pour you another glass?" She reached for the juice and the champagne.

"*No, no, grazie.* I will visit the contessa and be on my way. Your garden party was a lovely affair, and I fear some of my flock may require assistance getting home, even now." He laughed.

"Thank you, Father. I wonder how we could have had the event without your amazing resourcefulness." She shook his hand. Father Dom leaned forward and kissed her cheek.

"My pleasure. I understand you are unofficially the new contessa and a new member of my parish. Life will certainly be interesting in our little village. I look forward to many more gatherings." He bowed, turned, and walked into the house.

Later in the day, Father Dom returned with *El Doctori* and suggested Sebastian might want to sit with the contessa. The contessa asked to see Maddy in the afternoon. She fell asleep as the sun set on the vineyard, leaving them with her last wishes and declarations of love.

After the Honeymoon

Tanned and exhausted, they boarded the flight, both anxious to get back to their new home, yet sad to leave the villa and Father Dom. Sebastian was subdued on the flight. Maddy wondered if the ordeal at the villa and the funeral for the contessa had been more than he could handle—so many changes in such a short time. There had been the transformation of Bellmere, the villa was theirs and would require serious work, and the death of the contessa had left them feeling sad but disoriented—many questions were left unanswered, although many secrets had been disclosed. Maddy wasn't sure Sebastian was ready to hear why the contessa and Belle had fallen out—that he was the currency they had fought over; both had wanted him for their own. A conversation with Belle was Maddy's top priority.

Their honeymoon had been action-packed, with friends coming and going, the garden party, and the funeral arrangements. Belle had not travelled to Italy, vowing she was not up to travel, and Maddy wondered if Sebastian was worried about her as well. She was keen on getting home. He agreed and held her hand. Philippe was to meet them at the airport, as his flight was arriving before theirs—he had business in London and was anxious to share his plans for the vineyard with them.

Maddy kept taking side glances at Sebastian, worried he might not be feeling well. She noticed he was getting pale and pasty looking. His hands were cold, and he seemed unfocused.

"Are you feeling okay?" she asked tenderly, fearing the worst.

Pressing the call button, she asked for medical assistance on arrival.

She leaned over and kissed his forehead, telling him how much he meant to her, how much she loved him, and how she was looking forward to their life together. He felt clammy at her touch. She felt useless; all she could do was tell him over and over how much she loved him.

Walking into the terminal, leaving the jetway, Sebastian fell, gasping for air. Maddy dropped to the ground, cradling his head, calling for help. This could not be happening. She loosened his tie and looked around her helplessly. "Where are the paramedics? We requested medical assistance!" she shouted.

He was taken to the Royal Hospital by ambulance. Philippe and Maddy were allowed to ride with him. When Maddy saw him in the hospital bed, with tubes and machines hooked up to him, she burst into racking sobs. She sounded like a wounded animal. Philippe was unsure how to console her. She continued to sob, sliding down the wall and sitting on the floor. Philippe sat beside her on the floor and took her hand, waiting for her to cry herself out.

"He said he was taking energy from me, and I didn't understand. It took so long for him to feel comfortable with simple things like touching ..."

Philippe clucked his tongue "Maddy, my dear, we were raised at boarding school, where touching was forbidden; we went to university; and then we married women who didn't like to be touched ... What do you expect? It's just our nature." He added softly, "You have changed his life for the better, I know."

As the doctor approached, Philippe helped her up and stood beside her. Her eyes were red, her face streaked with the tracks of her tears. She tried to compose herself and prepare for the news. "Your husband is comfortable; that's the best we can do at this point. We'll do the remainder of the tests after he's had some rest. His heart condition will require some life changes, but we are optimistic he will be out of hospital in a few days. He's asking for you. You can go in for a short time, if you like." The doctor moved away after patting her shoulder and nodding to Philippe.

Maddy slowly walked into the room, her eyes stinging and her heart pounding as she saw Sebastian lying in the bed, hooked up to monitors and drips. She held his hand, leaning over to kiss his forehead, running her fingers through his hair. He opened his eyes and squeezed her hand.

"I'm sorry, Maddy; I'm supposed to be the strong one," he whispered. She moved her hand down his face, smiling at him. "We're going to be just fine. Please sleep and get strong enough so we can break out of this place."

"Don't go," he pleaded. "They said I could see my wife. My wife … it has a nice ring to it."

Maddy looked around the small room and smiled at him. "Philippe wants to see you. I'll be back. I can't sleep without you."

Maddy walked into the hall and motioned to Philippe. "I'll stay here tonight; he's awake if you want to see him."

Philippe nodded and entered the room. Moments later he came into the hallway, head down, rubbing his eyes. "I'll be back in the morning. I hate to see him this way. Be strong, Maddy; I'm here for both of you." He hugged her and walked away, turning once to look back and wave.

Maddy entered the room, dimmed the lights, and climbed onto the bed beside Sebastian, careful not to disturb the hookups. Sebastian moved to make room, smiling at how well she fit beside him.

"Maddy, it's easy to see why I'm crazy about you. What did you see in me? Why did you stand by me when I was so awkward and hopeless? I've wanted to know right from the beginning." His words were slurred from the medication.

Maddy thought for a moment, smiled tenderly, and stoked his forehead. "You were … calm."

"You mean boring?" he asked, amused.

"No … not at all. I lived in an aggressive, competitive, and emotion-charged environment for so long I thought that's how everyone lived. After a few days with you, I realized I felt safe and less guarded. It was nice. You didn't want to change me; you accepted who I am. We didn't talk much, but we were comfortable with each other, not angry or competitive with each other. Being with you makes me feel grounded."

"I wish I'd met you years ago," he said affectionately.

"We wouldn't have met years ago; you know that. Besides, I wasn't ready to meet someone like you." She looked up at his face, smiling. "I'm ready now, so go to sleep; we have a chance at happiness, and I don't want to miss a moment."

He closed his eyes, feeling stronger with Maddy beside him and the promise of tomorrow.

"Maddy, I don't understand you," he was shouting from the garden. "You save people from beatings, you gift homeless children to save a marriage, you basically marry two old people off, you babysit chickens, you kidnap a schoolboy, you organize people and their lives, and yet …" His tirade seemed to be losing steam as he came towards her. "And yet you cannot play bridge." He stood in the doorway, red faced and out of fight.

Maddy laughed until tears ran down her face. Sebastian tried not to smile but eventually broke into laughter with her. It was a happy memory. She fell into a deep sleep.

The duty nurse was about to enter the room and ask Maddy to remove herself from the patient's bed when the young doctor approached, asking how Sebastian had fared overnight. The nurse reported there had been no concerns. He smiled at her, taking the chart, and as if he knew what she was thinking, he reminded her that human touch was a great healer.

"Let them be. Mrs Walker is a volunteer here." The nurse turned in a huff and retreated. Standing by the bed, he touched Maddy's arm and winked. "How's your patient doing?" He looked up from the chart and watched Maddy stroke Sebastian's hand. "How are you doing, Maddy?" His voice was less businesslike, friendlier in tone.

"Oh, Steve, he slept through the night. It's good to see you," she whispered as she stretched. She and the young doctor had stayed in touch since the accident and the "buttons affair", as he called it. They met for tea or a quick break on her visits to the hospital. She was always pleased to see him and report on the buttons.

Sebastian stirred, opening his eyes, and reached for Maddy.

"Good morning, sweetheart; how did you sleep?" she asked, sliding off the bed, bending from side to side to relieve the stiffness and smiling at him.

"Sebastian, you remember Dr Steve Howe; he was the emergency doctor on call at the car accident when the buttons appeared. He also did some tests on George. He was at the farewell party. You are in very capable hands."

The two men exchanged greetings. Steve turned to Maddy. "Maddy, I'm going to take the job in Africa. Your friend could not have been more accommodating or convincing. They have offered to sponsor me for the year. Thank you. I just wish I had someone like you to come with me."

"No, you don't. You'll meet amazing people when you're there; I wouldn't recommend going with anyone you already know. I'm so proud of you. You'll be great." She hugged him.

Sebastian watched the exchange and shook his head. "Maddy, I fear you've interfered in yet another man's life."

"Steve thought he wanted a small country practice, but that was before he knew he could join Doctors Without Borders. He's a pilot, and he's never been out of the south of England. I think he needs to see the world. I just provided a connection," she replied guilelessly.

The young doctor laughed. "I must finish my rounds. I'm glad to see you are on the mend, Mr Walker. We caught this early enough, so you should be home in a few days. I don't anticipate any concerns with the stent. You may have to make modifications to your diet, but otherwise I believe you are in good hands—unless, of course you would prefer to check into a rehabilitation centre for some peace and quiet." He winked at Sebastian.

"Well now, that's a consideration. Maddy is the one who makes my heart race, so maybe it would be best …" Sebastian smiled at the doctor.

"You do know I'm standing right here listening to the two of you, right?" Maddy moved forward, hands on hips.

Dr Howe laughed, closed the chart, and started for the door.

"Cheers, Maddy. The patient is yours to do what you will. I'll stay in touch." Steve kissed her cheek. "Oh, why don't I have them bring you a cot for this evening? It might be less scandalous for the matron." He was chuckling as he left the room.

Sebastian was released into Maddy's care the next day. They drove to the seaside cottage, where they spent time walking on the beach, visiting with Belle, reading by the fire, talking about their hopes and dreams, laughing together, watching the sunsets, and enjoying their self-imposed exile from the world. Maddy prepared simple meals, which they ate outdoors on the deck. They shared more stories of growing up, disappointments and highlights, and favourite books and heroes. Neighbours who met them thought they radiated happiness, still on their honeymoon, so lovely together. The days seemed too short.

Sebastian could not imagine life without Maddy. He woke each morning looking forward to the day with her. He was no longer surprised when she offered to help milk goats, lead a bicycle tour for a media group, or design a website for a small retailer who might be struggling. She would be at home anywhere. He looked forward to watching a tennis match with her or discussing the latest news item. She still wasn't sure about cricket but committed to learning the game. They enjoyed football and watched the local teams play, meeting and making new friends.

Maddy fell asleep beside the love of her life and opened her eyes to see him watching her wake up. They started each day smiling at each other, thankful to be together. Several times throughout the day they would catch sight of each other and share a loving glance. Falling in love is not reserved for the young; they don't have enough life behind them to know when they have found the right person to grow old with: the person who makes their heart flutter with just a look; the person who is happy for their success, not self-serving; the person they can't live without. No, it takes time and some heartbreak to know when you are with the right person, truly in love, ready to be in love.

"I'm just running out to the market for a few things. Anything you want?" Maddy swept through the room.

"Just you." Sebastian smiled up at her.

"Will you be all right for an hour or so? I hate to leave you, but you should be resting. Can I get you anything before I go?"

"Stop fussing; I'm fine. I need to make a few calls, so the time will fly by. Off you go; I'll be waiting to hear who you saw and what you planned when you get back."

Maddy leaned over him and kissed his forehead.

"Don't run away with the first gypsy that comes by. See you in a bit." As she walked to the door, she suddenly turned. "Sebastian, Audrey and the buttons are hoping to come down this weekend; do you think they could stay at the house?"

"I don't see why not. Belle would be so pleased to have them in the house, and I know you would enjoy a visit." Sebastian wondered how Maddy had coped with being away from her friends for so long.

"Mrs B is coming early, so we can take a quick pass through and dust before they get here. You know Mrs B has been their favourite babysitter of late. Isn't that cool?"

Sebastian nodded, happy to see Maddy excited about the visit. "Off you go." He waved at her and continued to smile as he read the summary in his hands.

Maddy whistled as she walked up and down the aisles of the market. Audrey was coming to visit. Mrs B could check in on Sebastian, and Belle would welcome the chaos involved with the buttons. If only Henry were with them.

"Maddy, is that you?" A familiar voice interrupted her happy thoughts.

She turned and took a deep breath when she saw Rod standing before her. She had not seen him for months. "How are you, Rod?" They fell into a soft embrace. "Where have you been? We missed you at the funeral."

"I've been in Dubai for the last three months, on a contract. Glad to be home. I took my son with me, and it was a disaster; he wasn't ready to accept a new culture or entertain himself. I'm glad to be back. What funeral?" He couldn't stop staring into her eyes.

"George passed away about a month ago. I came back so I could see him before he passed." She broke away and held his hands in hers.

"Oh, Maddy, I'm so sorry I missed it. On the other hand, it's great to have you back. Are you staying here now?" He felt the ring on her finger, and suddenly it dawned on him; he had missed more than a wake.

"We're here for a few weeks. Sebastian had a health scare, so we're here for some recovery time. Please come and have dinner with us tonight. I'm sure Sebastian is getting bored with my company."

"I can't imagine it, Maddy." Rod felt faint. "Are you married?"

Maddy stepped back, realizing the air had changed. "Yes, we were married at the hospital before George passed."

Rod looked as though he had been punched in the stomach.

He looked at Maddy and realized he should say something congratulatory or at least pretend he was pleased.

Maddy sensed his discomfort and reacted. "Please come to dinner and we'll catch up. Chicken and dumplings with chocolate cake—best I can do." She smiled, and he found himself agreeing to come to dinner at six. She waved goodbye, leaving him standing in the aisle, unable to move. Maddy was married. He had missed his chance.

"Guess who's coming to dinner?" Maddy said, greeting Sebastian with a kiss.

He removed his glasses and waited for her to continue.

"I saw Rod at the market, and he's stopping by; you'll have someone else to visit with. Isn't that great? He's been in Dubai on contract, so you two should have lots to catch up on."

Sebastian was sure Rod would be disappointed to learn Maddy was taken, but he was anxious to see his old friend. "What can I do to help you?" He realized he had missed her, even for the short time she had gone shopping.

"You may create the most magnificent salad the world has seen." Maddy laughed at his serious expression. Their hands touched, and they gave each other a loving smile. Sebastian wondered how he had ever lived without her.

Rod arrived brandishing a magnum of champagne and apologized for being "a wretch" and not congratulating Maddy properly. They toasted to happy lives and friendship. Maddy gave both men cooking tasks; the three of them worked in the compact kitchen side by side.

"The kitchen was always off limits for me growing up," Rod shared with his friends. "My mum always made preparing meals seem like magic—a mystery only a mother could perform. We loved coming home with Sebastian and having meals with Belle. It's one of my best memories."

"Yes, our kitchen was always a treasure trove of exotic ingredients, most with names we couldn't even pronounce. We were only allowed to watch." Sebastian laughed. "Maddy introduced me to the joys of preparing meals, and I must say I'm finding it quite therapeutic … and delicious." He dipped his spoon in the gravy and gave it a thumbs up.

Maddy smiled at the two men reminiscing and laughing at their boyhood memories. She wished Henry were there with them; her heart would be full if they were all together.

After dinner they watched the sunset and played a board game, which for some reason brought on fits of laughter and more reminiscing. Sebastian tired quickly but refused to rest. Maddy looked so happy. As Rod was leaving, he shook hands with Sebastian and confessed he felt he never had a chance. Maddy was about to ask what he meant when the two men nodded and exchanged knowing looks. Rod hugged Maddy, thanked them both for a wonderful evening, and promised to look in on them again as he walked to his car.

Maddy and Sebastian waved good night, closed the door, and smiled at each other.

"It's way past your bedtime. I hope you're not too tired, but it was lovely to see you laughing tonight." Maddy took his hand and led him to their bed. It was the first time Sebastian had spoken about finding his parents and the villa in Italy; he was at peace with it now, and it had been heartwarming to hear him share the story with Rod.

Sebastian was indeed tired, but he felt like a young boy winning the prize at the fair.

"Maddy, we should get back to London and the house. Your friends are missing you, and I could see tonight you miss entertaining. I can't keep you here much longer."

"Don't be silly, Sebastian; I know Italy wasn't the honeymoon you imagined, but we finally got to spend some time alone here. I've loved every minute being with you. I want you to recover and be strong again. We have a lot of living to do. We don't need to be back in the city until your next check-up. Our friends, your work, and your club will be waiting for you when we're ready to go back. Right now, I'm happy here, with you. Is that okay?"

"Indeed."

Secrets

"Rod called today and invited us to attend an interesting session at the library this evening. Some psychologist is doing her thesis on a cold case her mother left in her notes. It sounds interesting. Shall we go?" Sebastian asked as Maddy walked into the room.

"If you like. Did you ask Rod to join us for an early dinner? We can go together." Maddy kissed his cheek and sat beside him. "What's the cold case?"

"Rod wasn't sure, but apparently the mother worked for the CIA and had operatives in Canada and New York State. When she passed away, the daughter found a letter a child had written while in her care. The mother was unsure if the child knew what was happening, and she protected the operative and the child by not leaving any names. She didn't specify whether the child was female or male; there is no way to trace the child. Her dissertation is about searching for the child after all these years. Apparently the operatives used a teddy bear to pass on information. It sounds like a good film."

Maddy could feel her heart beating fast; the blood drained from her face. She knew she wouldn't be able to stand, but she also knew she couldn't react to the news. She started taking deep breaths, hoping not to faint. What are the chances this would be happening to her now, after so many years had passed? Sebastian had returned to his reading. Maddy slowly walked into the bathroom, shut the door, and leaned against the wall, rubbing her hands on her thighs.

Memories from long ago crept into her mind, and she tried to fight them. She saw a woman with dark hair sitting on the floor across a teak coffee table. The woman was looking after Maddy for a few hours, as her father had to attend a meeting. The woman said she was working on a report that was very important. She gave Maddy a large pad of paper and a pencil and asked her to write a story about herself. Maddy chewed the pencil for a moment and then began writing:

> I am a kid—just a kid with a mom and dad. We were so happy, and then my mom lost a baby boy. There was lots of crying, and now my mom stays in her room.
>
> I feel bad that I did not want a brother; now my mom is sad. It must be my fault. Meryl wants me to write a story, as she is busy and she is babysitting me. My dad had a special mission. He took my teddy bear again, but that is a secret. Mom says secrets are how adults get stuff done. I will understand better when I get old.
>
> My dad takes me on business trips. We go to Paris lots. I have to learn French, eat French, and learn about France when my dad goes to work. Georges works at the hotel, and he helps me find good chocolates for Madame. She sneezes when we bring flowers, so I bring chocolates when we go for dinner. Sometimes she gives me one. I don't think she likes me. She yells at my dad not to leave me alone. Monsieur laughs at my stories. I think he is afraid of Madame. Sometimes we go to other places in Europe, like Berlin. They have a curtain in Berlin, but I never saw it.
>
> I like Moscow and Vlada, my friend. She buys me ice cream in Gorky Park. My Russian is not so good, but I will try harder. Spain is hot, and the food is really good. They say "muy bueno". I have to go to bed now, so this is a short story. I don't have much to tell, because I am just a kid and I can't tell you any secrets. M

Maddy left the pad on the table and went to bed, as directed. In the morning, her father came in to wake her and placed her teddy bear under her arm. He also had warm bagels and hot chocolate. They walked home together. She never saw Meryl again.

Is it possible this is Meryl's daughter? Maddy wondered. *Why does she want to find the child? What good would come from knowing who the child is? What would that accomplish now?* Maddy didn't want to know. She needed time—time to think about so many things. She wouldn't go this evening. Secrets are meant to be kept.

"Sebastian, would you be disappointed if I bailed on the seminar tonight? I'm not feeling up to it. You go ahead." Maddy was trying to speak slowly, hoping he wouldn't hear the fear in her voice.

He looked up, concern on his face. "Are you all right? Come here. Come and sit with me. We don't have to go or do anything. I'm happy to stay in. Maddy, are you all right?"

"Yes, I'm fine. I just have a lot on my mind. Hungry?" She kissed his cheek and turned towards the kitchen.

Sebastian watched her walk away, unsure why he felt she wasn't telling him something. Normally Maddy would have been keen to hear about an unsolved mystery. Rod would fill them in on the story.

Rod was enthusiastic about the speaker's story of the lost child and the writer who wanted to connect the dots between her mother, the Cold War, and her suspicions that a child was used to carry microfilm in her teddy bear, seamlessly crossing borders and security checks. Sebastian could not help but notice Maddy was quiet, not engaging in the mystery, not her usual self.

Lying in bed, Sebastian asked Maddy if she was feeling better. She nodded slowly, her head on his chest barely moving.

"Maddy, I sense you don't want to talk about it now, but when you're ready, I'll be here for you." He paused, not sure how to continue. "It's your teddy bear, isn't it?" he whispered into her hair.

Maddy nodded and drifted off to sleep.

If You Love It, Let It Go

Sebastian appeared to be agitated when Maddy returned to the cottage after her errands. After several attempts at being jovial, she gave up, believing he might be tired. As they lay in bed reading, Sebastian removed his glasses, placed his book on the bedside table, and cleared his throat. Maddy looked over, hoping he wanted to talk.

"Did you return the message?" he asked in a tight voice.

"What message?"

"When you were out, there was a message on your phone; I couldn't help but hear it. I wish I hadn't," he whispered, shaking his head.

"Is that why you've been moody all evening?" Maddy sighed. "I don't know what message you're talking about."

"It's on your other phone—the phone in the foyer."

Maddy threw back the duvet and padded to the foyer, picked up the phone, and checked the messages. As she heard the familiar voice, she sat down on the hall bench.

"Maddy, pick up. I know you're there. Pick up. Listen, the Morocco trip is leaving from the locker in Seville on Monday morning at 9 a.m. I'm giving up the locker, so if you want your bike, you'd better be there. Ah, Mad, there's been a cancellation, and you can join us. You've planned every detail of this ride, and I know you were looking forward to it. You can room with me. It'll be like old times. It'll be a blast. Just be at the locker, ready to go. Ah, I heard you might want to marry some old British guy. Don't do it; you'll be bored out of your mind. If you really want to be married, for goodness' sake, why didn't you say? Gotta go. See you Monday. I know you; you'll be there."

Maddy wasn't sure how long she sat there in the dark, replaying the message in her mind. She jumped when Sebastian touched her shoulder.

"Maddy, you want to go, don't you?" he whispered.

She nodded and watched Sebastian walk across the room to the bed.

"I want my bike back." She whispered to the darkness.

They sat in the cab, Maddy folded into his arms, joking with the driver about the early morning traffic and the bitter coffee. As they approached the locker compound, an urban storage facility, they could see a group of men preparing their motorcycles—packing saddlebags, checking oil, polishing windshields, and testing their communicators. The sound of motorbikes revving, the men shouting across the yard, the air blue from the exhaust—it was a familiar scene for Maddy.

"Come on; we'll get my bike and see them off." She patted his knee.

Sebastian didn't move. "You go, Maddy; it's what you want. You know where I'll be when you get back." He was staring ahead, afraid to look at her.

"Are you kidding me? This is the second time I've been dismissed in the back seat of a car by you. I swore I would never let that happen to me again." Maddy stopped to collect her thoughts and control her racing heart.

"We are here to collect my bike. You have two options: you can step out of the cab and come with me and we can carry on with our lives together—our perfect lives—or you can stay in the cab and drive away and never see me again. Simple. Your choice." Maddy was shaking with anger.

"Maddy, go and enjoy the trip. Get it out of your system and then come home; I'll be waiting for you." Sebastian spoke slowly, trying to sound impassive.

"That's not how it works. I made a commitment to you. We had plans to grow old together. You don't get to farm me out. Are you coming?"

Maddy looked across the road and back at Sebastian. He continued to stare ahead, not moving.

Maddy looked at the driver, who was watching her in the rear-view mirror. She shook her head and stepped out of the cab. She brushed the tears from her eyes and straightened her tunic, squared her shoulders, and walked across the road.

Sebastian could hear the welcome whistles and comments from the group. They were delighted Maddy was joining them. He forced himself to look over and saw a tall man holding his helmet place his arm around Maddy and pull her close. *That must be Dag.* He looked away and told the cabbie to drive him back to the airport.

"Are you crazy, mister? I would be following her. What's wrong with you?" The cabbie was pacing beside the car. He wondered what his wife would say when he told her about this fare. He watched the woman greet the riders and shook his head. He got in the cab, troubled by the scene he had witnessed. The couple looked so in love, and then this guy let her walk away. She didn't want to go; he could tell.

The cab moved around the corner and stopped. "Mister, I'm calling you another cab; my wife would be so angry if she knew I took you back to the airport and left that woman here. Sorry, man; I can't take you any farther." Sebastian nodded, threw some euros on the seat, and stepped out of the cab.

The roar of the motorbikes starting up and leaving the compound was overpowering. The convoy moved out in single file, spacing themselves and saluting the passers-by. As the roar subsided, the cabbie rounded the corner and ran out to the curb.

"You didn't go?"

"I never planned to go." Maddy stepped off the bike. "I only got the keys as they started up."

"What will do you now?"

"Don't know. I'll get on the bike and start driving … see where I end up. I don't know." She shrugged.

"Come home with me. My wife will be angry with me if I let you go on the bike without lunch and some plan … Come, follow me. My name is Liuni—it means 'lion' in Sicilian. You can call me Leo. Come on; I know your name is Maddy. Come, Maddy; you can't sit here." The cabbie continued to pace in front of Maddy, who was now sitting on the curb, her biking gear on.

Maddy smiled at Leo and burst into tears. She felt lonely and abandoned, and yet here was a stranger, a cab driver, trying to help her. She had no idea what she was going to do today, tomorrow, the next day …

"You're a nice man, Leo. Your wife is lucky to have you. Tell her that for me, will you?" Maddy wiped her eyes with her sleeve.

"The bike is secure for another month; everything is in order. Here's your new lock. Shall I roll it in?" The voice behind them made Maddy and Leo turn their heads quickly.

Sebastian offered Maddy his handkerchief.

"We'll come back and get the bike when you're ready to take me on your next adventure." He was standing in front of Maddy, his hand out to help her up from the curb.

Maddy looked away. "Go away, Sebastian; it's over. I'm getting on the bike and heading out."

"I know what you're thinking, Maddy, but I'm here to take you home and take care of you."

"You couldn't possibly know what I'm thinking right now." Maddy tried to stop the tears.

Leo watched the pair, nervous, not sure if he should leave or wait for Maddy, wondering what his wife would expect him to do.

"Maddy, I know you're angry with me just now, but I had to let you go if that's what you wanted to do—as much as it hurt. You chose not to go, so you won't look at me with regret when we get old together."

"You had a choice, and you chose to drive away; we're done here. Thank you for arranging the locker, but I won't be needing it."

Leo, the cab driver, nodded. She was right; the tall guy had chosen to drive away. Yet here he was, carrying on, looking after her. It was confusing.

"Maddy, I saw you get ready, and I honestly thought you were leaving with the group. I didn't see you when they passed by, so I rushed back here, relieved and happier than I deserve to be." Sebastian sat beside her on the curb.

Maddy stood up and walked over to the motorbike, grabbed her helmet, and was about to pull it on over her head when Sebastian grappled it from her hands and pulled her close. He kissed her cheek and tasted the salt of her tears. The pain and confusion in her eyes made him act on impulse. He kissed her slowly and passionately, hoping his feelings were relayed in that kiss.

Leo smiled as the couple before him seemed to reach an impasse. His wife would be pleased with the story of his day. She would want to know all the details, and he wouldn't have to embellish this tale at all; it was perfect. He turned to go, taking one last look at the couple. It was looking good.

Suddenly Maddy was getting on the bike and Sebastian was walking towards the office. Leo drove away wondering how he would end the story for his wife.

Real Estate

"Maddy, do you love the house in London?" Sebastian looked across the room at her.

"Hmm. I haven't really thought about it. I'm always happy here at the beach. I loved being in Italy. It doesn't matter where we are if we're together, right? Why do you ask?"

"Maddy, someone has put in an amazing offer on Bellmere. The buyer wants to move in as soon as possible." Sebastian looked up from his laptop. "Can you believe it?"

Maddy smiled, looking out at the waves washing over the rocks. "Well, it is a gorgeous house. Is it for sale?"

Sebastian removed his glasses and looked over at Maddy. She was biting the side of her cheek—a sign she was deep in thought. He waited for her response, wondering what was going through her mind. She loved their home, and they'd had so little time to enjoy living in it since her return, the honeymoon in Italy, and then his health scare. He had waited for her to return from Canada so they could live happily ever after in their glass house. Would she be disappointed? Would she be sad? He shook his head and smiled. Knowing Maddy, she was already onto the next move.

The incident in Seville with the bike had made them both realize they wanted a future together; where they lived was less important. Sebastian had been worried that Maddy would drive off and he would lose her, but in the end she agreed to return home with him. Leo, the cab driver, had circled the block when he saw Maddy drive away on her bike; he was sure Sebastian would need a ride to the airport. They had waited anxiously for Maddy to drive back into the locker area, and when she turned the corner, they both sighed in relief. Maddy invited Leo and his wife to dinner, and they spent a lovely evening reconciling the events of the day.

Sebastian felt very lucky and very loved. He didn't want to imagine a life without Maddy by his side. He also promised not to second-guess her love for him.

"Do you know who the buyer is?" Maddy continued to watch the waves.

"It seems you had a group of musicians over for a session, and they fell in love with the sound quality they recorded in the room. The piano reverberates against the glass, producing a wonderful sound for their album. They want the house and grounds for their next recording. Price is no object." He sounded mechanical as he read the message from Lambert.

Maddy continued to look out over the water, her fingers tapping the arms of the chair.

"Wow. A year ago, I wasn't sure where I would live, and now we have a beautiful home we haven't even broken in, our neighbours are moving away, we have a dream cottage overlooking the sea, and we have a sensational villa in Italy that needs our love and attention." She turned to meet his eyes.

"Audrey and Jeffery are considering moving the children to a less hectic locale, and after the weekend they wondered if Belle's house was available. They are asking Mrs B to live with them. She loves the children, and it would be a good fit. Don't you think?" No answer was required.

"Esme and Gordon hope to sell and move to Cornwall to be closer to their grandchildren. They've asked me to stage their house for the sale." She took a breath and continued. "The house down the street is almost ready to sell. You know, the housekeeper, Jasmina, suggested Audrey and I do whatever we thought we needed to do to sell; the owners were delighted to pay us to modernize the house and get the gardens ready for prospective buyers." She smiled as she recalled the conversation. The owners were so pleased with the condo downtown that they trusted Maddy to sell their ageing home. They were in no hurry for cash. What a world.

They sat in silence, Maddy looking for patterns in the clouds, and Sebastian digesting all the news he had just heard.

"Sebastian, did I tell you Mr Simpson is not well? We have contacted his son and a rare book dealer. The son hasn't responded, but the book dealer has been appraising the treasures and buying them. The poor man is going to die in that bookshop. We must help him. Wouldn't it be great to have a Starbucks or a trendy coffeehouse in the centre and let the customers browse the classics? We could offer the top ten bestsellers for sale at the counter and let people borrow the other books, returning the books when they come back for coffee. Just think about that. What a lovely legacy for Mr Simpson." Her cheeks were flushed as she sat forward in her deck chair.

"Slow down; someone offered to buy our house, and now you're taking over the future development of the neighbourhood." Sebastian was laughing. "Oh, Maddy, I guess it's naive of me to expect that you would be content just sitting here with me. That's why I love you. What shall we tackle first?" He reached for her hand and felt warm just seeing her smile.

"We have lots of time to grow old together. First we need to get Henry back from Australia and see him graduate and become a famous chef." She smiled at the thought.

"Where do you want to live?" she asked, a catch in her voice.

"Anywhere you are." He smiled tenderly.

"By the way, just in case you don't know, I love you and I would live anywhere with you." She stood over him, still holding his hand; she leaned over and kissed his forehead. Sebastian looked up at her; the late-day sun creating a halo around her head, and a soft breeze was moving her hair. Suddenly he realized there were tears on his cheek and they were his—tears of joy for having her in his life.

"Maddy, we have to be in Argentina for a few months. The startup is important, and I wouldn't even consider going without you. You can find us a place to live, and you'll finally get your tango lessons. How are we going to fit everything in?"

"No worries. This is so exciting. You'll love Argentina. When do we go? You'll see; we'll be fine with all the changes and challenges. It's not a problem; we can do it all." Maddy sat on his lap, her arms around his neck. "Don't you worry … We can do this." Her mind was racing. "Don't forget we have to be in Milan for the fashion show next week."

She stood and started pacing back and forth in front of him.

"We can do this. What a wonderful life we have. Aren't we just the luckiest people in the world to have so many options?" Maddy's cheeks were flushed; her energy radiated across to him.

"Indeed." Sebastian couldn't think of anything else to say.

Want more of Maddy and Sebastian as they build a future on the past?

Watch for *More or Less Reckless* - the next adventure - coming soon.

About the Author

Anne Marshall is an adventure seeker. She and her partner have travelled the world by small aircraft, motorcycle, by foot and more recently in a camper van. Her career in Hospitality has offered wonderful opportunities for lasting friendships and signature experiences. She calls rural Ontario, Canada, her home.

CPSIA information can be obtained
at www.ICGtesting.com
Printed in the USA
LVHW091102020919
629583LV00001BA/1/P

9 781982 233266